WHEN TERROR COMES

The man's left hand curled over the half-opened window. He bent over and stared into the car. In his right hand he held a gun. Beth looked up and saw glittering eyes and a frozen smile in the skull-like face. "Andrew," she breathed.

For a second she was paralyzed. Then instinct forced her to move. She jammed her left elbow on the door lock and turned on the ignition, stomping on the gas. The car jerked forward, and Andrew's hand smashed into the windowframe. He seemed to fall away from the car. Beth did not look back, but she heard Francie cry out, "He's gonna shoot!"

LITTLE
SISTER

PATRICIA J. MacDONALD

A DELL BOOK

Published by
Dell Publishing Co., Inc.
1 Dag Hammarskjold Plaza
New York, New York 10017

Dell ® TM 681510, Dell Publishing Co., Inc.

ISBN: 0-440-14743-3

Printed in the United States of America

July 1986

10 9 8 7 6 5 4 3 2 1

WFH

To my guys,
Big D and Mac, with love

Prologue

I_T started as it usually did. A barked command, a barbed insult, a festering grievance burst open into shouts too muffled to be understood in the far reaches of the darkened house. All that was clearly perceptible was a crackle of menace, like the creak and groan of shifting earth that bring a camper on a mountainside awake, alert, and clammy with fear and the knowledge that there is danger in the air.

The man's heavy tread caused tremors through the floors, and then he slammed the closet door in the large but shabby foyer, and the very frame of the house shook. He rammed his fists into the sleeves of his coat and turned his collar up high against the cold night air which seeped under the front door and circulated through the drafty house.

The woman, who had followed him from the kitchen where the fight started, pulled her sweater close around her and watched him with flinty eyes. "I don't know why I care. Why should I care?" she muttered in a low, disgusted tone. "I should have packed your bags long ago and thrown you out. You've never been anything but vile and selfish and crude. . . ."

The man turned to face her, and there was an odd expression on his face, almost a smile, as he spoke. "Well, you won't have to put up with me anymore now, will you? Let me tell you something. Walking out that door is going to be walking out the gates of prison. It'll be like having freedom for the first time after years in some stinking pit."

"You, you're so filthy. I always said that about you."

The man started to laugh in a high, hysterical tone. "That's true," he said. "That is true. You always did say that. If I heard it once, I heard it a thousand times. 'Filthy. A pig. Every breath I take fouls the fucking air.'"

The woman's thin hands tightened into fists, and she stepped up close to her husband. "So now you think you can do as you please. Run off with some little tramp. It's that teenager, isn't it? That little slut that works at the luncheonette. That's who you're running off with, isn't it? I've seen you looking at her."

The man curled his lip and seemed to be holding himself rigid with great effort. "Don't make me laugh. Do you think I'd want a woman, any woman, after you? I might never want a woman again. I don't think I could get it up for Raquel Welch. Not after being married to you."

"Don't be disgusting," she said with a shudder. "You're disgusting."

"That's right," he said, and then, gathering up the saliva in his mouth, he spit at her feet. The spit landed on her shoe and bubbled there. She stared down at it for a moment, stiff with revulsion. The man strode to

8

the door and reached for the doorknob. But the woman darted over and blocked his way.

"You're not going anywhere," she said. "You're not going to desert us for some little slut. Humiliate me in front of this town."

"Get out of my way," he said through gritted teeth.

The woman pressed herself up against the door and shook her head frantically. "I've been a good wife to you. I did everything for you. You had nothing when you met me. My father gave you that job. He left us this house. Now you think you can just abandon me here," she whined.

"Don't tempt me," he growled, slowly raising his arm.

"You're nothing without me. You'll always be noth—"

The blow from his meaty hand caught her on her cheekbone and jerked her whole upper body sideways. She slumped down to her knees, still resting against the door. In a daze she pushed her ash blond hair away from the darkening bruise on her face.

"I told you to get out of the way," he roared.

The woman struggled to her feet, her eyes still unfocused from the blow. "No," she whimpered. "Don't go."

The man bent down and, grabbing the collar of her sweater, lifted her up with both hands and shook her. "I'm so sick of you," he snarled, and then he pulled her forward as if he were about to heave her aside like an unwieldy bag of garbage.

Her eyelids fluttered as if she were going to faint. Then, suddenly, her gaze widened, and she stared over his shoulder with fearful eyes. "Look," she whispered. "Look out."

"What?" the man yelled, eyeing her suspiciously.

The woman raised a finger feebly and pointed. Dropping his hands from her neck, the man wheeled around and looked in the direction of her startled glance. "Oh, no," he whispered.

The two stared in the direction of the staircase behind them. There, on the landing, stood a small child, dressed in a pair of flannel slipper-footed pajamas decorated with rabbits and furry yellow chicks. The child was holding a large revolver pointed in the direction of the quarreling couple.

"You fool," the woman snarled. "I knew we should never keep a gun in this house. I warned you—"

"Oh, shut up," the man said, turning carefully toward the stairs so as not to frighten the child with any sudden movement.

"Put the gun down, baby," the man crooned. "We'll get you another toy to play with, won't we, Mommy?"

The woman curled her lip in disgust at her husband and then hurried forward toward the staircase.

"Go slowly," the man warned.

"Give me that awful thing," the woman demanded. "Give it to Mommy."

The child stood gazing at the two of them, the gun raised in a wobbling hand.

"Right now," said the woman firmly. "Do as Mommy says."

"Get back," the man warned, his frown turning to a look of disbelief. "Sweetie, put it down. Don't . . ." he cried, lunging toward the mother and child.

"Now," insisted the woman.

The crack of the shot rocked the quiet house. The man groaned, and the woman let out an agonized scream. Blood splattered and flew, like the tumbling dirt and stones that announce the landslide.

Chapter 1

PINK and green giraffes stretched their long necks to nibble from the leaves on the high branches of a tree, while a red monkey peeked at them from behind the trunk. A blue and purple tiger stalked the high grasses on another wall with little matching tiger cubs tumbling behind him. Rare toucans and parrots preened among the foliage with colors vivid as life, and a friendly rhino and his mate, one orange, the other yellow, gazed, horn to horn into each other's eyes.

Twinkling white lights arched around them all and threw a becoming glow on the tuxedoed men and women in cocktail dresses, who milled beneath the jungle murals, their heels clicking on the shining floors. At intervals around the perimeter of the giant rotunda were tables covered in white linen and manned by waiters in short red jackets, serving cocktails and an elegant buffet to the guests, whose laughter and murmurs filtered up above the fronds of the large tropical trees to the skylighted roof, where stars pricked the night sky.

The only indications that the party was not being given in the home of some eccentric big game lover were the sign reading EMERGENCY with an arrow over one of the doors and the row of wheelchairs which were lined up against one of the curving walls.

An attractive young woman dressed in a simple green silk dress stood alone in the midst of the buzz, surveying the scene with a critical eye and sipping her drink. Her gaze traveled restlessly around the room, and the look on her face was that of a parent watching a child perform in a school play, part anxiety, part satisfaction.

A sleek-looking man with silver at the temples strode up to her and interrupted her thoughts. "Beth," he said, "this is the architect's equivalent of a smash Broadway opening."

"I know, Brewster," the woman replied. "It did turn out great."

"Oh, look sharp," he demanded, nudging her. "I want you to meet someone. Bob," he called out, collaring a passing man, who joined them, "it's good to see you here."

The newcomer, a dark-haired man with heavy circles under his eyes, smiled and shook Brewster's hand. "This wing is a very impressive addition to the hospital," he said.

"Well, credit where credit is due," said Brewster. "Bob, I'd like you to meet Beth Pearson. This is the talented lady who actually designed the pediatric wing and saw it through. Beth, this is our city councilman, Bob Tartaglia."

"I recognized you," Beth said. "It's a pleasure to

meet you." She returned the councilman's firm handshake.

"Miss Pearson . . . is it Miss?"

Beth nodded.

"You should be very proud of the way this facility turned out. Truthfully, as a parent—I've got two daughters myself—and, God forbid, if I ever had to bring them to the hospital, I would feel more comfortable bringing them here than to any pediatrics hospital I've seen."

"That's the best compliment there is," said Beth.

"Really, I mean it."

"Well, we wanted to design a place that would be cheerful and even a little homey for the kids, while at the same time providing the latest in equipment and technology."

"And using her considerable feminine powers of persuasion," said Brewster proudly, "she managed to get the DiSeca brothers to bring it in on time and within the budget."

The councilman rolled his eyes. "Two concepts almost unknown to us in city government."

Beth felt the praise making her a little giddy, like champagne bubbles, and she laughed aloud. All the setbacks she had encountered in getting the wing done to her satisfaction seemed to be only a vague memory now, fading in the pleasant glow of compliments.

"By the way, Miss Pearson—"

"Oh, Beth, please . . ."

"Beth, then. Did you meet the mayor? I see him over there talking to Mrs. Forster, from the fund-raising committee."

"Actually," said Beth, with an ill-concealed flush of

gratification, "the mayor spoke to me earlier and said some very kind things."

"And well deserved," said Councilman Tartaglia. "Well, Brewster, I know you got the contract for the new condo complex by the river. Have you got Miss Pearson here on the case already?"

"Unfortunately not," said Brewster Wingate, frowning with mock disapproval at Beth. "Miss Pearson is not with Wingate, Stubbs, and Collins anymore. This pediatrics wing was her last project for us."

The councilman raised his eyebrows. "Did I just make a faux pas?"

"No, no," Beth said hurriedly, shaking her head.

"She won a contract for having the best design for a new hospice being built out on the Main Line and decided to go into business for herself. She's the competition now," said Brewster sternly.

"No hard feelings, I hope," said Tartaglia, a shade mischievously.

"Well, I wasn't happy about it," said Brewster. "You can be sure of that. But I did it myself years ago, so I can understand it. We miss her, though." He smiled at Beth like a proud parent.

"How do you like being in business for yourself?" asked the councilman pleasantly.

"It's nerve-racking," said Beth. "But so far, so good. There's a company moving here from California that I've been talking to about doing their headquarters. If I land that, I'll be in good shape."

"Well, good luck to you," said Tartaglia. "I think you're going to do very well."

"Thank you, I hope so," said Beth.

"Bob!" exclaimed a chunky woman in a red chiffon dress. "Just who I've been looking for!" She smiled brightly at Beth and Brewster. "Could you excuse us for a minute? I have been trying to get this man's ear all evening about a teeny-weeny favor we need for the school."

The councilman smiled and gave a little shrug of his shoulders. "Teeny-weeny favors are my specialty. It's been a pleasure," he said as his insistent female constituent locked his arm in hers and began to lead him away.

Brewster turned to Beth. "Have you enjoyed yourself tonight?"

"It's been wonderful, every minute," said Beth, "although I will admit to being a little tired. There was the dedication this afternoon and this affair tonight."

"And knowing you, I'll bet you spent the hours in between working."

Beth nodded sheepishly. "How true."

A dark-haired young man carrying a plate of grapes and cheese walked up and joined them, shaking his head. "You would think," he said, "that they would at least provide handmaidens to peel these things for you."

"Don't look at me," said Beth with a laugh.

The young man raised a hand as if to disavow any such intention and then extended his hand to the older man. "Hello, Mr. Wingate."

"Dr. Belack," said the older man, nodding his head. "It's good to see you. Well, I'm going to leave you two now. I promised Pris an early evening. Listen here, Doctor, take care of this girl, will you? See that she gets her mind off the work now and then."

"I'm gonna do my best."

Responding to a sudden impulse, Beth stretched up and gave her former boss a kiss on the cheek. "Thanks for the support, Brewster. I really appreciate it."

Brewster waved it off and threaded his way back across the room to his wife.

"He's an all right guy," said Mike Belack.

"He's been great to me," said Beth. "He really encouraged me when I needed the push. Not everyone would have done that."

"No. Especially since you were his pride and joy at the firm."

Beth smiled. "Hasn't this been a lovely party, Mike?"

"Yes, it has," he said, squeezing her gently around the waist. "Do you want a grape?"

Beth shook her head.

"You know, I'm glad to see you looking so happy. There were times I thought that between finishing this wing and starting the new business, you were on the verge of a collapse."

"There were times I thought so, too," she admitted, "although I'm sure that in looking back on it, I'll always regard it as one of the happiest times in my life."

"Well, of course," said Mike. "You met me. What more could anyone ask?"

Beth made a face and punched him lightly, but she smiled to herself, acknowledging the truth of what he said.

Mike popped a wedge of cheese into his mouth and looked thoughtfully around the room as he ate. Beth reached onto his plate and took a piece for herself.

"I just ran into Maxine over by the dessert table," Mike said. "Let me tell you, if there was a lampshade in this room, she'd be wearing it on her head."

Beth laughed. Maxine had been her assistant at the old firm and had allowed herself to be recruited when Beth struck out on her own. She was now Beth's assistant, secretary, chief troubleshooter, and sole full-time

16

employee. She was also a model of tact and efficiency who gave the fledgling company a polished veneer for prospective clients. The idea of Maxine's tying one on at the party tickled Beth's fancy. "No one deserves to celebrate more than Maxine," she said. "Sometimes I think Brewster regrets losing her more than me."

"Well, it's been a great night," said Mike. "But what do you say we continue the celebration privately, at your house?"

Beth looked around the room and nodded. "It sounds good to me. Besides, I've just got to get off my feet."

"Good," said Mike. "Let's say our good-byes and be on our way."

He put his plate down on a nearby table, and hand in hand they made their way toward the door, stopping every so often to say good night. Near the door they passed Maxine, who was holding two men spellbound with her tipsy charm. At the sight of them Maxine broke away and gave her boss an affectionate hug.

"Thanks for everything," Beth whispered. "See you tomorrow."

"Let's walk," said Mike as they donned their coats and stepped out into the crisp night air. Beth nodded agreement and linked her arm through his.

"You were a smash," he said, and kissed her cold cheek.

"Thanks." She glanced over at him as they strode along in the direction of her house. The streetlights brightened and then darkened his distinctive profile. She felt a surge of happiness, having him with her to share this magical evening. The streets of the city were quiet, emptied by the cold and the lateness of the hour. The night seemed both peaceful and enchanted to her.

"What are you thinking about?" he asked. "You're awfully quiet."

"Just feeling lucky," she said. "And happy."

Mike pulled her arm closer to his body. "We are lucky."

He uses "we" so comfortably, she thought. It was typical of his confidence, his optimism. Although she liked to think that meeting him was a small miracle or even destiny, if there were such a thing, she was still reluctant to bank on "we." How could two people who were such different types have hit it off so quickly, she wondered. He had an open, freewheeling approach to life, and he took their love as something natural, albeit wonderful. *I have to poke at it, prod it, doubt it*, she thought.

Still, we fit, she reminded herself, with a satisfied smile. *We go together.*

"Hold that smile," he said. "We're almost home."

They turned a corner and then walked, arm in arm, up the steps of Beth's town house, which was one in a row of carefully restored old brick houses on a quiet, treelined street. Mike shivered as Beth fiddled with the keys. "It's cold out here when you're not moving," he said. "January, ugh."

"We'll be warm in a minute." She opened the door and stepped into the foyer, and the warmth of the house seemed to embrace her. It was the first house she had ever owned, and she had bought it at a low price, for it had been in a sad state of neglect and disrepair when she found it. She had planned the renovations and worked side by side with the workmen and often long into the night after they were gone, both to save money and to have the satisfaction of transforming the place with her own labor. It gave her a little feeling of pride every time she walked into the home she had made for herself.

Mike took her coat, and Beth went in and turned on the lamps in the living room. "Do you want a nightcap?" Beth called out to him as he hung their coats in the hall closet.

"Just some club soda for me. I'm on call early tomorrow."

Beth poured them both some club soda and handed him one as he came into the room.

"What do you say," said Mike, wrapping an arm around her, "we take these upstairs, where we can be more comfortable?"

Beth smiled at him. "Sounds good to me. Just let me close up for the night."

As Beth went into the kitchen to check the back door and the windows, Mike looked around the room. "You know," he called out to her, "this wouldn't be a bad room to have a wedding, provided it wasn't too large."

Beth, who had turned on the back floodlights to check the garden, snapped down the switch and did not answer for a second.

Mike appeared in the kitchen doorway, his head cocked to one side. "Of course, we'd have to provide a lot of extra ashtrays."

Beth exhaled slowly. Her heart was beating very hard. "I never thought about it," she said, although this was not precisely true.

He had mentioned weddings before. Whenever he did, she felt a funny combination of happy excitement and, at the same time, a little ratlike scurry of fear through her intestines. And there it was again. *You are twenty-eight years old,* she reminded herself, *and this is the first man whom you could imagine being mar-*

ried to. Most of the men in her past had found her difficult, competitive, prickly. She had been called all that, and much more, before the door slammed and then were gone from her life. With Mike it had been different. Right from the start he had accepted her moods and applauded her accomplishments, as if they were the most natural thing in the world. With Mike she could bloom. She was sure of it.

But so much could go wrong between people. A marriage could turn so ugly and frightening. She knew that it could. She had seen it firsthand. But if you didn't chance it, didn't try . . .

"Never did, eh?" he asked in a jaunty tone. "Well, think about it."

Beth nodded and squeezed him tightly. "I will."

"I knew it," said Mike with a grimace as the demanding ring of the phone shattered the air. "Well-wishers no doubt."

"Let's not answer it," said Beth. "Whoever it is can wait."

Reluctantly he let her go. "It could be the hospital."

Beth nodded and walked over to the phone. "I guess this is what the life of a doctor's wife is like," she said teasingly. She blushed as she said it. Then she picked up the phone.

For a few moments she just listened to the voice at the other end. Mike watched as her normally mobile face with its lovely green eyes and fine features stiffened into a tight, expressionless mask. She made him think of a boat, clipping along with the wind, that hits a hidden rock and begins to sink without warning. He could not understand, from the monosyllables she spoke, what the call was about.

"All right," Beth said at last. "I'll be there tomorrow. Thanks for calling."

Beth replaced the phone on the hook and stood staring at it.

"What's the matter?" Mike asked. "Trouble?"

Beth raised her eyes from the phone and looked at Mike with a dull, distant gaze. Then she cleared her throat. "That was my aunt," she said. "My father died today, of a heart attack."

"Oh, baby, oh, no," said Mike. "Come here. I'm so sorry."

Beth backed away from him and waved off his concern. "No, no, it's all right." She frowned and bit her lower lip. "I'm—I'll have to go up to Maine tomorrow."

"Darling, what can I do?" Mike asked, coming over and putting his arms around her.

Beth shook her head absently. "I'll have to pack. Maybe you could call the airlines for me. I need to fly to Portland tomorrow."

"Sure I will. But talk to me. What's going on? Are you okay?"

Beth sighed. "Yeah."

"Darling, you should go ahead and cry if you want. Don't hold it in," he said.

"I don't feel like crying," she said. "Mike, could you just make that call for me? I'd better go up and pack."

"Okay," said Mike, watching her quizzically as she turned away from him and headed for the staircase. He picked up the receiver and quickly dialed the airline. It seemed to take forever to get a reservations clerk on the line, but he finally succeeded.

"Have you got any direct flights from Philadelphia to Portland, Maine, tomorrow morning?" he asked.

The agent informed him that he would need a connecting flight through Boston and left him hanging on the line while she checked the possible connections.

Mike cocked an ear toward the upper floor of the house while he waited, expecting to hear the muffled sound of sobs from the rooms above, but all he heard was the shush and slam of drawers opening and closing.

The agent came back on the line and gave him the flight times. Mike completed the arrangements and then hurried upstairs to the master bedroom.

Beth's suitcase was open on the bed, and she was methodically, if somewhat listlessly, choosing what to put inside it.

"It's all set," Mike said. "Tomorrow morning at ten. You change in Boston."

"Thanks," she said.

"Beth," he said, "why don't I come with you? I can arrange for someone to cover for me."

Beth looked at the two sweaters she was holding as if she were weighing them in her hands. She put one of them in the suitcase and returned the other one to the drawer. Then she looked up at Mike with confusion in her eyes. "I don't think I'll need both of them, do you?"

"What?"

"Both sweaters. I'll be gone only a few days. What do you think?"

"I think one will be enough," he said gently. "You know, it might help to have someone with you. I hate to think of you being all alone up there."

"Well, I won't be all alone. It's all right, Mike. But thank you anyway. My sister is there. And my aunt and uncle."

"You never mentioned that you had a sister, Beth," he said, a little surprised.

"I didn't?" Beth asked.

"I thought your father was it."

"Yes, Francie. She's much younger than I am. I guess she's about fourteen by now. I hardly know her."

"How long has it been since you've seen your family?" Mike asked.

Beth wrested a set of thermal underwear from the bottom of the stacking drawers in her closet. "It's bitter up there," she said, folding them into the suitcase. "I haven't been back in a long time. Years now. Since my mother died, I guess. And that was, let's see, about eight years ago. So I haven't seen Francie since she was, well, pretty young."

"Wow," said Mike.

"Wow what? What's the wow?"

"It's a long time not to see your family. That's all."

"I suppose so," said Beth.

"Take some turtlenecks," he advised her as she stood helplessly staring into a bureau drawer. Beth nodded gratefully.

"What happened to your mother anyway? How did she die?"

"She was in an accident," said Beth. "I'd rather not talk about it."

"Okay."

"I was pretty close to her. But my father and I never really got along. We never did. Anyway, I was up there after my mother died, and he and I had a huge fight. And then, well, that was it, really. There was the occasional call or letter. It suited us both that way."

Mike suspected that there might be pain behind the offhand explanation, but he could tell from the closed look on Beth's face that he should pursue it no further for the moment.

"What about Francie?" he asked. "What happens to her now?"

Beth, who was stuffing socks into the corners of her

suitcase, made an exasperated sound. "Why should you be so concerned about Francie?"

"I'm not concerned. I'm just asking," he protested. "Don't get mad."

Beth shrugged. "Sorry. You're right. I have an aunt and uncle who live up there in Oldham. That was my aunt May calling about my father. She's my father's sister. My uncle James is a minister there. They're older, but they're very nice people. Francie will go live with them. They've had two kids of their own, so they're happy to take her. There, that looks like all I'll need."

"Beth," said Michael, who was seated at the edge of the bed, "come here and sit down."

"Mike, will you water the plants while I'm gone?"

"Of course."

"I hope I won't be gone too long. I have to get back to work. As it is, this couldn't have happened at a worse time."

Mike grimaced at this remark and then tried to hide it, but Beth noticed it. She sighed and seemed to search for something to say.

"Look," she said, "I know what you're thinking."

Mike shook his head. "I'm sorry. I know you're upset, but I'm not used to seeing you like this. You seem so stiff and, I don't know, detached. And I know that's not you. You're not an unfeeling person. You're the farthest thing from it."

Beth frowned and jerked the zipper shut on her bag. Finally she said, "I'm sure you wouldn't feel this way if it were your father, but we all don't feel the same about our families. I can't help the way I feel. I know you don't understand, but I can't explain it to you. Not right now."

"All right, all right. I'm not trying to judge you. Believe me. Come and sit down here."

"There's the wake and the funeral. Then I'll have to go through the stuff in the house and get Francie settled in with my aunt and uncle, and then I'll be back. I figure three or four days. Five at the most. God, I hope it doesn't take longer than that. I won't be able to stand it." For a moment there was a note of real dread in her voice.

Michael stood up and, taking Beth by the arm, led her from where she was pacing on the rug to the edge of the bed. He sat her down beside him, and she did not resist his efforts. She stared out in front of her, her mouth slack with apparent exhaustion.

"I'll water the plants; I'll look after the house; I'll pick up the mail. Anything you need. Don't worry about it. And Maxine will look out for everything at the office. The world will not fall apart while you are gone," he said.

"I know. I know. I appreciate it, really." Her eyes were blank.

"What I'm worried about, though, is you. Are you sure you're going to be all right about this? I mean, I know it's a shock, but you shouldn't deny your feelings. Whatever they are."

"Please don't try to shrink me, Michael. I'll be fine."

"Okay, okay. Why don't you take a hot bath and we'll crawl into bed? You need the rest."

"I'm not tired now. I don't think I could sleep. You go to bed."

"Well, then I'll stay up with you."

"No, really. I just want to sit up for a while. By myself."

Mike started to protest and then thought better of it. She had every right to want to be alone at a time like this, he thought. He leaned over and kissed her. "Don't worry about the house or anything else. Just take care of things and hurry back to me."

Beth managed a smile and stood up. "I'll try not to wake you when I come up," she said.

"Don't stay up too late," he said. "Try to get some sleep."

"I will. Promise. And thank you."

Mike embraced her again, but Beth was wooden to his touch. Once he had released her, Beth left the bedroom, closing the door behind her. She could hear him opening the closet door as she went down the hallway toward the staircase. For a moment she thought of going back into the bedroom and crawling into bed beside him. But there was something hardening inside her that would not let any feeling, even for him, in or out. She thought suddenly of Brewster Wingate, beaming proudly at her, as if she were the best little girl in the world. It was funny sometimes how other people perceived you. *He should see me now,* she thought bitterly.

Beth descended the stairs in the quiet house. As she reached the bottom step, she felt a sudden chill run through her. She walked across the room and checked the thermostat, but the heat was at its normal level. She walked to the hall closet and reached inside for a sweater. As she closed the closet door, she could hear the sounds of water running in the upstairs bathroom while Mike got ready for bed.

Well, she thought, *I'm sure he's got a lot to think about. The girl that he thought he wanted to marry turns out to have an ice-cube tray for a heart. Her own father dies, and she cannot manage even to fake a tear.*

The idea of something warm in her stomach suddenly seemed very appealing. Beth went into the kitchen and turned the burner on under the teakettle. She stood with her back to the stove and stared out across the gleaming modern kitchen. *He might as well know the truth now,* she thought. *Get it out in the open. This is not the Brady Bunch he wants to marry into.*

The kettle whistled, and Beth turned and rubbed her fingers over the escaping steam. She poured the water into the teacup and then added a splash of brandy to it. The teacup shook in her hand as she began to shiver. Beth carried the rattling teacup into the living room and set it down on the coffee table. Then she walked over to the front windows to be sure they were closed. All three windows were shut tight. Outside, the tree branches snapped gently against them.

Beth was shivering continuously now. She walked to the hall closet again and dragged out a coat. She pulled it on over her clothes and her sweater, but the chills continued. Then she walked over and sank down into the corner of the sofa. She tried to pick up the teacup, but her hands were trembling so violently that she could not lift the cup to her lips, so she dropped it back onto the saucer.

As she pushed the saucer away from the edge of the table, her teeth began to chatter. For a few moments Beth stared blankly at the afghan, which was draped over the far arm of the sofa. Her mother had made it long ago, for Beth's hope chest, she had said. And Beth had always treasured it, even when the hope of a happy marriage had begun to seem as remote to Beth as the possibility of a walk on Mars. She leaned across the cushions, pulled the afghan to her, and bunched the heavy handmade blanket around her shoulders.

The image of her mother's face rose vividly to Beth's

mind despite the years that had passed since her death. It was a soundless image, for the memory of the voice was much harder to recapture as time passed. But the mild, wistful eyes were there, looking fondly at her. For a minute she stopped shaking. Then, gradually, her mother's face was supplanted by the gloomy visage of her father, the young man on whom her mother had pinned her hopes for happiness, long ago on her wedding day. Beth snorted in disgust and huddled inside the folds of the afghan, clutching it around her with fingers that felt stiff and icy. She realized suddenly, in recalling her family, that she had not even spoken to her sister. She wondered if Francie was with Aunt May. She had not even thought to ask. *She must be,* Beth thought. *Where else could she be?* Beth glanced at the antique gold clock on the mantel. It was much too late to call now. Besides, what would she say? It was just too late. "He's dead now," she said aloud. "It's too late."

Her teeth began to bang together with fearful force, as if her jaws were in an uncontrollable jerking spasm. Chills rushed through her body in waves. "I'm so cold," she muttered in amazement, and her chattering teeth clamped down in the inside of her mouth. A rush of warm blood spilled across her tongue. She wanted to reach up and stem the flow, but she found that her fingers were frozen to the blanket.

Chapter 2

T HE bus from the airport bounced along the narrow highway, which was scarred and pitted from a succession of brutal Maine winters. It wound through the harsh, rugged countryside, stopping in each of the scattered small towns along its tedious route. The bus was nearly empty of passengers, although it had held about two dozen when it began its milk run from Portland.

Beth gripped the seat in front of her and absorbed the jolts as they came, accustomed to them after the long ride. Occasionally she looked up to make sure her suitcase was secure on the rack above. Then she resumed staring out the window at the bleak, familiar landscape of her childhood.

It has its beauty, she thought. No doubt about it. But it was a desolate beauty for the most part. You got those days in winter that were dazzling with brilliant blue sky and snow-covered evergreens. And in the summer it could be heavenly when the wildflowers bloomed and the rivers sparkled in the welcome sun. But most often this was how she remembered it: gray and forbidding, with sharp-edged boulders covered by patches of snow and trees the color of lead against dank clouds that drifted like smoke through the mountains.

Beth sighed and checked her watch again, impatient with the plodding bus. It was nearly five o'clock, and she had already had a day of unending frustration. Everything had been late. Heavy fog in Philadelphia had delayed her departure. Then because of a snowstorm in Boston, she had missed two connecting flights. It was nearly four when she finally arrived in the Portland airport. The snow had turned to icy rain and then back to fog. She bought a ham sandwich wrapped in plastic and ate it at the airport bus stop. She had been tempted to rent a car at the airport, but she knew it would be treacherous driving on the icy roads, and besides, she didn't really need it. She could use her father's car when she arrived. There was no point in having two cars.

"Oldham next," the bus driver called out.

A woman with tightly curled hair and glasses and a cloth coat with a tiny fur collar jumped up and pulled her suitcases down from the rack above. Then she sat at the edge of her seat, eagerly craning her neck to catch a first glimpse of the town through the bus window.

Beth lifted her dark glasses and started to rub her eyes, but then she remembered her mascara and settled for massaging her forehead. She didn't really need dark glasses in the gloom of the late afternoon, but she felt as if they gave her some privacy and covered the weariness in her eyes. It had been nearly dawn when she had crept into bed beside Mike. Although she had applied her makeup with a little extra blush on her cheeks, she figured that by now her skin color was as gray as the landscape.

Up ahead she could see the few farmhouses getting closer together as they approached the town. The old houses looked shabby, unshielded by the bare trees. Each house boasted a barn on the surrounding land, and most of the barns were crumbling, their roofs sagging from the weight of snow and neglect. Hulks of rusting, broken-down cars without tires littered the rutted driveways. Beth shivered and gave a nervous tug to the belt of her wrap coat. Then she got up and pulled her suitcase down off the rack with shaking hands. *Not the chills again,* she thought. She edged down the bus aisle to where the woman in the fur collar was standing, exchanging pleasantries with the driver. *She can't wait to get there,* Beth thought. *We can't arrive soon enough to suit her.*

The bus turned off the road, rolled down the street past a garage and filling station, and pulled up in front of a convenience store on the other side. The woman in front of Beth stepped down, and Beth followed her out. She glanced around, getting her bearings. The filling station across the street had long been there, as Beth recalled, but the convenience store was new. At least the building was new. An old shed had once stood on this spot. The new building looked like a plastic shoebox with chrome borders and a lot of plate glass. *Progress,* thought Beth. The woman with the fur collar looked around at Beth as if to start a conversation, but Beth put her head down and avoided her bright glance. *The last thing I want to do is compare notes on how good it is to be back in Oldham,* Beth thought.

She looked at her watch again, wondering what time the wake was set to start. She had hoped to get in early enough to change clothes and take a nap, but now she doubted she would have the chance. *I'd better call*, she thought. Stuffing her suitcase under one arm, Beth crossed the narrow parking lot to the door of the convenience store and let herself in.

Leaning against the counter in a set of grimy coveralls was a stout young man with long, unkempt hair and a scraggly little beard. He was strumming on a guitar which was strapped over his shoulder, studying the positioning of his grease-stained fingers on the frets. Behind the counter a boy with dark hair and freckles scattered over his narrow features sat reading a paperback book which he had propped open on the counter in front of him. He was leaning on his elbows, his hands covering his ears, as if to shut out the sound of the guitar player's pickings. Both of them looked up and stared at Beth as she came in. The mechanic's strumming stopped abruptly.

"Do you have a phone?" Beth asked.

"Over there." The counterman pointed past a revolving rack of softcover books to a wall phone situated next to a display of potato chips and cheese snacks.

"Thanks," said Beth. She was conscious that they were watching her as she walked to the phone, and she was aware, with a wry sense of satisfaction, that she did not look as if she belonged in this town. From her sleek haircut to her fashionable black leather boots, she looked like a city person, born and bred.

She picked up the phone and dialed the house. The number rang and rang, but no one picked it up. "Damn," she whispered, feeling at once irritable yet oddly relieved. She realized that she was in no hurry to talk to Francie. Rummaging in her large leather pouch purse, Beth found her phone book and looked up the number of the parsonage. From behind her dark glasses she could see that the lady in the fur-collared coat had stepped up to the counter to pay for a box of candy and that the clerk was reluctantly distracted from his narrow-eyed scrutiny of her to wait on his customer. The guitarist, however, continued to gaze at her unabashedly.

Beth turned her back to them both and dialed the parsonage. Her aunt picked up the phone.

"Aunt May," said Beth, "I'm here."

"Oh, Beth," said her aunt. "How are you, dear?"

"I'm okay. I just got here. There was no answer at the house when I called. I'm wondering when the wake starts tonight."

"Well, dear," said May, "it starts in about forty-five minutes. Your uncle James and I are on our way to go. We're just about ready. Where are you? Are you at the Seven-Eleven?" May asked. "We'll come get you."

"Never mind," said Beth, knowing how long it took her uncle James to get organized. "Sullivan's isn't far from here. I'll walk over and meet you there."

"But, dear, you're tired. Let us come get you."

"No, really," said Beth, thinking that she would rather walk than hang around this store and wait. "I'll see you shortly. Yes. Bye."

Beth replaced the phone on the hook and put her address book back in her purse. She felt grubby and weary, and there was a headache starting to build at the base of her neck. She hesitated for a minute and then walked up to the counter. She picked out a pocket-size tin of aspirin from the display beside the cash register and asked the clerk for the price.

The boy finished the page of the book he was reading and then turned to the next. Beth noted the title, *Shoot-out in San Diego,* with a slight curl to her lip. On the cover was a guy in a safari suit, holding a blazing gun. "Excuse me," she said, rapping the tin on the counter.

"Fifty cents. Like it says," he told her, without looking up from his book.

Beth put two quarters down on the counter and picked up the aspirin.

"Do you have a water fountain here by any chance?" Beth asked.

The boy finally looked up from his book. "Nope."

Beth stifled a sigh and walked over to where the soda was stocked. She picked up a bottle of warm club soda and brought it back to the counter.

The counterman stared at her.

"How much?" she asked.

"Forty-five."

Beth tossed down the change and twisted the bottle top off with a snap of her wrist. She popped two aspirin in her mouth and swallowed them with the club soda. Then she started for the door. Beside the door was a large plastic garbage can with a swinging lid. Beth gave the lid a push and held the bottle over it.

"Hey," said the clerk, "don't throw that in there full like that."

"I replaced the top," said Beth.

"That don't matter," he said.

Beth felt her patience drain away. She dropped the garbage can lid and walked over to the counter. She set the bottle down on the counter with a bang. "There," she said sweetly. "Why don't you finish it?"

The boy with the guitar started to smile, but he tried to cover the smile with his hand. The counterman glared at him. Suddenly the boy with the guitar said, "Uh-oh, here comes Temple."

The door to the store swung open, and a heavyset

red-faced man, wearing a bow tie and a 7-Eleven jacket came striding in. "How we doin' today?" he called out. "How's business?"

I'm surprised he has any business at all with this creep working here, Beth thought. Turning her back on both the boys at the counter, she adjusted her suitcase strap on her shoulder, muttered a chilly "Excuse me" to the store manager as she squeezed past him, and left the store.

Time to face the music, she thought as she stepped out onto the chilly pavement. *Maybe the walk will clear your head.* She heard the door open behind her, and the boy with the guitar scurried out and across the parking lot toward the garage across the street. *The boss came back and spoiled all their fun,* she thought. *Serves them right.* She started off down the road toward the center of town. *Great to be back,* she thought. *Great.* The high-heeled boots were difficult to walk in, but they were the only black boots she had, and she'd worn them because she figured that she needed them for the funeral.

A couple of schoolgirls passed Beth on their bikes, chattering as they stood up on the pedals. They were bundled up in parkas and rubber boots, although Beth noted with rueful amusement that they were wearing Sergio Valente jeans. One of them could be Francie, Beth thought. She realized that she wouldn't even recognize her sister if it were she. One of the girls was pudgy, with a green knit hat squashing down her hair. Beth felt a little pang as she watched the girl ride by. *That was me,* she thought. All over. Plain, awkward, and out of it, even by this town's standards. Good in school and a social flop. What was it that her father used to call her? The dowdy dumpling.

Her father. Beth had been trying not to think about

35

the reason she was here. As she made her way along in her designer coat, high boots, and expensive haircut, which looked like something from a magazine, she suddenly felt dull, inept, and ugly. All of her life in Philadelphia—the business she'd built, the home she'd made, the wonderful man who loved her—seemed insubstantial. And it was just because she was here, on his turf again.

"Hey, there," a voice called out. Beth looked around and saw a station wagon with the 7-Eleven logo on the door slowing beside her. The driver was the counterman from the convenience store. "Do you need a ride?" he asked.

Recalling the scene at the store, Beth just frowned and waved him away.

"Hey, don't be mad," he said. "I was just in a bad mood 'cause Noah was driving me crazy with that guitar of his, and I was trying to finish my book before my boss got back."

For a minute she felt like saying, "Get lost," but she was tired, and the boy was obviously trying to be neighborly. Refusing the ride seemed like rather a childish, spiteful gesture. Beth nodded and forced a thin smile.

"All right," she said. "I'll take it."

The boy leaned over and opened the passenger door. Beth threw her bag in the back and slid into the front seat.

"It's getting dark," said the boy. "You have to be careful on this road. The other drivers can't see you."

"I hadn't realized it," said Beth, taking off her dark glasses and slipped them into her purse. "Which way are you heading?" Beth asked.

"Oh, I have to make a few deliveries. All over."

"The Seven-Eleven delivers?" Beth asked incredulously.

"Well, yeah. Here we do."

Beth peered into the back of the car and saw that the flatbed of the wagon had several boxes of groceries packed in it. Turning back, she caught the boy's eye in the rearview mirror, and he quickly looked away. She found something faintly charming about the way he nervously avoided her glance. She had a sudden sense of how exotic she must seem to him—a glamorous "older woman," visiting from some far-off place where the 7-Elevens didn't deliver. And here he was, looking as if he were just about old enough to have his license.

"Where can I drop you?" he asked.

Beth sighed. "Sullivan's Funeral Home."

"Oh," said the boy with polite concern in his voice, "who died?"

"My father." Beth felt a fleeting sense of embarrassment as she said it, and her voice caught for a second in her throat, even though she did not feel sad. She was here to bury her father. It did not seem real to her at all.

"Oh, that's too bad." There was a silence between them. *He's an all right kid,* Beth thought for a second. Then she looked out the window.

They drove along Main Street, passing the library, the laundry, the stationery store, and the luncheonette. The local doctor's office was at the end of the street, and Beth was surprised to see that Dr. Morris's name was still out front on the shingle.

"Dr. Morris is still alive," she said. "He must be a hundred by now." She wondered if he had been with her father when he died, trying to revive him with those strong, bony hands she recalled from childhood.

"Yeah, sure is. Are you from here originally?"

"I grew up here," said Beth. "My father was Martin Pearson. He worked for the electric company over in Harrison." As she said it, she realized what a feeble epitaph it was. But she did not know how else to describe him to this stranger without sounding strange and bitter. "I have a sister who lives here too," she added quickly. "You might know her, although she's probably a little younger than you. Francie Pearson."

The boy shook his head. "Doesn't ring a bell," he said. "Where do you live now?"

"Philadelphia."

"You came a long way."

"Yes. I had a hell of a time getting up here today."

The boy fell silent, and Beth wondered fleetingly if her mild oath had offended him. It didn't seem like something that would bother a teenager, but he could be really religious or something. "By the way," she said, "I didn't introduce myself. My name is Beth."

The boy looked a little startled, for he seemed to have been carefully thinking about the little Beth had said. "Nice to meet you," he murmured.

Beth waited for him to introduce himself. "This is it," the boy said suddenly. "Short trip."

He pulled the car up in front of the old, well-kept house which was the local funeral parlor. Beth had always thought it was one of the few handsome houses in town, except for the discreet signpost out front which reminded you that this was not a house for the living.

Beth reached into the back seat and retrieved her bag. "Thanks for the lift," she said.

"Anytime," said the boy, who waved to her as he steered the old Ford wagon away from the curb.

Beth's headache, which had abated somewhat in the car, now came back full force as she stood at the foot of

Sullivan's steps. She marshaled her strength as if it were a mountain she had to climb, rather than the six steps to the porch. It had been years since she stood here last, that terrible time when it had been her mother laid out in this house. *Well,* she thought, *nothing could be as bad as that.*

Taking a deep breath, Beth climbed the steps and opened the door to the funeral home. The foyer was quiet and carpeted, the dark green of the walls faintly illuminated by lamps which resembled gaslights. The air felt stifling and had an antiseptic smell perfumed by flowers, like the smell of a hospital without hope. The walls were lined with pictures of woodland scenes in dark wooden frames. They were the kinds of pictures you would never really look at.

Ahead of Beth were two sets of closed French doors curtained in white voile. Beside the doors on the left was a brass plaquette beneath a cross. The name Pearson was lettered neatly on a white card in the plaquette. Beside it was a lectern with a thin book for guests to sign lying open atop it. A bunch of white flowers in a permanent vase was attached to the lectern. The room was very quiet. The discreet strains of recorded organ music had not yet begun.

Beth heard footsteps coming up behind her and turned to see Mr. Sullivan in his old but impeccable dark suit, white shirt, and tie approaching her, his freckled hands extended in greeting. *He's probably the only man in town, besides Dr. Morris, who wears a suit to work,* Beth thought. She mustered a polite smile as Mr. Sullivan shook her hand.

"It's Beth, isn't it? My, how you've grown up. So sorry about your dad," he said in his kindly whisper.

"Thank you," said Beth.

"I spoke to your aunt awhile ago, and they should be along any minute with your sister."

Beth nodded.

"Here, let me take your bag. I can put it in the office if you'd like. Do you want a glass of water or something?"

Beth shook her head. "I'm fine."

"Perhaps you would like to have a few minutes alone with your dad before the others come," Mr. Sullivan suggested in a soothing tone.

Beth hesitated and then looked over toward the closed doors, feeling a mixture of duty and revulsion. The funeral director took her silence for assent. He walked over to the doors and opened them, motioning to Beth to come with him. Reluctantly she followed him into the room.

Several dozen folding chairs were set up in rows for the wake. *What do they need all these chairs for?* Beth thought. *He didn't have very many friends.* At the end of the dimly lit room the coffin rested amid a sparse array of flower arrangements that were banked on either side of it, like the winners' circle in a penny-ante horse race. The lid of the coffin was open, and Beth lowered her eyes to avoid looking at the familiar profile as she approached. Her mother's coffin had been closed because of the damage done by the accident. Beth felt a deep dread of looking at the body. For a second she felt faint. She steeled herself and followed Sullivan closer to the casket with leaden feet.

The undertaker nodded admiringly toward the taffeta-lined box. "He looks very well," he said.

Sullivan patted her arm and withdrew as Beth thanked him, leaving her alone beside the casket. Reluctantly she looked in.

People are always outraged by those words, Beth

thought. *"He looks well."* And in fact, there was something absurd about them. But what was a person supposed to say? *The truth?* she thought. *He looks awful. His skin is so white, and it looks as cold and dense and rubbery as an eraser. There is no light from within.* Not even the dark, scowling nimbus that often beclouded Martin Pearson's unyielding features. He had never looked like that, not even in sleep. All his demands, and his moods, and his intelligence and his opinions and his sarcasm and his occasional begrudging kindnesses were gone. *There must be such a thing as a soul,* she realized with a jolt of surprise. *This man's being has fled,* and that which was left behind looked amazingly unthreatening to Beth. Her fear ebbed away as she stared at the body. She wished that she could miss him, feel sorrow, but she felt only a blank space inside herself.

She had never been able to satisfy him, never been good enough to please him, much as she had wanted to. Even when she had been a small child, he would stride along ahead of her, impatiently barking at her to hurry and catch up. She knew, as she looked down at the body, that his soul would be a restless one. So she did something that she rarely did. She prayed. Her prayer was for her father's soul, that it would find peace, if peace was what it craved.

A door slammed in the foyer, and Beth heard the sound of raised voices, talking too loudly for the hush of the funeral home.

Beth turned her back on the body in the coffin and went down the aisle toward the door. As she reached the doorway the voices were clearly audible.

"It's not a party, Francie. We're not talking about a party, dear," said Uncle James in a soft, reassuring voice. "But it is customary for people to come in and have some refreshments afterward—"

Beth walked through the doors and saw a bespectacled young girl with messy ash blond hair to her shoulders and a face as white as chalk standing between the parson and his wife. "I don't care what you call it," Francie said in a loud voice. "That's what I call it. A party. And we're not going to have some goddamn party after my father's funeral. No!"

Mr. Sullivan had emerged from his office and was rubbing his hands together with a look of anxiety on his face. Apparently, despite the many manifestations of grief he had seen, he was still not used to it. Beth wondered briefly if he had an ulcer.

"Francie, dear," said Aunt May soothingly, "on sad occasions people need to gather together, and talk, and share their thoughts."

"Hypocrites," Francie announced.

"Beth!" exclaimed Uncle James, suddenly noting the presence of his niece in the doorway.

Beth stared at her sister for a moment. Behind her glasses the girl's wild-eyed expression narrowed into one of distrust at the sight of her sister. "You here for the party too?" said Francie.

"It's so good to see you," said Aunt May, rushing over to put her arms around her niece, who was a head taller than she. Beth awkwardly returned the embrace of her aunt and then her uncle.

"We're so sorry, dear," said Aunt May, "about Dad. Are you all right? How was your trip?"

"Exhausting, to tell the truth."

"I'm sure it was."

"Hello, Francie," said Beth evenly.

"Hello," muttered the girl.

"We were just explaining the funeral plans to

42

Francie," said Uncle James. "It's tomorrow morning at ten. Just a simple Christian service, which is what Martin wanted. And then we'll have the mourners come over to the parsonage afterward."

Aunt May nodded. "I think that would be best."

Beth looked down at her aunt's gray head bobbing in agreement with her husband and her patient, peaceful countenance. She had buried three other sisters and brothers, and Martin had been her youngest sibling. Beth wondered how May could have been so unlike her moody, intolerant younger brother. Beth looked up to see Francie glowering at her from red-rimmed eyes.

"That sounds fine," said Beth firmly. "Thank you for everything you've done."

"May," said Uncle James, "do you want to go in and have a minute alone with Martin? The others are going to be arriving any minute."

"Yes, dear. But perhaps the girls? Francie? Beth?"

"I've already been," said Beth.

Francie gave her head a violent shake.

Mr. Sullivan, who perceived that the crisis had abated, retreated into his office, perhaps to take an antacid and curse the day his father had left him this profitable business. Holding her husband's arm for support, May took a steadying breath and began the long walk down the room between the chairs to where her brother's body lay in its bier.

Beth decided to ignore the insolent look in her sister's eyes. *The kid is grieving,* she reminded herself. *She doesn't know how to handle this.* "How are you, Francie? How is everything?" Beth asked.

The girl looked at her incredulously. "Are you kidding? Do you want to talk about the weather? Or maybe my grades in school?"

"I didn't mean it that way," said Beth in a calm voice. "I was just concerned about you. It's been such a shock."

Francie didn't answer. She was staring stonily ahead. Beth noticed that her slip was showing under the shapeless dress she was wearing, and one of her knee socks was slipping down into her running sneakers. Beth forced herself not to comment on the inappropriate attire.

"I just couldn't believe it when I heard," said Beth. "Had he been sick or anything lately?"

"No," said Francie.

"When did it actually happen? Aunt May wasn't too clear on that."

Francie glanced quickly at her and then looked away. "Yesterday afternoon."

"I hope he didn't suffer," Beth said, but it sounded hollow.

"He just had a heart attack and died," said Francie impatiently. "Dr. Morris said it must have been coming for a long time."

"Was he home?" Beth asked.

"What difference does it make to you where he was?"

Beth's temper flared at Francie's words. "I'm just asking. Believe it or not, he was my father too."

"He was home," said Francie.

Beth looked at her. She was about to say that she didn't really care after all when she noticed a strange uneasiness around the girl's eyes and mouth that made her curious.

"Were you home when it happened?"

Beth was unprepared for the look of alarm that the girl directed at her. "Who told you that?"

"What's the matter with you? Nobody told me any-

44

thing. Aunt May told me he had a heart attack. Period. He did have a heart attack, didn't he?"

"Of course, he had a heart attack," Francie shouted. Mr. Sullivan came running out of his office at the sound of Francie's loud voice. "Why are you looking at me like that?"

Beth felt a knot form in her stomach at the sight of her sister's face, which was mottled now with patches that looked greenish in the foyer's dim light. The girl's expression seemed to shift somewhere between rage and fear. Francie turned her eyes away and would not meet her sister's gaze.

A bell tinkled faintly in the hallway, and they could hear the front door open and then the muted voices of the first mourners to arrive at the wake. Beth hesitated, trying to decide what to say. A couple of people dressed in somber colors, whom Beth did not recognize, entered the foyer and looked uncertainly at the two sisters, who were tensely deadlocked in place.

"Girls," Mr. Sullivan urged in a hushed voice, "you should probably be going inside now. People are arriving to pay their respects."

Beth did not want to press it further. *It's probably nothing,* she reminded herself. *Francie is just distraught.* But she could not let go of the nagging sense that for some reason the girl was lying to her.

"Let's get this over with," she said, inclining her head toward the double doors. She felt it getting hard to breathe in the room. Francie nodded stonily and preceded Beth through the French doors. Beth wished she could make the time race. All she wanted to do was just get away from here and cheerfully forget them both—her father and Francie—forever.

Chapter 3

T HE click and swish of the windshield wipers and Aunt May's sniffling into her hankie were the only sounds in the car as Uncle James drove toward the Pearsons' house on Wheelock Street. Sitting with her knees drawn up uncomfortably in front of her, Beth felt like a child, sharing the back seat with her sister and staring out past the gray heads of the grown-ups in the front at the drizzle and the shining streets.

Aunt May cleared her throat. "It's not supposed to rain tomorrow. I'm sure a lot of people will come."

"That's good," said Beth automatically. Francie appeared oblivious of her aunt's remark.

"You never know about the weather," said Uncle James, and the silence descended again.

A lot of people probably will come, Beth thought. *The same people who came to the wake: friends of Aunt May's and loyal members of Uncle James's parish.* She had hardly recognized a soul there tonight.

"Here we are," said Uncle James as he made a wide

turn at the entrance to Wheelock and proceeded slowly down the street.

Beth felt her heart catch in her throat at the sight of the home of her childhood with its dark brown shingles and faded roof. She had not been back in eight years. In a way she felt glad to see it. In another way it made her feel faintly sick.

As the car headlights swept past it and turned into the driveway, Beth noticed a Christmas wreath with a tattered bow, turning brown against the peeling paint on the front door. Uncle James pulled into the driveway and put the car into park.

Aunt May turned around in her seat and looked at Beth and Francie with kindly, puffy eyes. "Are you sure you girls won't change your minds and come have supper with us? We'd love to have you. It's no trouble, you know."

Francie shook her head and opened the car door on her side.

"I'm awfully tired, Aunt May," said Beth. "The sooner I get to bed, the better. Tomorrow is going to be another long day."

"I've got chicken in the refrigerator all ready," said May.

"Don't hound them, dear," said Uncle James. "They're big girls."

"Thanks anyway, really," said Beth.

"Good night," said Francie, getting out and slamming the car door behind her.

Aunt May sighed as Francie headed toward the house in the rain, her shoulders hunched up to keep the water from running down her neck, her sneakers squishing on the muddy path.

Beth leaned over and gave her aunt and uncle perfunctory kisses before getting out of the car. "See you tomorrow," she said.

She turned her collar up against the drizzle and waved as they backed out of the driveway, with Aunt May fussing at her husband to beware of the tree on the other side of the road. Beth shivered from the chill as she stood there. Hoisting her suitcase again, she turned and walked toward the house. Francie had already disappeared inside. At the door she looked back, but she could no longer see her aunt and uncle's car lights. She turned the doorknob and went into the dark house.

Francie was not in the kitchen when Beth entered, and she could not hear her in the house. Beth put down her bag and looked around. The kitchen was at once familiar and strange. The decorations which her mother had used to cheer the room were still in place but were covered with dust and grease. A little plant pot in a ceramic windmill on the windowsill was still there, but the plant had died long ago. The cupboard doors hung open haphazardly, and the cabinets were sparsely stocked with instant potatoes and cans of stew and spaghetti that just had to be heated to be eaten. Her mother's prized china was chipped and carelessly stacked, and a dull film seemed to have settled over it. In the corner the rocker still sat, although the cushion on it was ripped and had been patched with a piece of masking tape. Looking at it, Beth remembered that it had been her favorite place to curl up and read when her mother was alive, bustling around the kitchen.

With a sigh Beth passed through the kitchen into the hallway and hung her coat in the closet. Once she had taken her coat off, she suddenly realized how cold it was in the house. Pulling her sweater closer around her and rubbing her arms, Beth went into the living room to check the thermostat. As she crossed the room, she touched a few of the things on the dusty tables. There was a music box the family had always had. And an ashtray from her parents' honeymoon in Washington, D.C. As she ran her hand along the table behind the sofa, her fingers touched her father's glasses. They were lying there, open, on the table, and she suddenly had a vivid image of him, absorbed in a book, the corners of his mouth lowered, his eyes narrowed behind the lenses, as if the author were trying to deceive him. She drew her fingers back quickly as if they had been burned.

Briskly she crossed the room and pushed up the temperature on the thermostat. The heat kicked on with a rumble.

"You'd better turn that down," said a voice behind her.

Beth started and turned around. She could see the outline of her sister's form crouched on the darkened staircase, watching her.

"Don't be ridiculous," Beth snapped. "It's freezing in here."

"Too bad," said Francie. "The oil's low. We didn't pay the guy last month, so he didn't deliver."

"I'll pay them," said Beth evenly. "They can deliver it tomorrow."

"Not on Saturday they won't," said Francie. "Not till next week."

"Great," Beth muttered.

"What?" asked Francie suspiciously.

"Never mind," said Beth as she went back and lowered the temperature. She heard Francie stomping up the stairs and then the sound of a door slamming on the second floor.

Beth went and got her suitcase and then climbed

the stairs herself. The wind and rain outside were buffeting the house, and she felt as if every draft were whistling through the walls and cutting into her. *I'll get pneumonia from this damn trip,* she thought.

The door to Francie's room was closed, and Beth passed right by it. She went into her old room and put her suitcase down on the bare floor. Then she sat down on the edge of the sagging bed and pulled off her black leather boots. She rubbed her feet and looked around her old room. It made a dreary contrast with her cozy bedroom at home. She thought wistfully of the cheery chintzes that covered her stuffed chairs, the soft light of the reading lamp by her bed, and, most of all, Mike, coming through the doorway, toweling his hair after a shower. She wished she could talk to him, although she knew he was at the hospital tonight.

Beth remembered that she had not taken much with her when she left this house, but as she glanced around, it seemed to her that no one had even set foot in her room since that day she had walked out and slammed the door behind her. Her books had gathered dust in the bookcase, and the eyelet skirt on her preteen-size dressing table was gray and dingy. The glossy photos of TV stars she had thumbtacked to her walls were curled up at the bottom so that you couldn't see their faces below their noses. A picture of her mother in a silver frame smiled out at her from the night table by her bed. Next to it was a blue china vase with a silk rose in it, which she had won in a raffle at the church fair.

Across the room the window, hung with limp voile curtains, still had in it the same diagonal crack that had been there when she'd left.

"Home sweet home," Beth murmured aloud. Then she shrugged and unzipped her bag. She slipped into a pair of running shoes and tied them up. They didn't look right with her good slacks, but she thought ruefully, *Who's going to see me here?* Besides, it did not take long to fall back into the local mentality, which was comfort over style every time.

She opened the closet door and saw that there were a few wire hangers, along with an assortment of clothes from when she'd been a teenager. Despite her weariness, she decided to unpack right away. She hadn't brought that much anyway. She quickly placed her folded things into the musty-smelling drawers of the dresser, and then she lifted out the black dress she had brought for the funeral, shook it out, and looked at it critically. It had gotten pretty wrinkled from the trip. The last thing she felt like doing at that moment was ironing, but she knew that there would not be much time in the morning. *I'd better do it,* she thought. *If they even have an iron.*

The black dress folded over her arm, Beth walked down the hall and knocked on the door to Francie's room. There was no answer.

"Francie," said Beth impatiently.

"It's open," came a voice from inside.

Beth opened the door and leaned in, holding the doorknob. Francie was lying on her bed, her arms folded across her chest, staring at the opposite wall. Her blondish hair was all bunched up and matted on the pillow behind her head, and her glasses had slipped down off the bridge of her nose. She did not glance at Beth or make any move to get up when Beth came in.

"Sorry to bother you," said Beth. "I've got this dress to wear to the funeral tomorrow, and I need to iron it. Do you know where the iron is?"

"Under the sink," said Francie. "I don't know if it still works."

Beth glanced around the girl's room. Clothes were heaped on the chair and in the corner by the closet. "Have you got something to wear tomorrow?" she said.

"What do you mean?" Francie asked defensively, giving her sister a sidelong glance.

"Nothing," said Beth. "I thought since we're going to have the iron out, you might want to press whatever it is you're wearing. That's all."

Francie sat up on the bed, grasping the edge for a minute as if she were dizzy. Then she got up and went over to the chair that was piled with clothes. She rummaged through the dirty dungarees and pilled sweaters until she dislodged what appeared to be a large sweatshirt.

"I'm wearing this," she said. "It's my sweatshirt dress."

"You're supposed to wear black," Beth said stiffly.

Francie continued to gaze at the rumpled garment in her hands. "He made it for me," said Francie.

"Who?"

"Daddy."

Beth examined the shabby dress incredulously. The top was a blue sweatshirt with the neck cut out and the sleeves cut to cover about the middle of the forearm. The skirt, which was sewn to the top, had a drawstring waist and was cut along the bottom instead of being actually hemmed.

"He sewed it," said Francie.

"He couldn't sew," Beth said flatly.

"He did, though. I wanted one of these dresses, and I was going to try to make it on my—on Mother's old machine, but I couldn't get it to work. So he came in and said, 'I never saw a machine I couldn't operate.' And he sewed it."

Beth stared at the faded garment as if it had suddenly come alive. The girl was right, of course. What could be more appropriate for the occasion? So what if she looked like a hobo's daughter? A quick glance in the closet told Beth that everything the girl owned was shabby anyway. It looked as if he had never bought her anything new. He thought new clothes were frivolous, a waste of money. Just like the heat. What did he care if they all froze to death? But an image of her father, seated at the sewing machine, seemed to rise before her like some mocking specter.

"Wear what you want," said Beth.

"I'm going to," said Francie, staring back at her.

Downstairs a door slammed, and Beth let out a gasp.

"How come you're so jumpy?" said Francie.

"What was that?"

"Probably the screen door out front. That always happens in a storm like this. The hook is broken."

"Screen door?" said Beth. "It's January. Didn't he even put the storm doors up? God."

"He didn't feel good a lot of times. There was too much that needed fixing."

Beth thought of her own house and the constant maintenance chores it required. And she had Mike to help her and no teenage girl to worry about. Somewhat chastened, she said, "I'll look at it." Francie did not reply.

Beth left the room and trudged down the stairs. She laid her dress on the banister and went to the front door. *Maybe I can wedge the screen shut,* she thought, opening the door. *I don't feel like trying to fix it tonight.*

Beth threw open the door, and as she did, dried

needles from the brown wreath hanging there showered the front hallway. The red bow tied to it had faded to pink from the exposure to the weather. "We need this like a hole in the head," she said.

The screen door flapped and banged as Beth reached behind the wreath and struggled to untwist the wire that secured it to the nail in the door. Needles scattered and clung to her sweater as she attacked the twisted wire with a ferocity it did not warrant. Finally she freed the wreath, and pushing the screen door out, she tossed the wreath into the bushes beside the door.

That done, she turned her attention to the screen door latch. She flicked it back and forth with her finger, but it was clearly broken. "Didn't he do anything around here?" she said aloud.

But even as she said it, she thought again of the sweatshirt dress, and she felt as if something were rising inside of her, closing off her throat. He had made Francie a dress.

Beth rattled and shook the door latch as if willing it to fix itself. The handle flapped helplessly in her throttling grip. She glared down at the useless catch in disgust.

The wind moaned around her and the rain spattered her shoulders as she let go of the latch and looked around the doorway for something to use to wedge the door shut.

At the foot of the stone steps was the day's newspaper, still rolled up and secured with a rubber band. *It's all wet anyway,* Beth thought, spotting it there. *I'll tear off a page and fold it up.* Clutching her sweater around her, she skipped down the steps and bent over to pick the paper up. As she reached for it her gaze fell on the feet and then the bent legs of a shadowy figure, crouching in the bushes beside the steps.

Beth screamed and scrambled up, stifling her cry with her fist.

The figure jerked back, as if ready to run.

"Show yourself," Beth demanded in a shaky voice. "I'll call the cops."

The person hesitated and then stood up and edged forward into the arc of the porch light. Beth felt the scowl on her face turn into a blush as she recognized the young man from the convenience store, the one who had driven her to the funeral home. His clean, disheveled dark hair shone in the lamplight. He met her gaze with a wary, slightly sheepish look. His thin shoulders were tensely hunched up in his threadbare overcoat, his hands stuffed in the pockets.

"Sorry," he mumbled.

"What are you doing," Beth demanded, "creeping around here?"

The boy shrugged. "I didn't mean to scare you."

She was about to protest again when it suddenly occurred to her what he might be doing there. It hardly seemed likely, but she couldn't think of any other explanation. The boy had tracked her down. She peered at him more closely. He was staring shyly down at his own feet.

"I didn't expect to see you again," she said.

"Surprised you, I guess."

This is silly, Beth told herself. But at the same time she could not help feeling a little flattered. She tried to sound stern, but there was a trace of warmth in her tone, and she felt a smile tugging at her lips. "Well, for heaven's sake, do you always go lurking around in bushes like this?"

The boy laughed nervously and shrugged again.

"I don't remember telling you where to find me," said Beth.

"It wasn't hard. I figured you'd be here," he said.

Beth raised her eyebrows in surprise. "Aha, a sleuth." She tried to keep her tone brisk so as not to appear flustered by this obvious, unexpected display of interest. "Well, I'm flattered that you went to the trouble, but next time I think you'd be better off knocking on the door rather than skulking around like that—"

Just then a voice behind her cried out, "Andrew," and Francie came out of the house in her stocking feet, bounded down the steps, and threw herself at the young man. She hugged him around the neck and then quickly let him loose. She grabbed his hand and looked at him with shining eyes.

"Hey, babe," he said, giving her a sly smile and squeezing her hand.

For a moment Beth blinked at them in confusion, and then she felt the color rise to her cheeks.

"Come inside," Francie pleaded, dragging him by the hand toward the house. "It's wet out here. Oh, I'm so glad to see you." She pulled him to the step and then seemed to recall that Beth was there.

"Andrew," she said, "this is my sister, Beth."

"I know," said the boy, grinning and winking at Beth. "I already met her."

"You did. When?" asked Francie suspiciously.

"At the store today," he said. "I gave her a ride to Sullivan's."

"You did?" Francie frowned at Andrew and then looked at Beth.

Beth nodded, but her lips were pressed tightly together, and she stared at the boy with narrowed eyes. Andrew avoided looking at her.

"Well, that was nice of you," said Francie.

"Why did you say you didn't know who I was? Or Francie, for that matter?" asked Beth in a harsh voice.

Andrew shook his head and waved a hand as if to dismiss it. "It was just a little joke."

Beth glared at him. *Yeah, and I was the butt of it,* she thought.

"It was easier than explaining," he said, looking a little uncomfortable. "It was just—I don't know. I didn't mean anything by it." His eyes widened, as if he were hurt by her attitude.

Beth closed her eyes for a second and tried to stop herself from losing her temper. But she felt ridiculous, like some foolish old maid who thought every man was after her. And he knew he had embarrassed her. She was sure he did.

"Come on in," Francie whined. "It's cold out here."

"Go get your shoes," he said. "We're going for a walk."

"But it's raining," Francie protested. Then she looked at Beth and back to Andrew. "Well, yeah, I guess so."

"Are you aware," Beth said in a disapproving tone, "that there has been a death in this family? Do you really think this is the time to be out strolling around town?"

"We aren't strolling around," said Francie in a shrill voice. "We're just going out for a walk."

"Well, pardon me for saying so," Beth said, clenching her fists, "but it seems a little tacky to me. People generally show a little restraint, you know. A little respect for the dead."

Francie turned on Beth indignantly. "We aren't doing anything wrong."

"Never mind, babe," said Andrew. "Your sister's the boss. If she says it's not cool—"

"Who cares what she says?" said Francie.

"No, no. I probably shouldn't have come over. Look,

I'll see you tomorrow anyway. It's no big deal," said Andrew, backing away with his hands raised. "You do what your big sister says."

Beth looked down at Andrew as if to acknowledge his good sense and thought she saw his eyes piercing her with a look of rage so intense it made his face muscles twitch. But it was gone in a thrice, like a lightning bolt that flashes so quickly that you cannot say for sure if it was really there.

"Good night now," he said, smiling politely.

Beth looked uneasily into the bland, guileless face. "Good night," she said, but her voice sounded shaky. She pulled her sweater tightly around her, as if to protect herself from his vicious glance, even though it was nowhere in evidence.

Francie watched him go with a stricken look and then turned and ran into the house.

Leaving the screen door to flap, Beth slammed the front door behind her and locked it. She pulled her dress off the banister and went into the kitchen. She tossed the dress on the rocker and leaned back against the sink, pressing her fingers to her eyelids as if she could wipe away the image of Andrew's menacing gaze. *Oh, stop imagining things,* she thought. *You're so tired, you're exaggerating this.*

She turned and began to rummage through the cabinets until she found a box of stale saltines. She reached into the box and numbly began to transfer the crackers to her mouth, shaking her head and staring vacantly out into the kitchen. She felt her face redden as she relived the encounter.

It was embarrassing to admit to herself that she had tried to belittle Andrew in front of Francie, wanting to pay him back because she had felt humiliated by the boy. But in a way it was a relief to acknowledge it.

She glanced over at her dress heaped on the chair and decided to hunt up the iron. With a sigh she put the saltine box on the counter and then crouched down and scanned the collection of odds and ends under the sink until she located the iron. Then Beth went to the broom closet, pulled out the ironing board, and set it up. She plugged in the iron and stood waiting for it to heat.

If she wants to wear an old ragged dress to the funeral and run around all night with her boyfriend, what difference does it make to you? Beth thought. *She's the one who's got to stay here, not you. And she obviously feels that she's got nothing to prove.*

Let her be. Let her do what she wants. She's gotten along without your interference all these years. She and your father. They did just fine without you. So butt out.

The iron did not hiss, and Beth felt sure it must be broken. She reached down to touch it, and the hot metal burned her finger instantly. She squeezed her hand into a fist and held it to her chest, resisting the pain.

She walked over to the sink and turned on the cold water with her other hand. Then she stuck her finger under the stream and held it there, staring out the window into the darkness. The shadows of the night moved in shifting patterns from the wind, and for a moment she had the strange feeling that there was still someone out there.

She smiled ruefully. *There is no one out there,* she reminded herself. *No one at all. You couldn't be more alone.*

Rubbing her sore hand, she turned back to the ironing board. The rain spit at the windowpanes, and the storm, which had died down for a moment, resumed its restless prowling around the house.

Chapter 4

"COME on, dear," Aunt May whispered, nudging Beth, as the sounds of the closing hymn swelled from the organ and filled the church. "We go first."

Beth felt drowsy and heavy-limbed, as if someone had just awakened her from a drugged sleep. She dragged herself to her feet and blinked at her aunt. May was adjusting her black hat and prodding Francie to her feet as the shining coffin, accompanied by a group of men from the church, passed by the entrance to the pew.

Somehow Beth had managed to tune it out, not to hear more than a smattering of the words of Uncle James's tribute from the pulpit to Martin Pearson. She had spent the time studying the familiar altar, thinking about Mike, and wondering if everything was all right at home. She knew what he had been saying. Something about the good Christian, loving father and husband, but she was able to muffle the words with her thoughts of things outside the church, far from this place. Still, the service had seemed interminable, as if she were to spend the rest of her life rooted to the cold wooden bench, captive to the sounds of her uncle's halting voice, the isolated whimpers, the loud, harsh notes of the organ. She had thought about people in prisons and how they must cope with confinement. She had escaped through her thoughts to other places, but the tension had never left her body.

Now, to her amazement, it was over. It was as if someone had opened the door to her cell and walked away. She felt dazed and not certain that it wasn't a grim prank, that if she stood up and started out, she would be rudely pushed back in her place. She could see Francie waiting in the aisle. Aunt May reached for Beth's arm as she slid out of the pew and then took Francie's arm and walked slowly between them behind the coffin toward the back of the church.

Beth kept her gaze focused on the church doors in the back, never once glancing down at the coffin. She could feel the curious gazes of the mourners trained on her. She was a stranger in this town now, and she could imagine their gossip. She was not weeping. Her expression was completely blank. She knew they would talk about that. How life in the city had made her cold and indifferent, taken out her heart and replaced it with a lump of coal.

Numbly she put one foot in front of the other. She could feel May shaking beside her, and she knew without looking that she was weeping. But there was no way that Beth could accommodate the onlookers. They might be able to point her out to their children, in a way they deemed subtle, as an example of what happened when a young person went away. For a few of those young ones, Beth knew, this would serve only to pique their curiosity. There were always those who wanted to escape.

True to Uncle James's prediction, the rain had stopped, although the sky now had the impenetrable, cottony look that often precedes a snowfall. Beth made her way down the steps of the church, helping her aunt along, and watched impassively as the coffin was loaded into Sullivan's ancient hearse. Out of the corner of her eye she could see the others exiting the church and gathering behind them in a ragged horse-shoe formation as the church bell tolled its doleful notes.

The undertaker sidled up beside Beth, causing her to jump, and pressed the long stem of a red carnation into her hands. "For the grave," he whispered, in answer to her questioning look. "To place on the casket."

"Oh," said Beth. Having tucked the carnation under her arm, she reached into her handbag and pulled out her dark glasses, which she quickly put on. There was no sun in sight, but at least they offered her some shelter from curious eyes.

The undertaker had given May and Francie each a flower and was now instructing them to pile into the old Lincoln and they would follow the hearse the short distance to the cemetery. Beth could see the black-garbed people scattering to their cars like crows in flight as she wedged herself into the back seat beside May.

The silence in the car was oppressive as they sat waiting in the church driveway. The driver, clearly a local farmer who was moonlighting for Sullivan's, chewed gum in a quiet, steady roll of the jaw.

"What are we waiting for?" Beth asked impatiently.

"Uncle James is going with us," said May.

Beth stared out the tinted window of the car at her

uncle, whose vestments were billowing in the wind, the skin on his face and hands ruddy from the cold as he nodded in hushed conversation with stragglers, slowly making his way toward the car.

"It was a nice service," said May.

Francie pushed her glasses up on her nose after wiping her eyes underneath them. "God," she said, "I hate this."

Beth sighed and looked away with dull eyes, grateful again for her dark glasses. *Not too much longer,* she thought. She felt something slimy on her fingers and looked down. She had absentmindedly crushed and rolled the petals of the carnation in her fingers. May saw her glance. "Don't worry," she whispered as the car door opened and Uncle James got in. "We'll get you another one."

The car started to roll slowly in the direction the hearse had already gone.

By the time they reached the parsonage, after the cemetery, the kitchen table in Aunt May's house was already laden with plates and casserole dishes full of food. Beth was a little surprised to see the spread, considering that she had hardly recognized any of the people at the funeral. *I'm the uncharitable one,* she thought. *I'm the one who is judging them, not the other way around.*

There was a buzz of quiet conversation in the house, and as Beth made her way through the crowded living room, she was greeted with handshakes and awkward, brief squeezes. She responded as courteously as she knew how.

She went upstairs to her aunt and uncle's bedroom and put her coat down on the bed along with all the others piled there. Then she went into the bathroom and fixed her makeup in preparation for facing the people downstairs again. When she came out of the bathroom, she saw a young women of about her own age sitting in the window seat waiting for a turn. The woman had a wide face and a short cap of curly red hair. It took Beth only a moment to place her.

"Cindy?" she asked.

The woman stood up and nodded, reaching out a hand to Beth. She gave Beth an apologetic smile. "So sorry about your dad," she said.

"Cindy Ballard," said Beth, shaking the girl's hand, remembering her as she had seen her last, in their high school days when they had walked home from school together and shared dateless Saturday nights. "God, it's good to see you. It was so nice of you to come. It's been years."

"I know. How are you? You look great."

"Thanks," said Beth, clinging to the woman's hand, happy to see someone who had once been a friend. She studied the other woman's clear eyes, her neat figure in a plain navy dress. "You look good yourself. Tell you the truth, I'm so glad to see someone I really know. I hardly recognize most of these people."

"I don't know. Old-timers, I guess," she said with a bemused smile.

"I guess some of them might have worked with my father," Beth observed.

Cindy immediately became more sober. "Probably."

"Well," said Beth, pausing awkwardly as a man in a neat but shabby suit edged his way hopefully past the young women toward the bathroom. "Do you mind?" Beth asked Cindy.

The woman shook her head and indicated that they should move out of the way.

"So—" said Beth.

"How've you—" said Cindy at the same time.

"You first," said Beth. "It's so good to see you. What are you doing here these days? How's your family?"

"Well," said Cindy proudly, "I'm married now." She held out her ring finger for Beth to admire.

"Do I know him?" Beth asked.

"Billy McNeill," said Cindy. "He was two years ahead of us."

"Ahhh, one of the older boys," said Beth slyly. "How did you manage that? We could never get them to look at us in school."

Cindy blushed. "My luck changed."

"Mine too," said Beth. "Are you working?"

"I'm teaching. That's one reason I'm here. Francie is in my class at school."

"Oh," said Beth, "I see."

"A couple of her classmates are here too. They wanted to come. Although they were a little nervous. You know, kids."

Beth, who did not want to admit that she didn't have any idea about kids, simply nodded.

"Listen, Beth, there's something I wanted to . . . Um, I need to talk to you about . . . Concerning Francie. Do you have a minute? I know this isn't the greatest time, but . . . well, it's on my mind, and it's kind of important."

Beth shrugged. "Sure, I guess so."

"Beth," said Aunt May, who had just made her way up the stairs and encountered the two young women on the landing. "Oh, hello, dear."

"Hello, Mrs. Traugott," said Cindy.

"Beth, dear," said May, "may I borrow you a minute. I need to ask you something. Do you mind, dear?"

Cindy shook her head. "No, of course not."

Beth looked at her questioningly.

"It's all right. We can talk later or another time."

Beth frowned at the uneasy look in Cindy's eyes. "Are you sure?"

"Sure," said Cindy. "Besides, I want a chance to hear about you." She gave Beth a tight smile and then waved, noticing that the bathroom was again vacant. She went in and closed the door.

"What is it, Aunt May? Do you need me downstairs?"

"No, no. They'll manage just fine. Everyone here has experience. They all know just what to do."

"I guess so," said Beth.

"I wanted to ask your opinion," she said, starting purposefully down the upstairs hallway of the house. "I've been trying to decide which room to put Francie in."

Reluctantly Beth followed her aunt down the hallway, with its faded lily of the valley wallpaper. "I don't think you need to decide right this minute," said Beth.

"Now Tommy's room is bigger," said May, opening the door and peering into the room, which had twin beds and was still decorated with pictures of ballplayers and trophies, which Tom had won in high school. Beth looked in over May's shoulder, remembering her cousin, who was married now and lived in Colorado. She had thought him a most dashing figure when she was a child.

"Tommy's room is nice," she agreed patiently.

"Peggy's room is smaller, but it gets lots of sunlight, and it's such a pretty room," said May as she toddled across the hall and opened the door to the pink and white room with a canopy bed and ruffled curtains.

"Well," said Beth, "why don't you let Francie pick? They're both nice rooms."

May pressed her lips together, one finger tapping her cheek, and nodded, still staring into the room of her daughter, who now had children of her own. "We want her to be happy here with us."

"I'm sure she will," said Beth automatically.

May smiled bleakly. "She hasn't had it easy, the poor thing. Although Martin tried very hard, there was only so much he could do, working all day, trying to keep the house up. A lot of it fell on that child, I'm afraid. It must have been awfully tough for her, growing up without a mother the way she did."

"Well, whose fault is that?" said Beth in a flat voice.

May's mouth dropped open, and she turned and stared at her niece, who was leaning against the wall. "Beth," said May sharply, "how could you say that?"

"I didn't mean it the way it sounded," Beth said hurriedly.

May's face had become very pink, as if she were going to cry again, and she shook her head at Beth. "Your mother's death was an accident. You don't mean to tell me that you think Francie was responsible—"

Beth was patting her aunt on the shoulder and trying to quiet her. "No," she insisted, "I didn't mean that. Please, Aunt May. I only meant . . . these things just happen. Nobody's to blame for them."

"That's right," said May. "It's God's will. He never gives us more problems than we can bear."

"I know, I know," said Beth. "Listen, maybe we'd better get back downstairs. All these people have been nice enough to come."

"Well, yes, you're right," said May, composing herself like a plump bird rearranging her feathers. "I'll decide about the room later."

She went down the hall and started down the stairs. Beth followed her, greeting the various people they met along the way and responding numbly to the introductions. She could not tell, from May's calm demeanor, whether she had believed Beth's explanation of that chance remark. As soon as she said it she had wished she could snatch it back from the air.

"Did you eat something?" May asked when they again reached the kitchen.

"I'm not hungry," said Beth, but a woman in an apron decorated with a print of squirrels wearing frills and hair ribbons was handing her a sandwich. Beth accepted it passively and began to eat, although the food was tasteless to her. As she stood by the kitchen table, chewing dutifully, the sound of guitar music wafted into the house from the backyard. May excused herself from conversation with a neighbor and walked over to the back door, looking for the source of the music. Beth put the sandwich down and walked up behind her to look out over her aunt's shoulder.

A group of kids, huddled together in their heavy coats, whispering, giggling, and poking one another, were gathered outside in the cold gray afternoon. Seated on the front hood of one of the cars in the driveway was the young man from the garage, his long hair pulled into a messy ponytail, with stray bunches of hair being lifted by the wind. The boy's guitar was perched on his lap, and he seemed to be wrapped in the cocoon of oblivion that often surrounds people at their instruments as he strummed away, singing along to his tunes in a nasal voice. A little apart from the others, Andrew had one elbow propped on the car's roof, his shabby coat collar pulled up almost to the tips of his ears, which were red from the cold. Francie leaned against him, the ragged hem of her sweatshirt dress hanging out from under her parka. Occasionally she leaned up and whispered at his coat collar, and Andrew nodded with a bored expression.

May took in the scene with a deep frown of disapproval, which Beth noticed immediately. She felt a flash of anger at the braying guitarist, who clearly would take any opportunity to find an audience. Francie looked up and saw them in the doorway. Beth motioned for her to come over.

Francie walked over to where her sister and aunt were standing and looked up at them questioningly.

"Who is this guy?" Beth demanded in a low voice.

"Oh, that's Noah. He's a friend of Andrew's. Doesn't he play good?"

"Tell Noah," said Beth, "that this is a funeral, not a hootenanny."

"A what?" said Francie.

"Never mind." Beth sighed. "Tell him to quit playing that guitar. It's very rude."

Francie's face contracted into a bitter pout. "We're not hurting you," she said.

"I thought you were the one who was so upset about having a party after the funeral."

Francie glowered at her, but Beth could see that her remark had hit home. The girl turned her back on Beth and went over and spoke to Noah. The boy put his guitar down as if it were red-hot and looked up with a guilty expression on his face. The other kids, seeing what had transpired, scattered like a startled herd.

Thinking her aunt would be satisfied, Beth glanced at May and saw that she was still frowning, but there was more worry than disapproval in her eyes.

Beth tried to make her tone light. "Kids, you know. They can be pretty ignorant sometimes."

"Yes," said May distractedly.

"They don't know any better, I guess," said Beth.

"I'm afraid that's true," said May.

Beth studied her aunt's lined face, wondering how she was going to cope with a youngster of Francie's age. *You've got to expect them to act like idiots from time to time,* she thought.

"Well, I'd better see to the others," May said.

"Do you need help?" Beth asked.

May shook her head and started back through the kitchen, her shoulders seeming to droop more than they had before. Beth chewed her lip, watching her go, and then looked out the door again. Francie and Andrew were still standing by the car. Francie looked up and caught Beth's eye and then turned her back on her.

Beth watched them for a few moments, debating what to do, and then she pulled on an old coat from a hook by the door and, jamming her hands in the pockets, walked out to where they stood, trying to keep the heels of her black boots from sinking into the mud.

The pair straightened up at her approach, as if girding themselves for battle. "Muddy out here," said Beth.

Andrew nodded slightly, but his narrow face was tense, and he watched her warily. Francie let out a deep sigh and looked up at the sky.

Beth bit her lower lip and then pressed her fists farther down in the pockets. "Andrew," she said, "I—I think I should apologize to you for the way I acted last night. I was a little upset, and I hope you will understand that I didn't mean to be rude to you."

Francie turned and looked at her sister, her eyes widening slightly. Andrew kept his head cocked to one side, his eyes narrowed. "That's okay," he said.

"These times are difficult," said Beth, realizing how

pompous she sounded but unable to think of any other way to say it.

"Yeah," he said. "Well, sure. It don't matter."

Beth nodded. "Okay," she said. "Well, no hard feelings, I hope."

Without waiting for a reply, she turned and started back toward the house. She could hear them whispering behind her.

That's better, she thought, opening the door and going back inside the house. She hung the coat back up on the hook, and then she remembered Cindy, who had wanted to talk. She wandered through the rooms, looking at the various groups of people, but after a quick search she determined that Cindy had already left.

One of the guests saw Beth staring aimlessly around the living room and cleared a chair for her. Beth sat down with a grateful smile. The air in the house was stuffy, and she envied Francie out there in the clear air, leaning against her beau. She felt a stab of loneliness, and tilting her head back against the chair, she thought of Mike. She wished she could call him and at least talk, but he would be at the hospital now, in the thick of it. *Later,* she thought, closing her eyes. *It will give me something to look forward to.* The hushed conversation drifted around her, but she stayed slumped in the chair, feeling as if it were taking all her effort just to keep breathing.

Chapter 5

*B*ETH came awake suddenly in the narrow, lumpy bed and lay still for a minute, sweat beading under her arms as she tried to remember where she was. Then the childhood room regained its familiarity, and she sank back on the pillow with a sigh.

Church bells tolled faintly through the town, announcing the end of a service, although it was hard to tell which service it was, for the light through the window was a metallic winter gray that defied the passing hours. Beth rolled over and put her face in the pillow. *You have to get up*, she reminded herself. *You have a lot to do. This entire house has to be cleaned out.* The thought of it was so depressing that she closed her eyes again.

But sleep was beyond her now. She felt sluggish, as if her heart were barely beating, but she forced herself out of bed and toward the bathroom. *You have to face it sooner or later*, she thought. She opened the door of

73

the bedroom and heard sounds from downstairs. She hoped, briefly, that Francie was on her way out.

When she had dressed and gone downstairs, she was surprised to find her sister still in the kitchen. Beth looked at the clock. It was nearly noon, although she felt as exhausted as if she hadn't slept at all.

"Good morning," she said.

"Morning," said Francie.

"How did you sleep?"

"All right. I was tired."

"It was a long day." Beth agreed with a yawn.

Beth went over to the refrigerator and looked inside. "God, there's nothing to eat in this house."

"Sorry," said Francie sarcastically.

Beth ignored the sarcasm. She blinked at the meager contents, trying to assemble a meal in her imagination from what was there. "Is that little market on Main Street open today? I want to go get a few things."

"Not on Sunday," Francie said incredulously, as if Beth had asked if it were a good day for the beach.

"No, I suppose not." Beth sighed. She reached into the refrigerator and sniffed at the carton of milk.

"It's good," said Francie indignantly.

"Look," said Beth, "no one expects you to have kept up on the groceries at a time like this."

Francie made a little grunting sound, but Beth could tell she was mollified.

"What about in Harrison? Anything open there?"

Francie nodded. "There's a big shopping center with a supermarket that's open every day."

Beth shook her head. "Times have changed."

Francie got up and put her dishes in the sink as Beth shook some dry cereal into a bowl. "The Seven-Eleven is open Sundays too," said Francie.

"Well," said Beth, "there's a better choice at the

74

supermarket. After I eat this, I'm going to take a ride over there. Do you want to go with me?"

Francie hesitated, balancing on one foot in the doorway like a crane. "I guess so," she said.

"All right," said Beth. "I'll be finished in a few minutes."

Visiting the Harrison Shop-Rite in a car was a luxury to Beth, who was used to carrying home a single bag from the crowded neighborhood grocery on her corner in the city. When she was entertaining, she would sometimes have a large order delivered, but as a rule, a single bag every few days sufficed.

"Family size everything," Beth exclaimed, hefting a huge jar of tomato sauce in wonderment.

Francie, who was dawdling along behind the cart, turned her head away and made a face. "Very funny," she muttered.

"I think it's great," said Beth. "I'm not making fun of it."

"Who cares?" said Francie.

Beth made a clicking sound with her teeth and shoved the cart on down the aisle. The Muzak in the store cheerfully played on as they cruised the aisles, covering up their lack of conversation. Occasionally Beth consulted the girl about what she liked, but Francie was unwilling to give an opinion and kept insisting that she didn't care.

"Did Dad do the grocery shopping for the two of you?" Beth asked.

"No," said Francie shortly, "I did. While he went to the Laundromat." Beth thought she heard the girl's voice catch in her throat, but Francie had already walked over to the magazine section and was flipping through a rock magazine.

75

When Beth pushed the cart up to her, Francie eyed the cart, which was half full of ill-assorted items. "Can we get out of here?" she asked.

Beth nodded, realizing all at once that her sister had painful associations of her father here in this homogeneous, well-lit, unremarkable supermarket. She felt a stab of pity for the girl and a sudden urge to do something conciliatory, although it was hard to think of what it might be since Francie would not even admit which foods she liked. She thought of going to a movie. There was a theater right in the shopping center, and it would delay the inevitable return to the gloom of the house. But they had all these groceries in tow. Then she had a sudden idea. Company, any company, might make the evening less dreary.

"Look," she said, "why don't you ask Andrew to come to dinner tonight?"

Francie looked at her warily. "Do you want him to come?"

Beth summoned up the necessary enthusiasm in her face and voice. "Sure. I think it would be nice."

Francie's face cleared. "Okay," she said. "I think he'll come."

Beth pointed the cart back up the meat and poultry aisle. "All right," she said, pleased with the effect of her suggestion. "What do you think he would like to have?"

Francie frowned thoughtfully and then picked up some chopped meat off the shelf. "He likes hamburgers," she said.

"Okay," said Beth. "Hamburgers and what else?" More purposefully this time the sisters began to retrace their route through the store.

With the aid of a rubber spatula Francie swirled the instant pudding filling around in the ready-made crust and then stepped back to admire her creation.

Beth searched through the cupboards and finally turned to Francie. "Where do you keep the seasonings?" she asked.

Francie tore her gaze from the pie and licked the spatula. "What seasonings?"

"You know, spices. Oregano, basil, garlic. All that stuff."

Francie picked up the pie and deposited it on the refrigerator shelf. "There," she said with satisfaction. "I don't think we have that stuff. There's salt and pepper on the table."

Beth nodded and closed the cupboard door. "Do you want to put some onion or bread crumbs in these hamburgers?"

"No. Why would you do that?"

"I don't know. Just to jazz them up a little."

"We like them plain," said Francie. "What's wrong with having them plain?" There was an edge in her voice.

"Plain is fine," said Beth, reminding herself that it was Francie's company.

For a few moments there was silence in the kitchen as Beth set the table for three and Francie formed the meat into patties. Then Francie said, "Do you use lots of spices in Philadelphia?"

Beth stifled a smile at the way the question was put. "Well, I have my own business there, so lots of nights I don't bother to cook. I'm just too tired."

"I know what you mean," Francie said in agreement. She frowned in concentration as she molded the meat.

There was another silence between them, and then Francie said, "It must be weird living in the city."

Beth laid down the fork and napkin in her hand. "I've been very happy there. It's been a good place to live."

"I guess you must miss it already," said Francie, carefully placing the meat on the broiler rack in readiness for cooking.

"Not too much," said Beth. "Not yet." As she said it, though, she thought of Mike. He had seemed so far away on the phone yesterday. He had been very solicitous of her, but she had felt, as they were talking, as if it had been months, rather than days, since she had seen him. She felt a sudden desire to be home, to be normal, that was like a little ache inside her.

Maybe I should call him again, Beth thought as she began to tear lettuce leaves into a green Pyrex bowl. Francie had said that they didn't need salad, but Beth had insisted that it was no trouble to make. *No,* she thought, *don't bug him. You've got plenty to do around here. Get it done, and you can be home again. That's what you really should do.*

Beth finished the salad and pushed it back on the counter. "What time did you tell Andrew to come?"

"Six."

"Six? Lord, isn't that a little early?"

"That's when we eat," said Francie.

"Fine," said Beth. "Six it is. I forgot how things are done around here. Look," she said, "I've got a lot to do, so I'm going to get started."

Leaving Francie in the kitchen, Beth picked up an empty grocery bag, went down the hall and reluctantly opened the door to the room which her parents had shared. She felt like an intruder in the dark, stuffy room, though she knew that neither of them would ever return to it. The room was neat except for one of her father's shirts, which lay at the foot of the bed, two pens still clipped to the pocket. She looked around the room. Everything else in it was exactly the same as it had been when her mother was alive. For a moment she had the terrible thought that perhaps he had never bothered to clean out her mother's things, and it made her feel almost faint with dismay. She walked to the closet and opened the door with trepidation. Only men's clothes hung there. She let out a sigh of relief and then looked in again. The clothes would have to be sorted and folded into boxes. She did not feel like doing that right now. She reached up to the top shelf of the closet and pulled down a shoebox with one ripped corner. The contents clinked and shifted as she moved it, so she knew it didn't contain shoes. She put the box down on the bed without opening it. Then she walked over to her father's bureau and opened the top drawer. The drawer was filled with a daunting jumble of items. She took the drawer out of the bureau and dumped it onto the bedspread beside the shoebox.

As she looked down at the motley assortment, she was dimly aware of the doorbell's ringing, and then she heard Francie's footsteps clattering down the stairs in response. *Sir Lancelot has arrived,* she thought with a smile.

She sat down on the bed and opened the top of the shoebox. It was filled with a sparse selection of men's jewelry, army memorabilia, and other scraps of things such as toothpicks, matchbooks, and loose change. A wave of inertia swept over Beth as she began to pick through this collection. Every single item required a decision. Was it old or new? Valuable or worthless, gold or brass? There were broken watches and medals with ribbons attached. She knew that they must be me-

mentos of something, but she had no idea of what. Weariness engulfed her, and she felt like putting the lid back on the box and just turning her back on it. *Do it now,* she told herself. *Get it done. It won't just go away.*

She began to sort, throwing everything that she was in doubt about into the empty brown bag and trying to keep only the things she was certain were of value. After a little while the odor of the hamburgers cooking filled the house. She realized that she was hungry when her stomach growled, but she doggedly kept on with her task, trying to get as much done as she could before supper. She looked at the clock on the night table before she unplugged it and decided to put it in a pile designated for the church. Six o'clock. What an ungodly hour to have dinner. It was the very time that they had always eaten when she was a girl.

Opening another drawer in the bureau, Beth found the old, battered wallet that her father had always carried. It had a rubber band around it. Someone must have put it in there after he had been taken away by the undertaker. Beth removed the rubber band, opened it up and looked inside. There were a few wrinkled dollar bills in the billfold and a couple of cards in the pocket. She pulled them out. There was his faded Social Security card, his driver's license, and an ID card from the electric company with a photo on it of him, pale and scowling, that made him look like a convict. There was an insurance agent's calling card, and Beth dimly remembered speaking to the man after the funeral. He had tried to explain the terms of her father's small life insurance policy to her, although she had not felt like listening. The wallet also held a yellow paid receipt for a local plumber and one picture, a wallet-size school portrait of Francie. It was the only photo he carried. As if she and her mother did not exist, had never existed.

Beth stared at it for a moment, the old familiar resentment churning inside her. Gripping the wallet tightly, she pulled out the money and put that on the bureau. "More junk," she muttered, tossing the wallet and the rest of its contents into the garbage can.

She was suddenly aware that the cooking smells had faded away in the house. Opening the bedroom door, she listened and could hear Francie's and Andrew's voices in the kitchen. She heard another sound as well: the scraping of silverware against plates.

After closing the bedroom door behind her, Beth walked down the hall and into the kitchen. Francie and Andrew were seated at the table, finishing up their meal. Two serving plates on the table held the hamburgers and potatoes, although the juice from the hamburgers was congealing around the meat. The salad which Beth had made was sitting, wilted and untouched, on the counter. Beth's place at the table was empty except for the silverware she herself had placed there.

This dinner was my idea, Beth thought. *My idea to ask him here, to be nice, for Francie's sake.* Suddenly, like the one witch not invited to Sleeping Beauty's christening, Beth wanted to get even.

"Noah thinks he's going to send his songs to Kenny Rogers and then Kenny is going to fly him to Nashville," Andrew was saying with a sneer.

"Do you want some pie?" Francie asked. "I made it." She suddenly noticed that Beth was in the room. "Hi," she said. Then she turned back to Andrew.

Andrew looked quickly from Francie to Beth, who was still standing in the doorway, her arms rigid at her sides. Then he shrugged. "Sure. I guess so."

"Good," said Francie happily, pushing her chair back and going to the refrigerator.

"How ya doin'?" Andrew asked Beth, watching her stony expression with wary eyes.

"Hello, Andrew," Beth said in a tart voice.

She strode across the kitchen and reached in front of Francie, who was cutting the pie on the countertop. Without saying, "Excuse me," Beth jerked a plate from the cabinet above Francie's head and slammed the cabinet door shut. She walked over to the salad bowl and heaped some on her plate. A slice of cucumber flew up and landed on the edge of Francie's pie. Beth ignored it and walked over to the table. Francie made a noise of protest that stuck in her throat. She looked at Beth, who had dropped her plate on the table and stabbed a hamburger with her fork.

Francie carried the two dishes of pie to the table and put one in front of Andrew and one in front of herself.

"These are burned," said Beth, dumping the hamburger on her own plate.

Two red spots appeared on Francie's cheeks, but she said nothing.

Andrew began to gobble down his dessert. "Good pie," he said through a mouthful of food.

"Thanks," said Francie. "It's a pie I always used to make for my—"

"What grade are you in school, Andrew?" Beth interrupted as she tore her potato apart with her fork and knife.

Andrew swallowed the pie as if it were a wad of wet papier-mâché and wiped his mouth with his napkin. He looked quickly over at Francie, who was staring down at her plate, her mouth turned down in a bitter line.

"I'm a—uh, sophomore," said Andrew.

Beth nodded as if she were a state trooper examining an expired registration. "A sophomore," she repeated.

"Yes," he said. He frowned at Francie, but the girl's eyes were riveted to the bottle of milk on the table. Her face was white except for the spots of red in her cheeks.

"You go to school and work, too, is that it?"

"What do you mean?" said Andrew, nervously folding the corner of his paper napkin into triangle upon triangle. His eyes narrowed as he looked at her.

"At the Seven-Eleven. You do work there, don't you?"

"Yeah, I work there."

"Part-time," Francie cried in a shrill voice. She slammed her hand down on the table. "Mind your own business."

Beth put down her fork and stared coldly at her sister. "I was just making conversation. This may surprise you, but civilized people often make conversation at dinner."

Francie's eyes glinted behind her glasses, and she gripped her fork so tightly that her knuckles were white.

Andrew stood up from the table. "That was really good, babe. But I've got to get going."

"No, don't go," Francie wailed.

"Thanks for having me," he said to Beth with just the hint of a sneer on his face.

Beth nodded stiffly, unable to meet his eyes. Francie stood up and slammed her chair against the table. Without another word to Beth she followed Andrew out of the kitchen.

"Good night, Andrew," Beth said. There was no reply from either of them. Beth sat alone in the kitchen, staring at the salt shaker and forcing down her dinner. After a minute she heard the front door close and then the sound of her sister's footsteps heading up the stairs.

"Francie," she called out.

There was a moment of silence, and then a sullen voice said, "What?"

"Get in here and clean up this mess. I'm not going to clean up after you and your little friend."

Francie stomped into the kitchen and began to throw the plates into the sink.

"What a bitch," she muttered.

"Pardon me," said Beth, "I didn't hear you."

"I wasn't talking to you," Francie snapped.

"I didn't hear you when you called me for dinner either," said Beth.

"I don't have to call you for dinner."

"No, obviously."

"Thanks for ruining everything," said Francie. She turned and jerked the faucets on full blast. "Bitch."

"I'll do my dishes later," said Beth, getting up from the table.

She went into the living room and sat down in a chair by the window. She picked up a book and pretended to read it, but her heart was pounding, and the words were a blur on the page.

Very mature, she told herself. *You really handled that situation beautifully. Why didn't you just dump their plates in their laps, just so there would be no mistaking how you felt? What's a good temper tantrum without a little food throwing? And all this because they ate a hamburger without waiting for you.*

Beth put the book facedown on her lap and turned her head to look out the window at the night sky. The stars seemed to swim before her eyes.

Suddenly she heard the water stop running in the

kitchen. After a few minutes she heard Francie coming down the hall. She felt an urge to call out to her, to try to make up. It had been wrong to spoil the evening, to run Andrew off, now for the second time. But as she saw Francie pass the doorway she could not force the words out. Francie started up the stairs to her room.

"Good night, Francie," Beth said, but her voice was harsh. She had not meant it to sound that way.

Francie kept going and did not reply.

Chapter 6

A*NDREW* felt the chill of the night cutting through his coat as he walked, head down, his body angled forward. It was as if icy hands were closing around his narrow chest, squeezing him, making it hard to breathe. The walk itself did not tire him. He was used to walking. He walked everywhere. But he was hurrying to get back, and the food from that miserable dinner roiled in his stomach, threatening to rise up and choke him.

Car headlights appeared behind him, in the distance, and Andrew whirled around, sticking out his thumb. The car whizzed past him. "Fucking bastard pricks," Andrew muttered after the car, and jammed his hands back in his pockets. He smacked his arms against his sides as he increased his pace.

He forced himself to go faster and faster, sometimes breaking into a run, until he could actually feel himself sweating despite the cold temperature. The night was still and quiet but not safe. He tried to clear his mind of everything but his progress. But every now and then the trees would rustle, and it seemed to him that the night was whispering to him some low words of warning that he could not decipher. He had to get back.

As he finally reached the house he looked up and saw a dark silhouette hovering in the front window beside the sheer curtains. The silhouette disappeared as he got closer. Checking around on all sides like a spy, Andrew started toward the back of the house, but he did not go in the back door. Instead, he lifted the sloping metal doors to the cellar and scurried down the cinder-block steps. The cellar was dark and smelled moldy. He made his way by habit to the light cord and pulled it on. A dim bulb was illuminated, throwing a weak greenish light on the cold cellar.

Quickly and mechanically Andrew began to remove his clothes. He folded and piled them neatly on a white enamel-topped table that stood against one wall. He stood there, naked and shivering, under a shower head that protruded from a length of pipes along one wall over a drain in the cellar floor. Gritting his teeth, he turned on the faucets and waited for the blast of lukewarm water to hit his goosefleshed skin. Almost as soon as the blast came and he had begun to lather himself with the soap that rested on a little plate attached to one of the pipes, he thought he heard noises coming from the floors above. It was as if someone were shouting his name in a high, frightened voice. Andrew shut off the water and demanded in an angry voice, "What?"

There was no reply. Andrew clenched the faucet handles and turned them on again. He rinsed himself quickly and stepped from beneath the shower. There was silence in the house.

Andrew rubbed himself dry with the scratchy towel

which hung on another nearby pipe. Then he dressed in the clothes which had been placed on the enamel table. After slipping on his shoes again, he pulled off the light chain, groped his way to the cellar stairs, and then climbed to the door at the top. When he arrived there, he knocked twice and then began to drum his fingers on the stair rail in annoyance.

A soft voice came through the door. "Andrew, is that you?"

"Open up," he snapped. "Of course it's me." *I saw you in the window,* he thought. *You waited until you saw me.*

"Just a minute." He heard the bolt being drawn back, and then the door opened. She poked her head around the corner, a limp ribbon holding back her frowsy, dirty blond hair. "Peekaboo," she said.

Andrew tried to push the door open, but Leonora Vincent raised her arm to look at her watch, thus blocking his exit. Andrew stared at the arm for a moment, thinking of snapping it back, like a turnstile.

"Seven o'clock," she said. "My goodness."

"Get out of the way, Mother," he said.

Leonora lowered her arm, and her son squeezed past her, making sure not to brush against her.

"I had to stay late at the store tonight," said Andrew, starting down the hall. "Mr. Temple had some meeting to go to." He walked into the kitchen and opened the refrigerator. After taking out a bottle of ice water, he poured some into a glass and began to drink it.

Leonora followed him and stood in the doorway. She was wearing a huge, shapeless sweater, a tight pair of stretch pants, and scuff slippers. "I think our Mr. Temple is being too demanding of your time," she said.

"I didn't care about staying," he said, gulping down

the water and starting toward the door where she stood.

"Wait. Not so fast," she said, pushing a hand into his chest. He backed away from her touch. "I have your supper all ready for you." She shuffled over to the oven, reached in, and produced a plate with a grayish mixture of fish and macaroni on it that made Andrew feel as if he were going to be sick.

"I had a sandwich at the store," he said.

Her face fell into a pout. "I saved this for you," she said. "You need to eat."

"I'm not hungry," he said in a tight little voice, turning his back on her.

"I didn't think we were so wealthy that we could just throw food away," she said, shaking her head as she opened the refrigerator and stuffed the plate inside.

Andrew bolted from the room and started down the hall, but she was behind him in an instant. "I'm going to have to speak to Mr. Temple," she said. "I think he is taking advantage of you because you are such a good worker. The very next time I see him I am going to say—"

"Don't say anything," Andrew snarled as he went into the living room and snapped on the television set. He flopped down on a chair and focused his eyes on the screen.

"No, I'm going to have to," she said, settling herself among the cushions of the worn old sofa, "because I don't know where you are sometimes and I can't even reach you—"

"Stay out of it," said Andrew in a low voice. "It's my job."

"I even called there tonight, two or three times," said Leonora, "and I guess he wouldn't even let you come to the phone because Mrs. Temple answered, and she kept pretending that you weren't even there."

Andrew, who had been ready to snap back at her, suddenly realized what she was saying. She knew that he hadn't been at the store. A sick knot formed in his stomach, and he stared at the TV screen as if he had not even heard her. There was a cop show on. Guys were jumping behind cars, toting huge guns. His body had stiffened up in the chair, but he kept his eyes riveted to the screen, pretending he was inside the TV, pretending that she was somewhere else, far away.

"Is that what happened, Andrew?" she asked.

"Yes," he said automatically.

Leonora leaned back a little in the cushions, but he could feel her eyes boring into him as he stared at the television. Her silence seemed to be drowning out the voices on the set. He wanted to get up, and go upstairs, and hide in his room, but he was afraid to. He was not sure his legs would hold him up.

"This is your last chance," said the man on the screen, holding the gun into the other man's belly. "Tell me where the money is."

"I must know where you are at all times," said Leonora.

Andrew gazed at the screen. "Yes," he said.

"Good," she said.

The man with the gun in his belly swore that he didn't know, so the other guy shot him. Andrew's heart leaped as the guy grunted and toppled over.

"We won't be staying up until all hours watching TV, I can tell you that," she said. "I have to be at Dr. Ridberg's bright and early tomorrow. We have a busy week."

Leonora was a dental hygienist who worked in the office of a dentist in Harrison. She took the bus to and fro each working day because she did not enjoy driving. She was never late, and she never missed an appointment. She felt that good dental hygiene should be a required subject in school. It was a subject about which she had strong opinions.

"I had a man on Friday," she went on. "I don't think I told you about him."

Andrew clenched his jaw and tried to hear the words of the cop, who was searching for the guy with the gun.

"This man had a buildup of calculus in the pockets of his lower anteriors, and it was a miracle he hadn't lost his teeth altogether. I was scraping out the pockets," she said, demonstrating by lifting up a finger and crooking the top joint in the air, waggling it back and forth. "I came upon a filling that was ready to disintegrate in the back. This man kept insisting that he didn't need a new filling, but I gave it a good poke, and this man let out a yell—"

Andrew leaped from his chair, as if he were the unfortunate patient, and twisted the volume dial on the TV, and the sound boomed out. "I can't hear anything," he screamed.

Leonora rose to her feet, walked to the TV, and punched the off button. The sound died; the picture faded away.

They faced each other across the ancient console. "Don't bother to show me your temper," she said in a low voice. "We know all about your temper."

Andrew stared at her for a long moment, his hands gripping the corners of the set. Then he suddenly realized that he was on his feet. Without a word he turned his back on her, ran for the stairs, and bolted up them and down the hall to his room. Once inside, he slammed the door shut and leaned against it as if he had escaped some kind of danger. He could feel the tight, squeezing sensation in his chest again. He limped to the window and threw it open, gulping in the air.

The air felt good, although with the window open he could hear the night whispering again, and he thought it might be making fun of him for being trapped there. "Not for long," he said to the darkness.

He wondered for a minute if Francie might be at her window looking out, thinking of escape, thinking of him. The harsh lines of his face slackened as he thought of her. She was so smart and grown-up, and she belonged to him. She was always telling him stuff about how great he was, and how handsome. At first he didn't like it because he thought she was making fun of him the way the other girls did, but lately he realized that it was true. He had asked her to swear that she meant it, and she had. And he told her that she would have to prove it, and she said that she would.

The mocking voices of the night seemed to be drowned out by his thoughts of her. He began to pace his cell-like room, remembering those first days. She would come into the store, interrupt his reading, and keep on talking to him. It made him angry at first, because girls had always joked about him in school and would run away, laughing loudly with their friends, if he tried to be nice to one of them. But this one would come in and hang around the counter; the TV dinners she had chosen would sit thawing by the register as she asked him questions. And she didn't seem to be laughing. One day Noah said to him, "She likes you." Noah's saying that had made him furious, and he had yelled at him to shut up, but then afterward he began to think about it a lot and wonder about it. Then, one day, she brought him a present. It was a stupid present, a key chain with a bird on it. He didn't thank her or anything, but afterward he began to think that she was going to be his girl. One day he was getting off work, and she was there, hanging around, and he walked her to the top of her street, and he told her she was going to be his girl. She liked it. She said okay.

His girl. Pride welled up in him at the thought. She would do anything he asked her to. She said that she would.

Andrew heard the sound of his mother's footsteps coming up the stairs, and he froze for a moment. All thoughts of Francie vanished from his mind. He pulled a book from the shelf by his bed, and opened it. It was a new one he had started reading, *L.A. Gundown.* He crawled onto the bed and huddled near the headboard. He could hear her footsteps. He counted them coming, his hands trembling as he held the book. He willed her to go by, but the footsteps stopped at his door. He looked up and saw the doorknob turn and the door open. He slid off the bed and stood between the bed and the wall, having hidden the book under his pillow. Leonora poked her head around the door and then sidled into the room.

"Andrew," she said gently, "I don't want to fight with you. You and I are, well, we're partners in a way. I get mad sometimes, but you know how much I love you. More than anything. I would do anything in this world for you. I think you must know that."

Andrew nodded, but he remained pressed against the wall, his eyes wide, his breath labored.

"Don't be upset, dear," she said, coming over to the

foot of the bed. "You know I would never let anyone or anything hurt you. You can always count on me."

She came toward him, down the narrow corridor between the bed and the wall. Andrew shook his head and tried to turn his face away from her. She smelled of mints. She always sucked on a mint between meals. "Occupational hazard," she liked to say. "I have to keep my breath sweet at all times."

"Don't be mad," she said. "Now, give me a kiss, or I'll be worried and I won't sleep."

Andrew held his breath and, with cold lips, placed a kiss on her soft, rubbery cheek.

"That's better," she said. "Oh, let's close this window," she exclaimed, shuffling over to the window and slamming it shut. "You'll catch a cold in here. We can't have that."

The window firmly closed, she turned with a satisfied smile. "Good night, dear," she said.

She closed the door to his room behind her. Andrew stared at the door after she was gone, still trying to catch his breath. But the room seemed stifling, and the air smelled of peppermint.

Chapter 7

BETH paid the check and then caught up with Francie, who was waiting in the parking lot of the little restaurant where they had eaten lunch. They had an appointment with the lawyer in Harrison, and Beth had suggested brightly that they have lunch on the way, but although Francie had agreed, they both had been silent and uncomfortable during the meal, trying to avoid each other's eyes as they waited for the waitress to deliver the food.

Beth took a deep gulp of the air outside as she walked toward the car, relieved that the meal was over. Francie was waiting there, her hands stuffed in her pockets. Beth unlocked the driver's side and then glanced down at her watch. She gazed around the bleak countryside surrounding the restaurant like an Indian scouting the hills for buffalo.

"Whatsa matter?" said Francie.

"Well, it's only noon, and we're not due over there until one-thirty."

Francie nodded, knowing that they both had eaten quickly to get the meal over with.

"So," Beth continued, "I'm just wondering what we should do."

"I don't know."

"If it's okay with you, I noticed that we passed an antiques barn a little ways back, and I'd like to have a look."

Francie raised her eyebrows and gazed blankly at Beth. "You want to go shopping?" she said.

Beth pressed her lips together, remembering with a feeling of guilty embarrassment how she had berated Francie for wanting to go out for a walk the night before their father's funeral. Here it was, two days later, and she was out bargain hunting. "We have to do something to kill the time."

Francie shrugged. "I don't care," she said. She pressed on the door handle, and Beth quickly slid into the driver's seat and opened the door for her.

It was only a short distance back to the old farmhouse with the nearby barn that had an ANTIQUES FOR SALE sign on it. They walked up the driveway toward the open doors of the barn. Beth knew that there was not much traffic for this sort of thing in the winter, so there was a chance that she could pick up a few items that would go well in her house. There was not much in her father's house that she wanted. Most of it had unpleasant associations connected to it. But if you looked carefully in places like these, there were often inexpensive items that needed only a little care and restoration. It was always worth looking.

Francie, who had been quiet and glum all morning, seemed to find the old barn interesting once they got inside. Beth scoured the old proprietor's goods with a practiced eye and was a little disappointed to note that

there was very little that attracted her. Francie, however, picked up and examined the man's knickknacks
as if they were baubles in a treasure chest.

"How much is this?" Beth asked, holding up an old
earthenware pitcher and checking it for cracks.

The old man, who had a yellowing mustache and
was wearing a gray corduroy shirt with a spot on the
front, answered firmly, "Ten dollars."

"It's very nice," said Beth, knowing that it was probably worth a lot more but that she didn't really need it.

"This is pretty," said Francie solemnly from across
the crowded garage. Beth glanced over and saw her
sister holding up a silver necklace set with cranberry-
colored stones. She went over to have a better look at
it. The stones were surrounded by a delicate filigree
and were cut in such a way that they shimmered.
Francie stared at it as if mesmerized by it.

"That belonged to my wife," said the old man
proudly. "She used to wear it when she was only a
little older than you. It's really more for a young girl
than an old woman."

Francie looked at him seriously. "Don't you want to
keep it to remember her by?"

The old man looked perplexed, and then he
laughed. "Oh, no, she's the one who wants to sell it.
She never wears it anymore. No, no, she's still around.
Up there in the kitchen doing dishes, right this minute."

Francie looked relieved.

She thinks that everybody dies young, thought
Beth. "Do you want it?" Beth asked aloud.

Francie put the necklace back down on the display
of old jewelry. "No, I don't need it."

"How much do you want for that?" Beth asked.

"Well, it's not cheap. I'd want forty dollars for it. This is a valuable piece of jewelry."

"Try it on," Beth said to Francie.

The girl backed away. "No, I have no use for it. It's too fancy."

"Well, I'm sure that sometime you will." She took out her wallet and counted forty dollars into the old man's hand.

"It's too expensive." Francie yelped, as if pained by the thought of the price.

"No, it's worth it," said Beth, lifting the necklace from the makeshift jewelry case and handing it to Francie.

"There, it's yours," said the old man. He reached up on a shelf near the door and pulled down an old mason jar full of bills. He stuffed the forty dollars inside and put the jar back up on the shelf. "Wear it in good health."

Francie held the necklace gingerly. "It's—it's really pretty."

"Enjoy it," said Beth, feeling a sudden surge of triumph. She knew that she wanted the girl to have it, but it took her a moment to realize why. Sure, she had done it to be nice. But more than that, she had just bested her father. She had been generous and free with her money, the way he never was. Suddenly she felt ashamed, trying to get the better of a dead man. But Francie, who was carefully tucking the necklace into her pocket, did not seem to notice.

The woman who admitted them to the waiting room of the lawyer's office was middle-aged, cheerful, and quite smartly dressed, Beth thought, considering the local standards. She offered them seats and went back to her typing.

In a few moments the door to the waiting room opened, and a short man with glasses, wearing a charcoal gray suit and a bow tie, stepped in. "Miss Pearson," he said gravely, shaking hands with Beth, and then, repeating the greeting, he shook hands with Francie. "So sorry to hear of your father's death. Won't you come in. Would you like some coffee?"

Beth shook her head, and they followed the lawyer into his office. They sat down in the chairs in front of his cluttered desk. Beth crossed her legs and settled back, her arms draped over the chair arms in an attitude of determined nonchalance.

Mr. Blount looked over his glasses. "I hope you weren't waiting long."

Beth shook her head. "Only a few minutes."

"Good," he said. "Well, let's get right to it."

"Fine," said Beth.

"Now, this will was written when your mother was alive. Despite my best efforts, I could not induce your father to come in and update it after your mother's death."

"Does that mean it's not legal?" Beth exclaimed.

"No, no," said the lawyer. "It's quite legal. It has provisions for all circumstances in it. We took care of that in the event that they died at the same time. The fact that their deaths came some years apart does not affect the validity of the will."

"Oh, good," said Beth. "I'd hate to have the thing all tied up in court for ages."

"No, that's no problem," the lawyer murmured, flipping the pages of the document in his hands. "It is a fairly standard form, and I will spare you the reading of the whole thing, unless you wish me to." He looked up at them.

"Fine," said Beth, and then remembered to look

over at Francie. The girl was sitting very still in the chair, gripping the chair arms as if for support and looking at the lawyer with an intent, serious look on her face.

"All right then," said Mr. Blount. "You, Beth, have been named the executrix of your father's estate, being that you are over twenty-one at the time of his death."

Beth nodded, expecting this.

"All your father's property and the house and all its contents are left equally to the two of you. Naturally you are also responsible for any debts, the funeral expenses, and legal fees. As you may know, you will be taxed on your inheritance but not on any insurance he might have had."

Beth nodded, mentally calculating the small sum of money involved.

"You look confused," said Mr. Blount kindly, leaning toward Francie.

"I don't know what this all means," said Francie.

"What it means, dear, is that your older sister was named by your parents to settle all your family business. It will be up to her to see that all the bills your father owed are paid, and then, whatever is left, you and your sister will divide equally. Because you are a minor, we may have to put whatever money there is aside for you until you are eighteen."

"Oh," said Francie, "I see."

"I'm sure your sister will do an excellent job of taking care of all this. Now, do you have any questions?"

"I don't know. I guess not."

"Mr. Blount," said Beth, "how long, if at all, must we wait before we put the house on the market?"

"Well, there's no reason to wait at all. You may not

receive the proceeds until the will is probated, but that is just a formality."

"Wait a minute," said Francie. "What do you mean about selling the house?"

Beth turned to Francie, who was staring at her with her mouth hanging open. "Well, I don't see any point in holding on to it. And we can use the money."

"But where are we going to live?"

"Well, you're going to live with Aunt May. I have to go back to Philadelphia."

"I don't want to live with them."

"Francie, didn't Aunt May talk to you? They want you there."

"You were supposed to live with me. I thought we both were going to stay in the house."

The lawyer looked at Beth with a grim expression on his face. "I would have thought you might have already talked this over with your sister."

"Everything has happened so fast," Beth explained uneasily.

"Well, I think you'll have to straighten a few things out. You, not her aunt and uncle, are the girl's legal guardian."

"I'm sure we can work everything out," Beth said lamely.

Francie, who was sitting limply in the chair, turned and glared at her sister. She stood up and, without another word, walked out of the lawyer's office.

Beth got up. "I'll have to get back to you," she said to the stern-faced Mr. Blount before she hurried after her sister.

The woman in the outer office tried to usher them out with a pleasant good-bye, but Francie strode through the office, glowering, and slammed the door on Beth. Beth caught it just in time and ran after

Francie, who had crossed the street without looking and narrowly missed being clipped by a delivery truck. She ignored the call of the driver, who stopped to make sure she was all right, and continued walking.

Beth ran after her, feeling clumsy in her high-heeled boots. When she caught up to the girl, Francie just kept on walking. "Look," said Beth, trying to fall into step beside her, "I'm sorry about this. I thought you understood."

"No," Francie snapped. "How was I supposed to know?"

"I guess I shouldn't have assumed," said Beth. "It's just that May and James want to have you. Aunt May's already fixing up a room for you. And I know you don't want to leave Oldham, and all your friends, school—and Andrew."

Francie did not speak but kept on walking.

"They are such nice people. You get along with them. And this way you can finish school here, and then, if you go off to college, there will be money from the sale of the house, just waiting for you. You can go anywhere you want."

"You've got it all planned," Francie muttered.

"Hey," said Beth with a sigh, "are we going anywhere? I mean, let's head back to the car. We can talk there."

Without a word Francie turned and started walking back in the direction of the lawyer's office. Beth tried again.

"Francie, I don't know where you got the idea that I would be able to move up here and live with you. I have my own business where I live. A house." She was about to say "a fiancé," but she stopped herself short. She did not want to get into that right now. "I just can't."

Francie's face was stiff, as if she were trying to keep any feeling from showing there. "You could if you wanted to," she said.

Beth felt her face redden at Francie's accusatory tone. "Well, it's just not possible, and that's it. I wish you hadn't started thinking that. If I'd have known what you were thinking, I would have said something right away. Honestly, it's not as if I were throwing you to the wolves. You'll be with people who care about you, right where you're used to living."

They had reached the car, and Francie pulled the door open and hunched up in the front seat without a word. Beth went around and got in on the driver's side. "I'm sorry, Francie. Really. I'm sorry that this came as such a shock to you. I'm sure that in a day or two—"

"He said you would take care of me. That you would stay with me if anything happened to him."

Beth's face turned white. She stared at Francie. "Who said?"

"Daddy. He said you would."

Beth felt as if her heart were being crushed like a nut in a nutcracker. It was an old, familiar feeling. "Doesn't that figure?" she said tightly. "Isn't that typical of him? Telling everybody else what to do and how to do it. Never mind what I want. Never mind how I might feel about things. What difference does it make what plans I might have made? No, no, just go ahead and dictate, and heaven help you if you don't see it his way—"

"Can we go?" Francie muttered. Beth started the car without another word, and they drove home in silence, not looking at each other.

When they reached the house, Francie went immediately up to her room. Beth followed her inside wearily. The house was quiet. She sat down in the living room, rubbing her forehead, and then she picked up the local paper and tried to read it. Nothing in it was remotely interesting to her. The living room seemed gloomy, and she felt a stab of homesickness for her cheerful house and then, immediately after that, for Mike. Suddenly she knew just what she wanted to do. She went into the kitchen and closed the door behind her. She dialed his number and stood there waiting, sure that she would get his service but hoping against hope that he might be there.

"Hello."

"Hi," she said to the faraway voice. "Am I tearing you away from something?"

"For you, anytime," he said.

Beth felt a rush of happiness and curled herself into the rocker with the patched seat, twining the cord around her wrist. "How's it going?"

Mike gave her a rundown on his cases, just as he would if they were sitting together in her kitchen. It sounded as if he had had one crisis after another the last few days.

"Are you beat?" she asked.

"Me, beat? Nah," he scoffed. "Just mildly exhausted. How about you? You sound tired."

She could picture the strong face, sagging a little with fatigue, eyes thoughtful with concern for her. "We'll be a great pair when we get back together. All we'll want to do is sleep."

"Wait till you see how fast I recuperate once I get my arms around you," he said.

Beth smiled. "Good."

"So, what's happening? How's progress coming on straightening things out up there?"

"Well, we hit a snag today."

"Oh?"

"It seems that little sister and I had our signals crossed about the next phase."

"What do you mean?"

"Well, we went to the lawyer's, and it seems as though Francie thought that my program was to give up my life in Philly and come up here and mind her in the old homestead," Beth said sarcastically.

She waited for Mike to comment, but there was just silence from the other end.

"So"—she went on less confidently—"I had to break the news to her that I was only here for the cleanup, and that I would be heading back as soon as possible, and that she is going to be living with her aunt and uncle."

"Oh."

"This is all my father's fault really. He told her I would come live with her if anything happened to him. I couldn't believe it when she told me that. That's typical of him."

"It must have really thrown her. Was she very upset?"

Beth's temper flared at the question. "I suppose so," she said coldly. "But it's not my fault. My father was the one who went ahead and offered my services."

"Well, I know. But she was counting on you."

"Oh, fine. All right," said Beth. "Maybe I'll just dump my business and sell my house and come up here to live. Maybe if I'm lucky, I can get my father's old job at the electric company."

"No, no one's asking you to do that, but there are other possibilities."

Beth pursed her lips and chewed the inside of her mouth, staring out the kitchen window.

"Why don't you bring her to Philly? She could live with us."

"Live with us? Great. Now you're the one who is offering my services. Terrific. Did it ever occur to you that I might not want to do that?"

"I'm just trying to offer a possible solution. And I'm not offering your services. I said 'us,' and I meant it. I'll help out in any way I can. She'll be a part of our family."

"I don't believe this," said Beth, jumping up from the rocker and pacing the room. "You're just like him. Telling me what to do. Doesn't anyone realize that it's my life we're talking about?" Beth could hear her voice turning shrill and defensive, but she could not prevent the nasty, bitter words from tumbling out. It was as if he had pressed a button that opened some kind of garbage chute.

"I have to admit I don't understand your attitude," he said. "She's your sister after all. All right, so you didn't get along with your dad. And I can see why you might be angry at the way he handled the whole thing, but what I don't understand is how you can be so closed-minded about this girl. She's only a kid. She's now lost both her parents."

"You're right," said Beth. "You don't understand."

"What is it? Some kind of leftover sibling rivalry or something? You're an adult. She needs you."

Beth felt angry tears springing to her eyes. "It's been a big help talking to you," she said resentfully, although her voice was thick.

Mike sighed. "All right, let's drop it for now. Maybe we should talk again when you are feeling better."

Beth remained stubbornly silent and then heard a click. "I don't believe it," she said, holding the phone away from her. "He hung up."

"Beth, I'm still here," said Mike.

She held the phone to her ear, although her hand was shaking. If he hadn't hung up, then it meant that someone had hung up the other phone in the house. Francie had heard the whole conversation. Beth could feel her face suddenly get hot, as if she had been caught stealing something.

"What was that? Your sister on the phone?" he asked.

"Don't worry about it," said Beth with an indifference she did not feel.

"Well, there's no talking to you now," he said wearily.

"So hang up," she said. "I'm going to. Good-bye." She slammed the phone down on the hook and flopped back down into the rocking chair. She didn't know whether she wanted to cry or to throw something. She stared at the receiver, hoping that it would ring, that he would call back, but the phone was still. She wasn't surprised, not after that conversation. Once she walked over and lifted the receiver. She heard voices. She replaced it without listening and sat back down in the chair as the twilight turned to dark.

Chapter 8

*B*Y the time Beth woke up and came downstairs the next morning Francie was already gone. The house was quiet, and there was evidence in the kitchen, from some bread crumbs and bologna skins left on the counter, that Francie had made her lunch to take to school.

Beth forced herself to clean up the kitchen and make some coffee. She had hardly slept for thinking about Mike, wondering if this was truly the end of it. Around dawn she had decided that it probably was. His opinion of her was obviously so low that he would never want to resume their relationship. After all, he hadn't called back. And for her part, she could not ever marry a man who tried to tell her what to do anyway. These thoughts had raced through her head until the morning's gray light brought a fitful sleep.

Now, groggy and low-spirited, she did not want to think about it. She thought about calling her office to see how things were going but decided against it. Maxine had her number. Any problems that might come up would find their way to her ear soon enough.

She looked around the house in disgust. She still had to clean it out, and the project seemed more daunting to her than creating an entire building did at work. *Well,* she thought, *it will give you something to do. You don't have to think.* Picking up an armload of brown grocery bags from the kitchen broom closet, Beth decided to start on the hall closets, clean them first, and then move on to the other rooms.

Grimly she set about her task, crouching down in the dusty closets and sorting through a lifetime of belongings. She had several bags for garbage, a pile for the church bazaar, and another small pile for things which she and Francie might want to keep or give to her aunt and uncle.

After a couple of hours of methodical sifting and discarding, her back ached, and her brain seemed equally tired. The mental strain was as great as the physical. She had to be ruthless about the baggage of the past, trying not to feel guilty as she discarded family memories, however bittersweet they might be.

Straightening up, Beth was proud to see that she had knocked off all the downstairs closets, except for the kitchen, and most of the upstairs. Closets were the worst. She brushed the dust balls off her sweatshirt and jeans. Closets were the resting places for everyone else's indecision.

She knew she should finish her parents' room next, but she was out of paper bags and in need of packing boxes. After going downstairs, she looked out the window. There was a light snow falling, although it was barely visible against the pearl gray of the sky. Beth debated for a minute, then pulled on her high school parka, which she had found in her closet, and plucked the car keys from the top of the refrigerator. She could just take a run to the 7-Eleven and see if it had any boxes.

Shutting the door behind her, Beth stepped out into the cold gray day. The air felt refreshing to her after a morning of rooting through dark, close spaces, and on an impulse she decided to walk to the store. The snow drifted lightly down and brushed her gently as she set off up the street toward the center of town.

Alternately walking and jogging, Beth made her way past the row of stores to the 7-Eleven at the end of the route. *If they don't have any boxes*, she thought, *I can stop by Hale's on the way home*, but she felt that the convenience store was the sort of place that had a more thriving business and more frequent deliveries.

The glass front of the 7-Eleven was steamed up, and there were only a few cars parked out front. Beth went in and was met by a blast of warm air that nearly chapped her cheeks on the spot. She was greeted by the same heavyset man whom she had seen there the day she got off the bus. "What can I do for you?" he asked pleasantly.

"Well," said Beth, "I have a favor to ask. I'm packing up my family house, and I need some boxes. I was wondering if—"

The man waved a pink, beefy hand. "No problem. I've got a bunch in the back. Bring 'em right out."

"Thank you," said Beth.

The man left the counter and headed for the back of the store. "I'll be with you in a minute," he said to a customer he passed, who appeared to be heading for the register.

"Take your time," said a voice familiar to Beth. Beth turned and saw Cindy McNeill approaching the counter, carrying a container of yogurt and a diet soda.

"Hi, Beth," said Cindy.

"Hey, Cindy. How are you?"

"I'm fine. Just picking up some lunch."

Beth nodded, recognizing the calorie counter's special. "I guess it is lunchtime. I've been so busy all day."

"How's Francie feeling?" Cindy asked.

Beth shook her head. "I don't know. All right, I guess. She was gone before I got up."

"Oh," said Cindy, "she's not sick then."

"Oh, I get it," said Beth. "She's not in school."

Cindy made a face and shook her head.

"Well, she's having a kind of rough time lately."

Cindy frowned. "I know she is."

"I'll mention it to her tonight. I'm sure she'll be in tomorrow."

Mr. Temple, the store manager, came back with four cartons, one inside the other. Beth thanked him.

"Let me know if you need more," he said gallantly.

"I'm packing up the house," Beth explained to Cindy as Mr. Temple made change for her purchases.

The two women started for the door of the store.

"Beth," said Cindy, "remember I said I wanted to talk to you about Francie? Have you got a few minutes?"

Beth felt herself squirming slightly and started to say that she had a lot of work left to do in the house, but she realized immediately that it would sound terribly callous. She pictured again the disapproving look on the lawyer's face and felt her face redden.

"Well, okay," said Beth. "Do you want to come over to the house and have your lunch?"

"Actually," said Cindy, opening the door to a little red compact car in the parking lot, "I'm on my way over to my mother's to have lunch with my little girl. Why don't you come along? You haven't seen my mom in ages. I told her you were here, and she'd love to see you."

"Your little girl?" Beth exclaimed. "You have a baby?"

Cindy nodded happily. "Yep. Dana. She's eighteen months old. My mom keeps her during the day so I can work. These days you need both salaries."

Beth opened the car door and slid in beside Cindy, tossing her boxes into the back seat. "I can't believe it. How long have you and Billy been married?"

On the short drive to Cindy's mother's house the two old friends caught up on the course of their lives, and Beth continued to marvel at the news of the baby, much to Cindy's delight. They pulled into the driveway of the old Ballard house, and Beth felt a little surge of pleasure to be back at that familiar place.

Cindy's mother met them at the front door, holding a strawberry blond toddler who shrieked at the sight of Cindy and pitched forward into her laughing mother's arms.

"Look who's here," Cindy said to her mom, and Beth exchanged a brief hug with the older woman.

"Beth, I was so sorry to hear about Dad," she said.

"Thanks."

"Come in, come in."

They all trooped into the warm house, and Beth took a turn twirling the baby around the living-room floor and burying her face in the fragrant baby skin.

"Do you want lunch?" Mrs. Ballard asked. "I can't get this one to eat anything," she said, frowning at her grown daughter.

Cindy, who was feeding tiny bits of yogurt to baby Dana, just smiled. Dana alternately made faces and clamored for more.

"She already ate," Mrs. Ballard said, but Cindy nodded and continued the game.

Beth refused lunch, and Mrs. Ballard had begun to settle herself in a nearby chair when Cindy looked up at her mother and said, "Mom, I want to talk to Beth about something. Do you mind?"

Beth expected some resistance and was surprised when Mrs. Ballard nodded knowingly and immediately got up. "Do you want me to take the baby?" she asked.

"Oh, leave her here," Beth pleaded. Dana had hold of one of Beth's fingers and was trying to poke Beth with it.

Cindy and her mother exchanged sober glances, and then Cindy said, "She's all right here. Thanks, Mom."

The older woman withdrew, and there was a silence in the room. Dana gurgled questioningly.

"Well," said Beth, "about Francie. The little truant."

"Francie. Yes, and a few other things."

"Cindy, before you start, I have to tell you that I don't have too much to do with her comings and goings. But I know that she's pretty upset with all this about my father, and maybe, I don't know, maybe she just needed another day off."

"Your father." Cindy sighed. "That's another thing."

Dana had wandered off and picked up a ball with a bell in it. She began to shake it and listen intently. Beth watched as Cindy hopped up and took the ball away from Dana, giving her a doll instead to circumvent tears. A serious expression on her face, Cindy resumed her seat. She was quiet for a moment, watching her baby. Then she asked, "Do you know Andrew?"

Beth was a little surprised at the question, but she

nodded. "Sure," she said. "The teen heartthrob. Oh, wait. Let me guess. Andrew is not in school today either."

Cindy gave her a curious look. "In school? No."

"And you think that they are up to something together."

"This is not the first time," said Cindy.

"Well, if they are up to something, I hope she knows what she's doing. God, I didn't know anything at fourteen. Although kids do seem to grow up faster these days."

"Beth, I think you should know your father was very distressed about the two of them."

"Oh, I'll bet he was," said Beth, rolling her eyeballs.

Cindy's eyes clouded over as she absently picked at Dana's curls. "Francie's a good kid. And a pleasure to teach. I didn't want to get her into trouble. Maybe I shouldn't have butted in, but I felt he ought to know about it. It's hard, being a teacher, to know what the right thing to do is. Anyway, I worried about it a lot before I decided to tell him. I knew he was strict with Francie. She meant the world to him."

"I know," said Beth stiffly.

"Now, well, sometimes I feel as if I made a terrible mistake."

"Oh, I'm sure he yelled and hollered," Beth said, "although it doesn't seemed to have affected the lovebirds."

"That's just it. He was so worked up when I told him. He was—beside himself really. I tried to get him to calm down, but he was in a rage."

Beth could picture her father's wrath as Cindy spoke, and she felt sorry that Cindy had been subjected to it. "He was like that," she said.

"And then—that was it," Cindy said in a choked voice.

"What was it?"

"That was the last I saw of him. Not two days later he had the heart attack. And he died." Cindy looked at Beth with wide, anxious eyes. Dana, alert to her mother's distress, began to wail in sympathy.

Beth took some Kleenex from a box on the sofa and handed them to Cindy, who began to wipe Dana's tears. "It's all right," said Beth. "It certainly wasn't your fault."

"I'm glad I told you," said Cindy. "It's really been on my conscience."

"It was just a coincidence, I'm sure," said Beth. "Look, I'll bet if you told Andrew's parents that he was missing school, they wouldn't up and die over it, would they?"

Cindy frowned. "What do you mean, 'in school'? You said that before."

"Andrew," said Beth.

"Andrew's not in school, Beth. He doesn't go to school. He has a job at the Seven-Eleven. He wasn't there today when I went to get my yogurt, and that's how I'm pretty sure they are together."

"What did he do? Drop out?"

"Beth, Andrew is nearly twenty-one years old. He hasn't been in school for years."

"What?" said Beth.

"Didn't you know that?" Cindy asked.

Beth shook her head.

"That's why I've been so worried about Francie. Andrew is, well, there's something not quite right about that boy. Apparently he was always a little different. The kids made fun of him even when he was very young. I had him in my class one time. He never had any friends, his grades were bad, and he got into all kinds of fights. He's had one job after another since he got out. He can't hold on to anything for long. He's just—I don't know. I think he's a troubled young man."

"Young man, my eye," said Beth. "Twenty-one years old. Goddammit."

"I didn't want to upset you, but this is what I mean. Francie's kind of a lonely kid. And she's vulnerable right now. I think that the sooner you get her away from him, the better. Are you taking her back to Philadelphia with you?"

Beth was immediately guarded. "No, no, I'm not. I think she's better off here, with her aunt and uncle."

Cindy shook her head. "I was afraid of that."

"Well," said Beth, "I'm just going to have to talk to her about it," although as she said it, she realized that it was unlikely that Francie would listen to anything she had to say.

"I think you should," said Cindy.

"I can't believe this," said Beth. "He looks like a kid to me."

Cindy smiled ruefully. "Compared to us, he is."

"But not to Francie. Well, listen, Cindy, I'm glad you told me. Really. You did the right thing."

"I've got to get back to school," said Cindy. "Can I drop you at your house?"

"Thanks," said Beth, pulling on her jacket thoughtfully and heading for the door. Then, remembering the baby, she stopped and doubled back. Cindy was hugging the baby, reluctant to put her down. Beth leaned over and kissed the child on the cheek.

"Be a good girl," she said.

"She's always a good girl," said her mother proudly.

Beth smiled indulgently at them as Cindy bounced Dana in her arms.

"You know," said Cindy, "I remember when Francie was this size. Remember that? We were just about the age she is now."

"Yeah, I remember," Beth said in a dull voice.

"I was so envious of you, having a little baby around the house to play with. She was a cute little thing."

"I guess she was," said Beth. "It seems like a long time ago."

Chapter 9

"**Y**OU probably don't recognize where we are," said Andrew, leaning back in the seat and pressing his hands against the steering wheel.

Francie, who was looking out worriedly at the snow, shook her head. In fact, she knew exactly where they were, near a state park several miles from town, but she could tell that he wanted her not to know.

"I thought so," said Andrew with a satisfied smile, and pressed down harder on the gas. "Figured I'd surprise you."

"Not so fast, Andrew, please."

Andrew turned on her. "I'm doing the driving," he said.

Francie sat huddled in the seat, squeezing her hands tightly together. "The snow. It's dangerous."

"I went to a lot of trouble to get off today," he said, "to get the car. After you called last night, I had to go through a whole thing with my mother. I had to tell her it was my boss, and I needed the car for work today and all that, just so I could take you here today. Now all of a sudden you're complaining on me."

"I'm not complaining," Francie said hurriedly. "How come your mother never lets you have the car?"

Andrew flicked on the wipers, and the snow flew off the clouded windshield. "Because she's a pig," he said.

He accelerated again, and Francie stifled a cry with her hand as the car swerved and then righted itself on the lonely highway. Andrew jerked the wheel around and then hit the brake. The car screeched and then skidded to a halt in a little clearing between the woods on their right and the road.

He turned and smiled at her. "We're here," he said.

Francie nodded, her face white above her pale blue parka.

Andrew slid over toward her in the seat and began to finger her hair, crooning to her. "What's so scary to the little girl?"

"I told you," said Francie. "I don't like icy highways. I told you what happened."

"Oh, yeah," he said, sitting up, "you and your mother. The car flipped out or something."

"I told you," said Francie petulantly.

"Well, the little girl is safe now," he said.

Francie stared out the window, past the bare black trees toward the cottony gray skies. "You can't even see the lake for the snow," she said.

"How do you know there's a lake? I thought you said you were never here."

Francie bit her lip and then, after a second's hesitation, said, "Well, you can tell. There are no trees back there. It has to be water."

"Aren't we smart?" he said.

"What's the secret place?" Francie pleaded. "You said there was a secret place."

"There is," he said, getting out of the car. "Let's go." He made his way importantly toward a path through the trees, and Francie followed behind him, carrying the brown bag of sandwiches she had made for them.

Andrew took his time, picking his way down the path, avoiding the stones and branches that were partly concealed by the falling snow. The woods surrounding the lake in a wide apron were sloped down to the water's edge, and the whiteness of the snow made them appear deceptively light. There was not another soul to be seen as they emerged from the woods and looked out across the vast frozen surface in front of them. A few feet to their right was an arched wooden bridge with a few slats missing. The bridge spanned the fifty feet to a small island, on which stood an old stone skating house.

"It's beautiful," said Francie, clinging to the arm of his coat.

"Well, come on," he said, "I'll show you our hideout."

He clumped down to the foot of the bridge and then started across, the sounds of his footsteps muffled by the falling snow. The bridge looked rickety, but it was sturdy enough. He reached the door of the skating house and looked down, expecting the padlock which he had put on it to have been removed, but it was still there. "Look at that," he said. "No one ever comes here." He turned around to show Francie, but she was not behind him, where she was supposed to be.

"Francie," he called out, "where are you?"

His voice echoed across the lake, but Francie did not answer. Her silence annoyed him, but he did not call out again. If this was some stupid game she was playing, he would not fall for it. Reaching down under the wooden step to the door of the house, Andrew pulled out the key, awkwardly thrust it into the keyhole, jerked the padlock down, and roughly pulled the latch forward when it was freed.

He kicked open the door and stepped inside the house. There were two overturned crates he had left there for sitting on, and light was coming in through the holes which passed for windows. There were still his ashes in the empty hearth and a small bag of food garbage which he had left there when he discovered the place. Here it was, the secret he had arranged for her, and she was not even there to see it. He slammed the door behind him and sat down heavily on one of the crates.

"Andrew," Francie cried gaily from outside, "come see me."

Slowly he got up and walked out on the bridge. He heard a giggling noise coming from under the bridge, and then he saw her head poking out, gazing up at him.

"Look," she cried, "I'm skating." She pushed off from the underside of the bridge and began to slide around on the surface of the ice, laughing and shrieking, her arms outstretched as she made awkward turns in her rubber boots.

"Get in here," said Andrew in a tight little voice. "I'm waiting for you."

"I'm flying," Francie cried, running along the ice.

"Be quiet," Andrew ordered.

"Come down here," she pleaded. "It's fun." As soon as she said it, she tripped and fell with a thud on her back. The ominous sound of ice cracking emanated around her like a starburst.

"Andrew," she cried, "help."

"Serves you right," he said, turning his back on her. He went back inside the house.

"Andrew," she wailed.

That will show her, he thought. She had to have her little game. Andrew shut the door behind him and sat down on the overturned crate. He pulled his paperback book, *L.A. Gundown,* from the pocket of his coat. There was a man in a tuxedo on the cover, strangling a mean-looking guy twice his size. Andrew began to read, ignoring the sound of her whimpering from outside and then her footsteps, clomping across the bridge.

Francie opened the door, wiping her nose on the sleeve of her parka. Andrew did not turn around. Silently she went over and sat down on the crate opposite him, putting the brown bag down between them. She folded her arms tightly across her chest, her mittened hands tucked under her armpits. Slowly she began to rock back and forth. Andrew continued to read his paperback.

"Andrew," she said softly.

He did not reply.

"I'm sorry," she said.

"You'd better be," he muttered, his eyes still on the book.

"Don't be mad," she said. "I was just having fun."

Andrew looked up at her. "You call me and you beg me to see you. So I bring you to this place, make this surprise for you, and then you act like a two-year-old. I do not appreciate it when you act like a two-year-old. You're a grown woman. Why don't you act like one?"

Francie rushed over to him and knelt beside him on the cold floor of the skating house. "This place is wonderful," she said. "And you are wonderful. Please don't be mad. You are everything in the whole world to me."

Andrew tried to conceal his smile, but his face reddened with pleasure. "You don't mean that," he said. "That's just something you say."

"I do mean it," she said. "You're handsome and smart. I love those freckles you have." She put a mittened finger on the end of his nose, but he grabbed her wrist and pushed it away, covering his face with his own hand, as if to hide from her. Francie laughed.

"Come on," she said. "You know it."

Andrew raised his eyebrows over his hand, and then peering at her with a mischievous gleam, he crossed his eyes. Francie laughed again, and he pulled her close to him, burying his face in her hair.

He breathed in the scent of her hair, his gaze at once wistful and faraway. "Your hair smells so clean," he said.

"I washed it last night." Her voice came up, muffled by his coat.

"Do you know that no matter how much some people wash themselves, they never smell clean like that?"

He gripped her tightly, and his heart seemed to be thumping aloud. He thought that she could probably hear it, and it embarrassed him. She would know he was thinking about doing things to her. He put his cold lips down to her forehead. She tried to struggle up, but he held her there, kissing her.

"Andrew," she said, "I can't breathe. Let me go."

He released her, and she popped up beside him, her face flushed, her glasses crooked on her head. She smiled at him proudly, possessively, and then leaned forward and began to kiss him on the lips.

He clutched her arms in the doughy parka and kissed her back with awkward eagerness. The fearsome pounding began in him, flooding through him, and he felt himself at once falling away and struggling to stop it.

Gently she tried to move his hand from her arm to the front of her jacket, and helplessly he let her. But as he felt that change in the bodily terrain, even under the bulky fabric, the familiar panic filled him. He knew what was coming next, the explosion he could not control, the hideous humiliation, the spreading stain in his pants, and she would know. He had to stop it in time.

With a fierce push he unloosed himself from her and began to gasp for breath. Francie's elbow slammed against the edge of the wooden crate as she fell, and she landed on the floor, where she sat, rubbing the elbow with a resentful pout. "If you don't want to kiss me, just say so," she said.

Andrew jumped up and walked around the skating house, pretending to be looking out the window as he pressed his body against the cold stone walls, as if he could freeze and deflate the agitation that had mushroomed within him. "Of course, I want to kiss you," he said irritably. "But there will be plenty of time for that when we're out of here."

"Out of here?" said Francie, unzippering her parka and shaking her sore arm out of the sleeve to make sure there was no blood on her elbow coming through her sweater.

Andrew glanced over at her. It looked as if there were two tiny eraser heads poking up her sweater from the small swell of her breasts. "Put your coat on," he said angrily. "It's cold in here."

"Okay, okay," Francie grumbled, shrugging the sleeve back on and zippering her jacket, but she was pleased by his concern, and she smiled at him. Then she got up from the floor and sat down on the other orange crate.

Andrew exhaled with relief.

"What do you mean, 'out of here'?" she repeated.

Andrew came back and sat down on the crate opposite her. "Give me a sandwich," he said.

Francie dutifully reached into the brown bag and handed him a packet wrapped in aluminum foil. Andrew tore it open and began to wolf down the bologna sandwich. Francie watched him tenderly, waiting for a compliment on the lunch.

"It's time we were making our plans," he said, crumpling the wrapper.

"Plans for what?"

"You know what," he said. "I'll take another one." Francie made a face. "They're good," he said. She reached in the bag again. "What have I been telling you right from the start?" he went on. "It's time for us to get out of here."

"Run away," she said quietly.

"That's right," he said. "Split, leave. Get out of this place. Just you and me. We get on the road and we go."

Francie sighed. "I don't know. I'm so—I don't know, crazy, right now."

"What was that all about last night?" he demanded. "'Andrew, my sister won't stay. She's makin' me live with those old people,'" he mimicked.

"I know."

"You call me up, crying, yelling how much you hate her, and them, and everybody. You know this is a stinking town. What is there to stay for? We gotta go," he said urgently.

"What about school?"

"School?" He looked at her incredulously. "Who cares about it? What are you? A brain."

"You finished school," she said accusingly.

"You can go somewhere else. Wherever we end up."

"But where would we go?"

"That's easy," he said, snapping his fingers and making her smile. "We head for the Coast."

She frowned.

"California. My old man lives out there now. Yeah, I got a few cards from him. My mother doesn't know anything about it, but I did. He's got a nice place out there. And he says I could get a job easy. He'll help me."

"What does he do?"

"I'm not sure. He's kind of closed-mouthed about it. I think he might have something to do with the casinos or maybe the government. He says he goes to Vegas a lot."

"Do you think he's a gambler?"

"How do I know?" said Andrew impatiently. "We'll find out when we get there."

Francie huddled on the crate, her hands squeezed between her knees. "I don't know," she said.

"Oh, Andrew," he crooned in a high, singsong voice, "you're so wonderful. I'd do anything in the world for you." He sneered and shook his head. "Sure," he said in his normal voice.

"It's not something you can decide just like that," she said indignantly. "How come you never ran away before? You could have run away plenty of times, I'll bet."

Andrew stared at her for a long moment. Then he said in a quiet voice, "Because I was waiting for you."

It didn't make sense, and some part of Francie knew it, but it gave her shivers all the same, the way he said it. "I just can't decide like this," she said in a plaintive voice.

Andrew scowled and turned away from her. She watched him for a minute, feeling as if she were floating alone in the blackness of outer space. "Can we have a fire?" she asked in a meek voice.

"No," he snapped. "All the wood is wet."

"Andrew, don't be like this. Please."

He opened the paper bag and looked inside. Pulling out the remaining sandwich, he threw it on the ground by her feet. Then he began to gather up the other garbage and put it in the bag, as if he were getting ready to go. He picked up his book and put it in his pocket.

"Look," she said in an anxious voice, "how can we go anyway? We don't even have a car or any money. You can't get anywhere without money. We couldn't even get anything to eat. Maybe we should just save up for a while. I've got some baby-sitting jobs, and you could work, and then we could go. When we get some money. Otherwise, I don't see how we possibly could go."

"I've got some money saved," he said, "from my job."

"Oh," said Francie dejectedly, "but we don't have a car."

"We'll take my mother's car," he cried. "I got an extra set of keys she doesn't even know about. Remember the key chain you gave me?"

Francie's eyes widened. "We can't do that," she said.

"Of course we can," he said.

"But she might need her car," Francie stammered.

"No, she won't. She's a pig, I told you. Pigs don't drive cars." He laughed aloud at his joke. "Oh, it will serve her right. I wish I could just get someone to go there with a camera and take a picture of her face when she sees we're gone with the car." He wheeled around and looked at Francie. "Do you think Noah would do that? I would love to see that."

Francie shook her head slowly.

Andrew shrugged. "Fuck it then. Just as long as she suffers I'll be happy."

Francie squirmed on her seat. "That's stealing really," she said.

"Stealing? That old wreck? That was my father's car. He probably left it for me anyway," Andrew cried. He slid over to where she sat, grabbed her arms, and held them tightly. "Besides, I have that coming to me. She owes me that car. No. She owes me more than that." His eyes suddenly took on a kind of dazed, faraway look.

"It takes a lot of money to get to California," said Francie.

Andrew suddenly came back to life. "We'll have it," he said. "No problem. We'll get it along the way. There's lots of stores and garages. People's houses even."

Francie stared at him. The look in his eyes made her stomach drop like a roller-coaster car. "People's houses?"

"Because we're gonna have a gun, little girl. And with a gun you can get anything you want. We'll just go in when there's nobody around, and when we get what we want, we move on.

"It'll be easy," he said. "So easy. We say, 'Give us your money,' and they give it over. Nobody says no to a gun. And if they do, blam, we blow them away. And we're off to the next town before you know it. We take what we want when we want it. Don't you see? It's our turn to take what we want. We deserve it. The fucking world owes it to us. All our lives we've been kicked around and pushed down. I've been thinking about this. That's why you and me are so perfect together. Everybody holding us down, telling us what to do."

He rose to his feet as if uplifted by his image of the future. "Let them come after me. I can run faster than they can. And if they want to catch me, they can kill me first. I mean it, Francie. I'll shoot them down. I don't care if the blood is washing over my feet and your feet. They won't stop us when we get going. I think about this every day. You and me out there. Free of all of them. Nobody stops us; nobody hurts us; nobody dares to even come near us."

Francie put her hands over her ears. "Don't talk like that," she said. "You're scaring me."

Her words seemed to bring him up short, like a dog on a leash. The glow faded from his eyes, and he looked at her anxiously. He gave a jerky laugh. "Don't be such a baby," he said. "I'm just kidding."

"How can you talk like that, about killing people and things?" she cried.

He came over and, sitting down beside her, ran his hand over her hair. At first she pulled away, but then she let him stroke her head. "I didn't mean it," he said. "I was just talking."

"You meant it about stealing," she said.

"Don't worry," he said. "I'll think of a way to get some more money. I will."

But she continued to look at him warily, her eyes clouded.

"I think I know where there's some dry wood," he said. "I'll bet I could find some and make that fire."

Francie sat stiffly on the edge of the crate, looking away from him. Andrew watched her anxiously, and he took his hand off her hair, but he could feel the irritation rising in him as she continued to avoid his eyes. Finally he stood up. "Yes or no?" he barked.

Francie jumped at the sound of his voice and looked up at him with wide eyes. "What?" she asked.

"The fire. Yes or no?" he asked in an angry voice.

Francie pushed her glasses back up on her nose and stared at him. "Yes," she said. "Thank you," she added in a whisper.

Chapter 10

ALMOST as soon as Cindy dropped her, and the boxes, off in her driveway, Beth found herself chewing over everything she had heard. Try as she might to get back to the job at hand, she kept picturing Andrew and hearing his lies. First there had been the lie about not knowing Francie and then the lie about being a sophomore in school, and who knew how many more? The idea of the two of them being off together somewhere, reveling in the fact that they had fooled her made her feel like smashing something. There seemed to be little else that she could do about it. Then an idea occurred to her. She threw the last of her father's clothes into a box on the bed, went out through the kitchen, grabbed a coat, and got into the car.

The snow was falling heavily, and the roads were slippery. Beth drove carefully up to the service station and stopped her car in front of the open garage doors, beside the tow truck. *They'll probably be busy with that today,* she thought, although looking inside, she could see Noah, leaning against an oil drum and plunking away. *I wonder if he sleeps with that thing,* Beth thought.

Pulling up her coat collar, she got out of the car and hurried inside the garage. Noah looked up and gave her a wan smile.

"Need gas?" he said.

Beth shook her head. There was something at once dense and innocent about the boy. She almost hated to pick on him like this. It shouldn't be difficult to get some information out of him. She smiled a thin, insincere smile. "You're a friend of Andrew's, right?" she asked.

"Yeah," said Noah. "We're buddies."

The way he said it made Beth feel a pang of sympathy for him. She doubted that Noah had many friends. "Then I guess you know he's seeing my sister."

Noah screwed his mouth up slightly and lowered his eyes, clearly worried about ratting on his friend.

"This is not a trick question, Noah. I've heard all about it."

Noah shrugged. "So?"

"So my sister did not go to school today, and Andrew is not at work, and I want to know where they've gone off to."

"You seem kind of mad," Noah said, squinting at her.

"I'm not mad. I'm just curious."

"Well, ask her when she comes back."

"I want to talk to her now."

Noah shrugged and strummed a G chord on his guitar. "I don't know where they are."

"Well, how about this. Where does Andrew live? Maybe they're at his house."

Noah made a face. "I don't think so. His mother is real strict."

"I'll just drive by and see."

Noah's mouth had a stubborn set to it.

"Do you have a phone book here?" Beth asked evenly. "I'll look it up."

"Ah, he lives over on Berwyn Road, down the end. It's an old green-colored house. Do you know where Berwyn Road is?" he asked, clearly hoping that she did not.

"It's near the bus stop by the reservoir, isn't it?" said Beth, gesturing vaguely behind her.

Noah nodded. A woman wearing a loden coat drove up in a noisy car and came into the garage. "Do you have mufflers?" she asked meekly.

Noah signaled her to drive the car on in, and she went out and got back in the driver's seat.

"Well, thanks," said Beth.

"Andrew's a great guy, you know. I don't see what's wrong with being friends."

"I'm sure you're a very good friend to him," said Beth, and she walked back to her father's car. She left Noah to the problems of the lady's muffler and turned in the direction of the reservoir. *I'll just check out his house,* she thought. *At least I'll feel I've done something. If they're not there, I'll just have to wait until Francie gets home, and we can have it out then. I can't be chasing all over creation looking for them. They could be anywhere.*

Berwyn Road was several miles from the garage, and Beth thought about how far Andrew had to walk every day to get to work. Maybe his boss let him use the 7-Eleven car when he pleased. Still, she wondered why a young man of his age didn't have his own car. On her way to Andrew's house she passed some run-down farms and an abandoned ski slope, which boasted a rope tow and had done a pretty good business when Beth was a girl. It looked as if the slope had not been used in some years. Just past the bus stop on the main route to Harrison, Beth turned down Berwyn Road and drove slowly along. There was a trailer home on the corner lot and then a farmhouse across from an empty field. At the end of the street was an old house surrounded by a few scraggly bare trees.

There was no name out front, but Beth recognized the green from Noah's description and pulled slowly into the rutted driveway. The house looked deserted, but as she climbed up to the porch she thought she could see a light on in the back of the house.

She rapped twice on the front door, then stamped the snow off her boots and brushed it off her shoulders. She shivered as she waited, looking out over the unkempt yard. She knocked again and tried to peer into the house through the curtained side windows next to the door, but the house seemed quiet. *I guess they're not here,* she thought, and was surprised to feel a kind of relief. At least that meant that they were not holed up in his bedroom. She sighed, realizing all at once how uneasy she had been about that idea. She had turned to go when suddenly the front door opened about six inches and a woman appeared, dimly, from the darkness behind the door. "What do you want?"

Beth jumped, for she had not expected anyone to answer. "Excuse me," she said, spreading her hand over her thudding chest. "My name is Beth Pearson. I was looking for—uh—is Andrew here?"

"No," said the woman behind the door in a faintly patronizing tone. "Andrew is at work."

"Are you Andrew's mother?" Beth asked.

"Yes, I am," she said suspiciously.

Beth chewed her lip for a second. Then she said, "Could I talk to you for a minute?"

The woman appeared to be put out by the request and began to make excuses. "Well, I just got home from work, and I'm still in uniform. The weather, you know, was bad, and so the doctor insisted that I go home early. Cancellations, you know. And I haven't even had a chance to change."

"That's not necessary," said Beth. "This will only take a minute."

"Well, just a minute," said Leonora Vincent, and shut the door.

Beth frowned and then shook her head. *She's probably running around picking up newspapers and straightening cushions,* thought Beth, stamping her feet on the porch to keep warm. Her jeans weren't much protection from the cold.

The door opened again, wider this time, and Beth started to walk in, but to her surprise Leonora motioned her back as she stepped out onto the porch and shut the door behind her. She was wearing a nurse's white pants outfit and white shoes, and she had pulled on a heavy nubby sweater.

Leonora noted the surprise on Beth's face and waved vaguely behind her. "You don't mind," she said. "It's germs. You can't be too careful about germs in the house."

Beth tried not to take offense, wondering if this odd behavior had anything to do with the woman's nursing. Perhaps there was someone ill in the house. She pondered it for only a second, for she could see the tight, impatient expression around Leonora's mouth.

"I'm sorry to bother you Mrs.—uh—Vincent," Beth said, and waited for the automatic suggestion that Beth use her first name. The suggestion was not forthcoming.

"I just found out today that your son has been seeing

my little sister. You see, I don't live around here. I just came up here for my father's funeral. Well, anyway, I heard from Francie's teacher at school that Andrew and my sister have been hanging around together, and I'm afraid I don't really approve of it."

Beth half expected the woman to tell her to mind her own business, and she half felt that she deserved it, but when she looked at Leonora Vincent's face, she saw something else entirely. The woman had turned a deathly shade of white, and her eyes had a fierce expression which reminded Beth, inexplicably, of Andrew. Leonora's lips barely moved when she spoke.

"What are you talking about? I know nothing about this. Who is this girl?"

Beth suddenly felt her own irritation dwarfed by the woman's obvious rage. She decided to soft-pedal it a bit. "Well, I don't know how much they have been seeing of each other. It's just that Francie is only fourteen, and your son is quite a bit older. I'm sure he's a very nice young man, but—"

Leonora did not appear to hear what Beth was saying. She raised her eyebrows high above her oddly shaped eyes and stared out into the distance. "So," she said, "lies and deceit. Vile, filthy behavior with a young girl."

Beth could see that Andrew would be facing some tough accusations when he got home. She suddenly felt slightly guilty. She wanted to make sure that she had not implied more wrongdoing than she knew to be true.

"I'm not saying that they are doing anything improper, you understand. It's just the age difference."

"I have always said that the apple never falls far." Leonora went on. "Not far at all. I have done my best, Mrs. Pearson, to try to turn that tide. But there is only so much a mother can do. Even when she is trying—night and day, day and night. Despite the training and the punishments, the weakness is there. It's in the blood."

Beth began to feel distinctly uncomfortable. "I think it would be best not to overreact to this."

"Did you know that Andrew's father was just like that? Oh, yes, when Andrew was only a small boy, his father was running around with a young tramp. Just like your sister. He left us. Oh, it was a scandal. I'm surprised you don't know."

Beth felt that she was finding out more than she wanted to know about the Vincent family tree. Leonora Vincent's crooked eyes were trained on Beth now, and Beth could sense that she was gearing up for a diatribe against both her errant husband and her son. She seemed oblivious of the cold. Beth decided to cut it short.

"Well," she said, "I intend to speak to Francie about this and suggest that she find more friends her own age. All I wanted was to see if you might do the same with Andrew."

Leonora's train of thought had clearly been interrupted by Beth's remark, but she made an effort to focus on what Beth was saying. "I will speak to Andrew," she said.

Beth thanked her and went back down the porch steps toward her car. She grimaced at the thought of the tongue-lashing Andrew was in for. Overkill perhaps. *But that should put an end to it anyway,* she thought. She could feel Leonora's eyes still upon her as she got back in the car.

The trick, Beth told the mirror, as she penciled carefully around her eyes, *is to be calm and reasonable about it. She'll probably get all upset and weepy and protest that it's true love. You've got to meet her head-on with cool logic.* Beth sucked in her cheeks and applied some blusher to them, thinking about what Cindy had said, how her father had been so furious about the relationship. She could well imagine the kind of scene he had made, banging his fist down as he hollered. She remembered his anger very well. She had always been intimidated by those thundering rages. But clearly that tactic had not deterred Francie from meeting Andrew. Or perhaps it had, briefly, but now that her father was gone, Francie obviously thought the way was clear. Beth pursed her lips and applied a copper-colored lipstick. Well, it was time to get that straightened out.

She stood back from the mirror and examined her made-up face. For some reason she had felt the need to wear her makeup for this discussion. She hadn't worn it since the funeral. But it made her face look sharper, more definite. She held her head up and looked sideways into the glass. *You just explain to her that this is not going to fly. And that's it.*

The sound of a door slamming downstairs startled her, and then she glanced at her watch. Just about the time she'd be getting home from school. Taking a deep breath, Beth went downstairs and into the kitchen. Francie was sitting at the kitchen table, holding an apple. She was in her stocking feet but was still wearing her parka. Her glasses were fogged from the heat of the house.

"Still snowing?" Beth asked.

"It's letting up."

"That's good."

Francie took a bite of the apple and chewed without enthusiasm.

"How was school?" Beth asked.

"Fine."

"Oh," said Beth, turning her back to the girl to pour a glass of water from the faucet. "How would you know?"

Francie lowered the apple to the tabletop and looked up at Beth without speaking.

Beth turned around and smiled brightly at her. "I happen to know that you weren't in school today, that you were off somewhere with your friend Andrew."

Francie grunted and got up from the table. Dropping her parka on the chair, she headed for the living room.

"Hey, hold it," said Beth. "Get back here."

"Okay," said Francie. "So I cut school."

"Cutting school is not the issue. Everybody cuts school now and then. That doesn't bother me."

"I don't care what bothers you."

"It's Andrew that's the problem here, Francie."

"What about Andrew?" Francie put her hand on her hip and leaned against a chair.

"Francie, look, I know all about him. I know he's much too old for you. That he's got a pretty bad reputation—"

"I'll tell you something," said Francie. "I couldn't care less what you heard. Or what you think."

Beth pressed her lips together and then spoke as calmly as she could. "You have no business with a boy that age."

"You don't tell me what to do. Period." Francie turned and started to walk out again.

Beth bolted from the sink and grabbed Francie by the arm. The girl gave her hand a withering look, and Beth released her and pointed a finger at her.

"Now you listen to me," said Beth. "You do not have

license to do whatever you please. That means you do not skip school and go running around with some guy who should have friends his own age instead of putting the make on little girls."

"Go back where you came from, will you?" said Francie, curling her lip at her sister. "Butt out of my life."

"Francie, this is not a suggestion I'm making. I'm telling you that this is the way it's going to be. I'm your legal guardian, and I'm telling you that you aren't going to see that boy anymore."

"You're not telling me anything," Francie cried, picking up the chair an inch or two and smashing it back down on the floor. "I do what I want. Legal guardian. Don't make me laugh."

"Oh, no, you don't," Beth yelled back at her. She could feel her temper rising at the girl's defiance. With a struggle she reined it in. "As a matter of fact, I've made sure you won't. I went and saw his mother today, and you can bet she'll have something to say about this to him."

Francie took a step back and stared at Beth. Her eyes were wide with disbelief behind her glasses.

"You did what?"

Seeing that she had finally trumped her sister, Beth gave her a thin, satisfied smile. "I found out you were skipping school, so I asked Noah where Andrew lives, and I went over there to see if you were there. His mother was home, so I told her all about it."

"You stupid asshole. Why don't you mind your own business?"

Beth clenched her fist, resisting the urge to smack her sister. "This is my business," she said grimly.

"It is not," Francie shouted.

"Well, it gave my father a heart attack," said Beth coldly. "I'd say that makes it my business."

It was a low blow, and Beth knew it. She hadn't meant to say it, surely not that way, but now the words were out. *All right*, she thought. *Let the chips fall.* She reassured herself with the memory of what Cindy had said about her father. He *had* been upset. Furious. It was the truth.

Francie seemed stunned by her words for a moment. She staggered back a step and leaned against the table, her eyes lowered to the floor, staring, as if she were looking into a pit full of demons. Watching Francie slump over, Beth felt a little ping of elation, as if a voice inside were crowing, "Bull's-eye," but a stab of guilt pierced it like a pin in a bubble. She thought of apologizing and opened her mouth to speak.

But Francie had collected herself and drawn herself up, and she met her sister's guilty gaze with scorn in her eyes. "Oh, really?" she said. "You're so concerned about our father? You're so worried about how he got a heart attack? Don't make me sick. All these years you never cared one shit about him. You never came home, or called him, or bothered with us. And now you're so involved, right? Give me a break."

Beth glared at her. "Don't change the subject," she said in a brittle voice. "I happen to know he was furious about Andrew."

"It did not give him a heart attack," Francie screamed. "He would have had one anyway. The doctor told me himself. He said it was coming for years. He was tired a lot of the time. And sick. But how would you know? You wouldn't even call him. That made him sick more than anything. How many days do you think he spent worrying about that and suffering over you—"

Beth tried to drown out the words with her own voice, to protect her ears by shouting. "Admit it, Francie. Just admit it. He was so mad about Andrew that it killed him."

"Stop it," Francie growled at her. "Stop trying to make it that I hurt him. I didn't. You can't lay it on me."

"No, no," said Beth. "You're never to blame. You just happen to be there when the damage is done. First Mother. Now him."

At this Francie stopped dead, her face white as paper. "Mother?" she whispered.

Beth was shaking from head to foot. She could not meet Francie's eyes.

"I was only six years old," said Francie. "The steering failed on the car. Are you saying now that I caused that?"

Beth could not stop herself. The words were like a handful of knives that had been goring her for years. She was ripping them out, hurling them at her sister. "You knew she was hurt, but you just sat there by the car. If you had only gone for help, called to somebody. She didn't have to die. You were old enough to get help. You knew enough to do that."

"I was afraid to," Francie screamed. "I was afraid to leave her. I was afraid of the dark."

But Beth was not listening. There were tears in her eyes as she ranted at Francie. "And Daddy never said one word to you. His little pet. You'd think he was glad it was Mother, and not you, who got killed. And if he hadn't been so fucking cheap and seen to it that the car was fixed, but no—"

"Oh, God," Francie moaned.

"Well, it's true," Beth cried. "He sent her out on the worst night in that piece of crap—" She remembered, as she said it, having this same argument with him and being met with the same defiant stubbornness. He refused to take responsibility or to chastise Francie for letting their mother bleed to death while she sat there. He told Beth she was out of line, and he warned her never to speak about it again or to get out. She had left and never come back. Not until now.

"So that's why you're so rotten," said Francie.

Beth wiped the angry tears off her face and answered in a shaky voice, "Shut up."

"Like you were the only one who ever lost anything. You really don't care about anybody but yourself. You make me sick."

Beth turned on her, but she was almost too drained to reply. The ringing of the phone startled them both, and their eyes met for a moment. Then Francie stamped over to it and picked it up.

"Hello," she said angrily. Then, more softly, she said, "Hi."

Beth knew instantly who it was.

Francie was silent for a few minutes. Then she said suddenly, "Look, I'd better warn you. Something happened. My sister talked to your mother." She hissed on the word *sister*. "Yes. I don't know how. Oh, I guess Noah told her. Yes, I can come." Francie's eyes met Beth's defiantly as she spoke. She listened again and then nodded. "I'll meet you in a few minutes." She hung up the phone and walked over to the door. She pulled on her boots with a violent jerk.

Beth opened her mouth to speak, but Francie had the last words as she opened the back door. "You bitch," she said. And she was gone.

Chapter 11

A NDREW hung up the pay phone beside the men's room door and walked around, past the station office and the gas pumps, to the open doors of the garage. The back of Noah's greasy coveralls stuck out from under the hood of a battered yellow Mustang as he bent over the coughing engine.

Andrew walked up behind him, leaned over, grabbed a wad of the coverall fabric near Noah's shoulder, and yanked him up, banging the boy's head on the hood as he straightened him up.

Noah cried out in surprise, dropping the wrench that he held in his hand. The tool clanged on the cement floor, narrowly missing Andrew's foot. Andrew shoved Noah back against the car.

"What's the matter, man?" Noah yelped. "Cut it out."

"I just talked to Francie. She says you sent that bitch to my mother."

"Wait. What?"

"Her sister. What did you tell her?"

An uneasy look rose in Noah's eyes. "Oh, her. Yeah. She came over here all pissed off. But I didn't tell her anything. She knew all about you and Francie skipping school and all, and she asked me where you were, but I said I didn't know."

"How'd she end up at my mother's?" Andrew demanded.

"I don't know?" Noah whined.

"You liar," Andrew cried. "You told her."

"She would have found out anyway. She was going to look it up in the book."

"But she didn't have to because you told her."

"I'm sorry, man."

"Don't say 'man,'" Andrew snarled. "You sound like an idiot when you say that." Turning around, he nearly tripped over Noah's guitar, which was propped up against a pile of snow tires. He grabbed it by the neck, raised it, and smashed it against the metal doorframe as hard as he could.

Noah turned pale and let out a strangled cry. "Hey, goddamn you." He lurched forward and struck out wildly with his fist, just missing Andrew's shoulder. Andrew dropped the guitar, and it hit the floor with the crack of wood and the jangle of strings. Before Noah could strike him, Andrew sidestepped him and stalked out of the garage.

It was dark as Andrew crossed the parking lot to his mother's car. He had come by to fill the tank, just so that she would not know he had taken the car farther than the 7-Eleven. Provided she did not check the mileage, he would have been safe. *Well,* he thought, *now she knows. I could have saved the gas money. She knows everything. Thanks to Noah and that fucking nosy sister.* Acid flooded Andrew's stomach at the thought, and his heart felt as if it were beating out of control. He tried to stop the waves of nausea that were coming over him, but it was no use. He bent over the side of the car and threw up in the parking lot. He felt as if his stomach were turning inside out, and all his blood seemed to have rushed to his head, which was pounding. His hand, which gripped the tail of the car, was crablike and veiny, like the hand of a very old man. He stared at it while he took deep breaths, trying to calm his stomach. But his thoughts would not stop churning. She would forbid him to see Francie now. She would cage him in. Bind him tighter. There would be new rules. He knew it.

"Andrew?" a voice said softly. "Are you okay?"

Andrew straightened up and saw her standing there, her ash blond hair like an angel's halo in the lamplight of the parking lot. Her eyes were wide behind her glasses.

"Are you sick?" Francie asked.

"I'm okay now," he said. "Get in." He opened the door to the car. Francie looked worried, but she slid in.

Noah had finished with a customer at the pump and was staring across the lot at them, his arms hanging limply at his sides. Andrew turned on the engine.

"Where are we going?" Francie asked.

"I don't know," he said dully.

He pulled out of the lot and drove slowly along, staring blindly ahead. She waited for him to speak, but he seemed lost in his thoughts.

"Andrew," she said, "I can't take any more of her. First she had a shit fit about you and me. Then she said it was my fault that my father had a heart attack. And then that wasn't enough. It turns out that it's my fault that my mother got killed in a car accident when I was six. She really said that," Francie cried. "I couldn't believe my ears. She's sick."

"She told my mother," Andrew said almost incredulously. "My mother knows where I've been."

"Well, that's different," said Francie. "At least you're grown up and have a job and everything. You can do what you want. I can't do anything. Now she's saying I can't see you anymore. It's like she owns me, even though she hates me."

"I didn't think she would find out," Andrew said.

"I can't stand it," Francie cried. "Now she'll tell my aunt and uncle, and it will be the same thing with them. Why did she ever have to come here? I can't believe my father ever wanted her to take care of me. She is the meanest, rottenest—"

"Stop," said Andrew.

Francie turned on him with a wounded expression in her eyes.

"I'm—I'm trying to think . . ." he mumbled apologetically. He didn't like it when she talked too much. It was annoying, like something buzzing in his brain, making it impossible for him to hold on to anything in his mind. He needed her to be quiet and just to obey him. As if she could read his thoughts, she fell silent. He drove along, trying to avoid looking at his old man's hands on the wheel. The night seemed to whisper and laugh outside the car. He thought the windows must be rolled down, but he looked, and he could see that they were closed tight. He thought he could detect the faint scent of peppermint in the car.

"Andrew, I've been thinking," said Francie in a small voice. "And I've decided. If you still want to, I'm ready. I'll run away with you."

His head snapped around, and he looked at her with

a vacant, confused stare, as if he were groggy from a dream.

"Let's just go," she said. "Now. We have the car. We can go. Tonight. We can't stay here. If we stay here, they won't let me see you. Oh, let's get away from here." She turned her head and stared out the window into the night. "I hate this place."

Running away. How many times had he dreamed of it, imagined it? Pleaded with her to go with him. And now here was his chance. The little toy girl was looking at him with hopeful eyes, promising him that she was ready to run with him. It was too good to be true. Sweat beaded on his forehead as he looked at her, and he could feel his hands trembling on the wheel.

"We can't," he said, shaking his head. His own voice sounded foggy to his ears. "We can't. We have no money." He had just said the first thing that came to mind, but that seemed the real reason for the fear that paralyzed him, now that the opportunity was at hand. "We can't go anywhere without money."

"We could ask Noah," she said eagerly. "He could give us some money from the drawer, and then, when we got to your father's place and got jobs, we could send it back—"

Andrew was shaking his head. "No, no. We can't ask Noah. He wouldn't."

Francie fell back against the seat, silent.

Andrew rolled down the window and tried to take a deep breath. "Why not tonight?" the trees whispered. He had a sudden image of himself as an animal, bolting through that open door of the cage. His heart rose. Then he saw the hunter, sights trained on his scampering hindquarters. Calmly taking aim. "Why not tonight?" the trees mocked him.

"I know where we can get some money," she said.

Their eyes met in the darkness. He could feel a golden web enveloping him, spun from her hair and the silver glint of her glasses. "You do?"

Francie nodded.

"Where?" he whispered.

On the road to Harrison Francie told him about the old man's barn and the mason jar on the shelf. Andrew listened without replying, seemingly distracted by other thoughts. Every so often Francie pleaded with him to slow down, and then, when he did, she rolled down the window and peered around in the darkness.

Suddenly they came upon the little restaurant where she and Beth had had lunch. "Too far," she cried. "It's back that way."

"Are you sure there is such a place?" Andrew asked peevishly.

"Yes. But I've been there only once, in the daytime. And it's hard to see from the road."

Andrew sighed noisily, to cover his anxiety.

"Don't get mad about it," said Francie. "We're right near it. And then we'll have the money."

Andrew turned the car around and headed back in the other direction. After they had driven a short distance, Francie suddenly said, "Stop." Andrew put on the brakes, and Francie squinted out into the darkness. "This is it," she whispered.

Andrew pulled over to the side of the road and turned off the lights. The pair gazed over at the old farmhouse and the barn, which stood about a hundred yards back from the road. There were several lights on in the house, but the barn was completely dark.

"It'll be hard for you to see in there. You'll have to be careful," said Francie.

"You're the one who's going to have to be careful," he said.

"Me? I thought you were going to get it."

Andrew bristled. "Hey, this was your idea. You saw him put it away. You know where to find it."

"But—"

"But what?"

"You're the boy."

Andrew stared at her. "You say you want to run away. Are you ready to do what has to be done?"

"I'm afraid," said Francie. "Won't you go? I'll tell you right where the jar is."

"I have to drive the car. I can't do everything."

Francie flopped back on the seat and stared at the dashboard. "Let's forget it then," she said.

"All right," said Andrew in a tight, angry voice. He started the engine. "Get out. Go home to your sister. I have to be on my way."

Francie was silent for a moment. Then she said, "You'd go without me?"

"I don't want to," he said. "But if I can't trust you to hold up your end, I'm better off alone."

"All right," she said. "I'll do it."

Andrew exhaled with relief. "Good."

"You'll watch, though? Come in there if anything happens?"

"I will. Now go. I'll keep the car running. Hurry."

Francie opened the door. "I hope nothing happens."

"Go on," he whispered excitedly.

Francie slipped out the door, closing it quietly behind her. Then she looked all around before crossing the street and edging up the side of the driveway toward the barn.

Francie could feel her heart pounding as she approached the barn door. The winter grass was brittle, and it crackled as she tiptoed through it. The barn loomed before her, forbidding as a tomb. For a moment she wished that it were locked up tight so that she could not get in it. She would rattle the door and then just run back to the car and tell Andrew that it couldn't be done, that she couldn't get the money.

She reached the barn door and looked at the handle. It was shut with a wooden bolt that could be easily pushed back. She looked back toward the car. If she got the money, it meant a whole, new, happy life. It was that simple. Taking a deep breath, she pushed the bolt back, and the door began to swing in, almost as if it were exhorting her to enter. It creaked as it swung, and she grabbed for it, to stop the sound and carefully move it until it was wedged in a spot on the dirt floor.

The thudding of her heart made her whole body tremble as she sidled into the dark barn. She stood still and pushed her glasses up on her nose, trying to adjust to the darkness. *It's all right,* she told herself. *It's going to be all right. You'll get the money, and you'll go away.* To California. She pictured them there, in a little bungalow under palm trees, with big flowers growing all around. *Maybe we can get a cat,* she thought. *We'll all live together.* That thought made her feel a little calmer.

She could see more clearly now through the piles of junk which filled the old barn, and she tried to remember what some of the things were that only appeared to her as vague outlines now. There were a bunch of mismatched china pieces on one table and an old mantel clock against the back wall that she recognized. Hanging in one corner were some old clothes that looked like scarecrows in the dark. She felt guilty, making her way through the old man's things, but she pushed the feeling away. The old man had had his chance to be young and run away. Now it was her turn.

Slowly, carefully, she crossed the barn as if it were a minefield. Nothing fell over; nothing broke, although she had to act quickly to keep from knocking over a birdcage on a stand which she accidentally had brushed against. She reached the wall with the shelves and stretched to grope around for the mason jar. She could not get her hand up high enough.

Looking around in the dark, she discerned the outline of a straight-back chair. She tiptoed over to it, lifted it up, and carried it over to a spot just under the shelf. Then, gingerly, she climbed up on it, keeping her feet on the rim to avoid the caned seat, which might be weak.

The chair gave her the necessary height to reach the jar. For one moment she wondered if perhaps the old man emptied it each night and this was all in vain. Then she heard the clink of coins as she pulled the jar forward. She inched the jar toward the edge of the shelf, scraping it along through the dust, until it reached the edge and she grabbed it in her hand.

Clutching the jar to her chest with a feeling of triumph and relief, Francie steadied herself on the chairback to jump down. She had one foot off the chair when the barn door banged back. By the moonlight Francie saw the silhouette of the old man holding a shotgun. "Who's there?" he cried.

Heart pounding, Francie tried to freeze, but her weight was off-balance, and she pitched forward. The old man caught sight of the movement and wheeled around, aiming at the intruder.

"Don't—" Francie cried, but he did not hear. The shot exploded from his gun.

Chapter 12

ANDREW looked down at his watch. It was a digital camp watch that he had ordered from a soldier of fortune magazine that came to the 7-Eleven. He had mailed in a money order and had it delivered to the store. His mother didn't allow him to read such magazines, and if he had had the watch sent to the house, she would have opened the package and seen where it came from. So it was easier that way, sending it to the store.

Not too late, he thought. He might still be okay if he played his cards right. He just had to figure out what to say to her. It was like the watch. He had to tell her things that would convince her. He had fooled her before. One more time was all he needed. Then, by tomorrow, he'd have things his way.

Andrew drove fast, knowing that time was essential. He hadn't meant to leave Francie there, but it turned out that he had no choice. He had been sitting with his head back against the seat, trying to relax while he waited. Out of the corner of his eye he saw the front door of the house open, and the old man stomped out on the porch, holding in his hand something long that looked like a mop handle. The old man had stared out at the car where Andrew was sitting. He stared long and hard at it, and Andrew knew he was wondering what the car was doing there at that time of the night, just sitting.

That was why he had to go. If the old man had come out and started asking questions, there would have been trouble.

Andrew had hesitated for a moment and then drove off. In his rearview mirror Andrew could see the old man walk out onto the silvery lawn and then look in the direction of the barn.

Andrew intended to drive up and down a few streets and then circle back and pick up Francie. That *was* his plan as he drove away. He would just kill a little time until the coast was clear and then circle back for her. But as he drove slowly down the neighboring streets, he began to reconsider.

By now, he knew, his mother would be on the warpath. She might already be calling the police. If she did and they started looking . . . Even if they got the old man's money, they'd never get out of the county. And if they picked him up trying to run away, he knew his mother. She would tell them everything. Robbing the old man was one thing, but murder was another. Once the cops heard about that . . .

Andrew was getting closer to Berwyn Road, and he knew he had to think clearly. The problem with tonight was that the timing was bad. It was good that Francie was ready to come with him, but she had picked the wrong time. You had to plan something like this. You needed to be clever and have a head start on things.

Tonight was all-important, he thought. First he had to convince her that the story about him and Francie that the sister told was just a big lie. Then tonight he would make all the plans, get everything ready. *She'll never know what hit her.*

As he drove up to the house he could see that she was not waiting at the window. This was unusual for her, and the sick feeling came over him again. It was almost as bad as it had been in the garage parking lot. He got out of the car and breathed deeply of the chilly air, trying to fortify himself and stick to his resolution. As quickly as possible he hurried in through the basement and took the ritual shower. His clothes lay in a neat pile on the table, as they always did. This reassured him. She wasn't any more cunning than he. Whatever she might pull on him, he would be ready. He climbed the stairs and tapped gently on the door, trying the knob automatically. To his surprise the door opened, and he was able to let himself in.

"I'm back," he called out in a voice that was meant to sound casual. It echoed hollowly through the hall.

"I'm in here."

He followed the voice into the gloom of the parlor. She was sitting in the faded brown wing chair. Her fingers were curled like claws over the edge of the threadbare arms. In her eyes was that haunted, beleaguered stare that he had seen so often. No error in his behavior was too small to summon that look to her eye. It would be followed, he knew, by the tremulous inquiry, the opportunity she always afforded him to try to weasel out of an accusation, before she pounced on him, crushing him with her ironclad information. Tonight he was ready for her. He knew what to do. He had never felt so determined. Fear fluttered around in his stomach, but he was able to ignore it.

"Did you have to work late?" she asked.

"Well, no, not really."

She was silent for a moment, already surprised. "Well, where were you?"

"It's—sort of a secret."

"A secret."

"Yeah."

"I know all about it, Andrew."

"About Noah?" he asked.

"Noah? What's Noah got to do with this?"

"That's where I was. Covering for Noah."

"Don't give me that, Andrew. I had a visitor today. Do you want to know who my visitor was?"

"Sure. I don't care," he said calmly.

Leonora jumped to her feet and shook a finger at him. "You'd better care. It was the sister of your little girlfriend. The Pearson girl. She told me all about you and that little girl you are running after."

Andrew felt a little shaky, hearing the words, but he put on a smile. "Oh, that's the joke," he said. "It's not me. It's Noah she's running around with. She's so stupid. She got it all wrong. I'm just helping out my friend."

Leonora glared at him and came up close to him, atomizing peppermint into his face. He held his breath. "Don't lie to me, Andrew," she said, but there was a tiny doubt in her voice. "She said it was you. I was humiliated to listen to it. Vile, perverted behavior with a child. Oh, and I could well believe it. Filth. Just like your father. Filth."

Andrew stood perfectly still, clinging to the story in his mind like a sailor in a gale, clinging to the mast. "She made a mistake," he said. "It was Noah."

"Listen to me, Andrew. I did not sacrifice my whole life to protect you just so you could be like him, running around with some child. Oh, no." Her doughy face was right up against his, and her narrowed eyes were fiercely bright.

"It wasn't me," he said.

She stared at his forehead, as if trying to read his mind. He could see that she was unsure. "This whole day has been torture," she said. "Sheer torture."

He smiled blankly at her. "You shouldn't get so upset. I would never do that."

"I hope not," she said. Then her eyes narrowed again. "You hear me out, Andrew. If I ever, ever hear this again, that you are going around with that girl. One time is all, and I'll be asking around, you can bet. If I hear that—I won't tolerate it. All these years I have protected you from your punishment. If it weren't for me, you would be in jail or a mental institution. I'm sure you haven't forgotten that."

"No," said Andrew, squeezing his fingernails into his palms. "I'm grateful to you."

She gripped his upper arm in her stubby hand. "I've covered up for you, Andrew. I saved you from a life you couldn't even imagine. I'm not sorry. You are my son, and I would do it again. Any mother would. But I won't be humiliated by you. I won't allow you to run wild, flaunting your perverted lusts. I won't." She tightened her grip on him. "I can still lead the authorities to your father's body. And the gun. It's not too late for that."

Andrew turned and looked at her. He felt lightheaded, as if her breath were ether and he were floating away from her. He could smile and lie in the face of that lifelong threat. For tomorrow he would be gone. He would never have to look at her ugly face again.

Freedom was so close at hand. He and Francie would be gone, and they would never come back. "You're getting yourself all worked up over nothing," he said. "The stupid bitch made a mistake."

"Andrew," she said, releasing him, "don't use that word."

"I'm tired," he said. "I'm going up."

She let him go, watching him as he went but not saying anything more. He went to his room and sank down on his bed, a blissful feeling of relief washing over him. She had believed him. Now he had all night to plan.

After a few minutes of lying on the bed, he heard her footsteps on the stairs and a soft tap at the door. He stiffened at the sound of the tapping.

"Dear," she said, "I've brought you something to eat."

"I'm not hungry."

"Andrew, I've got this tray in my hands, and I can't open the door. Just open it a teeny bit, and take this before it gets cold. I've got some steaming hot soup."

For a minute he hesitated, and then a thought came to him. He leaped off the bed and threw the door open. "Give me the soup," he demanded, and jerked the tray up from her hand so that the bowl flew back at her and the steaming soup splattered all over her.

She yelped in pain. "It burned me," she screamed. She wrung her hands and ran for the bathroom. Andrew heard the water running.

"Sorry," he said, glowing inside at the success of his sneak attack. "Forget about the soup. I don't want it anyway."

He slammed the door to his room before she had a chance to reply. After a while he heard her going down the hall to her room and closing the door. He did not watch the clock, but he waited for a long time, until he was sure she would be asleep, before he started to stir. As he moved around the room he thought about guerrilla units, packing up camp and moving out in the dead of night. He had read a lot about them in the mercenary magazines. Silence, stealth, and cunning. Those were the qualities that you had to admire about them. That and their deadly resolve to carry out their mission at all costs.

First he went to his bookcase and dragged out the road atlas and opened it to the map of the U.S.A. There were so many places you could disappear to, a million towns where you could be free in the land of the free. The thought made his lips curl into a smile, although his eyes remained cold and riveted to the page. He had told Francie his father lived in California. He ran his finger up and down the California coastline. That was no problem. Once they got there, he'd just say he lost the address or something. He rolled up the atlas and put a rubber band around it.

Then he lay down on his back and ran his hands under the bottom of his dresser, peeling off the masking tape which held the large lightweight package wrapped in plastic. Andrew shook the package loose and took it out. It was a khaki duffel bag, neatly folded, which he had ordered from the same magazine as the watch and had hidden under the dresser. He had had to be very careful getting it into the house because he knew if she saw it, she would take it away, saying he didn't need it because he wasn't going anywhere.

Gently he shook the bag out and then, after easing open the creaky drawers of the dresser, took out some clothes he thought he would need. He took only light things, figuring it would be warmer where they were going. Plus he had to keep the bag fairly flat so he could hide it under the bed for tonight and the morning.

Now, he thought, zippering the bag, for the most important part. In the toe of his oldest sneakers, which he always kept stuffed with a pair of sweat socks, he pulled up the insole, and there it was. It was the key chain she had given him, the one with the bird on it, and dangling from the metal hook were two keys, one to the ignition and the other to the trunk of his mother's car. He had had them made in Harrison one day, when he drove her there to shop on a Saturday. It had been a daring move, although he had waited to run to the hardware store while she was in the beauty parlor having her hair cut. She had been suspicious of his whereabouts, but he made up a good story about trying on a pair of pants, and even though she made a fuss and said they couldn't afford new pants, she let the matter drop.

He stared at the keys now with an exhilarating feeling of power. Tomorrow she would be sure to take her set to work after the way he had kept the car out late today. He would pretend to go walking off to work as usual, but instead, he would go find Francie at school and convince her to come with him. Then he could come back for his things, and the car, after she had gotten her bus, and he and Francie would be long gone by the time she got back from Dr. Ridberg's.

As he formulated the plan in his mind he found the last thing he needed. It was an envelope of money, hidden inside a book which he had cut out the pages from, the way it was done in the movies. He had been saving the money for a car, but now they wouldn't need it because they had her car. After unzipping the duffel bag, he tossed the keys and the money back in and then carefully wedged the bag under the bed.

He attached it to the bedsprings so that it did not hang down under the wooden frame. He began to think about the car. She would probably describe the car to the police, and sooner or later he and Francie might have to ditch it and steal another car. For that matter, the money could run out, and they had to have a way to get more money fast. The one thing they still needed was a weapon, and he knew there was a gun in this house. Hadn't she been threatening him with that information for years? Tomorrow, when he got home, he would search the place until he found it. It didn't matter how he tore the house apart. He wouldn't need to put anything back. She could yell all she wanted after he was gone.

Andrew felt a surge of happiness all through him as he went over the plan in his mind. Tomorrow they would be gone. Free. He had never been able to do it alone. It was Francie who gave him the strength. His girl. They would do it together.

He got into bed, but he could not sleep, and the book that he had suddenly did not interest him. It was as if his veins were filled with an intoxicating drug. He would be free. His mother's voice, her smell, this house—all of it would be wiped away.

Let her tell. They would never catch him. Francie would be with him, and there was no end to what they could do. They would take what they wanted and have their own way.

He sat up in his bed, wide-awake, until dawn. His eyes were open, but he did not see his shabby room. He saw visions of himself and Francie, driving fast, mowing down anyone or anything that tried to get in their way, taking without asking. The images danced in his head, wreathing him in happy contentment, all night long, like visions of sugarplums on Christmas Eve.

Chapter 13

BETH walked up to the front door and rapped on it with the tarnished brass knocker. A frail old woman with unsmiling eyes opened the door.

"Good evening. I'm Beth Pearson. I've come about my sister."

The old woman indicated for her to come in with an impatient gesture. "Frank," she called out, "the sister's here." She indicated a stiff-looking chair in the corner of the dreary living room. "Sit down," she said. "I'll get him."

Without another word she turned her back on Beth and went down the darkened hallway to the other end of the house.

Beth sat down on the hard seat and looked around. The room was lit only by dim bulbs in ancient lamps with yellowed shades. A jumble of furniture filled the room, barely leaving a walkway between pieces. Framed sepia-toned photographs hung above the mantel. The only thing in the room that did not look as if it belonged in another century was the giant console TV, which sat opposite the sofa. The top of the TV was thick with dust.

Beth closed her eyes and rested her head against the scratchy upholstery of the chair. A grandfather clock by the staircase chimed eight o'clock, and Beth was surprised. It seemed much later than that to her. It seemed like one of the longest days she could ever remember.

After Francie had stormed out, she had wandered the house in a daze for a while. She had tried to call Mike but got only his answering service. Finally she had sat down in the living room and forced herself to go back over the argument with Francie. She had been shocked by her own outburst. She had not really been aware of the ugly, irrational anger she had harbored for so long. From there she progressed backward in her thoughts to the news of her father's death, the beginning of this visit. Then, like someone picking at a scab, she thought back to her mother's death and then, farther back, to Francie's birth. It was like a journey through a jungle, like trying to find a river's source. She hacked her way back through a tangle of old feelings, old resentments. She had started out with the conviction that she was a good person at heart. After a while, though, she became frightened. Nothing was clear anymore.

By the time the old man called she had already been watching the clock for several hours, wishing Francie would get back and wondering what she would say to her when she did. The call had unnerved her and then sent her flying out the house.

Beth heard the shuffle of feet in the hallway coming toward her and then heard the old man say, "Go on. Move."

The old woman came in first, shaking her head, as if confronted with a hopeless quandary. Beth stood up.

"They're bad," said the old lady. "They have no morals. What kinds of homes do they come from that they turn out this way?" She did not look at Beth but simply seated herself on the sofa.

"And a girl," the woman continued, shaking her head in disbelief. "A girl no less. These days they are worse than the boys."

"It's terrible," Beth murmured, "although I know she's never done such a thing before."

"Frank," the old woman barked impatiently. "She's a bad girl," said the old woman. "She's no good. They ought to lock her up."

Beth tried to conceal her annoyance at the old woman's words. She thought about saying something about Francie's difficult life in her defense, but just then she heard the others coming in.

She turned and looked. The old man was prodding Francie along with the tip of a cane, and the girl dragged her feet as she walked, her eyes down, her hands tied in front of her with a length of rope.

Beth stifled a yelp of protest at the sight. "Francie," she said, "what happened?"

Francie looked up at her a moment and tried to stick her chin out defiantly. But there was a lack of spirit in the gesture. She looked back down at the floor.

"I'll tell you what happened," said Frank in a peevish voice. "I caught her red-handed in my barn, trying to make off with my money jar. She had it in her hand, so there's no point in making excuses. She's lucky I didn't shoot her. I was mad enough to, I'll tell you."

"You tried to," Francie muttered.

The man poked her with the cane. "What's that?"

"I just want to thank you," Beth said hurriedly, "for calling me first, instead of the police. I feel this is a matter we can deal with among ourselves."

"It seems like you don't keep a very good eye on this kid."

Beth wanted to insist that the man untie Francie's hands, but she did not want to make him angry. She quickly decided that diplomacy was in order. "You're right," she said, "and there's no excuse for it. But our household is in a kind of chaotic state right now. Our father just died, and we have no mother—she died years ago—so there's been a lot of confusion."

The old man was unflinching. He turned to Francie and poked her again. "Is this the way you respect your father's memory—breaking into people's life savings?"

"It's a sin," said his wife vehemently.

Francie shook her head. "I'm sorry."

Beth fought back the urge to push the old man away and undo the rope. It was a tricky moment. The old man seemed in no hurry to give up his prisoner. *Eat a little more crow,* thought Beth.

"It's a terrible thing," Beth repeated. "I'm sure Francie will never do anything like this again."

"She must be punished," the old man insisted. "She can't just walk away scot-free from something like this. You people must think I'm some kind of a sucker."

"She will be," said Beth, wondering what it was that he wanted before he would let Francie loose. It began to seem less and less as if it were compassion that had kept him from phoning the police.

"After all," he said in a whining voice, "I can't have hordes of people breaking into my business. I'm not insured or anything like that. They come in, and they damage valuable things—not to even mention what they steal and run off with."

"Did you find the money?" Beth asked.

"Yes, I found the money," he said irritably. "That's not the point. She broke irreplaceable things in there. It will take me days to get things back in order. Not to mention my nerves. I may not even be able to work for a few days I'm so upset by this. . . ."

Beth suddenly understood that there was a financial penance involved. "That's true," she said, fumbling in her purse for her wallet and feeling glad she had brought some money with her. "I'd feel much better if you'd let me pay you for the damage done."

"Those things can't be replaced. They're antiques."

"I understand that," said Beth. "And I am sorry. I know that Francie is too. But if you would just allow me to offer you some money to start putting things back to rights . . ." She pulled out some bills from her wallet and pressed them into the old man's hand.

He estimated the amount with a grumpy snort and then exchanged a glance with his wife. Beth quickly leaned over and untied the rope on Francie's hands as he pocketed the money.

"I don't care," said the old woman. "No amount can pay us back for all this worry."

Beth began to edge toward the door with Francie straggling along in her grip. "I know. I'm so sorry. Thank you for calling me," she murmured, pushing the door open with her shoulder.

The old man followed them out onto the porch. "By rights she belongs in the police station."

"Good night," said Beth.

The old man slammed the door and turned the porch light off before they were even down the steps.

Beth and Francie stumbled in the darkness toward the car.

Once inside the car Beth turned on the radio. It played softly as they drove along without speaking. After a few miles Beth said in a calm voice, "I know this wasn't your idea. Where is Andrew? Did he run away and leave you there?"

"Don't start on Andrew again," said Francie in a voice shrill with weariness.

"I wasn't," said Beth. "I'm not."

They didn't say anything else until they got back to the house. Francie went inside and muttered something about going up to bed, but Beth stopped her. The younger girl waited in the kitchen while Beth took off her coat and hung it up. Francie kept her eyes trained on a spot on the floor, her shoulders slumped, as if waiting for a lashing that she knew she had coming.

Beth came into the room and cleared her throat nervously. She found herself knotting her fingers together like a child about to go on in a school play.

"I'll try to pay you the money back," Francie said in a tired voice.

"That's not—never mind that," said Beth. "Francie, I did a lot of thinking after you left today, and I feel really bad about some of the things I said. I owe you an apology, and I'm very sorry."

Francie blinked at her in surprise and then looked wary.

"I mean it," said Beth. "That stuff about Mother's accident. That was—" She shook her head. "Sometimes you just don't realize the awful thoughts you keep inside. I guess I was really hurt all these years, and I just took it out on you. I mean, blaming you was

—well, a terrible thing to do. Now Dad, I'm not so sure—"

"He felt as bad as I did," said Francie. "You just didn't know him."

Beth nodded and sighed. "Well, maybe you're right. I don't know. I don't seem to know anything today."

Francie pursed her lips, her eyes still on the ground. "I think I'll go up," she said.

"I want you to know," said Beth, "that I'm truly sorry."

Francie nodded and left the room. She didn't smile, but her face looked less drawn than it had when they walked in.

Beth sat down in the rocker, feeling relieved that she had at least tried to do the right thing. After a while she picked up a bag on the floor with some work she had for the business and put it on the table to look at it. She wanted to get her mind on something concrete and emotionally uncomplicated, like work. She heard the water running in the upstairs bathroom, and then it stopped. She wondered if Francie would be coming back down, and she forced herself to concentrate on the drawings in front of her.

A door opened upstairs, and Beth heard Francie call her name. Beth walked toward the foot of the stairs. Francie was hidden from view at the top.

"Thanks for helping me," she said.

"That's okay," said Beth.

She could hear that Francie had not budged. Beth wanted to say something friendly or consoling, but she could not think what it might be. After a few moments the girl's footsteps receded down the hall, and her door closed. Slowly Beth climbed the stairs, determined to try to start some kind of bridge between them. She walked to the door of Francie's room and stood outside. Inside, she heard the sound of the girl sobbing.

The sobs startled her. It was as if she finally had discovered evidence of Francie's misery. Beth put her hand on the doorknob. She wanted to go in and put an arm around her sister and speak to her. She felt her own loneliness answering the sorrowful sounds from inside the room.

You hardly know her, she reminded herself. *Don't intrude on her private feelings.*

Telling herself that the girl's sobs seemed to be quieting down, Beth let go of the doorknob and backed away from the door. With a quiet tread, so as not to be heard, she made her way back down the stairs.

Chapter 14

ANDREW hustled up the hill and cut across a field. He knew he would have to hurry if he wanted to catch Francie before her classes started. His plan was to catch her before she went into school. He knew that all the kids waited in the lobby for fifteen minutes to a half hour before the doors opened, so he had to be sure to get there on time.

He felt he should be tired, having been up all night, but he was tense and full of energy. His mother had been suspicious about his going off early to work, but she had accepted his explanation that he had not put up all the stock because he left early yesterday to cover for Noah. He had wanted to howl in glee when he said good-bye to her, knowing that he would never have to see or be near her again. While he hurried along there was a little skip in his step as he pictured her face when she came home and found him and her precious car gone without a trace.

He was slightly out of breath but not at all fatigued

when he finally reached the single-story building that served as junior high and high school for Oldham and three other nearby towns. It was a plain ocher-colored structure, built in the fifties to accommodate the increase in children that had resulted after the war, even in Oldham, Maine. Andrew had attended the school himself, and he felt a familiar shiver of revulsion as he approached the swinging glass doors that provided entrance to the building.

As he pushed back the door familiar sounds and smells assaulted him. The odor of pencil shavings and fresh wax mingled with the perfumes and after-shaves of the preening teenagers crammed into the foyer. Their chatter was deafening as they pretended to talk to their friends, all the while flirting and tempting with glances, gestures from beringed fingers, the flexing of young bodies in tight clothes.

He had never understood it, never been able to join it. Any awkward advances he had made had been mocked. He had been marked from grade school as weird, undesirable. He had always known it, although he tried to pretend that he didn't, or didn't care. Now, standing in the crush of the excited students, he felt his breath coming in gasps, and he broke out in a sweat. His clammy hand groped to pull the door open so he could run. Then, suddenly, he remembered. He was here to see his girl. He had a girl. The thought filled him with a creeping warmth. His heartbeat quieted. He looked up at the clock above the door. He had made good time. And his girl was here in this throng.

One of the teachers came to the inside doors and unlocked them. The students surged into the building, pushing and chattering. Andrew wanted to stop someone and ask him if he'd seen Francie. He wanted to say the words *my girlfriend* in these halls. He would ask some big, handsome guy. A guy who looked popular.

Just then he spotted her. She was edging up to the doorway in a crowd of children. They were the babies of the school, who endured the most shoving. They bounced along like pebbles on a tide.

"Francie," he called out, waving to her.

She looked up over the other kids and saw him there, smiling eagerly at her, gesturing to her. She pushed her glasses up on her nose, lowered her head, and pushed a little harder to get through the door.

Andrew glowered and called her name again, in a harsh voice. But she huddled in among the kids, and there was no doubt this time that she was ignoring him, trying to get away from him.

Andrew tried to elbow his way past the other students to get to her and caught a girl's barrette in the fabric of his coat sleeve.

"Oww . . ." the girl wailed, reaching for the crown of her head.

Andrew saw Francie carried through the door, her ash blond hair disappearing into the darkness of the main lobby. He jerked his arm back and forth, trying to free himself of the girl to whom he was fettered by the barrette.

"Cut it out," the girl shrieked, while her friends yelled, "Stop it," at him, and one girl tried to undo the clip from his waving arm.

"Let go of me," Andrew growled, searching the doorway for the sight of Francie, but she was gone.

"There," the girlfriend cried as the barrette popped open and her friend's hair was loosened from Andrew's arm. There were tears in the long-haired girl's eyes as she rubbed her reddened scalp. A clump of her hairs trailed from the arm of Andrew's coat as he threw down the barrette and started for the door.

"Don't say you're sorry, jerk," hissed the friend who had undone the clip, but Andrew was already breaking through the last few students who were dawdling on their way into class.

The main hallway of the building was large and gloomy with the auditorium on one side and the school offices on the other. He looked around, cursing, for he didn't know where to find her. The corridors branched off the main hallway, and after a moment's hesitation, he began to rove restlessly up and down them, looking for the eighth-grade signs outside the classroom doors. Teachers were coming out into the hallway and closing their classroom doors as Andrew rushed by, peering into their rooms.

"May I help you?" asked a crew-cutted teacher coolly as he looked Andrew up and down.

"No," said Andrew. "I'm just looking for my—uh—a friend." He glanced across the hall and saw the sign for O'NEILL, GRADE 8, lettered on oak tag beside the door. Craning his neck, he saw Francie, seated several rows back by the window.

"There she is," he muttered. "Scuse me." He hurried over to the classroom door. Mrs. O'Neill was not yet in her classroom, and Andrew stood in the doorway and called Francie's name. The girl sitting next to Francie nudged her, and Francie looked up and then back down at her desk, her face white.

"Come here a minute," Andrew insisted.

"Go away," she said.

"Get out here right now," he demanded. The buzz in the classroom subsided at the sound of Andrew's angry voice. Francie hesitated for a minute and then got up and walked out into the hall as the others watched. In a minute the chatter picked up again.

"What do you want?" Francie asked sullenly.

"Hey, smile," said Andrew. "This is our lucky day."

"Sure," she said with a snort.

"Listen, I've got a lot to tell you."

Francie looked up angrily at him. "Andrew, what happened to you last night?"

Andrew looked surprised. "Last night? What do you mean?"

"Where did you go? That old man caught me in his barn."

"He did?" said Andrew. "What happened? I guess he let you go."

"Yeah, he let me go finally. But first he tied me up, and he called my sister. And he almost called the police."

"Well, yeah. But everything's okay now."

"You left me there. He had a gun, and he shot it at me. How could you just leave me there?"

Andrew frowned at her as if he were concentrating on her question. "I had to," he said. "You'll see why when I tell you this."

"Forget it," said Francie, turning away from him.

He grabbed her arm. "Wait. Don't be mad. I have everything all arranged. That's why I had to leave last night."

"Arranged for what?"

"For us to run away!"

"Stop yelling," she said, looking up and down the hallway. People were still straggling into their classes, settling in for the morning. "Why should I go with you?" But her tone was more fretful than angry.

"You see, last night wasn't the right timing. I didn't have things ready. Now we've got everything packed.

I've got the money. All we have to do is go and get the car. Come on," he said. "I came here to get you. We can go right now."

"I can't," said Francie.

"Why not?"

"I can't just leave school. The teacher will call my sister."

Andrew glared at her and dropped her arm. "I've gone to a lot of trouble," he insisted. "Everything is ready."

His angry tone made her heart sink. She became immediately conciliatory. "How about later?"

"When?"

"After school."

"It's too late."

"My last period is study hall. I can skip that," she offered.

The door to the ladies' room opened, and Cindy O'Neill came out into the hall, smoothing down her skirt. She looked coolly at the pair in the hallway and then spoke to Francie. "Aren't you supposed to be in your seat?"

Francie nodded her head nervously and threw a glance at Andrew, who was glaring at the teacher with icy, piercing eyes.

"Three o'clock?" Francie whispered hopefully.

"The stone wall, by the post office," he said.

Cindy met his flinty gaze with her own. "I don't believe you're a student here, Andrew."

"I'm leaving," he said.

Francie nodded at him as he looked back at her. Three o'clock. It was too late. It messed up all his plans. He stomped down the hall and slammed through the front doors of the building. He would go to work for a few hours, maybe take himself a little going-away present from the cash drawer. Three o'clock would still give them a few hours' head start. It would have to do.

Chapter 15

*B*ETH lifted the lid on the old trunk with the broken lock, brushing away the cobwebs as she did it. She was feeling quite proud of herself, having gotten through almost everything else in the attic already. It was going well. She had developed a rhythm as well as a rather thick skin about saving things, and it looked as if the whole house might be done tomorrow.

You are going to be a success in business, she thought. *Good organizing skills.* She pulled an empty garbage bag up beside the trunk, prepared to toss out the contents. The lid fell back with a snap, and a boxful of yellowed lace filled her view. As she reached in to pull it out, Beth recognized her mother's wedding dress. She had not seen it in years.

Beth sat back on her heels and stared at the crumpled dress. She had played dress-up in it when she was little, but her mother had caught her and warned her not to rip it because she might want to wear it herself one day.

She saved it for me, Beth thought. She always was an optimist. Beth sighed and then smiled, thinking of her mother, as she held the dress absently on her lap. She had always been tenderhearted and sentimental. Beth remembered teasing her because she would cry and cry at those old black-and-white movies on the late show. Beth found herself wondering if her mother would have liked Mike. She pictured her mother's gentle, approving eyes, and she knew that her mother would have thought he was great. An ideal husband.

Beth shook her head and looked down at the dress. Her mother wasn't exactly the best judge of husbands. It wasn't as if the dress had proved to be so lucky for her.

Beth hesitated, trying to decide what to do with it. *Even if I ever do get married,* she thought, *I probably wouldn't wear something this lacy.* But she felt uncomfortable throwing it away. Her mother had dreamed of her wearing it. She had saved it for her all these years.

All right, Beth thought. *I'll find someplace to keep it.* She lifted the bulky dress, now crisp with age, out of the box, and carefully started to fold it into a manageable size for storing. As she turned it over she noticed a note pinned to the bodice of the dress. It said, "For Beth and Francie. Your mother's wedding gown." It was written in the unmistakably stilted script of her father's hand.

Beth stared at the note for some time, feeling slightly dazed as she realized that he was the one responsible for labeling the wedding dress and carefully storing it in the trunk. It took her a few minutes to realize that the ringing in her ears was the sound of the telephone.

Having dropped the dress into the trunk, she bolted

down the stairs and grabbed the phone. On the other end was Maxine, her assistant at the office.

"How's it going?" Maxine asked sympathetically.

"Not too bad," Beth said, chewing thoughtfully on her lip. "I should be back in a couple of days."

"I'm afraid," Maxine said, "you're going to have to get back sooner than that."

"Like when?"

"Like tomorrow. It's an emergency. Hanley just called from California. He's flying in tonight, and he wants to see you tomorrow, before he makes the final decision about the headquarters building. He's going to be here only the one day, and he insists on seeing you."

"Damn," said Beth. "We need to get that job. You couldn't stall him?"

"I sweet-talked him every which way," said Maxine. "I tried."

"I know," said Beth. "I know you did. It's just that I'm going to have to fly down there tonight and then turn around and come right back up here in a day or two. What a waste of time and money."

"I know it. I'm sorry."

The doorbell started to ring, and Beth groaned. "Hold on a minute, Maxine. This place is suddenly Grand Central."

Beth rushed over to the door and opened it. Cindy O'Neill stood on the front steps and looked worried as Beth threw the door open.

"Beth, do you have a minute?"

"Come in," said Beth. "Just a sec. I'm on the phone." Beth returned to the phone as Cindy stepped into the living room and stood there, looking around at the disarray.

"Take your coat off. Just hang it on a carton," Beth told her. She returned to her call.

"I have company," she explained to Maxine.

"Listen, Beth, I feel terrible about this. I wish I could have handled it for you."

"No, it's all right. We have to land this client. This job is gonna pay our salaries for the next six months. It's worth the trip. All right. I'll get busy with reservations. I'll be home sometime tonight, probably late. But I'll be in the office tomorrow morning at nine. You can tell him that I'm taking him to lunch. Make us a reservation somewhere nice, will you? La Famiglia, maybe."

Maxine agreed to it, and Beth sighed. "I might as well get a nice lunch out of it, right? See you tomorrow."

She hung up the phone and turned to Cindy, who was perched on the edge of a chair that had clothing on hangers draped over its back. "Sounds like big business," said Cindy.

Beth flopped down on the sofa. "It's a big headache, I'll tell you that. I have to go down to Philly tonight and then come back up here after I've taken care of this client's problems."

Cindy pressed her lips together and nodded.

Beth sighed. "It's not all bad, I guess. It will give me a chance to see my—the guy I go with. We really need a visit. This phone stuff is terrible. I thought things were over for good the other night. At least he and I can have a night or two together to straighten things out."

"Well," Cindy said, "I hate to add to your problems, but I had a free period, and I thought I'd better come over and talk to you."

Beth covered her eyes briefly with one hand. "Don't tell me. What did she do now?"

"Well, it isn't what she's done exactly—" said Cindy.

"Did you hear about last night?" said Beth.

"No, hear what?"

Beth waved it off. "It's a long story. Suffice it to say that she narrowly missed ending up in jail. I had to do some fast talking to get her out of a mess."

"You may be doing that again tonight," said Cindy.

"Hit me."

Cindy took a deep breath. "This morning I was in the ladies' room, and I overheard your sister and Andrew talking out in the corridor."

"Andrew? What was he doing there?"

"From what I heard, he came to talk Francie into running away with him tonight. And I believe he succeeded."

"Goddammit," said Beth, jumping up from the sofa and pacing around the cluttered living room. She nearly tripped over a box, which she promptly kicked out of the way. "That guy is a real pain in the ass. He is nothing but trouble. That's how she got into trouble last night. Because of him. I've had just about enough of this crap."

"I'm sorry, Beth. I feel as if I bring you nothing but bad news all the time."

"No, no," said Beth. "I'm glad you told me. What the hell am I supposed to do now? I have to go to Philadelphia tonight. Now Andrew comes up with this little stunt. What's the matter with him? Is he crazy? Didn't he ever hear of the Mann Act?"

"I don't know," said Cindy. "They're so mixed up at that age."

"Francie maybe," said Beth. "But there's no excuse for him. He is old enough to know better."

"Well," said Cindy, pulling on her wool hat and tucking her red curls up into it, "I heard them planning to meet at three o'clock up near the post office."

"We'll see about that," said Beth grimly.

"Don't tell her I ratted on her," said Cindy. "I feel bad about it, but I was afraid it could mean real trouble for Francie. And I like her. I mean, I've always had a soft spot for her because I've known her for so long, and she's your sister. I also think she's a sensitive, bright girl. Andrew is only going to mess her up. I'd hate to see that happen."

"Believe me, Cindy. I appreciate your telling me. I'll see to it that this little scheme never gets off the ground. You can be sure of that."

Beth waved to Cindy as she went down the driveway and got into her little red compact car. Then she looked at her watch as she went back into the house. She had a lot to do and not much time to do it.

She went upstairs to pack her bag for the trip to Philadelphia, and then she came back down to make her airline reservations. While she was at it, she tried to call Mike again but was only able to reach his office. She left a message saying the time she would be arriving in town and hung up.

Suddenly the door to the house opened, and Francie walked in. Beth jumped and then tried to conceal her surprise. They greeted each other casually, although Beth noted the high color in Francie's cheeks and the way she avoided Beth's glance. She immediately went up to her room, and Beth heard the sound of drawers being opened and shut. *Packing,* Beth thought grimly. *Okay. Here we go.*

After a while she heard Francie coming down the stairs. Beth waited calmly in the kitchen, going through her papers as if there were nothing unusual going on. Francie came into the kitchen carrying a blue backpack.

"I've got a baby-sitting job," she said without preamble. "I won't be back until late."

"What's that for?" Beth asked, nodding toward the pack.

"Books for studying. Junk like that."

"Oh," said Beth, "okay."

Francie twisted her hair absently around one finger. "Well," she said, "good-bye."

Beth kept her back to her sister and her head bent over her papers. "See you," she said as casually as possible.

Francie hesitated for a second and then headed out the door.

Nothing to it, Beth thought. *Just good-bye, and she walks out of my life.* For a minute she felt like kicking something, but then a rueful smile crept over her face. *That's the pot calling the kettle black,* she thought.

Beth waited for a few minutes to give Francie a head start. She cleaned up all her papers and put them back in their folders. They all had to go into her suitcase for the next day's meeting. Then she pulled on her jacket and picked up the car keys. She knew what she wanted to do, and she was ready. She would intercept the would-be runaways and have it out with the two of them then and there. There was no point in being nice about this thing. She was going to settle it once and for all.

The tomblike temperature in the car made her shiver as she tried the engine. She had not been out in the course of the day, and the engine balked at her attempt to turn it over. Beth shifted around in the seat and looked up the street. Francie was well out of sight by now. After rubbing her hands together anxiously, she tried the key again. She wanted to be able to take the two of them by surprise, but she certainly didn't want to give them a chance to get away from her. "Come on," she muttered, pumping the gas pedal. The engine gave a sustained wheeze and then sputtered to life.

She let the engine idle for a few minutes as she planned what she would say. She rehearsed her speech aloud, and her breath fogged up the insides of the car's windows. She flipped on the heat and the defroster, wiped the inside of the windshield impatiently with her gloved hand, and began to back down the driveway.

The afternoon sky was a dull, steely gray, and the clouds were like wide paintbrush strokes of a darker, more purplish hue. Beth could not see Francie anywhere on the street as she drove, and she hoped again that she had not let the girl get too far ahead of her. There was not much traffic on the road. A few pickup trucks passed Beth, going in the other direction. Beth slowly climbed the hill to the corner near the post office and glanced out. Sure enough, there was Francie, standing by the stone wall, looking up the street to her right. Beth quickly made a left and circled the block again. She came up on the corner from behind and pulled over into the parking lot of the little branch office of the savings bank. She could see Francie clearly now, though the girl's back was to her. She was shifting her pack from side to side as she peered in first one direction and then the other.

Despite the cold, Beth switched off the car engine, so that the sound of the idling car did not attract Francie's attention. *This shouldn't take long*, Beth thought. She made an estimate of the distance between her and Francie, wanting to be sure that when

Andrew's car pulled up, she would have time to make it up the hill before Francie could get in and they could pull away. *It's only a short sprint,* she reassured herself. *You'll have your hand on the door before she even gets that pack in the car.*

With a sigh Beth settled back against the seat and watched for Andrew, although she felt anything but relaxed. The car had heated up a little on the ride over, but it was getting cold again quickly. As Beth watched, Francie removed the backpack from her shoulder and rested it on the wall. She shifted her weight from foot to foot, occasionally pushing her hair back from her face when a gust of wind rearranged it.

Beth looked down at the dial of her watch. It was past three. Andrew should be coming around the corner any minute, she thought. She craned her neck to look up and down the street, but she had no view from where she was situated, so she settled down again. She would just have to rely on Francie's reaction to know he was coming.

Francie wiped her nose on the sleeve of her parka and stared in the general direction of Andrew's house. After a few more minutes she stamped her feet, crossed her arms in front of her, and pressed her hands under her armpits.

No gloves, Beth observed. That figured. She sighed, but at the same time she had a fleeting wish that she had an extra pair in the car to give her. She wondered whatever made Francie think that she could manage on her own with Andrew. *I sometimes feel I can't manage on my own,* she thought ruefully.

Beth yawned, but it was a yawn of nervousness, not of tiredness. She thought about turning on the radio, but she didn't trust the battery in the old car. She still had to drive it to the airport tonight. She looked down again at her watch. It was getting close to four, and Andrew had not yet appeared.

Francie turned around for a minute, and Beth ducked, afraid that the girl had sensed she was being watched and that she would spot her there, lying in wait. But Francie was only facing the wall to climb up on it and sit down. Once she had hoisted herself up on the stones, she wriggled around and sat there, her thin legs dangling in front of her.

She began to rock back and forth as she sat there, picking up her pack and clutching it to her chest like a mother trying to rock her baby to sleep.

Beth shifted in her seat, feeling pins and needles in her nether region that were partly from the cold and partly from the fact that her legs were going to sleep.

The sky had started to darken, the early winter night chasing away what little daylight there had been. The paintbrush clouds were turned to charcoal as the gray light drained from the sky and the darkness came on. A sliver of moon glowed weakly over the rugged horizon. The inside of the car was like a refrigerator now, but at least it wasn't windy. Beth was grateful for that. She could see the occasional gust lift Francie's hair and ripple the surface of her limp, well-worn jacket. Francie dislodged a hand from under her arm to push her glasses back up on her nose. Then she slumped back, her chin resting atop the pack with the forlorn look of a dog that has been banished from the room.

She looks like a waif, Beth thought, *huddled there in the cold, as if that wall were a raft and she were lost at sea, hoping for rescue. And look who she is waiting for,* Beth thought disgustedly. *Andrew. He's a weirdo. He's way too old, he left her in the lurch at the old man's barn, and he's a loser nobody likes. But there she is, waiting patiently. Why would she wait for someone like that?* Beth wondered.

But almost as soon as she asked the question, she recognized the answer. It caused a little thud in her chest, as it came to her. She looked away from Francie and caught sight of her own grim expression in the side-view mirror of the car. *Because she is a waif, and she is adrift, and she needs someone. You don't want to see it, do you?* she thought. *She is not an adult. She is still a child, and she is afraid. And she needs someone. Even Andrew.*

Francie had pushed herself off the wall again and was walking back and forth in front of it, dragging her pack and glancing up hopefully at any sound of a car's engine. But with each passing car her step seemed to get heavier.

Beth looked at her watch again and saw that another half hour had passed. She looked back at Francie. The girl was leaning against the wall now, her arms crossed in front of her chest, her head hanging down, the blond hair falling like a curtain around the sad, pinched face. She was jiggling her outstretched legs to try not to freeze.

He's not coming, Beth thought. All at once she was sure of it. *He left her last night, and today he's not even going to come.* Beth felt a stab of fury at his callousness and wished that she could punch him, but at the same time she was relieved. It was as if she had been given a reprieve, and she felt a sudden surge of energy through her and was happy, for the first time in days, it seemed. For a few minutes she debated what to do, but she already knew, in that instant, what it would be. She started the engine, and Francie snapped to attention at the sound. She looked up and all around and then sank back against the wall. Beth pulled out of the little parking lot, drove the short distance up the street, rounded the corner, and pulled up to where Francie stood.

The girl's head jerked up as the car glided to a halt in front of her, and then she frowned. Beth leaned across the seat and opened the car door. Francie bent down and looked in at her.

"Hi," said Beth.

"Hi."

"You must be getting kind of chilly out there."

Francie stuck out her chin and stared up the street.

"How about a ride?"

"How'd you know where I was?"

Beth hesitated for a second. Then she said, "A friend of yours told me."

"Andrew?" There was a wistful note in Francie's voice.

Beth resisted the urge to make a derogatory remark. "No, not Andrew."

Francie blinked rapidly as she stared into the distance, her shoulders sagging. Beth sat very still and waited, letting the motor run. After a few minutes Beth said, "Look, I have to go to Philadelphia tonight because I've got some business there first thing tomorrow."

Francie's gaze was impassive. *Go ahead,* she seemed to be saying. *Who's stopping you?*

"I was thinking," Beth went on, "since you're already packed— I know it's not what you had in mind, but how about coming with me? It would be for only a couple of days. Then we'll come back, so I can finish up here."

Francie stood up straight, and Beth could not see her face. The pack dangled from her hand.

"What do you think?" Beth asked. There was no reply.

Beth was just about to ask again when Francie bent down and tossed the pack into the backseat. Then she slid into the front seat and glanced briefly at Beth.

"Well?" said Beth.

Francie shrugged her shoulders, and then she nodded.

"Good," said Beth. Looking to make sure no one was coming, she pulled away from the curb.

Chapter 16

"WHAT do you think you're doing?"

Andrew jerked his hand out of the cash drawer and looked up into the red face and angry eyes of Lewis Temple. "Nothing," he said.

"You were taking money from me."

"No," said Andrew.

"And why have you got your coat on?"

"I have to leave early."

Lewis Temple looked at him incredulously. "Leave early? And what were you going to do? Just leave the store untended while you were gone."

"I was going to lock up. That's what I was just doing. Locking up the drawer."

Temple shook his head and pulled off his jacket. "It's a goddamn good thing I stopped in here." He turned back to Andrew and stared at his pocket as if he could see inside it with X-ray vision. "Just locking it up. I'll bet."

Andrew came out behind the counter and passed

the store manager, who was sputtering. "Gotta go," said Andrew.

Temple grabbed the sleeve of his jacket and poked a finger into his shoulder. "You're not going anywhere."

Andrew stared intently at the restraining hand on his shoulder. He wanted to break it off at the wrist and hear the man scream in pain. It was what he deserved. But he didn't want to start trouble in case Mr. Temple decided to call the police. Besides, he had the money in his pocket, and the store owner couldn't prove it wasn't his. "I'm in a hurry," said Andrew.

Temple let go of him with a little shove. "Don't come back, Andrew. You're fired as of right now. And don't come sniffing around for your pay either. I think you already helped yourself to it."

Andrew could barely control the desire to grin. He only wished he could tell the stupid prick that he could stuff his stinking job, that Andrew was not even going to be around after today. He forced himself not to say it, although the thoughts were loud in his head. He looked up at Mr. Temple's face and saw that it was puffy and discolored. There was a trickle of blood running from the side of his mouth, and his eyes were rolled back in his head. Andrew felt a surge of happiness.

"You've been nothing but trouble anyway," said Mr. Temple.

Andrew blinked hard and looked again. The bloody image had disappeared, and Mr. Temple's glittering eyes bored into him.

"I'll see ya," Andrew said in a bland voice. He did not wait for a response.

The wind snapped around him as he alternately walked and ran the distance to his house. He had plenty of time, he reminded himself. Plenty of time.

She never got back from Dr. Ridberg's until nearly six. By then he and Francie would have a big head start, and no one would know in which direction.

He laughed aloud, thinking of how Temple had just fired him from his job. That would be a good story to tell Francie in the car.

He reached Berwyn Road in no time, as if he had been flying, not walking. The day was cold and gray, and there was a smell of woodsmoke in the air. Warm lights beckoned from houses he passed, and Andrew pictured the families inside, gathered by the hearths, cheerful and smiling with their arms around one another, like a bunch of stuffed dolls.

No, it was California for him and Francie. Where the sun was always shining. You never had to stay inside there. He reached the end of the street and stopped outside the house, debating what to do. He always took a shower when he came in. It was the rule. But today he didn't want to go into that cellar and take off his clothes in the chill. He did not want to be blasted with that lukewarm water and emerge shivering, obedient, and clean.

What did it matter how angry she would be? She could never berate him for it, for she would never be able to reach him. Never again could she subject him to her disappointment and her peppermint breath, for he would be gone. Boldly he walked up the front steps, turned the doorknob, and stepped over the threshold, germ-laden and defiant.

The foyer was dark and chilly, but as soon as he closed the door he noticed the strange smell. Sniffing the air warily, he made his way down the hall. There was an odor of woodsmoke in the house. *A fire*, he thought. It couldn't be.

His heart beat fast as he approached the door to the

parlor. A bright gleam met his eye. He stopped and stared transfixed at the cheery glow of burning logs, crackling steadily in the fireplace, which had never, in his memory, been used.

From an armchair with its back to him the familiar voice assailed him. "Andrew," she said, without stirring from the chair, "what a nice surprise. Home so early."

Andrew was rooted in the doorway, trembling from head to toe.

"Why don't you come in and join me? I'm having a little bonfire."

Andrew entered the room as if in a trance and walked toward the hearth. As he reached it he saw an empty sleeve trailing out of the fireplace. It was one of his shirts.

Leonora's sour expression was made gargoylelike by the light from the flames. "I was wondering when you would be coming in. I decided to start without you."

Andrew looked from his mother's face to the open bag beside her chair. It was his duffel bag, torn apart and nearly empty. She was holding a poker in one hand and feeding his belongings to the fire as if she were roasting marshmallows.

"There," she said with satisfaction as the last of the clothing he had packed went into the flames. She reached into the open mouth of the bag and brought out the envelope of money.

"I have told you again and again, Andrew, that there are germs on everything and that we have to be very careful. I hope this will teach you a lesson about hiding things from me in this house."

Andrew's eyes were riveted to the gloved hand which held the envelope of money. "Put that down," he growled.

Leonora turned and shook the envelope at him. "How dare you try to keep this from me? I have given you everything, and you, you're that selfish—"

Andrew's eyes were wide, and the fire seemed to be licking his pupils. "Give that to me."

With the poker in her hand Leonora picked up the empty duffel bag and tossed it into the flames. The heavy canvas smothered part of the fire, and smoke began to fill the room.

Tears welled in Leonora's eyes, and she started choking. But she continued to rant at him between coughs. "Run away, will you? I knew you were up to something. I suspected it last night. So this morning I decided I would just find out." She again shook the envelope that held the money.

Andrew reached toward it, but she snatched it back.

"So I called up Dr. Ridberg and told him I was sick today. I did not like having to lie to him, but I had to find out what you were up to. And this is what I found." Leonora laughed, but there was despair in her laughter. "Did you really think you could hide this from me?" she said, shaking the envelope again.

"I need that money," he said, and his eyes were dull as he stared at it.

"I need that money." She mimicked him. "What for? To rent motel rooms with your little piece of trash? Oh, you are just like him," she cried. "And I suppose you need these too?" she said. She held up the set of car keys in her other hand, and they jingled as she waved them around in front of Andrew. The fire had burst through the canvas and was burning merrily. The keys glinted in the firelight, and Andrew stared at them as if he were hypnotized.

"Forget it, my boy," she said, coming up close to his face. "There's a little matter of your old man that you killed. I tell the police one word of that, and it's off to the loony bin for you. Or to jail. You pick."

Andrew tore his eyes from the keys and lifted his gaze to her pale, rubbery face, the mouth that seemed to be constantly in motion.

"What do you want from me?" he whispered.

The question seemed to stun her, and they stared at each other in the firelight, their endless struggle suspended for a brief moment. Her mouth started to work, but nothing came out. Then, like a dazed fighter rising from the canvas, her righteous anger reasserted itself. "What do I want from you?" she asked, drawing herself up. "That's a good one. What about you? What do you want from me? First you kill my husband. Then, after I protect you all these years, what do you do? You try to steal my car and my money and run away."

Andrew turned away from the sight of her wounded, contorted features. There was no way to win with her. She had always held it over him, from the beginning. And he had never won. Not once. Time and again she had whipped him and rubbed his nose in it. *But not this time*, he thought. This one was his.

"It's my money," he said in a calm voice. "And as for your husband, I didn't mean to kill him. It was you."

Leonora, who was preparing some sarcastic reply, took a second to register the words. Her mouth fell open, and her eyes took on a glassy look. "What did you say?"

Andrew smiled and nodded, trying to ignore the peppermint fumes that she was aiming at him. "You heard me. I said I was trying to kill you." He didn't really know whether it was true or not. He couldn't remember. But the effect of his words on her made him glad he had said it.

Her eyes widened, and she staggered back. Then she jerked back the hand that held the keys and smashed him across the face as hard as she could. "You—you liar." She wheeled around and tossed the money envelope and duplicate keys into the fire. "See how far you and your little whore get now," she cried.

The smile vanished from Andrew's face, and he lunged forward, trying to reach them, but Leonora kicked them farther into the fire with a hysterical laugh. "You're not going anywhere, you fool. Now go to your room," she shrieked, pointing a finger in his face, "and don't come out. Go!"

Slowly Andrew rose to his feet and came toward her, smacking her hand out of the way like an enraged bear.

"I told you to go," she cried, but there was fear in her voice, and the look in her eyes, as his hands closed around her throat, filled him with euphoria, as if he were levitating off the floor. She clawed weakly at his hands, and he could feel her feet kicking him, but it was like the faraway patter of raindrops on the roof. The leaping fire filled him with warmth, and as he throttled her and as she struggled he felt a happiness, a satisfaction he had never known. Suddenly she shuddered and went limp beneath his deadly grip.

In that instant her weight seemed able to knock him over, and her flesh was slimy to his touch. He released her throat, and she tumbled to the floor with a resounding thud. Her left thigh landed on his foot. He jumped back, repulsed by the feeling of her bulk against him. For a long time he stared down at her, almost in disbelief. It was as if he had just come home and found her like that.

The fire died away as he stood there. Rubbing his eyes, he backed away from the dead body on the floor and stumbled over to the sofa. He huddled in the corner and stared at the blank screen of the TV. After a while he got up and turned on the set. Then he resumed his seat.

Chapter 17

"RIGHT here. The second one on the right," said Beth, leaning over the seat of the cab. The driver pulled over to the curb and turned on the overhead light.

"Thirteen fifty," he said.

Francie scrambled out of the cab, clutching her pack, as if the cab were about to take off with her still in it. Beth paid the fare and got out, closing the door behind her. Francie was standing on the curb, looking warily up the wide, dark corridor of a city street, lined with parked cars and intermittent scraggly trees.

"This one's my house," Beth mumbled, pointing to the shuttered, brick-fronted row house. Francie nodded and continued to look around her. Beth followed her gaze. Piles of plastic garbage bags, looking slick and greasy under the weak streetlights, lined the curb at intervals, in anticipation of the morning's weekly pickup. Dirty chunks of snow and slush filled in the narrow gaps between the cars, and evidence of the neighborhood dogs decorated the spindly tree trunks up and down the block.

Beth walked quickly up the steps to her door and said, "Come on," to Francie. She rattled the key impatiently in the lock.

Francie waited on the step below her. "What's that smell?" she asked.

Beth sniffed the damp, night air. A familiar, unappetizing odor greeted her. "They refine oil around here. Some nights you can really smell it," said Beth. "That's how you can tell when you're back in Philadelphia." She tried to say it lightheartedly.

She opened the door and sighed as she entered the house. In the street a couple who were walking down the street together started yelling at each other, and the boy shoved the girl, who was teetering along on high heels, into the side of a parked car. Francie stared at them until the boy looked up at her and snarled, "What's your problem?" She hurried in behind Beth, who shut the door behind her.

Francie shuffled into the living room and waited there while Beth riffled through the mail on the foyer table. Then Beth went down the hall into the kitchen and checked the back door and the windows. Francie followed her at a distance.

"What are you looking for?" Francie asked.

"Just making sure everything's okay," Beth said.

"I've heard about the crime down here."

"Everything's perfectly fine," Beth said irritably.

Beth opened the refrigerator and poured herself a glass of ginger ale. "Want some?" she asked, holding out the bottle to Francie. Francie, who was still clutching her pack to her chest, shook her head. Beth put the bottle back in the refrigerator, finished the soda, and put the glass in the sink. "I'm tired," she said, mainly to fill the silence.

Francie nodded. "That plane ride took forever."

It was true. They had been delayed on both takeoffs, and then bad weather had provided a bumpy, nerve-racking trip. But Beth felt unaccountably annoyed at Francie's remark.

"It couldn't be helped," she snapped.

"I didn't say it could."

"Well, there's no point in dwelling on it," said Beth.

"Who's dwelling on it?" Francie sighed and rolled her eyes. "I was just saying—"

"I know," said Beth. "Forget it. I'll show you your— where you're going to sleep."

Beth led Francie through the living room. Despite the impassive look on the girl's face, Beth felt as if she could read her mind. The flowers on the coffee table were brown at the edges and drooping, but ironically they were the only sign of life in the room. Everything else was perfectly coordinated and neatly placed, as if no one had ever dented a cushion by sitting on it or removed a book from a shelf. Usually when she had visitors, they would exclaim with admiration that her home looked like something out of a magazine, and she would feel pleased and proud. Now she felt as if she were seeing the room through her sister's eyes, and the room did indeed look magazinelike—glossy and sterile.

Beth stamped up the stairs, turned right, and opened the last door in the narrow hallway. She turned on the bedside lamp in the guest room and pointed to an old woven suitcase stand at the foot of the bed. Francie walked over to it and deposited her backpack on it. Beth looked around the sparsely furnished room, noticing the dust on the bureau top and the thinness of the old quilt she had found for the bed. She had always liked the way the room looked, rather primitive and countrified, but now it suddenly seemed cold and uninviting. "This is it," she said curtly. Francie looked around the room but didn't touch anything.

"There's a bathroom next door, and I'll put a couple of towels in there for you. I have to get up early and get to the office, but you can sleep late or whatever. Watch TV," said Beth.

"Should I go with you to your office?"

"That's not necessary."

"I'd like to see it," said Francie.

Beth was taken aback. "You'd have to get up awfully early."

Francie shrugged. "That's okay. I'm always up early for school."

"And we'd probably have to eat breakfast out. I don't feel like fixing anything at that hour." She could hear the unfriendliness in her tone and tried to amend it. "I'm usually rushing in the morning, so I have to grab something out."

"That sounds okay," said Francie.

"Well, all right," said Beth. "I'll wake you up. Is there anything else you need? There's an extra blanket in that chest over there."

Francie shook her head and sat down on the bed. "This is a really nice house," she said. "I can't believe you have so much pretty stuff."

Beth shrugged, but the words made her feel a glow run from head to toe. "Thanks," she said. "It's been sort of my pet project these last few years. It was pretty much of a mess when I bought it, but I've been fixing it up as I got the money."

"You did it yourself?"

"Yeah," said Beth. "Everything I could do. I had an idea of how I wanted it to look, and I figured nobody else would be as careful about it as I would. You can see it's an old house, and I wanted to restore all the original details of it. Like that curved strip molding," she said, pointing to the window seat. "It took me three days to strip and refinish that."

"It's nice," said Francie, nodding. Then she yawned.

"Well," said Beth gruffly, "you're tired. And I'm rattling on about the house."

"Well, I can see why you like it," said Francie. "Thanks for asking me down here."

"Get some sleep," said Beth. "I'll see you in the morning."

She closed Francie's door behind her and went down the hall to her own room. After closing her door and kicking off her shoes, she lay down on the bedspread with her hands over her eyes. After a few minutes she leaned over, picked up the phone, and dialed. A sleepy voice answered.

"I woke you. I'm sorry," she said.

Mike rallied gamely. "No problem. When'd you get in?"

"A little while ago. Francie is here with me."

"Really? How'd that happen?"

"Well, this guy she's been seeing up there is a bad influence, to say the least. I got wind of the fact that they were planning to take off together, and I sort of intercepted her. I figured I'd get her away from there for a few days, maybe cool things off."

"That was a good idea."

"I hope so."

"I'm looking forward to meeting her."

Beth stifled a sigh. "I just wanted to be sure I'd see you tomorrow."

"Tomorrow night. Six-thirty sharp. I can't wait."

"I'm afraid we're not going to have much privacy."

"We'll manage," he said.

"Now that I've got her down here, I've got to keep her entertained somehow."

"Nothing to it," he said.

"You're always such an optimist," she said, feeling something between amusement and exasperation.

"It's all part of my charm."

"It's true. And I love you."

"I love you too."

"I'm sorry I've been so temperamental lately. This has been a rough week."

"I know it has. Don't worry."

"Okay."

"I'll see you tomorrow."

"Good night," she said.

She hung up the phone and leaned back, feeling more peaceful than she had in days. After a while she forced herself up off the bed, went and took a shower, and got back into bed with a book. Despite the late hour, she felt the need to unwind a little more before sleeping. After an hour she got up, put her book down, and made a last trip down the hall to the bathroom. As she was returning to her room she noticed that the door to the guest room was ajar. She padded over to it and stood outside. She could hear the sound of Francie's steady sleep breathing wafting through the door like a soft summer breeze.

She lingered there for a few minutes, and then she went back down the hall to her room. She was about to close the door, as she usually did, but then she changed her mind. Leaving the door open about a foot, she climbed into her bed and turned out the bedside light. She lay there in the darkness, listening. She knew it was impossible to hear the girl's breathing this far down the hall. But as she began to drift she imagined that she could. The soothing sound seemed to rock her, from far away, and she fell into a deep, dreamless sleep.

Chapter 18

*H*E was back in school again, although it was vaguely different from what school had been. All the students were dressed in similar drab gray outfits, and when he looked around, he saw that the windows were barred. The teacher stood at the blackboard, her back to the room, scratching out some indecipherable lesson on the slate. She was wearing the uniform of a guard, and he could hear the jangle of the keys at her thick waist and the squeal of the chalk as she wrote. He wanted to get up and leave, but he could not move, and he knew it, even without trying. She was almost finished writing, and he knew that soon she would turn around. He began to sweat at the thought of seeing her face. Although she still had her back to him, she began to speak to him in that familiar accusing tone. Among the words of gibberish on the board he recognized his own name. His heart constricted at the sound of her voice, although he could not make out the words over the mocking laughter of the other students. He under-

stood that he was being singled out for punishment
and that once she had finished writing her message,
she intended to come after him. He struggled to free
himself from the desk, but he was wedged into it. No
matter which way he turned it seemed to close more
tightly around him, making it hard for him to breathe.
He could see her now, putting down the chalk and
slowly rubbing her hands together to rid them of the
dust. The noise in the room was growing louder, almost like a chant rising, and it had to do with his
punishment. They all knew what she was about to do
with him. Terror rose in his throat as she started to
turn. He wanted to cover his eyes with his hands, to
avoid the sight of her, but they would not move from
his sides. There was no escaping what was coming.
The despair of his situation, the hopelessness were
crushing. Suddenly, like a miracle, he heard it. A bell
was ringing. The class was over. Relief and surprise
washed over him as he felt himself freed from the seat
and rising. The end of the class. He had forgotten all
about it, but now that bell was ringing and he was free
to go—

Andrew came awake with a start and sat up in the
corner of the sofa. Despite the chill in the room, his
face felt greasy, and his underarms were sticky with
sweat. The TV was still blaring. He could not remember having fallen asleep. The elation he had felt in the
dream vanished as he looked down and saw the body
of his mother sprawled, facedown, on the sooty hearth.
He closed his eyes again, wishing he could retrieve the
feeling from the dream. Then, suddenly, he realized
why the classroom bell had saved him. It was the
phone ringing. It had been ringing all along.

Fear and nausea warred for his stomach at the
sound. *Don't answer it,* he thought. But what if some-

one got worried and came to look in on them. *Answer it.* He gaze was glued to the revolting fleshy mass on the floor. He forced himself up on wobbly legs and dragged himself out into the hall toward the telephone table. He wondered how his voice would sound, if it would give him away, the way a virgin wonders if she looks different after her first night of love. His heart pounded in his ears as he lifted the receiver. "Hello," he said numbly.

"Hello, Andrew, is that you? This is Dr. Ridberg." A picture of the pale, balding dentist, round-shouldered in his white jacket, swam into Andrew's foggy mind.

"Hello," he mumbled again.

"Is your mother there?"

Andrew's heart jumped. He pressed the cold receiver to his ear and stared through the door at the rumpled mass lying on the grate.

"I know she wasn't feeling good yesterday, and I wanted to know if she was planning on coming in today. It's after nine." There was a faintly injured tone in the doctor's voice. "If she's sleeping, of course, she might not be feeling good still. I wouldn't want you to wake her, but I would appreciate knowing—"

"Just a minute," Andrew mumbled.

He dropped the receiver and buried his face in his hands, rubbing his eyes violently. Then he raked his fingers through his hair, pulling at his scalp. For one moment he felt frantic tears welling up in his eyes. He thought of picking up the phone and saying, "No, she's not coming in. She's dead. I killed her last night." He forced himself to take deep breaths, to squash the fearful impulse to confess. With trembling hands he fumbled for the receiver at the end of the cord and held it to his ear.

"Hello," he said. "She's still sick. She said to tell you she can't come in today."

"Oh, that's too bad," said the dentist with forced sincerity. "Well, all right. Tell her I hope she feels better. Will she be in tomorrow, do you think?"

"Tomorrow," said Andrew. The absurdity of the idea was amusing, in a ghoulish way. "I don't know," he said. "It depends on how she feels."

"Maybe she should see a doctor," said Dr. Ridberg.

"No, no," said Andrew. "It's just a bad cold." Then he had an idea, his first clear idea of the day. "She doesn't want to give it to any of the patients."

Andrew could picture the alarm in the dentist's eyes as he hurriedly agreed. "I'll just have to do the best I can without her. Maybe Mrs. Ridberg can fill in for her a little, at least get the phone and such. You tell your mother not to worry. Tell her to get plenty of rest. And to gargle."

"I will."

"Good-bye," said the dentist.

"Bye." Andrew hung up the phone and walked slowly back into the parlor. He walked up to the body and gingerly shoved it with his toe. The flesh just sank back to the floor. "You're supposed to gargle," he said aloud. At the sound of the words he was overcome with a fit of giggling. He tried to suppress the sound, as if he were in a library. Tears welled in his eyes and rolled down his cheeks.

Gasping for breath, he headed for the couch. He missed the cushions as if he were drunk, slid down the front, and landed on the floor with a thud. He wiped his eyes as the giggles subsided into hiccups. He sat and stared, his body jerking intermittently, as if he were riding on a bouncy road. On the TV set a pair of women with fluffy hair were talking animatedly, a bowl of flowers propped on the table between them. Andrew watched uninterestedly.

Suddenly he heard the sound of footsteps outside, the heavy tread climbing the porch steps. At once he was alive with fright. Dr. Ridberg had been suspicious and called the police. They were here already, to check out the nosy dentist's complaint. There was no way to pretend he was not home. They would be able to hear the shrill voices of those two bitches yapping on the television. It was too late to move, too late to hide her.

He stared at the doorway, his arms crossed over his chest to combat the shudders that shook him. He listened for the gruff demand to open up, the huddled decision to break the door in when he did not respond. Suddenly he envisioned the scene as they would see it when they broke in: his mother's body in a heap on the floor and him, sitting there beside her, the guilt naked in his eyes. At the thought of it, he felt the urine leak from him and run down his leg, the wet stain gluing his pants to his thigh.

The lid of the metal mailbox clanged shut out on the porch, and then the footsteps receded down the steps and out, across the yard. Andrew sank back into the couch seat, allowed himself to breathe, and tried to quiet his pounding heart. He noticed then that his hiccups were gone. Scared away.

No one knows, he thought. *No one will even miss her. She has no friends. The doctor thinks she's sick. There was no scream, no loud struggle, nothing to arouse suspicion. You are perfectly safe.*

A smile of blissful relief spread over his face, and his heart seemed to float lightly inside him. Suddenly he felt hungry. He decided to go see what was in the kitchen. After stripping off his wet pants, he left them in a heap beside her body. Wearing only his shirt and socks, he padded into the kitchen. He helped himself to whatever he could find. He ate cookies and canned sardines and drank soda for his breakfast, spreading crumbs, wrappers, and cans on every sanitary surface. Nothing had ever tasted so good. She was gone. He didn't have to listen to her ever again. The chill of the house did not bother him. He felt warm inside and free. He could do anything he wanted. He could have Francie if he liked.

Francie. The thought of her pierced his heart with pleasure. Licking his oily fingers, he walked back out into the hall, picked up the telephone, and dialed. He glanced into the parlor and stuck out his tongue while he waited for Francie to answer.

The telephone rang and rang. Cold air seeped under the front door and gave Andrew gooseflesh on his bare legs as he stood there. *Where is she?* he thought impatiently. *Maybe she went to school already.* It annoyed him that she wasn't there. The stupid sister wasn't even around to answer the phone. Andrew hung up and wandered back into the living room. He was feeling cold now and irritable. And the body was still there. Like a problem that you couldn't solve.

He reached down and picked up the stained pants from the floor. He pulled them back on and zippered them up absently, staring all the while at the inert human-shaped debris on the floor. It was safe for now. But it wouldn't last. He had to get rid of it. Sooner or later someone would wonder. He couldn't just bury it. Someone, the dentist probably, would demand an explanation of where she had gone. Leonora Vincent, dental hygienist, would not just quit her job without informing her employer and leave town on the first bus. She had never liked to leave Oldham, except to go to work.

His head filled with possible lies, and he weeded through them as he stared blindly down at the body. *Think of a good one,* he warned himself. *You'd better. And fast.*

Chapter 19

MIKE signaled the waitress to bring the dinner check and then turned back to Francie. "So it sounds as if you were having quite a tour for yourself today while your sister was charming her clients."

Francie shrugged. "I did walk a pretty long way."

"From Beth's office on Spruce Street to the Reading Terminal Market. I'd say that's quite a hike."

Mike's niece, Gina, a lively, round-faced girl, leaned over to Francie. "I love that market. You can really pig out there."

Francie nodded solemnly. "I had a bagelwich, a cannoli, and three kinds of chocolate chip cookies."

"Ugh," said Gina appreciatively.

"By the time she got back I was sure she had gotten lost," said Beth.

"No, I found my way around pretty easily," said Francie.

"And how'd you like Beth's office?" Mike asked.

"Nice." Francie nodded.

"Maxine adopted her right away," said Beth.

"I liked her. I wrote a letter while I waited, and she mailed it for me some kind of way like pony express where it gets there in one day."

"Overnight express," said Mike. Beth looked vaguely surprised at the mention of the letter.

"I didn't know they had that," said Francie.

"Everything is instant these days," said Mike. Then he looked around and spoke in a confidential tone. "Except, perhaps, for the service in this restaurant."

Francie and Gina smiled, and Beth elbowed him as the waitress appeared suddenly at his elbow with their bill. As Mike counted out the money, Beth indicated to the younger girls that they could start putting their coats on.

"I feel sick." Gina groaned as she pulled on her worn leather bomber jacket. "I ate so much." Francie gazed admiringly at Gina's jacket.

"You two ready?" Beth asked.

Gina nodded.

"That's a nice coat," said Francie.

"Isn't it excellent? I got it in a secondhand clothing store right here on South Street," said Gina proudly.

Francie shoved her hands into the pockets of her old parka and nodded. "It's really cool."

"We can go down there and look in the store," said Gina. "They're open at night." She turned to Beth. "Let's walk down there and show Francie, okay?"

"Sure," said Beth. They all had reached the front door, having threaded their way through the closely packed tables in the Mexican restaurant.

"Okay, Uncle Mike?"

Mike indicated the door. "Sounds good. Lead on."

"Did you like that Mexican food?" Gina asked Francie as the two girls pushed open the glass doors.

"Yeah. I never had it like that before. I've had chili, but what was that green stuff called?"

"Guacamole."

"That was good."

"I love it," Gina said in agreement. "I ate so much I could burst."

"This was a brainstorm," Beth said to Mike as they followed the girls out the door and slowly began to stroll down South Street.

Mike pulled her arm through his and smiled a little smugly. "I thought so."

"You'd think they were old buddies."

"Well, that Gina is a good girl. And she never met a stranger. I figured they'd get along. They're just about the same age."

"It's nice to see them having a good time," Beth said thoughtfully.

"What about you?" Mike asked.

"Hmmmm . . ."

"Are you having a good time?"

Beth nodded. "Yes." She watched the girls, who were chattering away, a few steps ahead of them. "I can't believe Francie's so talkative around you. She's always so silent with me. That business about Max mailing the letter for her. She never even mentioned that to me."

"She probably forgot about it."

"I wonder if that letter was to Andrew. I'll bet it was," Beth said in a gloomy tone.

"Why don't you ask her if you're curious?"

"I don't want to butt in like that. But I'll bet it was."

"Well, I wouldn't worry about it in any case. It was just a letter."

"I suppose," said Beth. "Anyway, it's none of my business."

A couple, both dressed in studs and black leather, with matching Mohawk haircuts were walking toward them. The young man's stripe of hair was dyed electric blue, and his girl's was magenta. She was wearing dangling metal earrings and a short leather skirt and ankle boots, while he was resplendent in crisscrossed bandoliers of metal studs. Francie stopped dead and stared at them as they went by, while Gina poked her and giggled.

As Beth and Mike caught up with them, they heard Gina saying to Francie, "South Street is sort of like the Greenwich Village of Philadelphia."

"Oh," said Francie, "I've never been to New York."

"Everybody looks like that in New York," Gina informed her in a confidential tone.

"Not everyone," Mike said with a wry smile.

"That's the store I meant," said Gina, pointing across the street. "Meet you there," she said to Mike.

Mike waved indulgently at them as they sprinted across the street in the direction of secondhand treasures.

"Amazing," said Beth, shaking her head.

"What?"

"Francie. She's having the time of her life."

"It's good to see her smiling," said Mike. "She's got a really sad aura about her. You can tell those eyes have seen some sorrow."

"It's true. They have."

"Well, if anyone can make them sparkle, Gina can. She's kind of goofy, like most kids, but she has a way of drawing people in."

"It's a gift," Beth said ruefully.

A bell overhead tinkled as Mike and Beth entered the musty clothing store. The two girls were trying on old hats with veils and making fun of each other.

Gina began to hunt through the racks of old clothes and finally pulled out a faded leather jacket with a crow of triumph. "Try this on," she insisted.

Francie looked at the coat. "That's a nice one."

"The lining's perfect," Gina pointed out.

Francie shrugged off her parka and tried on the coat, looking at herself in the cheval mirror in the corner. "Too big," she said.

"It's supposed to be big," said Gina. "That's the style."

Francie looked at it doubtfully. "I don't think so. I don't like it as well as yours anyway."

Gina pulled off her own coat and exchanged it for the one Francie was removing. She tried it on and admired herself. "Well, I like this better than mine." Impulsively she hugged it around herself and rejected her own coat, which Francie was holding out to her. "No, you keep mine, and I'll get this one."

Francie looked horrified. "No, I couldn't."

Gina forced it on her with a laugh. "Yes. I've got some Christmas money, and I like this one better than mine anyway."

Francie frowned at the jacket, her cheeks pink.

"Please?" said Gina.

"I'll pay you for it," said Francie firmly.

"No, no," said Gina. "Just get rid of that old parka so I won't be embarrassed to be seen with you."

A blush of humiliation began to creep up Francie's neck, but a glance at Gina's kindly smile seemed to reassure her. She put the coat on with a shrug. "How do I look?"

"Great," Gina shrieked.

Mike and Beth exchanged a glance. "She reminds me of you," Mike said.

"Who? Francie?" Beth asked in surprise.

"It's that stubborn little I-don't-need-nothin'-or-no-body streak. All genuine offers met with suspicion," he said in a bemused tone.

Beth was about to protest the unfairness of the remark, but she lapsed into silence instead as she mulled it over. After a minute she said, "You think I'm like her?"

"No, I think you're a little worse."

"Thanks," she said indignantly.

"Come on," he said. "We're gonna have to work to keep up with these two."

After a few more stops along the way Mike finally convinced Gina that it was time for her to go home and drove her down to his sister's house in South Philadelphia. Beth leaned forward and held the seat down as Gina started to climb out and then reached back to give Francie a hug.

"When are you coming back?" Gina asked.

"I don't know," said Francie.

"Well, let me know."

"I will."

Beth felt herself getting a cramp in her side as she held the seat at its awkward angle during the lengthy good-bye. They were congratulating each other on their coats again. *You'd think they were sisters,* Beth thought.

"Come on, girls," she said irritably.

"I had a great time," Gina caroled as she bounded up the stoop to the front door of her house. She waved as she let herself in.

"She's really nice," said Francie as Beth pushed the seat back and slammed the door shut. Mike drove to the corner and then headed back uptown in the direction of Beth's house.

"She is a nice girl," said Mike.

"She's your niece?"

Mike nodded. "The oldest daughter of my oldest sister. I have five other nieces and nephews too. Gina has two younger brothers."

"I know," said Francie. "She told me."

"Now my younger sister has only one child. A boy. But I am partial to him because he's named after me."

They chatted on amicably for the rest of the ride home, Francie questioning Mike about his family and Mike cheerfully filling her in. Beth sat silently in the front seat, staring out the window.

Mike and Francie were still chattering as Beth unlocked the house, and they followed her inside. "We're here," she announced.

"Anyone want a cup of coffee?" asked Mike as he headed into the kitchen.

"No, it'll keep me up all night," Beth said, hanging up her coat.

"No, thanks," said Francie. She flopped down into a chair in the living room. "That was fun," she said.

"I'm glad you enjoyed yourself," said Beth.

"I've never been in a city before. There's so much going on at once here. It's like a circus."

"I've always liked it," said Beth. She could remember very clearly her first time in the city. There had been a street fair going on, people smoking dope in the sunshine and Hare Krishna monks chanting on the corner. It had scared her a little but instantly convinced her that she wanted to stay. She wished that Francie would ask her about it or at least seem interested. Words to describe that kaleidoscopic day waited eagerly for an opening.

Francie took off her glasses and squinted at them. She fished in her pocket, found a Kleenex, and began to wipe them off. She was still wearing the coat that

Gina had given her. Beth thought for a minute of the necklace she had bought for her in Maine, the day they had gone to the lawyer. She hadn't yet seen Francie wear it.

"We'll be leaving fairly early tomorrow," Beth said in a stilted tone.

"Oh, okay." Francie sat up straighter in the chair and replaced her glasses on her nose.

"You'd better get some sleep. It could be a long trip again."

Mike came into the living room carrying a cup of coffee as Francie was getting up from her chair. "Going up already?" he asked.

"Yeah, I'm pretty tired."

Mike nodded.

"G'night, Mike. It was nice meeting you."

Mike smiled broadly at her. "The pleasure was all mine. See you again."

"Night," Francie said to Beth. "Thanks for everything. I had a good time."

Beth smiled briefly at her. "I'm glad. Sleep well."

Mike leaned back and sipped his coffee. "That's good instant," he said, smacking his lips.

Beth nodded, her face sunken into a frown.

"I thought the evening went swimmingly," he said.

"Mmmm," said Beth. "I guess so."

"They had a blast."

"Yeah."

"So you don't sound too thrilled."

Beth shrugged and sat up, hugging herself. "You know, Mike, I felt pretty good when she agreed to come down here with me. I—I don't know. I guess I thought we might be making progress. But—"

"But what?"

"I don't know. I feel as distant from her as ever. More than ever—"

"I thought she was quite friendly. She was clearly enjoying herself."

"I can't talk to her," Beth complained. Then she sighed. "Well, that's just the way it is. Too much has happened. All the arguing and the bad scenes up there. I should be grateful we can even tolerate each other and leave it at that. It doesn't matter all that much, the little we see each other."

"Can I tell you what I've noticed about you two?"

"Go ahead," said Beth.

"I think she wants to be friends with you. She seems pretty willing—"

"In other words, it's my fault," said Beth, running her hands through her hair. "Look, Mike, we're just not on the same wavelength. You don't understand. I can't just chatter away with her the way you can. I don't feel comfortable doing that. I'm not like that."

"Wait a minute. Wait. At the risk of sounding—well, it seems to me you're both willing. But you're being altogether too polite. I mean, you seem to keep on saying all the polite things, but you're not really saying anything. Maybe if you just jumped right on in. She's your family after all. You can talk at her if you want to. Say whatever comes to mind. You don't have to be formal with your family."

Beth shook her head. "I don't want to be the boring older sister. Besides, I don't think she's all that interested in my life."

"So you censor everything you want to say. You're cautious. You worry about what she will think. But the best thing about family is that you're entitled to be yourself, even if you're being a jerk. And they're entitled to tell you to stuff it. The whole idea is that in your family you are free."

"Your family must have been different from mine," said Beth. "It must have been fun."

"Just the way our family is going to be," he said. "But let's start with you and your sister."

Beth sighed, and stood up. She paced the living room while Mike drained his coffee, waiting for her to speak. Finally she stopped pacing and looked at him.

"Do you know, something so odd happened last night?"

"What?"

"I was in bed, getting ready to go to sleep, and she had her door open down the hall. I was going to close my door, the way I usually do. And then I decided to leave it open."

Mike nodded.

"I imagined that I could hear her breathing—you know, sleep breathing. I'm sure I couldn't actually hear it. She was too far down the hall. But I felt this peaceful feeling. I hadn't felt it in years. It had to do with her just being there, sleeping in that other room."

"It's called security," said Mike.

"I have security with you," said Beth.

"It's something different. I know what you mean. I feel it whenever I stay with one of my brothers or sisters. Especially my brother Ron. Whenever I stay at his place or he stays at mine, it's like we're safe, being there together. I'm not sure what it is we're safe from. Maybe it's like going back to childhood and not knowing the things that grown-ups know and worry about."

Beth nodded and looked at him in genuine surprise. "Yes," she said. "That's it. Safe. Isn't that odd?" She walked to the foot of the stairs and looked up toward the rooms above. "I hardly know her."

"I'm telling you," said Mike. "It's in the blood."

Beth turned and looked at him with an eyebrow raised. "In the blood. I see. That's a very scientific way for a doctor to talk."

" 'There are more things in heaven and earth, Horatio, than are dreamt of in your philosophy.' "

"Thank you, Will Shakespeare," said Beth wryly.

Mike shrugged. "I believe it."

But Beth was not listening. She stared up the empty stairwell, hugging the newel-post. The expression in her eyes was at once intent and perplexed as if she had sent a question up into the darkness and were waiting there, patiently, for her answer.

Chapter 20

*H*E waited until six o'clock, when the darkness outside was complete and almost everyone would be
home from work, huddling inside to avoid the cold,
probably eating supper. Then he began.

First he went downstairs and opened the door that
connected the garage to the basement. Using a flashlight, he located his old bike and tried walking it
around the perimeter of the car. The steady click and
whir assured him that the chain was not broken, and
the tires still had spring to them as they moved, so they
clearly were not flat. He had not used the bike in a
long time, and he congratulated himself on his luck.
Having leaned the bike against the side of the car, he
unlocked the trunk and then folded the bike inside. It
was also lucky that it was an old car, with such a deep
well in the trunk.

It was true, he thought as he lowered the trunk hood
and locked it, that the plan involved a major sacrifice.
He hated to give up the car. But it was a brilliant plan,

all the same, better than any in all the books of the decimater series that he had read. What made him think of it finally was Francie's mother. She had been snuffed in a car accident. The car had just flipped over on her on an icy highway. It was neat and simple. The roads were steep and dangerous around here. It could easily happen. Someday, when they were far away and it was long in the past, he'd have to tell Francie how she had inspired him with that story about her mother. She'd be proud of him, he thought.

Andrew tried the trunk lid for security and found it locked tight. That was good. He didn't need it springing open on him while he was driving. Then he opened the car doors and went back into the house.

Now came the hard part. He had to drag it down to the garage and then hoist it into the front seat. He went into the living room and looked down at the body. He had gotten used to seeing it there. That didn't bother him. But the idea of touching it, lifting it up was repulsive. The flesh was cold now. He tried not to touch it as he squatted down and lifted it up under the armpits. For a moment, as he hoisted up the dead weight, he had a sudden image of his mother's lifting his father's body this same way. He could not tell if he had actually seen it happen or just imagined it. There was blood all over both of them. His teeth started to chatter at the thought, and he felt weak in his extremities. He felt the body slipping down and willed the thought from his mind, rearranging his grip on the corpse and starting to pull.

She was not light, and each backward step involved an effort that made his arms and shoulder muscles burn. As they reached the doorway, the body became hooked onto a multicolored rag throw rug. It bunched the rug up into folds that became impassable. Cursing himself for this oversight, Andrew maneuvered the body onto its side while he freed the rug from beneath it. He tossed the rug onto a chair by the door and then turned the corpse over again and pulled it through the doorway. He began to back down the hall, hauling her under the arms. The stiff hands dragged along the ground, and the feet fell open, heels scraping grooves in the wood floor. He was nearly to the top of the cellar stairs when her foot caught the cord of the phone on the table in the hallway, and the cord twisted around the table legs and pulled the table over. It fell on top of her, the phone clanging and making a harsh ring as it banged off the corpse and onto the floor. Andrew jumped and let out a yelp of anger and fright. "Goddammit," he bellowed. Every moment's delay seemed eternal, every sound in the house sure to attract the police. He forced himself to calm down and decided not to drop the body in order to replace the phone. If anyone was trying to call him, he didn't want to talk to that person anyway. *Except Francie,* he amended the thought. But he would talk to her later. Once he had fixed everything for them.

Leaving the phone braying its off-the-hook signal on the floor, he started down the cellar stairs, pulling the corpse behind him. The body thudded down each step and then began to veer diagonally over the steps between the handrail and the stairs. At first he tried to right the direction, but then he realized that it was unnecessary. He let go of the shoulders and gave the back a shove. The body slid under the handrail and tumbled to the floor below, landing with a crack of bones breaking.

As he stared down over the rail at the crumpled corpse, shivering overtook him again. She had landed on her back, and the face, bluish and distorted, wear-

ing the expression she sometimes wore when she had
punishment in mind, seemed to be watching him. Andrew tore his eyes from her face and tried to examine
the body dispassionately. There was something wrong.
In a few seconds he realized what it was. He ran back
up the stairs and rifled the hall closet until he found
her coat. Then he ran down the hall and retrieved her
purse from the kitchen counter. She wouldn't go out
without these, he reasoned, no matter what state of
mind she was in. And even though he planned for
there to be little more than cinders left of her when
she was found, it was important to remember details.

He clattered back down the cellar steps and rolled
the corpse over again, his nerve returning. He forced
the stiff arms into the coat, cursing the body's immo-
bility as he worked, and then he buttoned up the coat
and sat back on his heels, exhausted by the exertion.
His stomach began to roll on him as the smell of the
body permeated the cold air of the cellar. He forced
himself to his feet. There was no time to waste. A great
deal to be done.

After dragging the corpse across the rough concrete
to the garage door, Andrew finally made it over the
lintel, down the narrow step, and over to the side of
the car. Holding the car door open with his body, he
took a deep breath, reached down, lifted with all his
strength, and stuffed the corpse into a kind of fetal
squat in the front seat. He sighed with relief, his muscles trembling, to see the job done. Leaning over the
body, he reached out and locked the car door on the
passenger side.

It took him a few minutes to catch his breath. Then
he went back into the house and checked all the doors
and windows to make sure they were locked. It distressed him slightly to see the mess the house was in,

but he did not have time to pick it up now. At least no one would be able to get in and find evidence of what had happened while he was gone. Turning his back on the parlor, he reached back into the hall closet and pulled out one of her old knit hats. He jammed it down on his own head. Now, if people saw him leaving, he reasoned, they would think that Leonora was driving.

Andrew hurried back down to the garage, raised the garage door, and slid into the driver's seat of the car. The body of his mother, quiet for once and hidden from view, rested on the seat beside him. He looked several times in both mirrors as he backed down the driveway. *It's going perfectly,* he reminded himself, but his breath came in short gasps, and his hands were damp on the steering wheel. He began to drive with the most exaggerated caution. *If someone stops you—* He could not complete the thought. He just had to keep on going.

The day had been damp and cold, and fog was now rising from the ragged, rocky hills outside Oldham. Although it made the road difficult to see, the fog suited his purposes very well. He drove north toward the mountain ridges outside town, constantly checking his rearview mirror as he went. The roads were deserted, as they often were on winter evenings. The local people eschewed all but the most necessary traveling on icy nights. Andrew drove along until he passed a sign for a scenic overlook, where he slowed and pulled off the road. Through the wooded mountainsides he could see the lights of Oldham, where he had come from. The deserted vantage point was ideal, he decided, looking hastily around. He hopped out of the car and ran around the back to unlock the trunk and dislodge the bike. He leaned the bike against a tree and then returned to the driver's seat. He jockeyed the car around, his hands trembling on the wheel, until it was aimed right at the wooden railing that surrounded the overlook. He jerked up the emergency brake after putting the transmission into park, then got out and looked around again. Panic was rising in him with every passing moment. Someone was bound to pass this way soon, and now the situation looked suspicious, even to the most casual observer. After reaching in and grabbing her by the front of her coat, he hauled his mother's body upright into the driver's seat and strapped on the seat belt. Making sure that the wheels were pointed toward the fence, he put the car in gear. Then he removed the itchy knit hat from his own head and jammed it down on her hair. He placed her leaden foot, and her pocketbook for good measure, on the gas pedal, and the engine revved. Releasing the emergency brake, he jumped back, prepared to push from behind. But it was unnecessary. The car was already rolling as he slammed the door shut. The blood pounded in his ears, and he held his breath as he watched the car lurch across the road, crash through the railing, and plunge down the mountainside, gathering momentum as it sailed, then crash into the hill and roll. It came to a halt in a clump of trees, the wheels spinning. Smoke rose from the wrecked vehicle, but there was no fire.

Sweat broke out all over him as he looked down at the car sitting there. *It's no good,* he thought. *She's got to burn. If she doesn't burn . . .* The inside of his mouth was dry as paper. He fumbled in his pockets. Maybe he had matches. He could throw one in the gas tank. But then how would he himself escape the explosion? It was a moot point, though, for he could not find a match in any pocket. Cursing himself for his forgetfulness, he stared helplessly at the car. Maybe there were matches in her purse. Why hadn't he thought to bring some? He had to try. If she were found like this, everyone would know.

After a few seconds' indecision, when he thought of just fleeing, he steeled himself and began to scramble down the hillside toward the car. Halfway to it he saw something bright flash under the hood. It took a second to register, and then his heart swelled as he saw a flame shoot up through the wreckage. But was it enough? he wondered. Would it catch? As if in instant answer to his question, there was a sudden deafening explosion that sent him flat against the hillside. He wanted to cheer, to cry out for joy, but there was no time. He scrabbled back up the hill like a crab, looking back once at the wonderful glowing fire, and then he jumped on his bike and started to pedal.

The route home was arduous because for every long slope there seemed to be a grade, but his heart was pumping like a champion athlete's as he pedaled along, feeling his power, his success. It was several miles before he saw an oncoming car, and then he crashed into the woods beside the road to avoid being seen. It was the beginning of the end, though. He knew it. She would be found now, and he had to be home when it happened.

He concentrated mainly on the ride, but occasionally he repeated his story to himself, the way he had planned it during the long day. When he finally reached the old house, out of breath and sweating inside his coat, it was the one time he could ever remember feeling happy to be there. Having stashed the bike in the back of the garage, he let himself in through the cellar. As he crossed the basement he thought about the shower. It would be good for him, he thought. He could take his shower, and then he would be all cleaned off, not a trace of the deed on him. Quickly, as if of his own free choice, Andrew stripped off his clothes and stepped under the dripping shower head in the dank cellar. There was still a towel and fresh clothes set out on the enamel tabletop. He made a mental note to put more down there. Then, dressing hastily, he climbed the stairs and hung his coat in the hall. In the dim light of the foyer he saw his face in the hall mirror. At first he jumped, startled by the shadowy visage, the wary eyes. Then, realizing it was his own image, he grinned. It was a sharp-eyed, mirthless smile. Even he could see that. *A killer's smile,* he thought. It made him feel good to think that. He admired himself in the mirror.

Andrew, said a voice. Her voice. *You were always a killer.*

The face in the mirror turned sickly pale. He wheeled around and looked. He was sure he had heard it. It was so loud. But there was no one there. He steadied himself, reminding himself that she was not there. Hurrying into the light of the parlor, he began to pick up, removing the evidence of what had been. He had just turned on the TV when he heard footsteps on the porch and a knock at the door.

Andrew's heart leaped in his chest. It was too soon. The police couldn't be here already. Impossible. They must have been right behind him. They must have seen him. Seen everything. They knew everything that had happened, and they were here to arrest him. If he opened the door, they would get him.

The pounding on the door came again. Andrew's stomach flopped around helplessly like a fish in a boat. He rubbed his clammy hands together. He had to open it. They knew he was here. He could not remember the story he was going to tell. It had left him completely. His legs were stiff. Too stiff to move. He made himself go forward and reach for the doorknob. He closed his eyes, like a man about to face a firing squad, and opened the door a few inches, picturing the badges, the guns.

Instead, he heard a woeful voice, slurring his name. Andrew pulled the door open wider and looked out. Noah stood on the steps, looking around, a large paper bag balanced on his hip, a beer can in one hand.

Andrew's heart flopped over again, this time with relief. At the same time he felt enraged at Noah's arrival. The terrible timing was just what he might have expected from Noah.

"What do you want?" Andrew asked harshly.

Noah wiped his hair off his forehead with his wrist, and some beer slopped onto the fake fur collar of his jacket. "I gotta talk to you, buddy. Somethin's up."

Andrew felt his usual irritation at the way Noah tried to sound cool. He was such an insignificant asshole. Besides, he was still dirty from the garage and probably germ-laden too. "I'm busy," said Andrew.

"No, man," Noah insisted. "This is important." He patted the bag on his hip. "I brought some brews," he said in a wheedling voice.

Judging from the bleary, mournful look in Noah's eyes, Andrew figured that he had already gotten a long head start on the beer. And now he was here with some stupid problem he wanted to maunder on about. Andrew felt like slamming the door on him, but a cautious voice inside reminded him that Noah's presence might look favorable for him should the police arrive anytime soon. Screwing up his face in distaste, he pulled the door open.

"Come on in."

"Thanks, buddy." Noah seemed to have forgotten

their fight in the garage and the smashed guitar as he thumped Andrew on the shoulder and shuffled into the parlor, fishing in the bag for a couple of beer cans. He handed one to Andrew, shook off his jacket onto the floor, and then sank down onto the sofa, popping the lid. Suddenly he sat up.

"Is your mother home?" he asked in a loud whisper.

Andrew shook his head, feeling his chest tighten in alarm at the question. He willed his voice to be calm. "No, she got pissed at me over some stupid thing and stormed out of here awhile ago. Drove off in a huff. She's probably out getting loaded somewhere."

Noah nodded understandingly. "Probably. Well, just as well. I know she's not big on company."

Andrew nodded, feeling a little surge of triumph. The story had fooled Noah easily. Of course, it would be different with the cops. They wouldn't be drunk—or simpleminded. Still, it had sounded good, convincing. It had made sense to him as he said it.

Noah was leaning forward, his arms resting on his knees. He shook his head sadly. "Buddy, I got big problems, and I had to unload them somewhere. So I came to you."

Andrew took a swig of beer and made a face. He didn't want to get drunk, but he wanted to seem normal. He forgot, until the beer hit his growling stomach, that he had not eaten since the sardine and cookie breakfast. He wiped his mouth as if to wipe away the taste. "All right," he said impatiently. "What is it?"

"I can't believe it," said Noah, leaping up and shaking his fist at the heavens. "I just can't believe it."

"Cut the crap, will you? Don't turn this into a fucking soap opera."

Noah turned on him and looked at him petulantly. "I'm trying to tell you how I feel."

Andrew shook his head in exasperation and chugged some more beer. It churned in his stomach like brackish water. "You haven't said anything yet. You're just proving how juvenile you can be."

Noah resumed his slumped position on the couch. "My folks lowered the boom tonight at dinner." He sighed and shook his head.

Andrew got up and turned up the volume on the TV. Then he sat down in the chair and began to stare at it.

"Okay, okay," Noah cried. "They're retiring."

Andrew kept his eyes on the screen. "So?"

"Will you turn that down?" Noah pleaded, holding out another beer. Andrew snapped the set off and glowered down at Noah.

"They're moving away. To North Carolina. My dad is leaving me the business."

Andrew snorted. "That's the big tragedy?"

"But my tunes," Noah wailed. "The music business. I was already thinking about going to Nashville. Now how can I?"

"You never would have gone," Andrew assured him.

"I would. I was gonna," Noah insisted, thumping his fist on his knees and spilling beer on the carpet. He was immediately apologetic, getting down on the floor and wiping it up with his old red and white handkerchief. "Do you think your mother will notice this?"

"No," said Andrew.

Noah sat back down. "I can't believe it, man. I'm gonna spend the rest of my life under a car. The best years of my life. When I could really make it in music. I know I could have."

The image of an upended, burning wreck of a car seemed to flame before Andrew's eyes. He felt a little light-headed, and his disgust for Noah felt less immediate. He swallowed some more beer. "There's no one who wants to stay in this stinking town, that's for sure," he said.

"That's right," said Noah. "I figured you'd understand. But what am I gonna do?"

Andrew frowned. "What's that?"

Noah sighed. "It's a car. Must be your mother coming back. We better clean these up. He began stashing the empty cans into his brown bag as Andrew stood listening, his heart thumping wildly. It was a car. Stopped outside the house.

"I better go," said Noah. "She's gonna be pissed to see me here. Why don't you come out with me? We can talk over at the garage." He began to teeter to his feet and fumble for his coat.

"Just sit there," Andrew hissed.

Noah took this as an invitation. He wiped his pale face on his sleeve and began to rearrange his ponytail. "I don't know. I probably should be mad at you after what you did to my guitar. But you've been my buddy for a long time, and friends are hard to come by in this town—"

The knock at the door made Andrew jump, even though he had been expecting it and had known it would come. Noah turned and blinked at the door as if he had completely forgotten that he had heard the car. "Who's that?"

"How should I know?" Andrew said, getting up and wiping his hands on his trousers as he headed for the hallway.

"Your mother's gonna have a fit," Noah predicted.

For one moment, as he pulled the door open, Andrew pictured her standing there, battered and burned, glaring at him, the ultimate triumph in her eyes.

"Andrew Vincent?" asked the cop who stood on the porch steps. He had a red mustache frosted with gray and tired eyes. The collar of his uniform coat was turned up around his ears against the night air. Behind him stood another, younger officer, staring uneasily away from Andrew.

Andrew nodded. "Yes?"

"Sorry to bother you. May we come in?"

Andrew shrugged and stepped aside.

Noah jumped up and jammed his hands in his pockets. Then his face lit up as he recognized the older officer. "Hey, Burt. How ya doin'?"

Burt looked over at Noah and greeted him solemnly. Then he turned back to Andrew before Noah could attempt to continue the conversation.

"Andrew, we have some bad news for you, son."

Andrew frowned.

"Leonora Vincent is your mother?"

"Yes."

"Well, son, I'm sorry to tell you this, but there was a bad accident up on Hawk's Ridge. Apparently your mother drove her car right off the road."

Andrew's eyes widened. "Is she all right?"

The cop pressed his lips together and shook his head. "I'm sorry," he said.

Noah let out a soft whistle. "Jeez . . ."

Andrew clapped his hand to his head. He could feel himself sweating, the blood draining from his face. His head started to throb. "What happened?" he whispered.

"We don't know for sure. Either she lost control of it, or she couldn't tell where she was going in the dark. There weren't any skid marks on the road. But that's a treacherous strip up there."

"It's impossible," said Andrew.

"Do you know what she was doing driving around up there at this time of night?"

"No," said Andrew. "Well, I don't know. We had an argument—"

"She went out in a huff," Noah said helpfully, as if he had seen her go. "You know, people should not get into cars when they're mad. I don't know how many times we've towed a wreck over at the station that started out with someone being mad." Noah shook his head. "His mother never drove that much anyway."

Andrew kept a hand over his eyes and felt a surge of adrenaline course through him as he heard Noah, in his ineffectual, plodding way, giving all the credence he needed to the story.

"Is there anything we can do for you, young man?" asked the officer named Burt.

Andrew shook his head.

"Jeez, Andrew," said Noah, coming up and gripping his shoulder, "I'm so sorry."

"I shouldn't have let her leave like that. You're right."

"No, no. C'mon. You didn't know this would happen."

The whine in Noah's voice and the sour beer on his breath made Andrew want to turn away from him, but he forced himself humbly to accept the condolences. He could feel sweat popping out at his hairline and trickling down his sides inside his shirt. His knees had begun to wobble underneath him.

"Can I use your phone?" asked Burt.

Andrew nodded and then clutched his stomach. "I don't feel well," he said. And it was true. The beer in his empty stomach, aggravated by the stress, was suddenly revolting on him. "I'm gonna be sick."

Freeing himself from Noah's treacly attentions, he

bolted for the front door. The clap of cold air felt wonderful, but it was too late to help his stomach. Grabbing the porch railing, he leaned over and began to heave up the rancid mix of beer and stomach acid.

The younger cop, who had been standing awkwardly to one side until that moment, rushed out after him, followed by Noah. One stood on either side of Andrew as he retched into the bushes below. Once the heaving had started, it was uncontrollable. Andrew wanted to scream at them to get away from him. Their nearness to him only made it worse.

Over Andrew's bent form the young policeman and Noah exchanged an anxious glance. "Poor kid," said the cop. "It's tough."

"Just let it out," Noah advised.

Noah reached over and patted Andrew on the back, murmuring encouragement.

Fools. You believed it, Andrew thought triumphantly as his stomach turned inside out on him again, and he gagged, sweating and moaning, in the chilly night air.

Chapter 21

BETH woke at dawn, awash in uneasiness, as if she had had a bad dream that she couldn't remember. Mike slept quietly beside her. She felt like reaching out for him, but she didn't want to wake him. With his exhausting schedule he needed all the sleep he could get. She lay back and closed her eyes, waiting for the night terror to subside and for sleep to overtake her again.

It must be the traveling, she thought. It was hard to get a good night's sleep when you knew you had to travel that day. *That's it,* she thought. *The traveling.* Her thoughts turned to Francie. Once she got her settled at Aunt May's and got the house put up for sale, she could come home. But perhaps she could get back up there to visit Francie one of these days. Or maybe Francie could come down to Philly and stay in the guest room. She tried to imagine herself proposing this to Francie and was struck by how unrealistic a plan it seemed. They had little common ground between them. Once this settling up was over, they would have even less.

She tried to change the subject mentally, making lists of things she had to do when they got back. It would be a busy few days. The prospect of it filled her with dread. *You're just exhausted,* she told herself. *That's the problem. You're overtired. You've been trying to do too much.* She thought of Francie, sleeping soundly down the hall. *Well, you've taken most of the burden of this off her. At least you did that for her.*

All of a sudden she heard the sound of the medicine chest squeaking and then the rush of the tap in the bathroom. After a moment she heard Francie's footsteps padding back to her room. *She can't sleep either,* Beth suddenly realized. *Probably taking an aspirin.* She could picture her sister, lying there awake, fretting about the trip back. For some reason the thought made her eyes fill up with tears. *She's anxious,* Beth thought. *We're both anxious.*

But instead of troubling her, that realization was oddly comforting. In a few minutes she had fallen asleep again.

The second time she awoke, there was sunlight coming through the slats of the pine shutters and Mike was leaning over to kiss her good-bye. Beth clung to his fingers and kissed him repeatedly until he laughed and told her he had to go. Reluctantly she let go of his hand.

"When will you be back?" he asked.

"Soon. A couple of days."

"Good," he whispered. "Tell Francie I'll see her soon." He slipped out the door with a wave.

"I love you," said Beth. She wondered briefly what he meant by seeing Francie soon. *Probably the wedding,* she thought. He always found a way to bring that up. She smiled and stretched. She hated getting out of the warm bed, but it was time to get started. It wasn't as warm, anyway, with Mike gone.

By the time she got dressed and made up and went downstairs, Francie was already in the kitchen. There was a pot of coffee on the stove and three bowls on the table. As Beth walked in, Francie was searching through the cabinets for cereal boxes.

"Beside the sink," said Beth, getting out some coffee cups. Then she picked up one of the bowls and put it back in the cabinet. "Mike leaves kind of early," said Beth. "He has to be at the hospital."

"Oh," said Francie, "I thought he was still here."

Beth smiled to herself, thinking that she had hoped Francie wouldn't even know he had stayed over if he left early enough. She was going to keep the thought to herself when she remembered what Mike had said the night before about being less guarded and saying what was on her mind. She hesitated, and then she said, "I didn't want you to know he stayed over."

Francie raised her eyebrows. "Why not?"

"Oh, some Victorian impulse, I guess. I thought you might be shocked."

"I'm fourteen," said Francie, as if that explained everything.

Beth recalled how naïve she had been at fourteen. Then she decided to say it. "I would have been shocked when I was fourteen." It came out sounding a bit disapproving.

Francie's face closed up again. "Things have changed."

"I think it's better this way," Beth said hurriedly. "I mean, it's better to know about things, be more accepting. Although I don't necessarily think it's good to get too much experience too soon."

Francie shrugged, and Beth felt as if she were prying. She wondered, as she often had, what the nature of Francie's relationship was with Andrew. She reminded herself that it was none of her business. She shouldn't have said anything about it.

"Knowing them doesn't mean you do them," Francie said, and Beth felt relieved and a little grateful to the girl.

"That's true," she said. "Well, I guess it seems stupid to you, but—I was worried about Mike's being here. I'm afraid I still think of you as a little girl."

Francie sat down at the table and began to eat her cereal. "He's a great guy," she said.

"Thanks," said Beth, feeling a little glow of pride. Then she reminded herself about opening up. "I think we're going to get married."

"Really? That's great. You're lucky."

Beth was about to get defensive. She caught herself reacting and tried, lamely, to turn it into a joke. "I tell him he's the lucky one, getting me."

"Well, yeah," said Francie earnestly. "You're both lucky to have someone, you know, who you belong to. You seem happy together."

Beth nodded, feeling a surge of warmth for Francie. "We are." She hesitated. Then she said, "I'm glad you like him."

Francie poured her coffee and began to sip it, her eyes looking past the steaming cup into the distance. "When's the wedding?" she asked in a diffident tone.

"Oh, we don't know yet," said Beth. "We have no definite plans."

Francie nodded, and Beth suddenly felt as if her sister thought she was evading the question. Perhaps she didn't want to appear to be angling for an invitation. "It's my fault really," Beth added hurriedly. "I've been a little bit—afraid, I guess, to go ahead."

Francie said nothing, clearly not wanting to pry.

Beth took a deep breath and plunged ahead. "I have this fear that I'll ruin it somehow. That it won't work out. It's irrational, really. But still—it's there. I remember Mom and Dad. It wasn't exactly a picnic with them. I wouldn't want to live like that."

Francie blushed to the roots of her hair, and Beth steeled herself, half expecting the girl to lash out at her for not respecting their parents' memory. After a second Francie said, "It doesn't have to be like that. You seem to get along really well together. I think you should do it. That's just my opinion, of course."

Beth smiled. "Thanks. I think you're probably right." They sat there in a rather awkward silence for a moment. Then Beth looked at her watch. "Well, we'd better get packing."

Francie nodded and jumped up to take her dishes to the sink. "When do we leave here?"

"About an hour."

"I'll be ready."

"Okay." Beth left the kitchen and went up to her room to repack. It did not take her long to get the few things she needed reorganized and stuffed into a bag. When she was done she went down the hall and rapped on the guest-room door, which was ajar.

Francie was sitting on the bed, staring out the window through the bare branches at the street. She jumped up as Beth came in.

"Not much of a view," said Beth, walking over to the window.

"I don't know. I kind of like it," said Francie, looking out. "There's always something going on out there. All

243

kinds of people coming and going. I could watch them for hours."

"Yeah," said Beth. "I like that, too, although it's a lot prettier in Oldham."

"It's pretty sometimes," said Francie. "But there's never anything new there. Here everything is different: the people you see on the street and all the buildings and the shops and everything. It's exciting."

"Some people think it's scary."

Francie shrugged. "I guess so. But I like it."

"You know, I think you're really a city girl at heart." *Just like me,* Beth added to herself.

"Maybe," said Francie, gazing out the window.

Beth studied her sister's profile out of the corner of her eye. There was already a suggestion of the woman's face that would be sculptured from the smooth, adolescent features. *The last time I saw that face, it was a child's face,* Beth thought. She had a sudden, panicky sense of time fleeting, of something lost.

Francie turned away from the window with a small sigh. "It was nice of you to have me down here," she said politely. She walked over to the bureau and picked up her comb and brush. She brought them back and stuffed them in the pocket of her backpack, which was lying on the bed.

Beth watched her movements with a growing tightness in her chest. She was overcome with an acute, unreasonable sense that she was being abandoned. She thought back over various guests who had occupied this room. She had always enjoyed the company, but she had also watched them pack with a secret sense of relief that she would have her home to herself again. But the sight of this strange girl getting ready to go made her feel as if she would never open the door to this house again without feeling lonesome.

The years will go by, she told herself. *You'll forget all about each other.* And this thought, meant to be reassuring, made her want to cry out instead. In that instant she knew exactly what it was that she wanted to say. But her voice was trapped inside her. She sat down on the edge of the bed and nervously began to fold and unfold the corner of the quilt. Maybe it was the wrong thing to do, she thought. Maybe it wouldn't work out.

"I'm ready," said Francie, "except for this."

"What?" Beth asked in a small voice.

"This jacket," Francie said, pointing to the parka on the bed next to the leather jacket from Gina. "I can't fit it in the pack."

"You going to wear the leather one?"

Francie looked at her incredulously. "Yeah. Of course. But I still think I should keep the other one. You know, for rainy days and stuff. Could you fit it in your bag maybe?"

Beth looked at the jacket lying on the bedspread. It was faded and without body. But it was clean and had a kind of shabby dignity to it. Francie rested a proprietary hand on it, as if to prove that she would not deny it, despite its obvious shortcomings.

Beth stared at it for a long moment. Then, without looking up, she heard herself say, "Why don't you leave it here?"

Francie shook her head and repeated patiently, "I might need it."

Beth recognized the opportunity to retreat. Francie had not understood. She licked her lips, aware of the dryness in her mouth. Then she said, "I know. What I mean is, leave it here and you come back."

Francie looked at her and shook her head uncomprehendingly.

"Come back with me when I come back."

The younger girl frowned as if she were having trouble hearing her sister.

"I'd like you to come back," said Beth. "You could live here with me. This can be your room."

Francie's face slackened as if she had been punched, and Beth suddenly felt panic-stricken by what she had said. It was too late to take it back, but she couldn't think what had possessed her to say it. Maybe Francie would refuse. She looked at her sister. Behind the lenses of her glasses Francie's eyes were fearful.

Beth's panic subsided like a squall that blows out to sea and was replaced by a sudden protective impulse toward the girl. "You'd have to give up your friends and start a new school. And I don't know if you'd like it here, but well, I'd like to have you here. If you want to . . ."

Francie bit her lip.

"I guess you'd really miss Oldham, and your friends. And not seeing Andrew—"

"I'm not gonna see Andrew anymore. I wrote him a letter."

"You did? Oh."

The room was silent for a moment. Then Francie said, "That's really nice of you, but, um, I can live with Aunt May. I don't mind."

"No," said Beth, "I'm not being nice. I'd like you to come here."

"You don't have to say that," said Francie. "Really. I understand you're busy and all."

"I'm not that busy," said Beth. "I just like to appear busy. It makes me seem important."

"Well, besides, you're getting married. You don't need somebody else around."

"Mike is all in favor of it. Believe me."

"Was it his idea?" Francie asked.

Beth hesitated. Then she pressed her lips together and shook her head. "No," she said. "This is what I want."

Francie smiled briefly, although there was a look of concentration in her eyes, as if she were at work on a complex equation.

"I think we'd do pretty well together," said Beth.

"I like it here," said Francie.

"What do you think?"

"I don't know. Are you sure?"

Beth picked the parka up gently off the bedspread and arranged it on a hanger. "I think we can just leave this in your closet."

"Okay," said Francie. "That'd be good." They smiled at each other and then quickly looked away. Francie began to fiddle with the buckles on her pack, as Beth placed the hanger on the closet bar and firmly closed the door.

Chapter 22

*T*HE empty church echoed the sound of Andrew's footsteps as he walked down the center aisle and then, crossing in front of the first pew, stepped up on the altar. He looked around to his left and saw the door that the pastor had mentioned when he called. Andrew opened it and walked through. To his left was another door. He opened that and saw the stairs leading up to the pulpit. He stared up them, remembering how when he was little, before the—before his father died, his mother used to bring him to church. And he would marvel at the way the pastor suddenly appeared in the pulpit. He had thought that the pastor must somehow fly up there or maybe just materialize there, while people had their heads bowed over the hymnals. He had tried to watch closely, but he always seemed to miss it. He always looked away at the crucial second, and then, when he looked back, there was the pastor, high above them—triumphant after his magical, invisible flight.

Now, looking up the pulpit stairs, Andrew felt something cold and empty inside his stomach. It had been no magic, no miracle. There was no such thing. He had just been too young to know it. He could barely remember the feeling.

"Andrew."

Andrew wheeled around and closed the door. Pastor Traugott was standing in the chilly hallway, calling to him.

"I'll be just a moment longer, son." The pastor indicated a small pew outside his office door. Andrew nodded and seated himself on the wooden bench. Pastor Traugott went back into his office.

The hallway was bare except for some paintings of scenes from the Bible. Andrew scuffed his feet on the concrete floor and huddled up against the chill. The old pastor had called first thing in the morning to offer his condolences and ask if he could come by to discuss arrangements. Andrew didn't want him at the house, so he had offered to come to the church. He didn't care anything about arrangements, but he decided that he had better go for appearances' sake, and also, he thought that the old man would probably know where Francie was. He had been calling there all night, after the police and Noah had left, wanting to tell her the good news. But no one had answered. Then, at 3:00 A.M., he could stand it no longer. He thought there might be something wrong with the phone. So he had gotten dressed and walked over to the Pearson house. The house was dark, and the car was not in the driveway. He had peered in all the windows, but finally he had had to go home. There was no sign of her. He had not been able to sleep for wondering where she was. He was bursting to tell her the news—that they were free now. Free to be together always. It was what they had dreamed of, and he had made it come true.

Andrew felt suffused with a giddy warmth when he thought about the policemen last night. They had believed him completely. Even felt sorry for him. He could hardly believe that it all had worked out so well.

The office door opened, and the pastor walked out in the hall. He was dressed in his black tunic and white collar. Over that he wore an old gray cardigan sweater. "Come in, my boy," he said, putting a hand gently on Andrew's arm.

Andrew shrank from his touch but followed him into the office and slid into a chair. The old pastor sat in a chair beside him. The office was warmer than the hall by virtue of a quartz space heater that stood in one corner. All the furniture in the room was worn and mismatched, as if it had been salvaged from garage sales. The pastor offered Andrew a hard candy from a bowl on his desk. Andrew shook his head.

"I'm sorry about Mother," said James.

Andrew nodded, not knowing what to say.

"I haven't seen your mother for some years. After she stopped coming to church, I tried to call on her, but she asked me not to."

Andrew shifted in his seat. "Because of germs," he said shortly.

James patted the boy's knee. Andrew stiffened. "I know your mother had a number of ideas that must have been, well, difficult for you to live with."

"Not really," said Andrew.

"I think you were a very good son to her. Staying with her as you did. It's not always easy for us to understand one another, especially parents and children. I know your life has not been an easy one."

Andrew stared at the old man, wondering how he

knew so much about it. He felt as if the old pastor could see inside their house, inside his brain. A chill ran through him. What if the old man suspected what had happened. Maybe the police had discussed it with him, and this was a trap they had set up. The old guy would try to pretend he was all sympathetic and get him to break down and confess. Andrew looked at him with steely eyes. He would not be conned by this kindly old pastor act. He was ready for any trick.

James went on, oblivious of Andrew's suspicions. "I thought if you liked, we could just have a short grave-side prayer service. I know that your mother had lost touch with many of the . . . friends she used to know. So we might not want to have a whole service at the church. But something, short and respectful. At the cemetery. How does that strike you?" James looked up questioningly at Andrew.

He doesn't know anything, Andrew thought. *He couldn't, or he'd be asking me a lot of questions about the accident.*

"Andrew?"

"Okay."

"Good. I'll take care of everything for you. Mr. Sullivan and I. Shall we say tomorrow? In the afternoon?"

Andrew nodded.

"Try to be strong, son. I know this is a difficult time for you."

Andrew stared at him.

"And I also hope, now that Mother has passed on, that you may feel like coming back to the church. We all missed you, although we knew that you were abiding by your mother's wishes—"

"Where's Francie?" said Andrew.

James looked a little startled by the abrupt question, but he tried to mask his surprise. "Well, uh, Francie and her sister went down to Philadelphia for a day or two. Beth had some urgent business there. They should be back soon."

"When?" said Andrew.

"I'm not sure," said the old man. "Mrs. Traugott talked to Beth before they left. It might be today. Or tomorrow. I know they will be most upset to hear of your loss."

"Probably today then," said Andrew.

"Maybe."

"I have to go," said Andrew, getting up from the chair.

"Of course."

Before James could get up, Andrew was on his feet and heading out of the office. "If you have any questions about the service—" said James, but Andrew had already slammed the door behind him. James heard a shout that sounded like a curse in the hall.

Andrew crossed the altar and stalked back down the center aisle of the church. As he reached the front doors he felt as if he were being watched from behind. He whirled around to confront the spy. The figure of Christ, wounded in the side, the thorns pressing into His forehead, hung on the cross above the altar, watching him.

Andrew stared back at it, feeling a band of pain gripping his own head and a sensation like a white-hot knife plunging through his body. For a moment he could see himself, hammered there, at the mercy of his tormentors. He tore his eyes from the icon and burst through the doors of the church, gasping for breath.

She had gone off on him without a word. His mind reeled at the thought. He staggered down the church steps and started off in the direction of his house. Her face filled his head, and she was laughing at him. Laughing, after what he had done to free them. He felt as if he were choking. His fists were clenched tight as he stumbled along, and he tried not to think of her, but the wind crooned her name, and he could not obliterate the sight of those ungrateful, stupid eyes dancing before him.

A mail truck was parked at the end of the driveway as Andrew approached the house. The uniformed driver got out and started toward him across the brown stubble of lawn as Andrew reached the porch. Andrew's heart began to hammer as the man came near. It was a trap. The police had sent the mailman to get him. They knew about his mother.

"Andrew Vincent?"

"Why?"

"Oh, for heaven's sake," the mailman muttered. "I have an express package here for you." His breath was visible in the chilly air. He thrust the envelope at Andrew. "Here." He turned and began to walk away.

"I won't sign anything," said Andrew.

"You don't have to," said the mailman, heading back toward his truck. "It's all yours."

Andrew looked down at the large brown envelope suspiciously. The return address was from Philadelphia. Then, all at once, he realized whom it was from. He caught his breath and stared at it. With trembling fingers he worked the envelope open. Inside was another, smaller envelope. In the upper left a printed business address had been crossed out, and the name F. Pearson was carefully written. Andrew studied his name and address on the cream-colored envelope, examining her writing, which was unfamiliar to him. He ran his finger gently over it as his heart rose, and ballooned in his chest.

Francie. His very own obedient girl. Here she was, gone only one day, and already she had written to him. It was probably a love letter, apologizing for having gone off without telling him, promising to make it up to him when she got back. Relief filled him, warming him. Nothing had changed after all. Everything was fine again. She was still his.

He did not want to open it right away. He wanted to savor the triumph. It was his reward for all he had done. Stuffing the envelope in his pocket, he let himself into the house. He stopped in the cellar, took off his clothes, and put them to one side, making sure that the precious envelope was nowhere close to the water from the shower. Then he stepped under the shower head.

The lukewarm water felt voluptuous on his skin. He threw back his head and let it run over his eyelids, into his mouth. He felt the anxiety easing out of him. As he slid his hands down to his genitals, he imagined her kneeling piteously before him, pleading for his forgiveness. He massaged himself, imagining how he would withhold his pardon, making her wonder if she would ever be returned to the warmth of his good graces. The image was wonderful and exciting. And she deserved to beg a little, for having made him worry. She would have to learn her lesson. But just as he was about to accept her pleas, he lost control of himself. Shame spread all through him as he felt the filthy gush of his semen. He washed himself off quickly, loathing the smell and feel of his body. He put back on the dirty clothes which he had been wearing and, feeling for the letter in the pocket, hurried up the stairs.

Ripping the envelope open unceremoniously, he pulled out the single handwritten sheet inside and began to read it in the dim light of the foyer. The message was short. "Dear Andrew," she wrote. "I have gone away for a few days with my sister. I was going to wait and tell you when I got back, but I decided to get this over with. I don't know why you didn't show up to get me last night. I waited where you said, and then I gave up. It was just like at the old man's place. You said you would do something, and then you didn't do it. I'm tired of you doing that. I don't want to see you when I get back, so please don't call me anymore. Don't think this is just because I'm mad. I am a little mad, but mostly I think we might be wrong for each other after all. Please just leave me alone after this. Francie."

Someone was knocking at the door.

Andrew reread the letter twice while a series of knocks was repeated on the front door. Then he crushed the paper in his hand. With wooden steps he walked to the door and opened it.

A plump woman in a green car coat stood on the porch, holding a large shopping bag. A late-model Ford station wagon was parked in the Vincent driveway. The plump woman looked up at Andrew as he opened the door, a sober but kindly expression on her face.

"Andrew?"

Andrew stared at her.

She smiled nervously. "I don't think we've met. Well, maybe once, but anyway I know you from your picture. I'm Estelle Ridberg, Dr. Ridberg's wife?" She looked for a sign of recognition in his blank red-rimmed eyes, but he seemed to be looking right through her. "Well," she went on, "Dr. Ridberg and I heard about your mother's terrible accident on the radio this morning. It is just a tragedy. I know you must be—well, she often spoke to the doctor of how close you and she were."

Andrew stared out past the driveway. He saw something move behind a tree across the street. It was her. The blond hair. The glint of her glasses. She was watching him. It was all a joke. She wanted to see what he would do when he got the letter. It was her idea of a little fun. Then she was going to run out, laughing, and throw her arms around him. He squinted at the tree and saw that it was only the tall, bleached grass, rustling behind it, the weak gray light of the day reflecting off a broken bottle lying there.

"I thought," said the plump woman, squirming slightly under the young man's trancelike gaze, "I'd just make you a little something to tide you over." She reached into the bag she had brought and began rummaging around.

No. It was impossible. Francie would never do this to him. She belonged to him. She would never leave him like this. She was going to run away with him. She had been all ready to. It had even said so in the letter. She had been waiting for him, until the sister took her away.

All at once the dark morass of unbearable feelings inside him was penetrated by a clear, bright beam of comprehension. That was it. Of course. The sister. It was the only possible explanation. Francie was taken away by the sister and forced to write that garbage. That's what she was trying to tell him in the letter. It was a kind of code between them. A way of letting him know that the sister had taken her prisoner. Andrew felt a white-hot halo of rage begin to tighten around his head. That bitch. He should have known.

"There," said Estelle Ridberg, her rounded cheeks flushed pink. She held out a dish covered with aluminum foil and pressed it into Andrew's hands. The warm dish seemed to startle him.

He stared at it as if it had dropped from outer space. "What are you doing here?" he demanded. "What do you want?"

"This is a chicken and noodle casserole," she said. "You just take off this foil and pop this in a moderate oven. Now there's also some salad in the—"

"Who told you to come here?" said Andrew.

"Dr. Ridberg and I are concerned about you. You have to keep your strength up at these times. You have to be sure to eat."

Andrew peered at her as if seeing her for the first time. He had to force himself to think, to figure out what was happening, even though his mind kept veering back to the letter. "I don't know you," he said.

"Well, as I said, we never met, but your mother—"

His mother. He knew it had to do with that. There were probably drugs in this food. The police would feed him drugs and then wait for him to confess. There was probably a tape recorder in that bag that they wanted to get into the house.

Andrew removed the aluminum foil and looked down at the yellowish chunks and strands in the bowl. "I don't want your drugs," he said. With that he overturned the bowl and dumped the contents into the bare bushes beside the steps.

Estelle Ridberg's mouth dropped open in astonishment, and then she drew herself up indignantly. "Wait one minute. Look here—"

With one swift movement Andrew reached down and picked up the bag, drawing it back like a discus and hurling it across the yard. It landed on the hard, rocky ground and fell open. Paper napkins issued from the top and fluttered in the air like white paper birds.

Letting out a weak cry, the dentist's wife hurried down the porch steps and retrieved the bag, picking up its littered contents as she went.

Andrew rushed after her. "Now stay away from me. Don't bother spying on me. And tell the others too. Don't try to pull anything on me."

"Oh, my Lord," mumbled the dentist's wife. "What is wrong with you?" She hurriedly reassembled the things in the bag.

Andrew loomed over her. She reached out to pick up a head of lettuce, which lay, still wrapped, on the ground, but as her gloved fingers touched it, Andrew drew his foot back and kicked it viciously, sending it sailing out across the street.

Clutching the bag, Estelle scrambled to her feet, hurried to her car, and quickly locked herself inside. She switched on the ignition with shaking hands and stared out at Andrew, who was looking at her with a wild, unfocused look in his eyes. He shook his fist at her. "Get out of here," he screamed.

As the engine turned over and the car began to roll, Estelle opened her window a crack. "Your mother would be so ashamed," she cried.

He started toward her car, but she poured on the gas and was out the driveway before he could reach her. He turned and stalked back up toward the house. Estelle cradled the bag on the seat beside her almost apologetically, her pink cheeks quivering as she sped away.

Chapter 23

THE old Fairlane sedan thudded to a halt in the driveway, and Beth switched off the ignition with a loud sigh. "God, I thought we'd never get here. I feel like all we do is travel lately."

Francie nodded. "It takes so long."

"It's changing planes. If there were a direct flight here, it wouldn't be so bad. But as it is, it takes all day." She looked out the window at the bare trees, black against the bleak sky. The clouds seemed to have settled in low on their side of the mountains, their variegated grays reminding her of a wash drawing in india ink. "What time is it?" she asked.

Francie looked at her watch. "About four."

"Well, we'd better heave-ho. I've got a lot of phone calls to make before five o'clock. A lot of places will be closed tomorrow since it's Saturday."

Francie got out and pulled her pack from the car. She trudged up toward the front steps. Beth came up behind her and shivered in the chill as she waited for

Francie to unlock the door. "I don't mind admitting that I'm glad I've—we've only got to make that haul one more time," said Beth.

"It's kind of fun, though. The plane and everything."

Beth groaned. "Flying is fun when you're young."

"What?"

"Did you ever hear that story about the kid who stowed away on airplanes?"

Francie pushed the door open, shaking her head.

Beth bent down and picked up the two newspapers, still in their plastic sleeves, on the front steps. "Well, it seems there was this little boy who liked nothing better than to stow away on airplanes—"

"Is this true?" asked Francie, reaching for the mail in the mailbox and then snapping on the inside lights in the house.

"Yes, I heard it on the news one time," said Beth. "So they finally catch him after he has done this about a dozen times. And before they take him home, they say to him, 'Why do you keep on doing this all the time? Stowing away on airplanes?' and the kid says, 'Because flying is fun when you're young.'"

Francie smiled. "That's great."

"Isn't it?" said Beth. "I love that story." She tossed the newspapers onto the kitchen table and looked in the refrigerator for something to drink. "Want some juice?" she called out.

"No, thanks."

Beth put a hand on her hip and looked around. "This place is a shambles," she said aloud. "Oh, well."

Francie joined her in the kitchen. "It does look bad."

"Well," said Beth, "let's get on with this. We need a plan of attack if we're going to get this all done and be on our way home by Sunday."

Francie nodded.

"Now first, I've got to call the real estate agent and arrange to give them the keys. Then the gas and electric company. Also, we've got to see if we can get somebody with a truck to come over here and load up all this stuff and take it to the dump."

"There's a guy, Richie Ferris, who has a truck. Dad used to have to call him sometimes."

"Perfect," said Beth, writing it down on the list she was making. "We need to arrange for a headstone. I'll ask Sullivan's about that. We are going to have a lot of chores tomorrow. We can divide them up. What about you? This is a kind of fast move for you. You think you can manage?"

Francie nodded. "But I don't know what to do about school."

"That's no problem. I'll call Cindy. She can arrange things for you here. We'll get you transferred to a school down in Philly."

"Maybe I can go to school where Gina goes."

"I think we can arrange that," said Beth. "Do you have to get anything from school, notebooks or anything?"

"Yeah. I have to clean out my locker. I'd better do that this afternoon. It won't be open tomorrow."

"That's a good idea. You'd better get over there." Beth picked up the phone and started thumbing through the phone book.

Francie pulled the sleeve off the newspaper and began to unroll it.

"That's another thing," said Beth. "I've got to stop the newspaper. I'll do that right now. We don't want to advertise that the house is empty once we're gone."

Beth called the newspaper delivery number and the real estate office in rapid succession. She was just fin-

ishing with the electric company when she noticed
that Francie was staring dumbly at the newspaper, her
face pale, her hands gripping the paper as if for support.

"What's the matter? You look sick."

"Andrew's mother," said Francie, "while we were
gone."

Beth looked where Francie's finger was pointing.
The crumpled, smoldering wreck of the car was pictured on the front page.

Beth sat down heavily in the chair and scanned the
article. "Wow," she said, "I can't believe it." She
looked up at Francie and saw that there were tears in
the girl's eyes as she gazed miserably at the paper.

"Poor Andrew," Francie murmured.

Beth felt a queasy sensation in her stomach as she
watched her sister's shoulders start to shake. "That's
too bad."

"He must feel so awful," Francie said in a teary
voice.

Beth thought of her encounter with Leonora Vincent and wondered how bad Andrew really would
feel. Then she chastised herself for the uncharitable
thought.

"It's such a horrible way to die." Francie groaned,
clutching the paper to her narrow chest. Beth recalled
their mother's death—the lonely car wreck out on the
highway and a terrified child sitting helplessly by.
Gently but firmly she pried the paper from Francie's
grasp and put it aside.

"Come on now," she said. "Don't get yourself all
worked up. You've been through too much yourself
lately. This is bound to hit you very hard. Come on."
Awkwardly she stroked Francie's arm.

Francie took a few deep breaths, but she continued

to stare down at the crumpled paper. "Maybe I should call him up," she whispered.

"Well, maybe." But Beth felt her stomach knot up at the suggestion. She scolded herself silently for her reaction. *Don't be a monster. The boy's mother is dead. Have a little pity, however much you dislike him.* "I guess it wouldn't hurt to call him," she added.

Francie shook her head, her eyes sad and faraway. "And I just wrote him that letter too. On top of this. It isn't fair."

"Well, you had no way of knowing this would happen."

Francie started to sob. "I know. But now he's all alone. Just when the worst thing in the world happens to him."

Beth pressed her lips together and continued to pat her sister's arm. It made her ashamed to see Francie's obvious grief and to realize what it must have cost the girl to maintain her stoic front at their father's death. She had not even questioned it. She had just accepted Francie's impassive exterior and never bothered to look beneath it. Now as Francie keened for poor Andrew, alone in the worst of situations, it was so clear that the girl was describing herself as well. "I know," Beth murmured. "I know."

"He probably got the letter today. Oh, God."

"The timing is pretty bad," said Beth. "But you didn't do it on purpose. It just turned out that way."

"I can't just turn my back on him when this happens."

Beth felt the queasiness in her stomach again. "Well, I thought you had decided. I mean, you're going to be leaving town."

"I know," said Francie.

"So I don't see how you can get back with Andrew now."

"I don't want to get back with him. It's just that I feel guilty. Like I should try to be a friend to him now, you know?"

Beth nodded. "Sure." They were silent for a moment. "But I'm just saying that you don't want to lead him on or give him any false hope. If you've really made up your mind to leave, that is."

Francie wiped her eyes and sat up straighter. "No, I'm leaving all right. I want to go. But maybe—well, that letter was pretty mean. Maybe we can part friends. I think I should at least try to be friends, after hearing about this." She pointed to the newspaper.

Beth nodded, although she felt like protesting. She knew that Andrew would see that Francie was vulnerable and would do everything he could to convince her to stay with him. It hit her, in that instant, that she did not want Francie to change her mind. She wanted the girl to come live with her. It was as if all the doubts she had had vanished once the commitment had been made. She watched worriedly as Francie got up and dialed the phone.

Francie let the phone ring about ten times, but there was no answer. "He's not there," she said.

"Oh," said Beth, feeling a temporary relief. "Well, you can try him later."

"Maybe he's over at the garage with Noah."

"I thought you said they had a falling-out."

"They always have fights. They make up, though."

"He could be anywhere."

"Yeah. I guess so." Francie sat dejectedly at the table for a minute. Then she stood up. "Well, I have to go over to school anyway, so maybe I'll do that and then stop at the garage on my way back."

Beth looked at the clock. "It's kind of late. Do you want a ride over there?"

"No, they have after-school activities until six or so. I'll be able to get in. And I might see a couple of people I want to say good-bye to." Francie zippered up her jacket and started for the door. "I want to show off my coat," she said, a strained smile on her face.

Beth waved her off and sat at the table, contemplating the crumpled newspaper. There was no point in worrying about it. In a few days they'd be gone. Andrew would just have to accept that. She tossed the paper into the trash and resumed making her phone calls. She talked for a long while to Cindy, who greeted the news with delight and approval and promised to facilitate the transfer for Francie. Then she called her aunt and uncle, who had more mixed feelings.

"We really wanted her to be with us," said Aunt May.

"I know you did."

"But you're sisters. You should be together."

Beth smiled. "I guess so."

"I think your father would be very pleased."

Beth frowned at the phone but didn't reply.

"You heard about Andrew's mother?" her aunt added in a whisper.

"We saw it in the paper," said Beth.

"He'll really run wild now," said May. "He was here to see James and acted very peculiar about the whole thing."

"Well, it's a shame," said Beth in a noncommittal tone.

"That's the one thing I'm glad about," said May, "is that Francie will be getting away from that Andrew."

"I think it's for the best."

"Will you come see us before you leave?"

"Tomorrow," said Beth. "I have a carload of stuff to drop off for the church."

"Good," said May. "I'll see you then. Bye, dear."

"Bye," said Beth. She hung up and looked down at her list. She still had to clean the bathroom linen closet and the medicine chest, and the house would be done. "Might as well do that now," she said aloud. As she started up the stairs, she thought about what her aunt had said about Andrew. He had acted peculiar about the whole thing. *I'll bet he did*, she thought. *This is a peculiar young man. And no wonder. With that mother.*

Beth grabbed a box from a pile still in the hallway and opened the door to the linen closet. The shelves were piled with towels, washcloths, and sheets, the nub faded on the terry cloth and the sheets soft and threadbare from repeated washings. Beth had the urge to throw the whole lot out, but she knew they were still useful. Uncle James, scavenger for the needy, would delight in them. There was a shelfful of soaps, creams, and various cough and muscle ache remedies that she put into another small box for the church.

She packed until her back ached, but finally she had the shelves cleaned out. Looking outside, she saw that the sky was dark and a round moon was up. She figured that it was after six, and she wished that Francie would get back. Almost as soon as she thought that, she heard a soft thudding sound from downstairs.

"Francie?" she called out.

There was no answer. She went to the top of the stairs and looked down the stairwell. The dim hall light and the faint light from the kitchen were the only lights visible in the dark house. "Francie?" she called again.

The house was silent. *Wishful thinking,* she thought. She returned to the bathroom and decided to begin on the medicine chest. She opened the mirrored door and looked inside. On the top shelf there were a number of orange plastic bottles, most of them expired prescriptions, some of them with her mother's name on them. With a sigh she tossed them into the trash. There were medications for angina and high blood pressure for her father, and she felt a little guilty looking at them. She hadn't even known he had a heart condition. She tossed the rest of them into the trash, along with shavers and shaving cream. She saved only some nail clippers and aspirin that she found there.

Picking up a sponge by the sink, she wiped off the empty shelves. Then she ran water over the sponge and squeezed it out. *That's done,* she thought. With a sigh she closed the door of the medicine chest and glanced up into the mirror.

A pair of glittering red-rimmed eyes bored into hers in the mirror.

Beth shrieked and whirled around, clutching the sink.

Andrew blocked the door of the narrow bathroom, staring at her.

"What the hell are you doing?" Beth demanded, her heart hammering wildly, despite her belligerent tone. "You scared me."

Andrew's face did not register her question. "Where is Francie?" he said.

Beth stared at him, still gripping the sink for support. He was gaunt and disheveled, as if he had been wandering for days without shelter. His eyes burned in his head but were strangely lifeless. He took a step closer to her, and Beth stifled a yelp. "She's not here," she said quickly. "She's out."

"Where is she?"

"I don't know. She was looking for you, as a matter of fact."

Beth felt as if his presence were sucking the air out of the narrow bathroom, making it hard for her to breathe. She wanted to get out, but he was planted in the doorway, and she was wary of antagonizing him. An aura of instability shimmered around him, like some volatile chemical that might explode if you jostled it.

"Where did she go to look for me?"

"I'm not sure," Beth said cautiously. "Noah's, I guess. She read about your mother in the paper. That was a terrible thing." Beth edged toward the door. "Excuse me," she said politely.

"She's sorry," Andrew said.

"We're both sorry about your mother," said Beth. She was right beside him now. He smelled of soap, mixed with something foul and decaying. "I need to get by," she said.

"About the letter," said Andrew. "She's sorry about the letter."

His tone demanded that she confirm what he said. Beth tried not to inhale the smell from him, which seemed to surround her. "That may be, Andrew. I don't know. You'll have to ask Francie about that." She pressed herself against the doorframe and slipped by him, her body brushing his as she passed. He turned on her but did not stop her. She hurried to the stairs and started down. He followed behind her, practically stepping on the backs of her shoes.

"She said that she wanted to break up with me in the letter, that she didn't want to see me anymore."

Beth could hear his voice rise and feel him bear down on her. She tried to keep her own voice calm, although her stomach was in a knot. "I don't know what she said in the letter, Andrew. She didn't tell me."

"She said that it was over with us and that she didn't want to see me anymore."

Beth hurried down the hallway toward the light of the kitchen. But before she could reach the doorway, Andrew barred her way.

"I'm sure that's very hard on you," Beth said softly, "but if that's what she wants—"

"You knew what was in the letter because you made her say it," he shouted.

Beth stared at him with wide eyes. His face had turned a mottled purplish red, and the cords on his neck stood out as he yelled at her. He was baring his teeth like an animal.

Uh-oh, she thought. *Okay. I get it. I'm to blame. That's what's going on here.* She took a step back but kept her eyes glued to his face. *Be very careful what you say to him. This guy is a little out of control here.* She swallowed hard and licked her lips. "I'm telling you the truth, Andrew. I didn't know anything about it."

"You lying bitch," he snarled. "Don't think I don't know what you're up to."

Beth was about to protest, but she stopped herself. There was no point in arguing with him. It would just antagonize him. God, they were right about him. Cindy and her father. Everyone. *He really is crazy,* she thought. She had to get him out of here somehow, but she couldn't think how. She looked nervously into the kitchen.

"What are you looking at?" he demanded. "Look at me when I'm talking to you."

"I was just looking at the, uh, phone," said Beth. "I was thinking I could have Francie call you when she gets back and you can talk with her and straighten this thing out."

"I'm waiting right here," he said. "You won't even tell her I was here."

"It's just that—well, you might have to wait a long time. I don't know when she'll be back. You could call her yourself, if you don't—if you want to be sure she gets the message."

Andrew put his face close to hers. "This is your favorite game, isn't it?" he said in a low voice.

Beth's heart skipped a beat. "What?"

"Telling everybody what to do. You call the shots."

"It's just an idea, Andrew. Why should you wait around here when you could be—"

At that moment the kitchen door opened, and Francie came in, lugging a bag filled with notebooks, her gym suit, a box of candy, and some books. "I got everything," she said, kicking off her boots. "Beth, I saw Mrs. McNeill, but she said you already called her."

"I did," said Beth, trying to sound composed. "You've got a visitor."

"I do?" Francie's pale cheeks were reddened from the cold, and her glasses were steamed up. She took them off and wiped the lenses and then put them back on and looked at the darkened doorway.

Andrew sneered at Beth and then dropped the arm that barred the doorway. He took a step toward Francie. "Hey, babe."

"Hi," said Francie. She avoided his outstretched arm. "I was looking for you. I heard about your mom. That was terrible. You must feel awful."

"Let's get out of here," he said, cocking his head toward the door.

"I can't," said Francie. "I've got to put this stuff away."

Beth watched Andrew from behind, uncertain what to do. He seemed less agitated now that Francie was here, but it reminded her of the sickly stillness of the sky before a tornado.

"I ripped up the letter," he said.

Francie grimaced. "I feel bad about that."

"I know you didn't mean it. Don't worry. I threw it out."

Francie opened her mouth to protest, but Beth said quickly, "Andrew is very upset about the letter," in a warning voice. Francie looked at her with a perplexed expression on her face.

"Who asked you?" Andrew demanded, turning on Beth.

Beth shook her head and looked down.

"Come on," he yelled at Francie. "Let's go."

"No, Andrew, I can't," said Francie. "I have a lot to do. I have to get ready to—to go," she concluded softly.

Andrew's eyes narrowed. "To go where?" he asked.

Francie sighed and made a face. "Look, there's something I have to tell you. I know you're going to be mad, but—"

"What are you talking about? Where do you think you're going?"

"I'm going to Philadelphia. To live with my sister," Francie whispered.

Beth steeled herself as if for an explosion. He was looking at Francie incredulously, as if the information were taking a long time to register. But then, instead of the eruption she anticipated, Beth saw a calm, sly smile spread over his face.

He gave a short laugh. "Oh, don't worry, babe. You don't have to listen to her. She can't make you do anything."

"Andrew, she's not. Listen—"

"Look," he said, "I have fixed everything for us. I know you're mad 'cause I didn't pick you up when I said. But there was something important I had to do. It was for us, believe me. That's why I didn't come get you the other night. But everything's perfect now. I'm not going to tell you about it in front of her." He gave a curt nod in Beth's direction. "But we are free now. We can be together now, just like we planned. No problem. Don't be afraid of her. She can't make you go with her. You've got me here to protect you now."

"She's not making me go, Andrew," Francie wailed. "Really. I want to get away from here. I don't want to live with my aunt and uncle. And I like it in Philadelphia. But it doesn't mean I'll never see you. You could come down and visit me there."

Andrew looked wildly from one sister to another, and then the sly look returned to his eyes. "She's making you say these things."

"No, she isn't," Francie insisted. "She asked me to come there to stay, and I said I would."

"Do you want me to go in another room?" Beth asked Francie. "Maybe if I'm not here—"

Andrew turned on Beth. "Shut up," he screamed. "You can't tell her what to do. Don't give me this crap. 'I'll go in another room.'" He mimicked her. "You can hear through the walls." He turned back to Francie. "She's forcing you. It doesn't matter what you want. Not to her. Oh, no." He shook his head at Francie. "I understand," he said. "Believe me. I know what's happening." He shook his head slowly, staring at Francie. Then he turned on Beth. "You cunt." He spit the word at her.

Francie gasped.

"All right," said Beth. "That's enough. You get out of here." She pointed toward the door, hoping he could not see her hand shaking.

Andrew's eyes blazed at her, and for a moment she thought he was going to come at her. Beth glared at him. "I mean it," she said. "Get out of here, or so help me, I'll call the police."

Andrew gazed at her for a moment as if appraising her threat. Then a mirthless smile sliced his face. "I know what you're up to," he said. "You can't put this over on me. I know every trick there is. Every one of them has already been done to me. I know how you can make people say what they don't mean to say, no matter what they want. You can make them do it. But you won't get away with it, this time. Oh, no."

"I told you to go," said Beth. She could not conceal the tremor in her voice. He had hunched over into a kind of crouch, as if he were going to spring at her.

"Don't be mad, Andrew," Francie pleaded. "Please."

Andrew turned to her and then straightened up and, with a gentle, faraway smile, reached out to stroke her ash blond hair. "I'm not mad. I understand. Believe me. I'll see you later." Without another look at Beth he headed out the door into the night.

Beth ran to the door, slammed it shut, and shot the bolt. Then she leaned against it and looked at Francie.

"I can't believe the way he was acting," said Francie.

"He's crazy," said Beth.

Francie looked at Beth with troubled eyes. "I

273

shouldn't have sprung it on him like that. His mother, and now me leaving. It's all just too much for him."

"Look, I don't care why. He sneaked into this house. He practically threatened me. You heard how he was talking."

"I don't think he meant all that stuff."

"Don't kid yourself, Francie. He's ready to snap."

Francie did not reply.

"Keep this locked tonight," said Beth. "I mean it."

Slowly, sadly, Francie nodded agreement.

Chapter 24

*H*E burst through the tower doors, his machine gun blazing as he mowed down the last of the guards. Francie turned from the barred window, her face pale from months of imprisonment and held out her arms to him. "I saw you leading your men this way," she whispered as she crushed herself to his chest. "I couldn't believe my eyes." His camouflage fatigues were soaked with sweat and blood from the battle, but she didn't seem to care. He picked her up and carried her down from the tower and out onto the balcony of the palace. Outside the palace walls hordes of people were chanting his name, blessing him for saving them. He waved to them, acknowledging their homage. Then he guided Francie over to the edge of the wall and pointed with the gun into the courtyard below. The tyrants were there, prisoners now, lined up against the courtyard wall. A firing squad stood at the ready, waiting for his signal. One of the prisoners looked up at them where they stood, the shouts of the crowd still ringing around them. It was a woman, her eyes defeated, her face haggard. She was gazing up at Francie, pleading for mercy. "She wants you to save her," he whispered to Francie. "She thinks you'll let her go free." He looked down at the ash blond head. Francie was shaking it from side to side. He squeezed her to him and raised his gun. "Fire," he screamed. "Fire."

A light flashed on in the darkened trailer down the street as Andrew approached his house. He heard the sound of his own voice echo in the frosty night. The door to the trailer opened, and a man's silhouette appeared, framed by the doorway. He looked up and down the street and then called out, "What the hell are you yelling about?"

"Sorry," Andrew called back. "I didn't mean . . . sorry." The man shook his head and then slammed the door of the trailer.

Andrew hurried up to the house and entered through the basement. Quickly he undressed and had his shower, straining to listen, through the cascading water, for the sound of the phone upstairs. She was sure to try to reach him. But as he emerged from the shower he was surrounded by silence.

He rubbed himself off with a stained, soggy towel that lay on the floor and then put his dirty clothes on again. He buckled his belt and trudged up the stairs, realizing, with each leaden step, that the call would not come. She would not be able to call. She would not be allowed to use the phone.

His head began to throb as if someone were tightening a metal band around it. He tried to recall the fantasy of rescuing her, but the pounding in his head prevented it. He went to the front window and stared out into the black night. He had no weapon, no army.

He didn't even have a fucking car to get them out of town. For the thousandth time he regretted the loss of the car. He didn't even have the money to buy a car. Andrew ground the palm of his hand helplessly against the throbbing in his eyes. The band seemed to tighten around his forehead. There was no money in the house. His mother never kept any around the house, and he had gone through her purse before he put it in the car with her, and she had only a few dollars on her. He knew she had some money in the bank, but he couldn't get at that. He had tried to get money from her accounts once and found out that he was "unauthorized" to take it out. That's what the zit-faced teller had informed him. Unauthorized. His mother had laughed when she heard it. "I figured you would try that," she had said, her eyes flinty, despite the laughter. "I'm always one step ahead of you." But even as his skin prickled at the thought of her ugly, laughing face, he suddenly realized that things were different now. She was not ahead of him any longer. She was gone, and he was her sole survivor. Her heir. All he had to do was find her will and wave that under their noses at the bank. They'd have to give him the money. It would be his by law.

The thought excited him, and the band around his head seemed to loosen. All he had to do was find the will. He bolted up the stairs to his room and picked up her keys. She had always kept the door to her room locked. She had never let him come in. That's proba-bly where the important papers were stashed. He went down the hall and unlocked her door. He shud-dered a little as he pushed the door open and thought he detected the scent of peppermint. Moonlight threw the lace pattern of the curtains onto the frayed rug. Andrew hesitated for a moment and then rushed to the bureau and switched on the dim pink bulb under the tasseled shade. He looked around warily.

The room was neat and still, a light coating of dust on the furniture tops. His heart thudded in time with his headache as he tried to decide which drawer to open first. *Go ahead.* He prodded himself. *She is gone.* With a defiant movement he threw open the jewelry box on her bureau and reached in. He pulled out a handful of worthless ropes of beads that trailed from the box like shiny intestines. He threw them down on the floor and plunged in again, unclasped pins sticking into him as he clawed through her junky collection in search of his legacy. He turned the box over, and the last few earrings tumbled out, but there were no documents. He tossed the box aside and began on the drawers.

One after another they yielded nothing but worn clothes, scarves, and underwear. Andrew tore through them, cursing her as he went, wanton piles of ripped clothing collecting on the floor around him as he emptied closets and drawers.

He had ransacked every hiding place he could think of when the trunk caught his eye. He had seen it as he scanned the room but had paid no attention to it. She used it as a piece of furniture. It was covered with a lacy cloth and an assortment of flowerpots holding the withered remnants of plants. But now, as he looked at it again, he noticed that its hasp was padlocked. For a moment he thought triumphantly that he had found it. She would keep her secret papers locked up like that. Then, in the next instant, he went weak all over as he realized what might be in there.

It was large enough. There was no doubt of that. Andrew sank to the floor, surrounded by wads of peppermint-scented clothing, and stared at the metal trunk. She had never told him what she'd done with the body. Wasn't it possible? He felt as if he could see through the metal sides, beneath the cloth and the rust-colored pots to the hideous contents of the trunk. Was there flesh left, or only bones? He imagined eyes bulging from the skull, wisps of hair still attached to rotting flesh, the old blue coat sheltering a putrid skeleton. She would keep it here, her evidence against him. Countless times she had threatened him with it, refusing to say where she had hidden the body.

Andrew's heart hammered against his knees, which he had drawn up and clasped to his chest. He could not take his eyes off the trunk. He had to know. But he was unable to move. Finally, as he began to ache from sitting in that fetal position, he put his hands on the floor and struggled to his feet.

With halting steps he approached the trunk. Bending over, he grabbed the edge of the lacy cloth and pulled it with a sharp, forceful yank. The flowerpots spun up and cracked against one another. They fell to the floor, dirt and roots spilling out across the carpet.

Andrew faced the naked trunk. Crouching down, he fumbled through the set of keys and, with shaking fingers, tried the smallest one in the padlock. The third key he tried turned and clicked, and he pulled open the stiff lock and slowly removed it from the hasp. He opened the hasp and then put his hands on the lid. He tried to summon every image of horror to his mind, so that when he lifted it, he would not be too shaken. He tried to steel himself, but he felt about as solid as gelatin. Swallowing hard, he pushed up, threw the lid open, and jumped back.

Over the rim of the trunk the corner of a brown envelope stuck up. Andrew leaned over and looked inside. The trunk was filled with papers.

Andrew exhaled and threw his head back, gulping in air. He fell on his knees beside the trunk, laughing exultantly as he reached in and pulled out ledger books, envelopes, and folders. It had to be here. There were old tax returns, yearbooks, photo albums, and receipts from ancient bills piled high inside it. Andrew began to toss them out and strew them around the room as if they were so much confetti. Papers fluttered and settled around him as he delved in again and again. But as the trunk emptied, the last will and testament of Leonora Vincent was nowhere to be found. Andrew's sense of triumph began to dissipate as he neared the bottom.

All at once his hand met something hard and heavy. He drew back with a cry and then slowly reached in again. He pulled out an old cloth bag and opened it. A box of ammunition fell out of it, and bullets rolled across the floor. Startled, he reached back into the bag and drew out a gun. It was a .38 caliber revolver, dark and pitted with age. Andrew stared down at it in amazement. It was the gun he had shot that night. He fell back on his heels and gazed at it. This was where she had hidden it all those years. This was her evidence against him, his baby fingerprints carefully preserved on the butt and now smudged over by his adult hand.

He stared at the gruesome souvenir of his childhood with a twisted sense of satisfaction. *She can't use it on me now,* he thought. He turned the gun around in his hands and examined it curiously. The barrel appeared to be clear, and when he snapped out the cylinder, he saw that it was empty but undamaged. He groped through the bullets on the floor, slipped the shells into the open weapon, and then snapped it shut again. He pretended to take aim at the pillow on his mother's bed.

From all his reading of mercenary magazines he knew quite a bit about guns, but it was a different thing altogether to hold one in his hand. It felt good to him, as if it belonged there. And it was a weapon, something he and Francie might need.

The thought of Francie and their needs made him turn his attention reluctantly back to the trunk. Placing the gun on the floor beside him, he resumed his search. But it did not take him long to realize that the will was not there. He found a couple of bankbooks with money in the accounts, but he tossed them aside in irritation. What good were they without the will? He couldn't prove that she had left her money to him, and the bank people would never believe him.

Her face rose before him again, mocking him. "I gave them strict instructions down at the bank not to let you near my money. I guessed that any boy who would do what you did to your own father couldn't be trusted. Oh, no. That's my work and my pay. I won't have you stealing from me, running around and spending my paycheck." She had laughed and laughed, delighted that another trap she had set had been sprung on him. Andrew slammed down the top of the trunk as if he were guillotining her head with the lid. There was no will here. She had still gotten the better of him, even now.

And then it hit him. Her paycheck. That was it. Relief flooded him. He would go get it from the dentist. Andrew's mouth fell open in amazement at his own ingenuity. It would work. It was perfect. The dentist would give him the money, and he would have enough to get a car. Noah always kept old cars around the station. It wouldn't be a great car, but it would be enough. Enough to get away from here. He was sure that eventually the bank would have to give him Leonora's money. He was entitled to it now that she was dead. But if there were no will, that would probably mean a lot of legal hassle. And he had no time to wait. He had to get Francie away from here. The bank could send him the money at his new address. His and Francie's.

Andrew rose to his feet as if in a trance, his mind alert with the details of his plan, despite the lateness of the night and his lack of sleep. He picked up the gun and carried it with him down the stairs to the foyer, where it had last been fired, years before. He took it to the closet and stuffed it into the deep side pocket of his overcoat. Then he went back into the parlor, to await the gray-gold light of dawn. He had been awake all night, and his nerves were frayed, but he was not tired. He felt like a man who was spending his last night in prison, now able to count the time in hours until he was free. He only wished that he did not have to wait those last few hours for the world's business to begin, so he could put his plan in motion. He thought that this must be how a general felt on the eve of a major attack. He was powerful.

At nine o'clock sharp he dialed Francie at her house.

"Hello," said the voice.

"Get Francie," he said.

There was silence at the other end, as if she might not obey. He was about to scream at her when he heard her place the phone down, and then he heard the squawk of her voice calling Francie's name. In a few moments his girl came to the phone.

"Hello?"

"Hey, babe," he said.

"Hello."

"I know you can't talk with her there, but I want you to meet me today."

Francie made a soft, snorting sound. "Where have I heard that before?"

"What?"

"Nothing," she said. "Anyway, I can't."

"Yes, you can. And you have to."

"I don't have to do any—"

"The funeral's today. I know you want to come."

There was silence at Francie's end.

"I came to yours, didn't I?"

"I know, I know."

"Just tell her," said Andrew. "You have to go. She can't say no to that. It's at two o'clock. At the cemetery."

There was a note of defeat in Francie's voice. "Okay, I'll go."

Andrew smiled. It was going to work. "Tell her to go fuck herself," he said softly.

"Andrew," Francie protested.

"I'll be with you later, babe." He hung up and closed his eyes, relishing the glow of success. Then he reminded himself that he still had things to do. He looked down at his military watch. He didn't have time to waste today. Andrew pulled his coat from the closet, locked the house, and started up the street to where his mother usually caught the bus to Harrison. An icy drizzle made the roads slippery, and it took him longer than usual to get up to the bench beneath a tree that served as a bus stop. He looked impatiently up the road, the rain dripping down his collar. The bus seemed to take forever to arrive, but finally he saw it coming. He climbed on board and shoved his last few dollars in the driver's face for the fare. The driver eyed him coldly as he counted out his change into Andrew's gloved hand. Andrew was too absorbed in his own thoughts to notice.

He found a seat near the back, next to a window, and arranged his bulky overcoat around him so that the gun in the deep side pocket rested in his lap. He had almost forgotten that he had put it there the night before. But it made him feel good to know he had it with him, even though through the fabric of his coat it felt cold against his leg. The dreary landscape rolled by as he looked out, his face pressed to the window. The cold glass felt good against the feverish warmth of his cheeks and his forehead. Although he seemed to be studying the passing farms and rocky hillsides, he could not see very much through the sheet of sleet that was now coming down, pelting the bus window with little icy missiles.

In the seat across the aisle a small child was crooning, despite his mother's best efforts to keep him quiet. The child's cries seemed to rake across Andrew's nerves. Andrew turned to look at the child and caught the mother's eyes. Her apologetic expression turned offended when she saw the look on Andrew's face, and she pulled the child to her and encircled him protectively. The child quieted down, and Andrew resumed looking out the window. Once he got the car, he would never ride a bus again, he thought. It was like riding with a herd of barnyard animals.

The houses and buildings were appearing in clusters as the bus neared the town of Harrison. Andrew sat upright in the seat, ready for the stop. The woman across the aisle shoved her child's arms into his jacket and then zipped him up. She picked up the child, and as the bus pulled up to stop just at the edge of the Harrison business district, she stood up and started to edge out of her seat. Andrew waited until she was halfway into the aisle before he jumped up and barged past her, making sure to crack the child with his elbow. The baby started to yell again as Andrew bolted down the aisle and got off the bus.

He looked up and down the deserted street and then started walking back in the direction the bus had come from. The dentist's office was in the ground floor of his home, which was on a corner of Main Street, a few blocks from the town. Andrew had been there several times before, and he had no trouble finding the place as he walked quickly along, his collar pulled up against the sleet, his leather soles slipping along the sidewalks. There were no other walkers in the miserable weather. A few cars passed him, going slowly along, their windshield wipers plowing away the sleet as it struck. The Ridbergs lived on a corner surrounded by trees and brown, brambly bushes. A white sign out front announced the dentist's practice. Andrew peered up the driveway and noticed that the station wagon was not there. There were lights on in the dentist's office but none in the house. He was relieved to see it, realizing that the wife was probably not at home. He did not really want to run into her after that business with the shopping bag and the casserole. She was probably still pouting because he hadn't wanted her dinner.

Andrew climbed the front steps and reached for the doorknob. A three-by-five card was taped to the pane in the door. The message on it was neatly typed: "Closed at 10:30 today due to funeral. Dr. Ridberg."

Andrew looked down at his watch. It was after 10:00 A.M. He had gotten here just on time. He pushed the door open and went inside. A bell tinkled faintly as he opened the door. The waiting room was on his left as he walked in. The music from a mellow listening radio station filled the empty room. The easy chairs in the waiting room were empty, although there was one coat hanging on the coat tree. The air smelled of antiseptic and room deodorizer. Through the door to the examining room Andrew could see his mother's desk, all neatly arranged, an artificial flower in a vase on it and a picture of himself in a red plastic frame. He sat down for a minute and then jumped up again and wandered around the stuffy room. From inside the office he could hear two voices chattering. Andrew walked over to the gurgling aquarium in the corner and began to tap nervously on the glass sides. Inside, a dozen tropical fish swam purposefully about, exposed by the eerie light of the tank. Andrew bent down and watched them in fascination, wishing for a moment that he could make himself one of them and be inside there, drifting endlessly along, not feeling anything.

An old man's loud voice said, "Thank you, Doctor." Andrew sneaked a glance over his shoulder and saw an elderly man with thick glasses coming out of the office. He plucked his coat off the clothes tree and went out the door, never even acknowledging that Andrew was there. Andrew was tempted to yell out, "Hey, you old bastard," just to see the man jump, but he stifled the urge. He didn't want the dentist to get testy on him.

After going through the door, he walked up to where Dr. Ridberg was making notes in a file on his desk.

"Hello, Dr. Ridberg."

The dentist looked up, surprised, and then his lips tightened at the sight of Andrew. He attempted to square his narrow, round shoulders. "I didn't expect to see you here today, Andrew."

Andrew shrugged. "I needed to get something from you."

The dentist looked down at the watch on his thin wrist. "I should think you would be home getting ready."

Andrew looked at him in surprise, wondering how the dentist could know anything about his plans. "For what?" he asked warily.

"For what?" Dr. Ridberg asked incredulously. "For the funeral, of course. Didn't you see the sign in my window? I'm closing early so I can get changed and have lunch."

"I'm ready," said Andrew.

The dentist sighed and looked back down at his folder. "My wife was going to come with me, out of respect for your mother, but," he said in a chilly voice, "after what happened yesterday when she was kind enough to try and bring you that food—the way you treated her . . ."

Andrew smiled to himself as he watched the man fussily rearranging the folders in a drawer. "I came for the money," he said.

The doctor, who had been expecting an apology or at least an explanation, looked up at him indignantly. "The money? What money?"

"Her pay," said Andrew.

The doctor shook his head and made a soft, clucking noise. "I am surprised at you, Andrew. I really am. Thinking only of money at a time like this."

"Don't try to get out of it," said Andrew. "You owed her her paycheck. So give it to me."

The dentist looked at him indignantly, and his balding head gleamed with a halo of perspiration. "I have no intention of trying to cheat you out of this money. Your mother earned it, and I suppose she would want you to have it. But when I think how she would feel if she knew, on the day of her funeral, that you were more concerned with her paycheck—"

"Just give it," said Andrew.

The dentist gave the young man a withering look and then opened a desk drawer. He hunted around in it and then pulled out a checkbook and opened it. He pulled a ball-point pen from his pocket and began to write. "After all she did for you. The way she sacrificed for you."

"Not a check," said Andrew. "I want cash."

Dr. Ridberg clicked the pen closed and put his hands on his hips. "Andrew, this is not a savings bank. I don't keep cash around here. I have always paid your mother by check."

"I want the cash," said Andrew.

The dentist was about to protest again when something he saw in Andrew's face made him reconsider. "Oh, very well. I'll see what I have." He opened another drawer and pulled out a metal box, which he opened with a key on his key chain. "You know, Andrew, I am really disappointed in this behavior of yours. I'm sure this has upset you very much, but perhaps you should think about going for counseling." He was counting out bills as he spoke.

"How much is there?" said Andrew.

"What do you think you're doing here?" came a voice from behind Andrew in the waiting room. He turned around to look.

Estelle Ridberg had come in, holding an animal carrying case in one hand. A small dog, which could not be seen, was making sharp yipping noises inside the box. She looked angrily from Andrew to her husband as she set the case down on the floor.

"Hello, dear," said the dentist. "What did the vet say about Pepe?"

"He gave me some pills for him. What is going on here?"

Andrew stared at her as she marched up to the desk and looked into the open cashbox.

Dr. Ridberg sighed. "Andrew has come for Leonora's paycheck. He's asked for it in cash."

Estelle stuck out her plump, pointed chin and spoke to her husband as if Andrew were not there. "Don't give it to him," she said.

"I think it would be best just to settle this matter right now and be done with it," said the dentist, clutching the bills in his right hand.

"After what he did to me? That cash is there strictly for emergencies. This is no emergency." She turned on Andrew, her face screwed up in distaste. She did not feel afraid of him now, on her own territory, with her husband to back her up. "What are you doing here on the day of your mother's funeral? Have you no shame at all? I can't believe you would even show your face here. We should kick you right out of here."

"Estelle, Estelle." The dentist tried to soothe her. "Please. I have the cash. I'm sure she'd want him to have it."

But the dentist's wife would not be appeased. "No, I'm sorry. This is wrong. Leonora would never have approved of this behavior." She turned on Andrew and waved a pudgy finger in his face. "You should be here apologizing, never mind scrounging for the last few dollars your poor mother—"

Andrew decided, quite calmly, to point something back at her. He pulled the gun from his pocket and leveled it at the woman's head.

The dentist and his wife both gasped, and he pulled his wife back toward him. No one spoke. The dog yipped anxiously in the background, as if trying to sing along with the music on the radio. Andrew relished the moment and the alarm which had replaced the smug looks on their ugly faces. He could hardly keep himself from smiling.

"Why don't you give me the rest of the cash in that box while you're at it?" he said.

Dr. Ridberg raised a hand as if in surrender, and it trembled as he gestured for Andrew to calm down. "All right, son. All right. Now look. You put that away, and I'm going to give you this money we owe you, and we'll forget all about this."

"I want all the money," said Andrew.

The dentist opened his mouth as if to argue, then thought better of it and picked up all the cash in the box with pale, fumbling fingers. "There's no need for this, Andrew," he said, handing over the cash. Andrew stuffed it greedily in his pocket. "I know you're distraught over what happened to Mother. But this—this is robbery."

The dentist's wife was shaking, partly from fear but also from anger. She looked as if she would like to claw at him, for the indignities they had suffered at his hand. "We've just tried to be nice to you," she said in a shrill voice. "And this is our reward." Her husband put a hand on her arm to try to quiet her, but she was determined to speak up boldly. "You won't get away with this, you know. Unless you give that money back, we'll have to call the police. And we'll tell them all about you."

Andrew looked at her quivering flesh, her mean, haughty little eyes, and he felt as if there were something hot and glowing inside his skull, threatening to burst it open. "No, you won't," he said.

Then he fired.

The bullet hit the dentist's wife square in the chest,

between the open flaps of her car coat. A look of horror and amazement flashed across her face as she pitched forward. Dr. Ridberg cried out and grabbed for her, but Andrew fired twice again, and the dentist's hands left his wife and grasped the bloody front of his white examining shirt. Then he, too, crumpled to the floor.

Andrew looked down at the two of them, heaped together there. His ears rang from the noise, and the smoke from the barrel of the gun curled up and filled his nostrils, making him cough. He bent down for a closer look. Their eyes were open in the blank, startled stare of death. Andrew kicked their sides gently and met no resistance. He straightened up and looked at the gun in his hand as if it were a stranger that had just said something mildly surprising. Then he looked back at the bodies.

He had not meant to do it. He was sure that he had not intended it when he came over here. He didn't even know if the gun would fire after all these years. But now it was done. For a few moments he had the panicky, nightmarish feeling of being on a stage and not knowing any of the lines to the play. But as the shock wore off and he recovered himself, a sense of satisfaction began to creep through him. *This is what it means,* he realized, *to get what you want when you want it. To have your own way. To silence the people you hate. To take what you are entitled to.*

Andrew stuffed the gun gently back into his pocket and then stepped over the bodies and emptied the metal cashbox on the dentist's desk. Then, after a moment's hesitation, he rummaged through the dead man's pockets, emptied his wallet, and helped himself to the cash contents of Estelle Ridberg's purse. He emptied the desk drawers, but there was no more money in them.

After running back out into the waiting room, he went from window to window, peering out to be sure no one was coming. As he did so, he saw the Ridbergs' car in the driveway. For a minute he felt elated. He had noticed the keys in her purse. All he had to do was take it and run. It was tempting and filled him with a sense of reckless excitement, but he forced himself to be cautious about it. If he had the car, he would be easy to spot. The police would be looking out for the stolen car. As it was, he thought he was pretty safe. He was sure he had not told anyone where he was going, and he didn't think he had been seen coming in here. The old man in the office hadn't even noticed him. He was still wearing his gloves, so there was no problem with fingerprints. Taking the car would just mean taking an unnecessary chance. *You got away with your mother,* he reminded himself. *If they catch you for this one, you're finished.*

He tried to think what to do next. He would have to go out the back way. He knew there was a back way because he had picked up his mother there from time to time. Taking one last look out the windows, he started back toward the office. The dog in the carrying case was barking wildly now and thrashing around in the box. Andrew reached in his pocket and grasped the gun, staring down at the box. Then he shook his head. The dog never hurt anybody.

He pulled his hand from his pocket and looked down at his watch. He couldn't take the bus back because he couldn't leave town on the main road. He could hitchhike, he decided. Someone was bound to pick him up in this weather. He would get a ride to the garage and get a car from Noah. Then he'd be set. With money to spare.

He felt the euphoria returning as he thought of the future. He and Francie would be on their way this very afternoon. Money, a gun, a car, and freedom. It was too good to be true. He stepped over the bodies sprawled on the office floor and headed for the fire exit at the back door. He poked his head out to be sure no one was in sight, and then he started down the steps. He pulled the door shut on the office as the languid recorded voice of Johnny Mathis began singing "Chances Are" on the radio.

Chapter 25

"*I* don't want you to go," said Beth.

Francie put down her comb and turned to face her sister, who was standing in her bedroom doorway. "I have to."

"I think it's a bad idea," said Beth. "You saw the way he acted last night."

"Well, it's probably because of his mother and all."

"I don't care what his excuse is. The guy is unbalanced. Dangerously unbalanced, if you ask me."

"You don't really know him," said Francie. "He's very temperamental. But he doesn't mean anything by it."

Beth stared at her sister, uncertain what to do. She could forbid her to go, but that would imply that she had the final word on Francie's actions. She wasn't Francie's parent after all. She didn't want to start demanding obedience just when they were getting ready to start this new living arrangement. She didn't want it to seem as if obedience were a condition of the move to Philadelphia.

"Look," said Beth carefully, "I'm not passing judgment here. But you must admit he's acting very bizarre, and I think you should stay as far away as possible from Andrew."

Francie pulled on a sweater and buckled the belt on her jeans. "I don't feel like going, believe me. Just what I want to do. Go to another funeral."

"So don't go," said Beth.

"I have to. I can't just ignore it. You might not believe this, but Andrew made me feel a lot better at Dad's. The least I can do is to be there for him today."

"I'm sure he did," Beth said, chastened by the implicit reminder of her own chilly reserve of the week before. "And believe me, I applaud your loyalty. I know you want to do the right thing. But I have a very bad feeling about him. I'm worried about you."

Francie took a Kleenex from her purse and cleaned off her glasses. "It's no big deal. I'll be back in no time."

"I'd better go with you," said Beth, "to be on the safe side."

"I don't think you should," said Francie firmly. "That's only gonna make it worse. Look, Uncle James is going to be there the whole time. Nothing can happen. Besides, you've got a list a mile long of things you have to do if we're ever going to get out of here."

Beth sighed and chewed her lower lip. "We could get it all done afterward."

"What about the headstone?" asked Francie. "You promised you'd get that, and the place is a half hour's drive from here."

"I thought we would do that together," said Beth.

"There won't be time. Beth, I've got to do this. And you promised we'd get that stone."

Beth grimaced. "I wish Mom were buried here. Then we could just add his name to hers. It would make it easy."

"Why wasn't she?" Francie asked. "I never understood that."

"Her family had a plot near Boston, where she grew up. She always wanted to be buried with her parents." Beth did not add her personal suspicion that her father had wanted to save the expense of the plot and the stone.

Francie stuck out her chin. "Well, you said we could get something nice for Dad."

"I thought you were going to help," said Beth peevishly.

Francie threw her hands open in a helpless gesture. "I didn't know this was going to happen."

"All right, all right," said Beth. She pointed a finger at Francie. "I'm gonna drop you over at Uncle James's. I want you to promise me you'll get a ride back with him."

"I will," said Francie irritably.

"All right, get your coat," said Beth.

"I'm just going up there so I don't feel guilty, and then I'll come back. In fact, I'll meet you at the parsonage later."

"Okay," said Beth. Gathering together her boxes for the church and her packages for the post office, Beth followed Francie out to the car. She drove to her aunt and uncle's and watched as Francie started up the walk to the door of the parsonage.

"Borrow an umbrella," Beth called after her. "You'll get soaked."

Francie ran back to the car, tipped the front seat forward, and rummaged around behind it. She held up a beat-up folding umbrella and showed it to Beth.

"Ready for anything," said Francie.

Beth smiled begrudgingly and watched after the sturdy, sensibly outfitted little figure as she trudged up the walk and disappeared into the house. *You can't spend the day worrying about this,* she admonished herself. *Concentrate on what you have to do.*

With a sigh Beth started off on her errands. Her first stop was the real estate office, where she dropped off the duplicate keys. Next she went to the post office, where she encountered a line, long for Oldham, of three people waiting at the window. Once the packages had been posted, she stopped in the luncheonette next door and ordered a cheese sandwich. While she ate at the counter she scanned the local paper, noting, as she turned the pages, the follow-up article on Leonora Vincent's death. Her former employer, a Dr. Ridberg of Harrison, was quoted as praising her work and deploring the road conditions in the mountains around the area. The article said that Andrew could not be reached for comment.

Yeah, he was too busy harassing us, Beth thought. She pushed her plate aside, her appetite spoiled by the mention of Leonora Vincent's son. The thought of his appearance in the house the night before made her shudder. She turned around abruptly on the revolving stool and looked behind her, half expecting to see him there, glaring at her. Then she shook her head and looked down at her watch. The funeral would be starting any minute now. The sooner it started, the sooner it was over. *And the sooner we can get out of this town,* she thought. *And away from that guy. The sooner the better.*

Beth left her money on the counter next to the paper and ventured out into the wet afternoon. She got back into the car and drew a blank on what she was supposed to do next. Then it came back to her: the headstone. She sat there for a few moments, trying to think of a way to get out of it, but finally she turned on the motor, pulled out, and headed out in the direction of the monument place.

Francie's estimate of a half hour drive proved accurate, and Beth felt her customary impatience with rural distances and inconveniences by the time she arrived. At first glance DiAngelo's monuments looked almost like a roadside souvenir stand. The front walk to the office was flanked on either side by crowds of stones and statues. There were angels and virgins, urns on pedestals, granite scrolls carved in stone, animals, birds, and even a horse's head among the gravestones. The clutter of gray effigies was almost cheery in appearance. Beth walked up to the door, pushed it open, and walked in.

Loud, jerky-rhythmed music that sounded as if it had been written by a computer blasted out of a portable radio on the lone desk in the room. Behind the desk, a T-shirted fellow of about fifteen contemplated a submarine sandwich, which was spread out before him on waxed paper, dripping grease. He looked up and gave Beth a wan grin when she came in.

"Do you work here?" Beth asked.

The boy turned the radio down and said, "What?"

"Do you work here?"

The boy looked around the room as if he were unsure of the answer and then shook his head. "Not really. I'm just filling in for my grandfather. He's out putting a stone in."

"I see," said Beth.

"He should be right back, though."

"What's right back?"

The boy shrugged. "I don't know. Ten, fifteen minutes. Why don't you wait?"

Beth looked at her watch in annoyance. *Half an hour to get here, and there's no one to take care of you,* she thought. She sighed.

"Here," said the boy cheerily, "have a seat. You can look this over while you're waiting." The boy handed her a buff-colored folder. "A Permanent Memento of Love" was the title emblazoned in gold lettering on its front. There was a grease stain on the corner, an apparent runoff from the hero sandwich.

"Thanks," said Beth in a flat tone. She took a seat and looked around. The office was decorated like a living room from a mail-order catalog. Everything from rugs and drapes to furniture coverings had a synthetic, highly flammable look to it. The walls of the office were adorned with calendars, topped with color photos of headstones, most of them profusely banked by flowers. Despite the flowers, the photos had, at best, a static appearance.

The boy at the desk gave her another smile. "Do you mind?" he asked, pointing to the sandwich. Beth shook her head and opened the folder she was holding. The boy turned up his radio again and dived into the sandwich. Beth began to read the long, wordy explanation, abundant with euphemisms, of the importance of picking the right memorial.

What am I doing here? she thought, throwing the folder down on an end table beside her. *I'm the last person who should be picking a memorial for him. An enduring memento of resentment. I don't know why I agreed to do this.* She sighed again and looked out the window. DiAngelo's statues stood like sentries in the icy rain. *You're doing it for Francie,* she reminded herself. *You promised.*

The tune on the radio ended, and the half-hourly newscast began. "Our top story today," intoned the announcer, "is the brutal slaying of an area dentist and his wife in an apparent robbery-homicide this morning."

"Did your grandfather say what time he'd be getting back?" Beth asked above the voice of the announcer.

The boy wiped his mouth with a paper napkin and swallowed. "I don't know exactly. He left about half an hour ago. It's not too far from here where he's going."

Beth nodded and sat back in the chair.

"Dr. Alan Ridberg, fifty-two, and his wife, Estelle, fifty, were discovered this afternoon, brutally slain in the offices of—"

The boy turned the radio down and raised his head as if he were listening for something outside. "I think I hear his truck," he said. He turned off the radio and began to gather up the napkins and empty soda cans on the desk.

"Turn that back on," said Beth.

The boy looked up in surprise.

"The radio," Beth ordered. The boy turned the volume knob.

"—no leads at this time," the announcer concluded. He went on to a story about a local lobster hatchery.

"I'm not supposed to play this in here," said the boy. "My granddad gets pissed."

Beth waved her hand to indicate that he could turn it off and slumped down in her seat, frowning. The boy walked to the window and looked out, peering over the fog his breath made on the glass.

Ridberg, Beth thought. *It's the same dentist Andrew's mother worked for. First the mother. Then the mother's boss. In two days.* Was that a coincidence? It

300

had to be. It *had* to be. But Beth could feel her insides recoil as if from some repulsive odor. She kept picturing Andrew's face. The blank red-rimmed eyes and the raving accusations as he stalked through the house after her. She had felt the physical menace coming off him in waves. But no. There was no reason for him to hurt those people. It was impossible. It was just a coincidence.

"It's him," said the boy at the window.

Beth looked up, startled. Then she rose from her seat.

"I can't wait any longer," said Beth.

"But he's here," protested the boy. "What about your monument?"

Beth looked distractedly around the room. "I don't know," she said. This was stupid. The man was right here. She had promised Francie she would get the stone. But anxiety was crowding out all other concerns. *I knew I shouldn't have let her go to the funeral with Andrew,* she thought. *But that's ridiculous. He didn't do anything. He's a little warped, but he's not a murderer. He just happened to know all those people. To be closely associated with all of them.*

She felt as if her mind were as knotted as her stomach. Francie would want her to stay put and get the headstone, just as they planned. Here she was, tempted to race all the way back to Oldham, and it was probably for no reason at all. This trip would be completely wasted. But as much as she tried to reason with herself, a warning was sounding inside her, like a siren, drowning out the voice of rationality.

You're probably just doing this to avoid having to pick out this monument for your father. That's probably it. She scolded herself. *Any excuse. That's what Francie would think. You can't even bring yourself to do this one last thing for him.* She remembered all of Francie's accusations against her: how she had abandoned her father, had never called, had never even known he was sick. And then she thought of Francie's screaming at her when they left the lawyer's office: "He said you would take care of me. That you would stay with me if anything happened to him."

Suddenly Beth felt a calm sense of resolution come over her. *That's right,* she thought. *Maybe I am imagining things, but I don't trust Andrew. I am worried about my sister.* Her mind flickered with the image of her father, dim but still powerful in its hold on her. *You may have to do without the stone, Dad,* she thought. *I'm going to do what you wanted me to. I'm going to look out for her.*

"He's coming right in," the boy assured her.

"It'll have to wait," said Beth.

"He's gonna kill me," said the boy, rolling his eyes.

"No, no," said Beth. "It's not your fault. I just remembered something important. First things first."

She bolted out the door and slammed it behind her. She passed the old man from DiAngelo's as he came up the walk. Beth did not hesitate but continued running straight for the car.

Chapter 26

*F*RANCIE held her umbrella up high and tried to angle it in such a way that the spill-off would not land on Andrew's back. She did not really want to get too close to him because of the strange odor that was coming off him, even outside in the windy cold.

"It's a terrible day," she said. "I'm sure more people would have come except for the weather."

Andrew nodded and looked around the cemetery with an indifferent expression on his face.

It was practically empty except for the two of them. Francie felt embarrassed and hurt for him that the turnout had been so scant. Besides herself and Noah, there had only been three other people. One of them was a lady from Harrison who said she was a patient from Dr. Ridberg's. And then there was an old couple from the church who went to all the funerals as their macabre form of entertainment. At least Andrew had not seemed to notice. He had shifted from one foot to the other as if he had had to go to the bathroom and had kept his eyes on Francie, seemingly oblivious of Uncle James's simple elegy. When it was over, he had all but elbowed the old pastor out of the way, explaining to him that he had to talk to Francie and assuring him that he would bring her safely home, despite Francie's nervous protests.

Now he stood gazing happily down at her. "I got a car for us," he said.

"Oh, good," said Francie in a flat tone.

"Come on," he said. "It's over there."

Francie looked over to where he was pointing and saw the ancient green Pontiac parked in the dirt roadway of the graveyard. "That's great that you got a car," she said. "I know you needed one."

"She's gonna be good to us," Andrew said proudly. He started picking his way along the paths between the graves toward the car.

"I wish I could hang out with you," Francie said, following behind him, "but I've got so much to do."

Andrew did not answer. He had already reached the car and was unlocking the front door. Francie walked up beside him and turned around, looking back at the field of gravestones. "It's unbelievable," she said. "To think we were here last week for my father. And now your mother. We must have a jinx on us."

Andrew grabbed her by the sleeve of her jacket. "Hurry up. Get in."

"Don't. You'll tear it."

"How long are you gonna stand around here?" he demanded.

"Sorry to keep you," Francie muttered as she climbed into the front seat. Andrew went around to his side, slid in, and tried to start the engine. He cursed as it refused to turn over.

Francie pressed her face to the window and looked

at the graves. Bare trees stooped by the weather stretched empty branches out like supplicating arms. She felt guilty leaving her father's grave here, knowing that she might never be able to visit it or even to see the headstone. She felt as if she were abandoning him to endless loneliness and silence.

"There," Andrew said exultantly as the engine started its raggedy hum. "Let's get out of this creepy cow pasture."

Francie sighed and looked over at Andrew. "You know, you don't seem very sad, considering this was your mother's funeral."

Andrew smiled, and his eyes glittered as he turned out of the cemetery gates and onto the road. "I'm not sad. I'm happy. This is the happiest day of my life."

"That's terrible," said Francie. "What a terrible thing to say."

"All right," he said. "I'm sad. I'm crying. Boo-hoo."

Francie shook her head. "Never mind. It's none of my business."

"Babe, how can I be sad when we're on our way?"

Francie made a face. "I said, 'Never mind.' Just drop me at my corner, will you?"

"No, no," he said. "We're going for a ride." As if to emphasize his words, he whizzed past the turn for Francie's street and headed toward the back roads out of town.

Francie sat up and looked indignantly at him. "Stop it, Andrew. I haven't got time to go for a ride. I have to get back."

"Babe, we've got all the time in the world. This is it. We're taking off."

"What?"

"Right now," he said. "Bye-bye, you dirtbag town."

"Taking off where? I'm not taking off anywhere."

"Look in back," he said pleasantly.

Francie scrambled up and looked over the seat. There was a packed duffel bag wedged in the well behind the seat. Francie stared at it for a minute, pushing her glasses back up on her nose. Her heart thudded in her chest. She looked over at him with wide eyes.

Andrew met her gaze with a leering smile. "California, here we come," he said.

"This is stupid," she said uncertainly. "Take me back right now."

"All right," he said. "I know it's a surprise. But I had to do it this way. It's the only way we could get away without your sister screaming. So I decided we would do it today. It was what we planned anyway. Right, babe?"

"Andrew, I told you in the letter I changed my mind about all that."

"Oh, the letter. I knew she made you write that. She's been plotting against us from the very beginning. She tried every trick there was to keep us from being together, but luckily I didn't buy it. What if I had believed her?" Andrew slowed the car as they approached the junction of a two-lane highway going south. He put his turn signal on and peered up the rainy intersection.

"I'm not going away with you," said Francie. She reached for the door handle and jerked it up. "I'm getting out."

"Don't open that door," he said, "or I'll wring your neck."

Francie's hand froze on the handle. She turned and stared at him, a sickening sensation in her stomach.

Andrew flashed her a false, skeletal grin and stepped on the gas. The car lurched out onto the main road.

There was silence in the car for a few minutes, and then Andrew's voice assumed a light, cheery tone. "I know it's late in the day to get started, but I figure we can cover a few states before we stop for the night."

Francie did not say anything. She stared out the window, gripping the door handle with bloodless fingers, as the familiar landscape shot past them. At first it was all she could do to breathe, so constricted did her chest feel. She wondered if this was what it felt like to be having a heart attack. She thought, in that instant, of her father and then was overwhelmed by a sense of weakness in all her limbs.

"See, I figured she'd be keeping watch on you," said Andrew, leaning back against the seat as if he were relaxed, although his neck and arms were stiff and taut. "That's how I thought of the thing about the funeral. I figured if you could get up there, that would be our chance to get away. It was perfect." He gave a harsh, angry laugh. "Now, once we get far enough away, we can be married. They'll never find us. We can use false names. It's just like we planned. Right, babe?" His cold eyes turned on her, demanding a reply. "Right?" he repeated.

"I don't have any of my stuff," she whispered, hoping against hope that he might relent and turn back.

"What?"

"My clothes and all that stuff."

"We'll buy some when we get to California."

"But it's expensive to buy all that stuff. Why don't we go back and get it? I can just run in the house. My sister isn't home anyway." She tried to keep the desperate edge out of her voice.

A Budget rental truck which had been coming up on them from the distance now pulled out alongside them and started to pass. A spray of gray slush shot up from the truck's tires and pelted the windshield.

"You fucking asshole," Andrew cried. He sped up and pulled out into the left lane, trying to pull out ahead of the truck. As he pulled out, he saw a small foreign car coming toward them, its fog lights cutting through the curtain of sleet. Andrew clenched his jaw and dropped back behind the truck to let the car pass.

"I could get my camera," Francie pleaded, "so we could take pictures of our trip." *As if this were a regular vacation,* she thought, swallowing the lump in her throat. *Oh, please turn this car around,* she prayed silently.

"We don't need any goddamned pictures," he yelled. He pulled back out into the left lane and pushed down the accelerator. Francie watched the speedometer climb as the car churned along. The truck did not slow down to let them pass. Instead, it put on some speed and pulled smoothly away from them.

"Slow down," Francie whispered in a hoarse, frightened voice. "We don't need to catch him."

"I'll show that son of a bitch," Andrew said through gritted teeth. He seemed to forget that Francie was there. He pushed the car to a faster speed and then began to slip from left to right on the road. Andrew held tightly to the vibrating wheel, his eyes burning into the rear of the truck.

"I'm gonna be sick," said Francie. She breathed hard through her mouth, trying to quell the nausea and calm her pounding heart.

"Shut up," Andrew cried. "We've got him!" They had come to a steep grade in the road, and the truck lost considerable speed because of the load it was carrying. Andrew gunned the engine, sweat breaking out on his forehead, and pulled out to the left again, inching up ever closer, despite the double yellow lines in the road that indicated no passing. As he pulled up to the side of the cab, he rolled down his window and began screaming obscenities at the driver as he honked his horn wildly.

Francie looked up and saw the driver glaring down at her and mouthing words she could not hear.

Andrew let out a howl of glee as he pulled out in front of the truck. He turned to Francie, a jubilant expression in his eyes. "Did you see that?" he cried. "I got him."

Francie realized, looking in his eyes, that there would be no conning him into turning back. It was no good pretending that she was willing to run with him. She spoke out in a quavering voice. "I don't want to go anywhere with you, Andrew. I don't want anything to do with you. Take me home."

The manic joy in Andrew's eyes vanished, like a doused flame, and his face turned ashen. "What?"

"I don't want to go with you. I don't want to marry you. I'm only fourteen. I just want to go back right now."

Andrew began to breathe hard as if there were a clamp on his chest. "Shut up," he said. "Shut your— you think you can just leave me? Do you know what I did for you? Do you know what I've done for you?"

For an instant it was as if he had forgotten he was even at the wheel. The car lost speed as he turned to her and tried to grab at her throat with a free hand. The truck, which was still behind them, seized the opportunity and surged out beside them. As he went to pass, the truck driver deliberately closed in and swiped the side of Andrew's old car as hard as he could.

Andrew grabbed for the wheel with both hands as the car went into a skid, and the truck roared off in the distance. Francie, who was huddled in the corner of the seat, having tried to escape Andrew's grasp, let out a scream as the car began to spin slowly around until it was no longer facing ahead. Andrew pitched forward and smacked his chin on the wheel as the car slid out across the highway.

It was as if it were happening in slow motion. Francie saw the car start to turn, and she flung herself down on the seat. *This is it,* she thought. *Oh, no, oh, shit.* The image of her mother at the wheel, that awful night on the highway sprang to her mind. The horrible splintering sounds would be next, she knew. She could see her mother's horror-struck face so clearly in her mind. Now she was going to die. She wondered if she would see her mother in death. *I'm too young,* she thought. *This can't be all.*

The car bounced, and Francie covered her head just in time as she felt herself hit the dashboard and then fall back against the seat. Twice more the car seemed to leap into the air, and then, with a scrape and a thud, it stopped.

Francie sat up in the seat and blinked. She checked her glasses to see if they were broken. She put them back on and looked around, amazed to be alive. She looked over at Andrew. He was groaning and holding his chin, but he was not bleeding. The car was resting on an angle in a gully beside the highway. For a second Francie felt like laughing for the joy of being alive and unhurt. Then she looked back at Andrew, and her heart froze with a newfound fear of him.

"That son of a bitch," said Andrew. "Look what he did to us."

Francie stared at him. *I have got to get away from*

him, she thought. He was jamming the key into the ignition and turning it, but there was only a grinding noise in the engine.

"I'll get this thing started," he cried. "It's slow to get started. That's the only problem. I'll have it going in a minute."

"It's stuck here," said Francie. "We'd better go call a garage."

Andrew turned on her in a fury. "What do you know about cars? Nothing."

"We were almost killed," said Francie in a trembling voice. "I know that."

"Shut up," said Andrew. "I can't think with you talking."

Francie saw her chance. She hesitated for a moment, and then she moved. Reaching out quickly, she unlocked her door. "I'll go for help," she said. In one swift motion she forced the door open and jumped out of the car. She landed on her ankle in the gully, turning it sideways, but she did not even feel it. She scrambled up the bank toward the road, just as she heard the car door slam on Andrew's side.

"Get back here," he shouted, starting after her.

"Help," she cried as she reached the highway and began to run along the icy road. Behind her she could hear him gaining on her. A car was coming in the distance. She waved her arms wildly as she ran. The fog lights of the oncoming car were getting brighter. "Please," she cried out.

Then she felt his arm reach out and grab her from behind.

Chapter 27

DESPITE the speed with which she made it back to town, there was no one at the cemetery when she arrived. Beth got back into the car and drove to the parsonage. Uncle James's car was in the driveway. Beth exhaled with a slight sense of relief. They were back.

Beth parked the car and ran up to the front door through the icy rain. She knocked on the door as she opened it. "Anybody home?" she called out.

Uncle James met her in the hallway. He reached for her wet jacket, which she shrugged off. "You'd better catch your breath," he advised. "What's the hurry?"

"That funeral didn't take long," said Beth. "I was just up at the cemetery."

"Oh, my, no," he said, shaking his head and leading her into the living room. "It was a sorry sight, Beth. I'll tell you that. Four or five people there, one little flower arrangement. That dentist she worked for all those years didn't even come. And the weather was so miserable, we had to keep it short."

Beth shivered at the mention of Dr. Ridberg. She decided not to bring up the murder. "It's wet all right." She looked over his shoulder through to the empty dining room.

"So you girls all packed up to leave us?"

"Just about," said Beth.

Aunt May emerged from the kitchen and greeted Beth. "I've got some hot tea if you want it."

"Where's Francie?" Beth asked.

"I left her with young Andrew," said Uncle James. "They seemed to want to talk to each other."

"With Andrew?" Beth cried. "Why didn't you bring her back?"

"He had a car," said James. "He promised to bring her back."

"I can't believe you let him drive off with her," Beth said in a shrill voice.

"I told him that when he got back," said Aunt May. "She has no business driving around with that Andrew Vincent."

"They are friends," said Uncle James, a wounded expression in his round blue eyes. "She wanted to talk to him. To console him, I'm sure. It's only natural at a time like this."

"She wanted to," said Beth curtly.

"They were talking together, and I'm sure now that she's going away, they just wanted a little time to share this grief, say their good-byes and so forth. I didn't see any harm in that."

"So she took off with him," said Beth. "Goddammit."

"I'm sorry, Beth," said Uncle James. "I didn't realize you felt so strongly about this."

"She promised me she would come back with you."

"These young ones have minds of their own," said James.

"May I use your phone?" Beth asked.

Aunt May pointed to the kitchen.

Beth went in and dialed her father's house. The phone rang and rang. She hung up and went back into her aunt and uncle's living room. "She's not home," she said angrily.

"I'm sure they'll be back soon," said Uncle James. "Here. Sit down and visit with us for a while. Once we drop you at the airport tomorrow, who knows how long it will be before we see you again?"

Beth sank down into a chair and stared blankly ahead of her.

Uncle James and Aunt May exchanged a glance. Then James said, "I feel terrible about this, Beth. I had no idea you wanted me to bring her back."

Beth shook her head. "No, never mind. It's not your fault."

"I'll get you some tea," said Aunt May. "James, why don't you help me?"

Beth stared into the unlit fireplace as the old people headed for the kitchen. She had gone off with Andrew. Beth could hardly believe it. After that whole conversation this morning about how she was just going to put in an appearance so she wouldn't feel guilty. She had deliberately lied about it. No, that wasn't fair, Beth rebuked herself. It was probably just a romantic impulse of the moment. To go off with that lunatic. It was unbelievable.

"Beth, you're a million miles away," said Aunt May, handing her a teacup.

"I'm sorry. What is it?"

"I sent James out to get those boxes out of your car."

"Good," said Beth absently.

"You're worried about Francie," said her aunt.

"I'll tell you, I'm more mad than worried. You should have seen the way he was acting yesterday. And she takes off with him anyway."

"Thank goodness you'll be getting her away from him. That's all I can say."

"Mmmm," said Beth. *I should call home again,* she thought. *Oh, the hell with her. If she wants to stay out all night with him, let her.* But her aunt's tea did little to soothe the angry, anxious knot that had formed in her stomach.

"Maybe I'd better just head home," said Beth, putting down the cup on the table. "I've still got things to do."

"I wish you'd stay," said Aunt May.

Beth thanked her. "If Francie should show up here," she said, "tell her I left—"

At that minute the phone rang. Beth jumped at the sound. Aunt May answered it and rushed back into the living room.

"It was for you," she said to Beth. "It was Francie. She's down at the police station. She wants you to pick her up."

Beth's heart leaped to her mouth. "What happened?"

"I don't know. She hung up."

Beth ran for the door, grabbing her coat in the hallway.

"I'm coming," said Aunt May, following her into the hall.

"No, no, you stay here. I'll call you. I promise."

"Call me right away," said May as Beth raced out the door. Uncle James, who was outside in his black

315

brimmed hat, locking up the shed where he kept the church donations, waved as Beth jumped in the car.

She imagined every kind of disaster on the ride to the station house. Drugs, robberies, car wrecks, and rapes jumbled together in her mind in a breathtaking array of possibilities. *At least it's not the worst,* she reminded herself. *She's alive.* The news report about the dentist and his wife sprang again to mind, but she pushed the thought away. There was no point in thinking about that.

Noah's tow truck was pulling into the parking lot at the police station at the same time that Beth arrived, the beam of its rooftop light flashing ghostly in the fog. Beth saw the stout ponytailed figure get out and go into the station as she was parking her car. She got out hurriedly and followed him into the station house.

The first person she saw when she came through the door was Francie, huddled in the corner of a wooden, pewlike bench beside the main desk. She looked around and saw Noah and Andrew conferring across the room. The police officer at the main desk was opening the wrapper on a packet of peanut butter crackers. He looked up at Beth.

"Could you close that door?" he asked. "It's a little chilly for air conditioning today."

"Sorry," said Beth. She went back and shut the door. At the policeman's words Francie looked up and saw Beth.

"Hi," she said, getting up from the bench. "Thanks for coming."

"What the hell is going on here?" Beth asked coldly.

Francie glanced nervously over at Andrew and Noah. "Andrew ran his car off the road. Luckily this policeman saw us and stopped."

At that moment Andrew spotted Beth and elbowed

Noah aside. "What's she doing here?" he demanded, striding across the cracked linoleum to where Beth stood.

"Get away from me," said Beth.

The cop came out from behind the desk. "Are you the sister?" he asked.

Beth nodded as Andrew turned on Francie. "How did she know you were here?" he demanded.

"I called her," said Francie wearily.

"What's the matter with you?" Andrew demanded loudly. "You know she's against us."

"Hold it, hold it," said the officer. He turned to Noah. "Are you the guy from the garage?"

Noah nodded. "We're gonna go get my buddy's car. I've got my tow truck right outside."

"All right. Well, why don't you just get going and do that?" the cop suggested, giving both Andrew and Noah a little shove toward the door.

Andrew turned back on Francie. "You know she'll do anything to stop us. What does it take to get through to you?" he growled.

Francie turned her face away from his, covering her eyes as if to shield them from too harsh a light.

"If I were you," said Beth, "I'd get out of here before that big mouth of yours gets you into more trouble than you bargained for."

"You shut up," Andrew snarled at her.

"All right now, that's enough," said the cop. "Get out of here. Go on. I don't want any more out of any of you."

Noah grabbed Andrew by the arm and started to drag him toward the door. Andrew stared back at the two sisters, his eyes bright with rage.

"He's insane," said Beth flatly.

"I know," said Francie.

"And you took off with him, so what does that make you?" Beth demanded.

Francie's mouth dropped open, and she shook her head.

"Okay, okay. Everybody go home now and get a good night's sleep."

"Let's go," said Beth irritably.

"Thank you," Francie said politely to the officer.

"Between you and me," said the cop, "I think your sister's right. He is bad news."

Francie nodded and followed Beth out into the parking lot. She hurried to catch up with her sister. "Look, Beth," said Francie as they reached the car, "I didn't go with him on purpose. He made me go with him."

Beth folded her arms across her chest. "I see," said Beth shortly. "How did he do that?"

Francie shook her head and threw open her hands. "I was just talking to him after the funeral. He got this new car, and he insisted on giving me a ride home in it. I wanted to make him feel better, so I went. Then he drove right by our house, and when I told him to stop, he said we were leaving town. He had his bag all packed and everything. It was just lucky for me that we had this accident and I was able to get away. I was running down the highway and this cop came by and he picked us up."

"So you're saying he kidnapped you," Beth said sarcastically.

"Really, yes, he did."

"Well, that's a crime, you know. Why didn't you tell the police that when they picked you up? Wouldn't that have been the obvious thing to do?" Beth's voice trembled with barely controlled anger.

Francie's eyes narrowed behind her glasses, and she

stuck her chin out. "Yeah, I should have. And I'm sure they would have acted just like you. I mean, he didn't use a weapon, and he's a friend of mine, and I got in his car of my own choice. I'm sure they would have been very understanding. Just like you."

Beth felt her face redden. She looked down and did not reply.

Francie jammed her hands in her pockets and shook her head. "I don't know why I called you. That was stupid. I thought you would take my side." She gave a short, harsh laugh, and then she spoke again, her voice quivering with anger. "You know, I'm beginning to wonder about this whole thing of going with you. Why should I have to try to convince you that I'm telling the truth? He could have hurt me out there. I didn't know what was going to happen—"

Beth put up a hand. "Wait," she said. "Wait a minute. Okay. You're right." She took a deep breath. "I thought—I don't know what I thought. I thought you were running off with him or something."

"I told you why I had to go to the funeral."

"I know you did."

"You didn't trust me," said Francie.

"I was . . . worried. Goddammit, I was really worried."

Francie nodded. They stood in silence for a moment. "No reason you should have trusted me, I guess," said Francie.

"It was him I didn't trust," said Beth. She shivered in the cold, damp air. "Let's get out of here," she said.

Francie nodded and got into the car. They drove home in silence, but the atmosphere between them was not tense. The sleeting rain had stopped, but the roads were still foggy, and Beth peered intently ahead as she drove, although her thoughts were not really on the road.

They reached the house, went inside, and turned on the lights. For the first time since they left the police station parking lot, Beth spoke. "Francie, I'm sorry about that misunderstanding. I mean it."

"That's all right," said Francie. "I can see why you thought that."

"I've been thinking about something else."

"What?" Francie pushed her glasses up on her nose and looked curiously at her sister.

"Andrew."

"What about him?"

"He's dangerous, Francie. I'm convinced of it. Especially after this incident today." She thought of mentioning the dentist and his wife and decided against it. There was no point in making an accusation like that. It was pure speculation, and it might just make the girl feel she had to defend him. "He's obsessed with this idea of getting you back. I don't think it's safe to be around him."

"He was bad this afternoon," Francie admitted.

"I was thinking about it on the way home. All day really. I don't think it would be wise to spend another night in this house."

"Do you think he'd try to get in?"

"I don't know what he'd try to do. I wouldn't put anything past him at this point."

"I don't think he's that bad," said Francie.

"I don't want to find out," said Beth. "Anyway, I think we should leave tonight."

"Tonight?" Francie mulled it over for a moment. "Well, we can't. Our plane's not until tomorrow, right?"

"What I'm thinking is that if we leave tonight, we

can drive down. You've got a lot of stuff to bring, and I think Dad's car can make the trip. It'll save Aunt May's having to mail all your stuff and dispose of the car. If we get tired, we can stop on the way and spend the night in a motel. What do you say?"

Francie's shoulders slumped as she looked around. "It's so sudden."

"It won't be any easier to leave tomorrow," Beth said.

Francie nodded. "There's a lot I still wanted to do."

Beth walked over to the window and looked out into the charcoal gray sky. "Every time I glance outside I think I'm going to see him there, circling us. Maybe I'm just imagining things. I hope I am. But why should we take a chance? For the difference of one night. The sooner I get out of here, the better I'm going to feel."

Francie sighed and looked sadly around the room. "You're right. It won't be any easier to leave tomorrow."

"It really won't."

"I guess it would be fun to stay in a motel."

"There you go," said Beth. "We'll make a good time out of it."

"All right," said Francie. "I'd better get busy."

"Good," said Beth, turning to the window and glancing out again. "Hurry."

Because they worked steadily, it did not take them long to do their remaining packing and get the house in order. Beth called her aunt and explained the new plan while Francie feverishly filled boxes with her things. Beth finally dragged the last of the suitcases down to the kitchen and called out for Francie. A voice answered from outside, behind the house.

Beth pulled on her jacket and went out. Francie was standing in the backyard, staring at the dilapidated old house, its lighted windows glowing in the night, the naked branches of the side yard trees arching over it.

"Finished?" Beth asked.

Francie nodded. "I already put my stuff in the car."

"The old place looks kind of cozy with those lights on in the dark, doesn't it?" said Beth.

Francie nodded but didn't speak.

"Maybe some nice family will get it and fix it up," said Beth. "It needs a little loving care."

"I hope so," said Francie in a thick voice.

"I think so," said Beth. They stood there in silence for a few moments. Then Beth said, "Come on. We'd better go."

"Good-bye, house," said Francie.

"I'll just get my bags in the kitchen," said Beth. "You get in the car."

Beth went back in the house and made one last check of windows and doors. Then she went back into the kitchen and picked up the two suitcases full of odds and ends she was bringing back. *Haul away*, she told herself.

Just as she passed the phone in the kitchen, it started to ring. Beth jumped. She turned and stared at the shrilly ringing phone, feeling a twisting in her stomach. It was him. She knew it.

The kitchen door opened, and Francie stuck her head in. "Do you want me to get that?" she asked. She walked over to the phone.

"No, don't," said Beth.

Francie looked at her in surprise, her hand poised over the receiver.

"Let it ring."

The two sisters looked long at each other as the insistent ringing came to a halt.

"Let's just go," said Beth. "Now."

Francie nodded and went out the kitchen door, slamming it behind her. Beth began to lug the heavy suitcases toward the door.

Just as she reached the door and turned the lights off in the kitchen, the ringing began again. Beth turned and looked at it, her eyes narrowed. "Go ahead and ring," she said. "Ring your bloody head off." She fixed the lock, slammed the door behind her, and hurried toward the waiting car.

Chapter 28

ANDREW hung up the receiver on the pay phone beside the men's room and went back into the garage through the office. Noah had the main doors of the garage closed against the cold.

He walked up to Noah, who had the hood of his old Pontiac open and was tinkering around with a wrench on the engine.

"What's the matter with it?" said Andrew.

"Well, I've got a pretty good idea, but I'm gonna have to put it up on the lift."

"Don't play games with me, Noah. Just tell me how long it's gonna take you to fix it."

Noah slammed the hood down and pointed inside the car. "Take your junk out if you want anything in there."

Scowling, Andrew opened the back door and removed the bag from the well behind the seat. He clutched the bag to his chest, imagining that he could feel the outline of the gun, which was in there, stashed among his clothes. The sight of the cop this afternoon, pulling up just as he had gotten hold of Francie, had practically made his heart stop. He was sure that the cop would search the car, go through his bag, and find the gun. They were probably looking for a gun now, a weapon that might have been used on the dentist and his wife. Luckily Francie had been good as gold. She had whimpered a little, but the cop assumed she was just upset about the accident. He hadn't even bothered to look in the car. Andrew set the khaki-colored duffel bag down on the cold cement floor of the garage, and Noah proceeded to activate the lift. Andrew watched in frustration as his new car left the ground.

"How'd you manage to do this anyway?" Noah asked as the car rose slowly up into the air.

"I told you. Some asshole truck driver ran us off the road. Me and Francie were leaving town."

"Mmmm . . ." said Noah. He stuffed his hands in the pockets of his coveralls and walked under the car. He squinted up at the grime-blackened workings on the Pontiac's underside. Then he rocked back and forth in his work boots. "That's what I figured," he said.

"You couldn't figure your way out of a paper bag," said Andrew. "Just cut the crap and tell me what it is."

"Well, if you're so smart, you tell me," said Noah.

"Do you know or don't you?" Andrew asked.

"Yep. It looks to me like you hit a rock when you went off the road."

"Brilliant," said Andrew.

Noah pointed upward. "See that? You've got no fluids. That's why the car won't start. When you hit the rock, you tore off the oil pan, and all the oil drained out. And the transmission pan is hanging on by a thread. All the fluid's gone from there too."

"All right, all right," said Andrew. "Can you fix it?"

Noah sighed. "Well, it can be fixed. I don't know if you want to put that kind of money into an old car like this. It'll cost you almost what you paid for the car."

"I didn't ask for your opinion. I asked if you can fix it."

Noah shook his head. "You're a nice guy, Andrew."

"Oh, Mr. Sensitive." Andrew looked down at his camp watch. "Just tell me how long it's going to take. Francie and I want to get on the road again. She's waiting for me. I've got to let her know what time we can get going."

Noah laughed. "What time? Oh, you can forget the watch. Try looking at a calendar."

Andrew stared at him.

"I've got to order the pans. For a car this old I'll be lucky if I can even locate them. It'll take them maybe two or three days to come in. Then I've got to fix the thing."

"Use pans you have here."

"I don't have any here. It's a special order. I'm telling you. I wouldn't lie to you about it."

"Can't you fix the simplest thing without all this crapping around?" Andrew shouted.

"You wanna fix it?" Noah asked.

Sweat broke out on Andrew's forehead, and he looked at his watch again. Then he looked down at the duffel bag. "I can't wait," he said. "I need it now."

"I'm sorry," said Noah. "That's the way it is."

A car horn sounded out by the gas pumps. "I've got a customer," said Noah. "You decide what you want to do. I'll be right back."

Noah stumped away across the garage as Andrew stared up at the metal underbelly of his car. It was black and broken, and for a moment Andrew had the ugly sensation that it was like looking inside himself. "Why don't you work, you fucking piece of junk? One goddamn day, not even. That's all you were good for," he muttered. The frustration seemed to be filling his throat, choking him. His means of escape hung there above him, useless as a severed limb.

For a moment the anger left him, and weariness rushed in, like a tide into an empty inlet. They were sure to catch him now. Someone would remember seeing him in Harrison. Maybe someone on the bus, that woman with the bratty kid maybe, had watched him when he left the bus, watched him turn up the walk to Ridberg's house.

The bitch was probably thinking about it right now. Figuring that as soon as she got that snotty kid to bed, she would call the cops and tell them. She'd probably seen it on the news about the murders, and being nosy and thinking she was smart, she'd put two and two together. She'd describe him to the cops, and once the Oldham police got wind of it, they'd remember him from this afternoon.

Fear crashed over him, and he thought he could hear a woman's mocking laughter inside his head. He shouldn't have killed the dentist. It was stupid. He hadn't meant to. But the wife had driven him to it. His eyes turned hard as he remembered her pink, quivering face.

But then he straightened his shoulders a little. A flash of defiance returned. It had felt good. Good to see that self-righteous little sow cower at the sight of his gun. His face broke into a wintry grin as he recalled the fear in her eyes.

Well, it was not too late, he thought. He still had his gun. He could still get Francie, and she would stand by him. They'd get away from the cops somehow. If he had to kill them all, they would.

Noah opened the side door to the garage and came back in. He walked over to where Andrew stood and glanced up at the mangled underside of the car. "So," he said, "Francie's waiting for you to come and get her. That's why you're in such a hurry to get this fixed, right?"

Andrew bristled at the smug tone of Noah's voice. "That's what I said."

"Well, that's funny," said Noah, bending over his toolbox and selecting a screwdriver. He stood up and began poking at the transmission pan, prying it loose. " 'Cause she and her sister were just here, filling up their car. Seems they're on their way to Philadelphia. Leaving tonight, they are. The both of them."

Shock jolted through Andrew like an electrical charge. "What?"

"Yeah. The car was piled high with suitcases."

"She can't do that."

"Well, she was doing it." Noah poked at the car again. "Seemed pretty happy about it too."

Andrew did not reply.

"Anyway, about the car," said Noah, "now that I'm looking at it again, it looks like you tore a hole in the exhaust system too. I can fiddle with that while we wait for the pans to arrive. As I said, it'll take two or three days. Then a day to put the pans in. But I don't know if it's worth it really. I can't recommend it. Even if I give it to you at cost, it's too much money to put into a car this old. It's up to you."

He looked out from under the car at Andrew, who was staring fixedly at the doors of the garage.

Chapter 29

"**Y**OU'RE awfully quiet," said Beth as she drove along one of the two-lane highways leading out of Oldham.

"I know," said Francie.

"It's hard leaving a place you lived in all your life."

"Was it hard for you when you left?"

Beth hesitated. "It was different. I wanted to get away. You've been kind of pushed out before you were ready. But yeah, in a way it was strange for me too. I didn't know what to expect. I felt a little like I was stepping off the edge of the world."

"Yeah," said Francie in a small voice.

"You'll be surprised how fast a new place can start to seem like home, though."

"Maybe. I hope so." Francie was quiet for a few moments. Then she went on. "It's not like I was so happy there all the time. But I knew everybody and and where everything was. . . ."

Beth could hear tears in Francie's voice, and she had

the impulse to interrupt, to try to change the subject, but she stopped herself. *Let her talk if she needs to,* she thought. She murmured, as if to encourage the girl.

"The house and school." Francie went on. "I don't know how I'll get along with the other kids there in Philadelphia. They'll probably think I'm some kind of hick and won't speak to me."

Beth felt as if she were experiencing every one of Francie's fears as the girl enumerated them, and a little sense of panic rose in her. "Don't worry," she said, as much to reassure herself as Francie. "It'll take a little time to adjust, but it'll all work out. It'll be easier than you think."

"I guess so," said Francie, her voice a little less shaky. After a few minutes she said, "Did you get that headstone for Dad?"

"Uh, no," said Beth slowly. "I didn't. I had a problem there."

"Didn't you find the place?"

"I found it all right. There was nobody there to help me when I arrived."

"Did you wait for somebody to come?"

"Nooo," said Beth. "That is, I waited a little while, but—the truth is that while I was waiting I started getting concerned about you and Andrew, and I decided to come back."

"Just like that. All of a sudden?"

Beth chewed her lip for a second. "It was because of something I heard on the radio. It was silly, I guess. It's not important now. Anyway, I figured I could ask Aunt May to pick out something and send me the bill. I'm sorry I didn't get it."

"That's okay," said Francie in a doleful tone.

"Speaking of the radio, do you want some music?" Beth asked with forced brightness.

"Sure," said Francie. She leaned over and fiddled with the dial until she found a music station. She sat back in her seat as if she were relaxed. Beth looked over at her out of the corner of her eye. Francie's eyes were weary, but her hands were clasped tensely together. Beth felt as if the mention of Andrew's name had summoned his presence between them, and the song that blared out of the radio did not dispel it.

"It's been a rough day," said Beth.

Francie nodded. "That's the truth."

"You know," said Beth, leaning over and turning down the radio volume, "I'm still feeling a little guilty about today and accusing you of going off with Andrew."

"I didn't want to go anywhere with Andrew," said Francie.

"I know. The point is, we're going to be living together now, and I'm going to try not to jump to any conclusions like that. I mean, I should have given you the benefit of the doubt." Beth gave a shaky laugh. "You'll have to be a little patient with me."

"I think you'll turn out all right," said Francie.

Beth smiled. They lapsed into silence, the radio playing softly between them. Beth peered out at the road ahead. It was still foggy, but at least the sleet had stopped, although the road remained a little icy. Once they hit Route 95, it was a clear shot to Philadelphia, or at least to a motel room somewhere in Connecticut. Meanwhile, she had to negotiate a series of two-lane highways, some of them in a rather pitted condition. There was no problem in staying alert, she thought. Her nerves were jangled after the day's upheavals and the rush to get on the road. *Take it easy*, she reminded herself. *You're on your way home.* She had a sudden image of herself opening the front door of the house, the warmth of it rushing over her as she ushered Francie inside and closed the door behind them. She thought that maybe she'd build a fire in the fireplace when they got in tomorrow. It would be lovely to relax in front of a fire, the flames dancing cheerfully in the grate.

As if to echo her thoughts, a flashing yellow light caught her eye. She looked up into the rearview mirror and saw that the vehicle with the flashing light was behind them, coming up rapidly on their tail.

Francie sat up and noticed it too. "It's the cops," she said.

"I'm afraid so," said Beth. She looked down at her speedometer. "I wasn't speeding," she said.

"Maybe it's not for us," said Francie.

"Maybe," said Beth, "but there's nobody else around." She kept driving, her hands tense on the wheel, but when she glanced up in the mirror again, the flashing light was still on their tail.

"It's too big to be a police car," said Francie.

"Must be one of those vans."

"They do patrol these roads," said Francie. "Thank goodness. But what did we do?"

"Nothing that I know of." Beth sighed. "I'd better pull over. See what he wants."

Beth put her right blinker on and eased the car slowly over to the shoulder. She jerked the gearshift into park as they stopped. "What a pain in the ass," said Beth, but her voice had a nervous edge. "They make you feel guilty even when you haven't done anything."

"I know," said Francie.

The police vehicle stopped some ways behind them.

Beth opened her purse and hunted for her license. Then she gasped and looked at Francie. "I hope the registration is in the car. I never even bothered to look. Open that glove compartment."

Francie pushed the button, and the metal door dropped down. She looked around inside, rummaging in the collection of objects stored there. "What does it look like?"

"It'll probably be in an envelope with a window."

"I can't find it."

"Let me look," said Beth. She leaned across the seat and peered into the lighted cavity. "Oh, shit," Beth muttered. "Where is it? Don't tell me it was somewhere in all those papers. Shit. I knew I'd throw out something important."

Francie sat up and looked back over the seat. She could see the man from the parked vehicle walking up to their car. She frowned and said, "Don't they usually wear hats?"

"Got it," said Beth, sitting up in the seat and rolling down the window.

The man's left hand curled over the half-opened window. He bent over and stared into the car. In his right hand he held a gun. Francie screamed, and Beth looked up and saw glittering eyes and a frozen smile. "Andrew," she whispered.

For a second she was paralyzed. Then instinct forced her to move. She jammed her left elbow down on the door lock, turned on the ignition, and stomped on the gas. The car jerked forward, and Andrew's hand smashed into the window frame. He seemed to fall away from the car. Beth did not look back, but she heard Francie cry out, "He's gonna shoot."

Almost as soon as the words were out Beth heard a crack and thud from the gun, and the back window of the car exploded. The wheel turned crazily in her hands as he fired again, and she tried to steer away from him. The car began to skid on the icy road, and she saw a tree appear in her headlights and heard the crunch of metal as the impact of the collision threw her back against the seat, bumping her head on the roof of the car.

For a second she sat there, stunned, as if she still expected the car to be in motion. Her hands, sweaty and weak, gripped the wheel. She looked over at Francie, who was holding onto the seat as if she were on a roller coaster, her eyes wide behind the lenses of her glasses. Their eyes locked in shared dread. He was beside them again, the barrel of the gun poking through the window.

"Open the fucking door," he said. "And get out."

For a moment Beth hesitated, trying to think of an alternative. But the gun barrel mocked her, assuring her of her impotence. "I have to do it," she said, half to Francie, half to herself.

Francie nodded.

I knew it, Beth thought. *I knew he was crazy.* It was no comfort. Slowly she opened the door and, with leaden limbs, pushed herself out of the car.

"You, too, babe," he said to Francie.

Francie got out, her eyes trained on his face.

"We're going back to my truck," he said. "Move it."

"Someone will see our car," said Francie.

"So they'll see your car. You had an accident and you left it there. Just like we did this afternoon. No one will care."

Francie gave him a baleful look and joined Beth, who was slumped against the back of the car.

"Get going," said Andrew, gesturing with the gun.

"Don't wave that thing," Beth muttered.

"What?" said Andrew.

"Come on." Francie urged her.

They walked back toward the vehicle parked by the side of the road. As they approached it, Francie exclaimed, "That's the tow truck from Noah's."

"That's right," said Andrew with a satisfied smile. "Fooled ya." He poked the gun into Beth's ribs, and she lurched forward.

"Did you steal it from him?" Francie asked.

"I borrowed it."

"He would never lend that truck to you. You stole it, didn't you?"

"No," said Andrew. "I convinced him to give it to me as a present. With this." He brandished the gun.

"He'll call the police," said Francie.

Andrew's eyes had a vacant expression. "No, he won't. He won't be calling anyone."

"Did you hurt him?" Francie asked.

"Don't even talk to him," Beth whispered.

"Don't tell her what to do," Andrew screamed at Beth, poking the gun in her cheek.

Beth felt the cold metal on her flesh, pressing up against her teeth. Her stomach flipped over.

"You've told her what to do for the last time," said Andrew. "I knew when I saw you what you were like. Bossing her around. Thinking you owned her. Well, we'll see who owns her. Get in the truck," he said. He indicated the driver's seat to Beth. "You're driving."

Slowly Beth pulled the door open and climbed in. Andrew turned to Francie. "Come on." He steered her around to the other side.

Beth sat in the cab, staring numbly at the dashboard of the truck. "I can't drive one of these," she said. "I've never driven one."

The passenger door opened, and Andrew climbed

in, pushing Francie ahead of him. He dragged her onto his lap and forced her head down. "You'll drive it," he said. "It's not that different from driving a Volkswagen when it's not towing anything. Now move it. Make a U-turn. We're going back this way."

Beth turned on the ignition and fumbled anxiously with the stick shift, her foot sliding on the clutch. She looked both ways, but there was no one coming. She pulled out and around for the U-turn. The truck bucked and stalled as she lifted her foot too quickly off the clutch.

"Be careful," Andrew screamed. "You don't want this to go off accidentally." He pressed the gun to Beth's side.

Beth licked her lips and shook her head. Where was he taking them? she wondered. It was like a nightmare come to life. Slowly she put the truck back in gear and eased up on the clutch as she gave it gas. The truck started to roll down the highway.

"We're by the lake," said Francie.

"That's right. By our place," said Andrew.

Beth felt her palms sweat on the wheel. *What place?* she thought. She tried to force herself not to panic. He was still holding the gun on her while he stroked Francie's hair with his free hand. Beth wet her lips again and spoke in a shaky voice. "Andrew, listen," she said, "there's no need for this. We're not strangers. We can talk this over, and no one will be hurt."

"That's far enough," Andrew cried. "Turn off here. And shut up. Go down that dirt road."

Beth hesitated, unable to see the dirt road in the darkness.

"Go," Andrew shrieked.

"I can't see it," Beth cried.

Andrew leaned over and grabbed the wheel, turning it sharply to the left. The truck jerked sideways and slid across the road. As they were upon it, Beth saw the entrance and straightened the wheel out just in time to ease them off the highway. The truck bumped along down the path, the headlights picking up the bare trees and bushes as they crunched over rocks and fallen branches.

"Sure, you want to talk it over," said Andrew, a sneer in his voice. "Well, no wonder. You think you can talk your way out of what's waiting for you. That's a good joke. I'd want to talk it over, too, if I were you. But I'll tell you a secret. You've got nothing left to say."

Beth tried to ignore his words and concentrate on the dirt pathway. *Maybe someone will come along,* she thought. *Please, someone, come along. Please.*

"Stop here," he said. "All right now, get out. You, too, babe."

While Beth and Francie climbed down from the truck, Andrew reached behind the seat and pulled out a large spool of wire and some wire cutters. He jumped down from the cab and cut off a length of wire, which he handed to Francie.

"Here," he said, "twist this around her wrists good and tight."

Beth could see that Francie did not want to take the wire. Andrew shook it at her, and Francie's terror-filled eyes met Beth's. Beth held out her wrists. "Behind her back," Andrew growled.

Slowly Francie began to wind the wire around her sister's hands. "Tight," Andrew ordered. "I want it to hurt. And hurry."

Francie did as she was told. She wrapped the wire around Beth's hands and twisted the ends together. Andrew came over and twisted it several more times, making Beth cry out in pain. Francie stifled a protest by putting her fist to her mouth.

Andrew smiled at Francie. "Good job," he said. "Now you're going to have to get back up in the cab."

Francie glanced fearfully at Beth and then climbed back up into the truck.

"That's far enough," said Andrew. After tucking the gun in his belt, he unrolled several other lengths of wire and then snipped them off. He threw the wire clippers under the truck and then wired Francie's hands and feet. "Sorry, babe," he whispered. "It will be for only a little while."

"What are you doing?" Francie cried.

"I'll be back soon. I have to take your sister with me. I have to punish her for all she's done."

"She didn't do anything, Andrew," Francie whimpered. "Don't hurt her. Please don't. Let me come along with you. I don't want to stay here alone."

Andrew laughed indulgently. "I won't be gone long. Then you and me can get going."

Francie squirmed away from him. "I don't want to go anywhere. Where are you taking Beth?"

"Stay here, Francie," Beth said in a shaky voice. "I'll be all right." The words sounded hollow. Beth felt as if her stomach were being twisted on a skewer.

"Don't tell her what to do," Andrew cried. He pulled out the gun and whacked Beth in the face with the butt. Beth heard a crack in her cheekbone and felt it throb.

Andrew took a handkerchief from his pocket and used it to gag Francie. Then he pushed her down on the seat of the cab. "Stay here, and I'll be right back." He reached back behind the seat and pulled out the duffel bag. Slinging it over his shoulder, he slammed the truck's door, locked it, and dropped the keys into his pocket.

Francie struggled up in the seat.

"Go on," said Andrew. "Move." He pushed the gun to Beth's back, and she fell forward. She took a breath of the cold, damp night air, and it felt like a stabbing in her chest. Looking back, she saw Francie's face pressed to the window, her eyes frantic, her mouth held down and open by the filthy gag.

"Hurry up," said Andrew, shoving her forward. She stumbled and then regained her balance. She kept on walking.

Chapter 30

ANDREW unzipped the duffel bag and pulled out a flashlight. He switched it on, but he kept it trained on his own path, leaving Beth to negotiate her way in the dark. He nudged her as she went, and she slipped and slid on the icy surface of decaying leaves, occasionally tripping across the branches that littered the rutted path. Every so often she would be smacked square in the face by the low-hanging branches because she could not use her hands to shield her face.

As she stumbled along, she felt her heart thud loudly in her chest, but it was from fury as much as fear. She was furious at herself for having stopped the car, for having fallen for his trick. They had been in the police station just this afternoon, and she could have pressed charges against him for kidnapping and had him locked up. And if she had, she would not be here, at the mercy of this madman with a gun. She thought that if she'd had her hands loose, she could actually kill him. She had never felt that sensation before. But even as she thought that, she realized that it was more likely he would kill her. Perhaps very soon.

She tried to calm herself, to assess the situation and think clearly. *He is dangerous, it's true,* she thought. *And you can't hurt him. But you may be able to outwit him. You are a lot smarter than he is. You have to think of something.*

They broke through the woods into a clearing and came out upon the lake. Its slick surface shone in the moonlight. Andrew switched off his flashlight. About fifty feet from shore Beth saw a small house with a bridge leading out to it. Otherwise, there were no buildings or any signs of life around the lake's dark perimeter. She felt Andrew step up behind her and thrust the gun into her back. His warm, sour breath befouled the clean night air.

"Across the bridge," he said. "Go on."

Okay, Beth thought. *Maybe he is going to leave me here. Maybe I can talk him into that. But then he'll go back and get Francie.* The thought of Francie's being forced to go with him made her feel physically sick. He prodded her in the back with the muzzle of the gun.

"I'm going," said Beth. The touch of the gun made her blood run cold, but she also felt, with a shaky hopefulness, that he was not necessarily going to kill her. He seemed calm and pretty rational under the circumstances. If he were going to shoot her, he probably would have done it at the car. *Play your cards right,* she thought. *Your life may depend on it.*

They reached the doorway of the skating house, and Andrew held her by the arm as he pushed back the bolt that secured the door of the little hut. He had stuffed the gun in his belt, and Beth stared down at it. She pictured herself kicking him, trying to knock him over and run, but caution warned against it. Her hands were bound, and he did have a gun. If she tried to attack him, he might lose his cool and shoot her after all. *No,* she thought, *the only hope is to try to reason with him.* If she could convince him, and he ended up leaving her there, she would be able to get out eventually. It was Francie she was really worried about. Once he took off with her, there was no predicting what he might do.

"Andrew," said Beth as calmly as possible, "I know you see me as the enemy, and I know you think I'm trying to come between you and Francie, but I want you to know it's not true. I'm just concerned about her, and I want her to be happy just as you do. I think if we could just talk it over, we could find a good solution for all of us." Her mouth was dry after her short speech.

Andrew pushed the door open and looked inside. Then he reached out and shoved Beth as hard as he could into the house. Beth tried to keep her balance, but he had caught her off guard, and she did not have the use of her arms. She pitched forward and landed on the floor of the skating house, scraping her face against the cold, rough floor. For a minute she just lay there, her face bleeding, her arms aching. She half expected to hear the door slam shut behind her, to be left alone like a prisoner in a dungeon. Instead, she heard him enter the room and drop his duffel bag down on the floor.

Beth hesitated for a moment, and then, with all her strength, she pulled herself up and faced him, resting her back and her numb, bound hands against one of the walls.

He was crouched down over the duffel bag, rummaging around inside it. She could see that he was removing some items from the bag, but she could not tell what they were in the darkness.

Try again, she told herself. *Don't give up. Try to get him to talk to you. He's a human being. He has feelings. Appeal to him. Give him a chance to be the hero.* She could feel a vein throbbing in her neck, visible evidence of her fear if he chose to look.

"This isn't the way it should be, Andrew," she said gingerly. "You're an intelligent, sensitive person. I've heard a lot of good things about you. You're not the kind of guy who is going to keep a couple of helpless women tied up and make them suffer, no matter how unfairly you've been treated in the past. The future can be very different for you."

Andrew rocked back on his heels and looked around the skating house. "This is our place," he said. "Me and Francie. I found this place for her."

Fine, Beth thought. *Okay. You pick the topic.* She felt a flicker of hope. *Whatever you want to talk about.* "It's a nice place," she said. "No wonder you were so happy here."

Andrew's head snapped around, and he looked at her with narrowed eyes. "How do you know what we did here?"

"I don't," said Beth hurriedly. "I never even knew of this place. I just know that Francie was happy when she was with you. And I assume some of those happy times were—"

"Nobody ever comes here," he said. "That's what I always liked about the place. We had it all to ourselves. No intruders."

Beth closed her eyes for a second and licked her dry lips. She struggled to keep her voice steady. "It's good to have a place of your own."

Andrew came over to where Beth sat and studied her for a moment. Beth tried to keep her breathing shallow and even, although the smell which emanated

343

from him made her feel like gasping. Suddenly he reached behind her and unwrapped the wire from her wrists.

Beth felt the wires loosen on her hands and then come off. She looked at him wonderingly as he pulled her freed hands forward. She forced herself to remain as still as possible, so as not to alarm him with any sudden movement or loud exclamation. *It's working,* she thought. *Thank you, God. Maybe he just wanted to scare me.* She squeezed her hands slowly open and shut, trying to get the blood circulating again. "That feels better," she said softly.

Andrew reached into his belt, pulled out the gun, and trained it on her without speaking for a moment. His eyes were flat black in the darkened room. "Unzip your jacket," he said abruptly, "and take off your shirt."

Beth closed her eyes and felt the room start to spin around her as if she had been punched in the stomach. *Oh, Lord, no, not that.* It had not even occurred to her. A flash of hatred for him jolted her like a lightning bolt.

"Hurry up," he said, waving the gun. "Do it."

"Andrew," she said in a voice strained through clenched teeth, "this is enough. Stop this, now." Angry tears were forming behind her eyes, but she willed them back.

"Go on," he shouted.

Beth's hands balled into fists, and she glared at him, but he leveled the gun at her head. She hesitated, and then, with leaden fingers, she unzipped her jacket and removed it. The temperature in the skating house was near freezing, but she could feel sweat breaking out all over her.

"Now the blouse and the pants. Everything. Come on," he insisted.

She undid the top two buttons and then stalled at the middle button, pretending not to be able to free it. Andrew's hand shot out like a hook and ripped the blouse open. Beth jumped back and stared at him. "I'll do it," she cried.

"Do it fast," he said, his sharklike eyes fastened on her.

She did not hesitate further. There was no way out of it. She knew he was capable of using the gun. He had already proved it tonight. She tried to pretend to herself that she was at a doctor's office, undressing in front of an uninterested stranger. She felt a little cry form at the back of her throat as she pulled off her jeans and crouched before him in her underwear. She forced the cry down and waited for him to order her to remove her underwear. Her head was pounding now, but she told herself that she could survive this. She tried not to think of him pressing himself against her, penetrating her. The idea of it caused bile to rise to her throat.

The order to remove her underwear did not come. She stole a look at Andrew and saw that the expression in his eyes had not changed. There was no lust or desire on his face, only an implacable look of loathing. He pointed to the pile of her clothes on the floor beside her. "Those are very messy," he said. "Pile them up neatly."

Beth looked at him in disbelief. "What?" she asked.

"Fold them in a neat pile," he ordered.

Beth shook her head and then saw that he was serious. She did not want to unwrap her arms from her chest, to expose herself further to his view. She turned away from him and then scuttled over as quickly as possible to the strewn garments and folded them with rapid, economical movements.

"Good," he said. "Now turn around and put your hands behind you again."

Beth knelt beside the clothes, her head bent, her whole body shuddering from the chills. "No," she said, a catch in her voice.

"No?" Andrew repeated incredulously.

"Andrew, you have to stop this. Don't do this. This is a crime, Andrew. If you leave now, if you just leave me here, you won't be in trouble," she pleaded with him.

"I told you to put your hands back," he growled. With that he grabbed her right arm and wrenched it behind her. Beth felt her arm snap back like a twig. She put the other one back behind her and felt him wrap the wire back around her wrists. Then he pushed her back against the wall.

This is it, she thought, steeling herself. *Here it comes. Oh, God.* She closed her eyes and waited. *Try to think of other things,* she told herself. *Try to pretend that this is not your body. If he has his way with you, he may just leave. Think of what you'll do after he leaves. How you'll get out of here.* She did not want to think about how long she could survive before hypothermia set in. *I'll keep moving,* she told herself. *I'll get the clothes wrapped around me somehow. And then I'll get free.*

She could hear him rummaging around, but she did not look. She did not want to see him approach her. *Let it be fast,* she thought.

He was beside her now, his breath fetid on her face. *You can take it,* she thought. *Picture yourself getting revenge.*

Even as she thought it, she heard his voice close to her ear. "Time to wash up," he said.

346

Beth's eyes flew open, and she stared at him, as he leaned back on his heels. In front of him were a Thermos, a dirty rag, and a bar of soap. She watched in horrified amazement as he poured some water out of the Thermos onto the rag and wiped it perfunctorily across the soap. Then he looked up at her. The expression in his eyes was all the more frightening for being so very detached. He reached the rag out toward her face.

Beth cringed, and her flesh crawled as the tepid water on the rag touched her cheek.

"It may be too late for this," he said. "You've brought so many germs into this place it may be contaminated. This place already smells from your being here. We have to wash you first. Clean you. Hold still."

He rubbed the rag across her face in a rough, circular motion and then began moving down her neck. Once he stopped and wet the rag again from the Thermos.

"You were raised like a pig," he said. "I was raised the right way. I was always clean. I did as I was told. 'Don't speak, stay here, be clean. And no one will ever have to know. I'll protect you from them. If they catch you, they'll put you away in a dark prison. Things will crawl over you in the night.' But do you know what?"

Beth shook her head. He was rubbing her flesh as if he were sanding it with the rag, his eyes intent on his task. But his words made no sense. He seemed to have slipped over the edge. "Here's the joke." He laughed. "I was already in prison, and I didn't know it."

His spittle landed on her cheek as he spoke, and his eyes were lit by some inner madness. She realized, watching him, that there would be no reasoning with him, no compromising with his plan. She was shivering uncontrollably, the water on her skin evaporating in the frigid air and turning her skin blue.

"Now," he said, "this is what you want to do to Francie, and it's up to me to save her from you. She has to be free of you."

He pushed the strap of her bra off her shoulder. "I'll take this off," he said calmly as he ran the rag down the slope of her chest.

Beth felt everything in her recoil from that hand, which slithered like a snake across her breast. She knew in that instant that she could not just submit to it. No matter what happened. She jerked her shoulder out from under his grasp. "Get away from me," she shrieked at him. "No!" The revulsion came in waves, loosening itself in screams. "You're crazy. Don't touch me." He rocked back, shocked for a moment, and then he reached out and hit her, as hard as he could, across the face.

Suddenly he gasped. "Quiet," he snarled. Beth opened her eyes and saw him pick up the gun and hold it trembling in his hand as he stared at the door, and they both heard the sound of footsteps coming across the bridge.

Beth hesitated for a moment, then she cried out, "Help." Andrew turned on her in fury, and they both heard the growl outside, followed by insistent barking on the other side of the door.

Andrew's stiffened body relaxed, and then his chalky face broke into a malevolent smile. The dog rooted around the door for a minute, continuing to bark. Then, frustrated by the lack of response, it retreated back across the bridge. Andrew ran to the door and opened it a crack, peering out.

"He's gone," he said.

Beth slumped back, her fleeting moment of hope

crushed. Andrew turned a vicious smile on her. "Help." He mimicked her. "Asking a dog for help. Very good." He shone the flashlight on her face, which was bruised from where he had struck her earlier. Beth winced and tried to turn away from the blinding beam of light.

"Disappointed?" Andrew asked. "You shouldn't be. I told you nobody ever comes here."

Beth leaned back and closed her eyes again, trying to block out the sight and sound of him. She licked her lips and heard him put the gun and the flashlight back down on the floor. Then she heard something else. Without opening her eyes she said, "What's that?"

"What?" he said.

"Listen."

She gazed boldly at him, and in that moment he heard it. It was a faint, blaring noise, long, steady, and shrill. It cut through the quiet night like a high-pitched foghorn.

It took a moment to register, and then he jumped up. "That bitch," he said. "She's leaning on it. What is she trying to do?"

"She's trying to get help," said Beth.

Andrew kicked into Beth as hard as he could, and she fell sideways on the floor. He grabbed her scarf from the pile of clothes and jammed it into her mouth. "She can't do this to me," he said. He ran from the hut, stopping just long enough to shoot the bolt behind him.

Chapter 31

*T*HE cold rose through the floor, and Beth felt as if she were lying on the icy surface of the lake itself. Everything in her ached with a deep, threatening kind of pain, as if it would overcome her if she moved. She heard his footsteps pounding across the bridge as he headed back toward the truck and Francie.

At the thought of Francie her heart felt as if it were being squeezed, and hot tears spurted from her eyes and trickled down her cheeks. He would be enraged when he reached her. There was no predicting what he might do. Francie had betrayed him, called for help, refused to obey. It was treason. The thought of those maddened eyes turned on Francie sent a shudder through Beth's body that had nothing to do with the cold. She struggled to pull her hands apart, and the wire burned into her wrists. She wondered if Francie knew the danger she was in. He would be coming after her, ready to kill. Maybe someone would hear the horn and rescue her. It was the only hope.

Beth could picture Francie there, leaning on the horn, her glasses resting on the end of her nose, that defiant look on her face. It was a look she had often turned on Beth those first days, a look that could infuriate her. She had labeled it petulance and snottiness. Now she recognized it as Francie's shield. It was her armor against a life that constantly hurt her. She was like a little guerrilla fighter, determined not to give in to the extraordinary woes that life seemed to hurl at her. And that one, unreadable expression was her badge of grit.

Beth marveled for a moment at her sister's bravery. Alone and defenseless in that truck, she had acted, not just waited to see what would happen. She had waved a red flag at the bull, knowing that she would enrage the beast and knowing she could not protect herself against him. But she wasn't just going to sit and wait for the ax to fall. She had chanced it.

Through her tears Beth felt a rush of pride in her sister that transcended even her fear. She wished she could shout to the world, "This is my sister. She did not just give in." But in the next moment a wave of hopelessness crashed over her as she acknowledged the danger they were in. They would probably not even survive to whisper it, much less to shout it.

The door of the skating hut rattled, and Beth heard the bolt slide back. She jerked up from her slumped position. He couldn't be back already. The horn was still blaring. The door was pushed open, and moonlight illumined the slight, bespectacled figure in the doorway, moonbeams glistening on her ash blond hair.

Beth stared at her for a moment and then tried to say her name, but she made only a gurgling sound through the wad of scarf in her mouth.

"Beth?" Francie glanced back over her shoulder

and then rushed in and pulled the scarf from Beth's mouth. "Oh, my God. What did he do to you? Are you okay?"

Beth nodded. "I can't believe it. How did you . . ."

Francie pulled the wire clippers from her pocket and reached for Beth's wrists. "Hold still," she said. She clipped the wires off Beth's hands and then gathered up the pile of clothes and handed them to Beth, piece by piece. "I didn't know what I'd find in here," said Francie. "I feel sick."

Beth rubbed her numbed wrists and then pulled on her shirt and jeans, which Francie had handed to her. "How did you get away? And the horn?" she whispered. "Oh, God, I'm so glad to see you."

"He didn't tighten the wire on me like he did on you. 'Cause he loves me, I guess," said Francie with a grim smile. "I hooked the wire over the door handle and wriggled my wrists out. While I was doing it, I accidentally beeped the horn, and that gave me an idea. When I got out, I wedged a stick between the seat and the horn, so it would keep on blowing."

"Brilliant," said Beth delightedly as she shrugged on her jacket. She grabbed Francie's hands to squeeze them and saw, even in the darkness, the bloody, abraded wrists. "Oh, Francie," she said. She lifted one of the wounded hands and pressed it to her own cheek.

"I came down the path," Francie continued, "and hid by the foot of the bridge. He passed me on the run. Didn't even see me. But we have to get out of here quick. He'll be back as soon as he finds it."

"You're right," said Beth.

"I think we should go out across the ice," said Francie. "I know this lake, and our car is over that way." She pointed in the opposite direction of the bridge. "We'll never get around the lake through the woods. He'd catch us. But if we cross the ice, we can get right to it."

"As the crow flies," said Beth. "Will the ice hold us? It's been raining."

"I think so," said Francie. "I was on it the other day, and it's pretty thick. Just a little thin around the edge."

"Let's try it," said Beth.

They slipped out the door, scanning the woods as they left, and then dropped down, one at a time, from the bridge to the little island that held the skating house. They scurried around to the back of the house and stared out across the lake.

"I hope it'll hold us," said Beth.

"It's better than being shot," said Francie.

Beth nodded. "Let's go."

Francie stepped out carefully on the ice. "It's okay," she whispered. Beth held out her arms for balance and followed her out. A faint, ripping sound below the surface made her stop dead, uncertain whether to go forward or back.

"Come on," Francie urged. "I told you the edge was thin. It's okay out here."

Beth took a deep breath and stepped out, like a sky diver stepping out of a plane. The ripping sound started again, but it ceased as she reached the spot where Francie waited.

Without another word they started across. The soles of their sneakers provided some traction, but Beth could feel her knees wobble beneath her as she tried to hurry along, sliding on the slick surface, guided only by the moonlight. The two of them were like comic dancers on a vast, empty stage, running with sideways steps, flailing their arms occasionally to keep their balance. *This would be fun,* Beth thought, *if it weren't so awful.* She looked over at Francie, who gestured in the direction that they had to go.

As she headed toward it, Francie slipped and landed with a cracking sound. Beth rushed to her, feeling as if she were wearing buckets on her feet. Beth tried to help Francie up but also slipped.

"It's a wet spot," said Francie. "Let's crawl."

On hands and knees they crawled across the slippery surface. Finally Beth was able to scramble to her feet, the flesh on her hands stinging as if it had been ripped off by the ice.

As she reached out to help Francie up she heard the sound of the car horn abruptly stop. The sisters looked at each other, wide-eyed in the dark. The silence around the lake was eerie. Beth shuddered. Francie pushed her glasses up on her nose. Then she stuck her chin out. "We're almost there," she said.

They were more than halfway to the bank of the lake. Clinging to each other's jacket sleeves, they hurried the rest of the way, adjusting their weight to balance themselves as they skidded along. They whispered encouragement and instructions to each other, each trying to keep the frantic note out of her voice.

"What do you think he'll do?" Francie asked, clutching Beth's sleeve as they neared the edge of the lake.

"Don't think about it," said Beth. "We're right there."

They hesitated for a second, looking at the bank. It was dark around the edge of the ice, and Beth felt queasy looking at it. "It doesn't look frozen," she said.

"I know," said Francie. She turned and glanced back toward the hut. "Look," she whispered.

The unsteady beam of a flashlight was visible bobbing across the bridge toward the skating house. They both watched it for a second. Then Francie turned and looked at the shore with a calm, assessing gaze. "It's not deep here anyway," she said.

Letting go of Beth, she made a few running steps and leaped out across the dark edge to the bank. She scrambled to her feet and held out her hand to Beth. "Hurry."

Beth crouched down and pushed herself off. One foot hit the ice with a splitting sound, but the other extended out and landed on the shore. She threw her weight forward and fell into the bank.

Francie helped her up. They looked back and saw the flashlight retreating across the bridge. "How far to the car?" Beth whispered.

"It's right up the hill through these woods. Not too far," said Francie.

"We'd better run," said Beth. "You know the way?"

Francie nodded and began to scramble up the bank. Beth followed right behind her, finding a foothold and rising to her feet. "I think we're okay now," said Beth.

"Oh, no, you're not."

The beam of a flashlight hit Beth full in the face. She threw a hand over her eyes as Francie stumbled back against her. They looked up to see Andrew's face, skull-like above the shaft of light. He held the gun trained on them. "Don't bother running," he said. "You're not going anywhere."

Chapter 32

T HE crazed satisfaction of victory was in his eyes. He had won the game. Their terror was his prize. He looked as if he would burst with the gruesome joy of it.

Beth and Francie stared in disbelief at the distorted, leering face. As they looked at him they heard a man's voice, thin and faint, drifting across the moonscape of the lake calling, "Mick, here, boy. C'mere, Mick."

Beth felt light-headed, as if she were going to faint. The flashlight on the bridge belonged to the man looking for his dog, the dog that had come sniffing around the skating house. She felt weak in all her limbs, and she could hear the beating of her pulse in her ears.

Andrew giggled as if he could read her thoughts. "It's such a nice bright night," he said. "The two of you made a pretty picture crossing the lake. I could see what you were up to right away. So I just went back to the truck, drove around to this side, and waited for you."

Beth felt as if someone were ringing a giant bell

inside her rib cage. No sound came out, but the clanging inside was shaking her. He had them now. This time he would not let them go.

Francie pushed her glasses up and spoke in a quavering voice. "Andrew, please stop doing this. Okay, I know you're really mad—pissed off, but please just stop this. You're really a nice person under all this." She started to edge toward him, holding out her hands.

Beth gasped as if she was watching her walk into the path of a rattler. But Francie paid no attention to her. "We can talk if you want. I still like you. You remember all the things we talked about. We can still do them."

He watched her approach him with unblinking, reptilian eyes, and Beth felt as if he were coiling back to strike as Francie unwittingly came closer, thinking she could pet him into submission.

"Come on, Andrew," Francie said. "You and I are close. We shouldn't be here like this."

"You cunt," he snarled. His hand flicked out and gripped her wrist. "I treated you like you were special. Different from the others. I should have known, the way you threw yourself at me like a whore. You're shit, just like the rest of them."

"We're friends, Andrew," Francie cried.

"Friends?" He said the word incredulously. "I have no friends. All I know are whores and creeps. Friends."

He shoved her away, and she fell on the ground. Beth crouched down to help her up, but Francie was already up on one elbow.

Andrew sneered down at them, relishing his moment of power. Beth felt revolted by him. All the power he had was in that gun. He was a weak, pathetic tyrant. But with the gun he held them captive, and she was sure that there was no mercy in him.

"I was thinking about a little pain for the two of you," he was saying. "I was hoping I could make it so bad for you that you would beg me to kill you. I'd like that. It would serve you two scheming bitches right."

Beth tried to stop the flow of his words from entering her head. She had to think, she told herself. She was still crouched down at his feet, supporting Francie. She looked at Francie's face. Her eyes were glassy, and her lips were white. Her mouth was hanging slack. Beth could feel the girl's body shaking with an uncontrollable tremor. The flashlight glared off her spectacles. Beth had the sudden realization that Francie might be going into shock. *It's all crashing in on her, crushing her. The mind has a way of withdrawing from unbearable pain.*

"I don't have time unfortunately." He was rambling on. "You see, they're going to be after me soon. They'll find Noah sooner or later. And that dentist and his ugly wife. I don't have a lot of time to fool with you two, although you deserve it the most. Next to my mother, of course."

He was confessing to murder, but his words had a strange, calming effect on Beth's mind. Suddenly everything was crystal clear to her. He was a killer on a rampage. There was nothing to speculate about, no hoping against hope. He was a killer, and he was proud of it, to judge from the tone of his voice. It made him feel good. She could feel Francie fading in her grasp. Francie was listening, thinking about what he was saying, and it was draining her.

Beth glanced up at him. The gun was pointed at her head. The man who was looking for his dog had long since gone on his way, and all was still and silent.

There was no help in sight and no doubt in her mind. Andrew was going to kill them. There was only this moment, and she had a simple choice: Sit still and be killed or try something, anything—no matter how reckless. At least try.

It was an easy choice now that she faced it. There was a sturdy-looking branch about a foot away from her. She studied it for a moment, picturing what she was going to do. She had read once that an athlete could improve his results by visualizing his performance just before the event. Beth went through the motions mentally. Then she took a breath, shoved Francie down with her left hand, and grabbed for the branch with her right. She swung it upward and smacked him in the hand with it as she followed through.

Andrew let out a cry of surprise as the gun flew up in the air, landed on the surface of the lake, and skittered across the ice. With a bellow of rage he tried to strike her, but Beth scuttled out of his way, dragging Francie. Andrew slid down the bank and lunged out onto the ice toward the gun. There was a loud, sharp crack and then a hoarse cry as the ice broke beneath the weight of his landing, and Andrew plunged down through the ice into the water.

Beth and Francie leaped up and scrambled down to the edge of the lake, galvanized by the sight of the black, jagged hole in the ice. Suddenly Francie started to scream. Andrew was crying out for help, pleading, although they could not see him.

"The flashlight," Beth mumbled. "Where is it?" She began to search the bank frantically, and then she laid her hand on it. She picked it up and clicked it on, sweeping the light over the surface. The light caught and rested on Andrew, who had bobbed up and managed to grip the slippery surface surrounding the hole he was in. He could not see them, but his eyes stared into theirs with an expression of the purest terror.

"Help," he screamed. "Help me."

Beth felt as if she were locked in place, staring at him as he hung there, clinging for his life to the sliding sheet around him.

"Oh, God," Francie whispered. She took a step out on the ice, and they suddenly heard a loud, splintering noise, and Andrew's anguished screams as the edge he was holding broke off and he sank below the surface.

"Oh, Christ," said Beth.

"Andrew," Francie screamed, wringing her hands. "Find him," she demanded.

Beth swept the beam of the flashlight out over the ice. They began to call out to him. The surface was slick and glassy, and the shadow play beneath the ice made it hard to determine where he was. But they could hear the bump of his body under the ice, the dull thudding as he pounded with his fists underneath and then sank back down.

"Give me that branch," said Francie.

Beth ran over and grabbed the branch she had used to knock the gun away. Francie snatched it from her and laid it down on the ice. "I'm going to try to reach him," said Francie. She crouched down and then stretched out on the icy surface and inched her way across to the black hole he had disappeared into.

"Don't," Beth screamed at her.

"He'll die. He's dying under there," Francie wailed.

Francie held the branch awkwardly in one hand and began to smash at the ragged edges of the hole, breaking it up and making the hole larger. All the while she called Andrew's name. Her hands went into the frigid water, but she pulled them out again and continued to flail away, making the hole larger.

"No," Beth screamed. "Come back." Beth trained the flashlight on her, screaming all the while. "It'll break. Leave him there." But Francie ignored her cries.

Suddenly, out of the black water, Andrew's arm shot up and groped for the edge. Francie threw the branch aside and caught his hand, pulling at him. "I got him," she cried.

Andrew's head came up out of the water, and he clung to Francie, but his soggy weight was much greater than hers, and as she started to scream, she slid toward the hole in the ice.

Beth shoved the flashlight in her pocket and crept out onto the ice. Flattening herself out on the surface, she crawled toward Francie and grabbed her out-stretched legs, pulling her back from the hole and lifting Andrew, who clung to her.

Desperately Andrew began to thrash, for he could not hoist himself in his waterlogged clothes out of the water. Suddenly, beneath the cries and the splashing, Beth heard the ominous cracking sound again. She tried to tug Francie back, but it was too late. The ice broke beneath her, and Francie plunged head and shoulders into the frigid blackness.

"Francie," Beth screamed, and tried to pull her out, but Andrew's weight was holding the thrashing girl down below the surface.

Then, in the darkness, Beth saw him emerge from the water. He was rising up, hand over hand on Francie's back, using her submerged upper body as a ramp, hoisting himself by grabbing fistfuls of her clothing as Beth held onto her sister's legs.

In the moonlit darkness Beth and Andrew were

only a few feet apart, Andrew straining to get his heavy, sodden-clothed body up and out while Francie struggled helplessly beneath the water. Beth watched his ascent over her sister's bent form for only a second, but it seemed like an eternity. Their eyes met in the darkness. He seemed unconscious of the fact that he was holding Francie down with his weight. His eyes glittered with determination. He might have been climbing up on a log.

In the next second Beth acted. Anchoring Francie's feet with one arm to her chest, she reached into her pocket and grabbed the flashlight she had used to find him. She lifted it up as high as she was able and cracked it down again and again with brutal force on Andrew's grasping hands.

"Oh, no, you don't, you bastard," she cried.

Shocked by the blows, Andrew let go of his hold on Francie and slid back with a shout of rage. Beth crawled forward, ready to smash him again, but he was sinking. With a strength she didn't know she had, Beth hauled her sister back from the hole as Andrew disappeared, howling, into the icy water.

Francie did not seem to be conscious, but Beth did not stop to be sure. Praying for the ice to hold, she dragged Francie slowly toward the edge and then, pulling her up under the armpits, hauled her off the ice to the bank as Francie's limp arms and hands brushed against her sides.

She laid the girl down and fell down beside her, cradling Francie's soaking head and shoulders on her lap. She bent over and listened to Francie's ragged breathing and then turned her head to the side and pumped down on her chest. Francie coughed and retched. Water spurted from her nose and mouth. Beth smoothed the wet matted hair off her face as

Francie continued to cough and then abruptly struggled to a sitting position and retched. She started taking deep breaths, and then her teeth began to chatter. Beth thumped gently on her back.

"I'm okay," Francie managed to stutter out.

Beth reached around her and tried to cover her with her own jacket.

"Are you sure?" Beth asked.

Francie nodded. "I guess so." She wiped her nose and then looked up at Beth. "Andrew?"

Beth glanced at the hole in the ice. There was no sound from it, and the surface was still. All traces of him were gone. Francie followed her gaze.

"Do you think he's dead?" she whispered.

"He must be," said Beth. "He must have drowned."

Francie began to shiver violently. She rocked back and forth, her arms wrapped across her chest.

"I had to," said Beth. "He would have drowned you."

"I know."

They huddled together on the bank, staring at the frozen lake. Finally Beth said, "We've got to get you somewhere warm."

"That s-s-s-ounds good," said Francie through chattering teeth.

"Can you walk?"

"I think so." Francie got up unsteadily and leaned against Beth, who held out an arm to encircle her. Slowly she urged Francie forward.

Francie reached up and groped around her eyes. "I lost my glasses in there," she said.

"Seen one moonlit lake, you've seen 'em all," said Beth.

Francie nodded and laughed and then began to sob.

"I know," said Beth, hugging her tightly. "I know."

363

She looked back fearfully at the black hole in the ice. Then she turned her back on it. Clutching her sister, she started up the bank on wobbly legs toward the car and the road home.

> "Gruesomely effective.
> A scary, engrossing book."
> —**Stephen King,**
> author of *Firestarter*

The Unforgiven

by Patricia J. MacDonald

Maggie tried to forget the body of the man she loved, the murder trial, and the agonizing punishment. Now she was free to start a new life on a quiet New England island—until the terror began again.

"A terrific psychological thriller." —Mary Higgins Clark, author of *The Cradle Will Fall*

"...one of those rare books that, once started, you can't put down." —John Saul, author of *When the Wind Blows*

A Dell Book   **$3.50**   **(19123-8)**

Stranger in the House

by Patricia J. Macdonald

After ten years, no one believed her, but Anna knew her missing child was still alive. And now her faith was rewarded: Paul had been found! He was coming home. But Anna would never forget that day fear walked in the door—and a danger that threatened her family, her marriage and life itself. Someone had a secret. Someone still wanted her son. Someone who would not give up until Paul was dead and gone—forever.

A DELL BOOK   18455-X $3.95